C000212430

Win a Luxury Weekend
at the Brooklodge & Wells Spa

to enter simply text the answer to the following question to 53131:
Ciara has two brothers, one is a priest. What is his name?

(Answer to be found in this book)

LOVE
HURTS

LINDA KAVANAGH

POOLBEG

Published 2004
by Poolbeg Press Ltd
123 Grange Hill, Baldoyle
Dublin 13, Ireland
E-mail: poolbeg@poolbeg.com

Typesetting, layout, design © Poolbeg Press Ltd.

1 3 5 7 9 10 8 6 4 2

A catalogue record for this book is available from the British Library.

ISBN 1-84223-196-0

Typeset by Patricia Hope in Palatino 9.7/13.6
Printed by
Litografia Rosés S.A., Spain

www.poolbeg.com

About the Author

Linda Kavanagh has worked as a journalist for several Irish newspapers and magazines, and was a staff writer on the *RTÉ Guide* for fifteen years. She lives with her partner in Dun Laoghaire, Co. Dublin.

Acknowledgements

My heartfelt thanks to the Poolbeg team for their patience and professionalism, to Denise Deegan for encouragement, Catherine Lee for keeping in touch, Eve Holmes for the great photographs, and my kids Susan, Elaine and Robert for their unwavering support.

Finally, special thanks to Mike Gold – without whose love, arse-kicking and computer skills, this book would never have seen the light of day!

PROLOGUE

The woman sat down at her computer and began typing. The words formed swiftly as her fingers flew over the keyboard, and before long she had filled the entire screen. Oblivious to the darkening room as evening set in, she continued typing as though possessed. Vitriol poured onto the screen, as though a dam had burst inside her. She typed on and on until her fingers began hurting, her hatred spurring her on.

Finally, she stopped typing, exhausted but relieved. This was just the beginning. There was still so much more that she needed to write before her story was told. This was the sad story of her life, and her justification for what she had done to Ciara. No one would ever see her words, but letting out her anger was a cathartic experience. She pressed 'save', then closed down her computer. Tomorrow she would continue with the next stage of her story . . .

BOOK 1

CHAPTER 1

"It was a beautiful service," said Ciara's mother Annie, as the first of the guests began arriving back at the house after the funeral. Ciara nodded numbly. Since her husband's sudden death four days previously she'd been walking around in a daze.

At first she'd been hysterical, then unbelieving. She and Niall had been so happy together! They had a lovely home, no money worries, good friends and an enjoyable lifestyle. Niall ran a successful public relations company, while she earned a good income from her painting. They'd enjoyed each other's company, shared many interests and had a healthy, if somewhat volatile, teenage daughter. Ciara gulped. They'd even been planning to take a holiday together the following month!

At the thought of the holiday that would now never be, Ciara's eyes filled again with tears. It just wasn't fair! She felt cheated of that last idyllic time they might have shared together. In some ways, anger was a more manageable way of coping with the pain. It briefly eased the terrible ache inside her, which kept welling up and threatening to choke her.

There were times when, she realised, Niall's death hadn't yet registered with her at all. Momentarily her mind would play tricks. She would look up and expect to see him coming through the door. He was too young to die. It was simply too devastating to accept that this man in his mid-forties whom she'd adored since her schooldays would never walk through the door again.

Hastily, she took around a plate of sandwiches. It was comforting to see so many friends, neighbours, family members and work colleagues of both hers and Niall's. Yet the situation all seemed so unreal. At gatherings like these Niall had always been there in their midst, cracking jokes and filling up glasses.

"Are you all right, Ciara?"

Her old school friend Kate was at her elbow, looking concerned and caring. "Here, let me take those."

Kate tried to take the plate of sandwiches, but Ciara clung on as though the plate was a life-raft in a raging sea. "I'm all right, really. It's better if I have something to do."

"OK, love. But don't tire yourself out. It's been a tough day for you."

Ciara nodded her thanks through eyes brimming again with tears. Any show of concern from friends or family overwhelmed her. Maybe handing round the sandwiches wasn't such a good idea after all. Quickly, she abandoned them to the sideboard and headed out to the sanctuary of the kitchen.

Gazing unseeingly out the kitchen window, Ciara recalled all too vividly the events of that fateful evening just four days ago. She and Niall had just finished dinner and were considering what to do for the rest of the evening. They'd debated the merits of watching television, or walking down to the local pub for a leisurely nightcap.

"I think I'd rather stay in tonight," Niall had eventually said. "I'm not feeling too good. Maybe I'm just a bit tired. If you don't mind, I'd rather unwind with a movie. Is there anything decent on?"

Ciara suddenly wondered how Sarah, her daughter, was coping. Many of Sarah's friends had come to the service and graveyard, anxious to give Sarah support but embarrassed and uncertain of what to say. Most of them had never had to face death at such close quarters before and were unsure of how to behave. Ciara had been deeply touched, knowing that their presence had required greater effort than many of the older people, some of whom positively thrived on funerals. So as they'd left the graveyard, she'd given Sarah a wad of notes to buy drinks for her friends at the local pub.

Annie had been shocked when she'd discovered that her granddaughter was in a pub on the day of her father's funeral, but Ciara dismissed her mother's misgivings. This day, of all days, Sarah belonged in the bright world of the living. The child would have to do her grieving soon enough.

Startled from her reverie, Ciara turned as Charlie Somers entered the kitchen. Charlie had been Niall's best friend since schooldays. Without saying a word Charlie put his arms around her, holding her tightly, both of them united in a fresh wave of grief. Sobbing together, there were no words needed. They had both lost someone they loved dearly.

Dee, Charlie's wife and one of Ciara's closest friends, joined them and they all stood together, arms linked and holding each other in wordless communication. Over the years, they had all shared so many milestones. It was impossible to accept that Niall would not be there to build more memories in the years ahead.

Gradually, the kitchen began to fill up with people bringing in food. Delicious hams, cold meats, salmon and salads had appeared on the kitchen table as if by magic. Ciara realised with gratitude that her neighbours and friends must have organised it all. Fires had also been lit in both dining-room and drawing-room, creating a cosy and welcoming atmosphere. She was now angry with herself for being so self-indulgent. Niall would have expected her to look after the guests properly. After all, these were the very people who had come to pay their respects to his memory.

People were still arriving back from the graveyard, and Ciara heard the deep booming voice of Liam Golden in the hall. Leaving the kitchen, she hurried outside to greet him, needing to feel the warmth of his embrace as he enfolded her in his huge arms.

"Ciara, love . . ." He held her tightly, smoothing her hair as one might soothe a small child. No words were necessary. They had known each other for years, and Ciara found comfort and solace in his affectionate embrace.

Since her art college days, Liam had been her mentor

and friend. As owner of the Domino Gallery, Liam had spotted Ciara's talent and given her a solo exhibition when she was still an unknown. It had been a wonderful opportunity for a young art student, and to everyone's surprise but Liam's her work received rave reviews and the entire exhibition sold out within a week. Since then, despite offers from bigger, more impressive galleries, Ciara had continued to work exclusively with Liam and his gallery. She might have made more money elsewhere, but to Ciara money wasn't everything.

Suddenly, Ciara became aware that there was a woman standing just behind Liam smiling sympathetically at her. Simultaneously, Liam released Ciara from his embrace and turned to introduce the woman to her.

"Ciara, this is Ita. She wasn't sure if she should come, but I said . . ."

"You're very welcome, Ita," said Ciara, extending her hand. "Any friend of Liam's is a friend of mine."

Ita smiled shyly as they shook hands. "Thanks, Ciara. I'm very sorry about your husband."

"Maybe you two can get together some time," said Liam eagerly. "Ita just loves your paintings."

Ciara felt a sudden surge of affection for Liam. He was transparently anxious that she should like this woman. She now recalled that Liam had casually mentioned a new woman in his life. When he'd mentioned her there had been a gentle smile at the corner of his lips, and Ciara had thought, 'Uh-oh, this one might be different.'

Ciara would have willed herself to like any woman who was important to Liam, but in any event she didn't

9

find it difficult to like this tall, beautiful and effortlessly elegant woman. Ita seemed to have an empathy about her, and Ciara was pleased to think that Liam had found someone he evidently cared for.

Just at that moment, Annie edged her daughter aside.

"Are you all right, love?" she asked, "would you like a cup of tea? I'm just going to make a fresh pot."

Ciara shook her head. For as long as she could remember, a cup of tea had been her mother's answer to all the woes of the world, but Ciara felt in need of something stronger. As though anticipating her need, Dee appeared with a brandy.

"For medicinal purposes," she whispered, winking, as Ciara gratefully took the glass.

"Are you OK?" Dee asked, giving her arm a squeeze. Ciara nodded. At least she had managed to keep her composure so far.

Ciara was glad to see that people were enjoying themselves. Having shaken off the sombre atmosphere of the church and graveyard, they were all relaxing now and sharing jokes, chatting about their families and careers as though the morning's event had never happened. In fact, Ciara observed dispassionately, there was the makings of a good party underway already. Yet in the midst of all the chat and camaraderie, Ciara felt terribly alone. Everyone else seemed to be with their lover or partner, whereas hers was gone forever.

She now recalled how tired Niall had looked that night. She'd noticed the first streaks of grey in his previously black hair, and his skin had an unhealthy pallor too. Not unreasonably, he'd been unusually quiet since Eamonn Merrigan, his friend and contemporary from the golf club, had died of cancer a few weeks earlier. Therefore she'd assumed that Niall's lethargy was a reaction to the loss of a friend, tempered by fears about his own mortality. Now, memories of that unnatural colour haunted her. If she'd realised its significance, she might have acted faster and been able to save him . . .

Why hadn't some sixth sense warned her? Surely after living with a man for years, there would be some form of telepathic communication between them? Yet when she'd brought two cups of coffee in from the kitchen after dinner, Niall had been lying on the floor, groaning and clutching his chest.

The next few hours had passed in a daze. She vaguely remembered ambulance personnel asking her a series of meaningless questions, Niall being taken out on a stretcher, the interminable drive to the hospital with the sirens wailing. In the hospital, she'd just stood there twisting the buttons on her cardigan as the clamps were applied time and time again to Niall's chest. His body had shuddered like a rag doll as the electrical charges went through him.

Then suddenly, the emergency team weren't trying any more, and a hush had descended over the room. Then they had all turned to face her, with pity in their eyes. And she'd felt like an outsider, watching a ghastly play in which she had no part.

As she now crossed the room aimlessly, she was welcomed into a small group that included her younger brother Cillian, and his wife Betty. Ciara and her younger sibling had little in common, but she was glad he'd been able to get here. As a busy surgeon, he'd probably had to rearrange his entire schedule.

Thanking them for their solicitations, she glanced around the large room at the cousins, aunts and uncles from both sides of the family. Many of them she would never see again, or at least not until the next funeral. She shivered as she remembered seeing photographer Alan Moore at the church. He had a nerve turning up, after all the harm he'd caused her! How she hated that man, with his insolent grin and knowing eyes. Thank goodness he hadn't come back to the house – that would have added insult to injury!

Her heart pounding, she headed towards the drinks cabinet. Perhaps another brandy would help her to keep going.

"I'll get that for you . . ."

Ciara's brother Kevin had spotted her empty glass, and seen her moving in the direction of the drinks cabinet. Ciara nodded gratefully. Kevin was the eldest of the family and home on leave from Africa. As a priest, his work involved travelling over hundreds of miles of rough terrain each week to places where there were no roads, where water was always scarce, and where electricity and flush toilets were non-existent. Added to that was the never-ending horror of hunger and disease, and the hopelessness of people living constantly on the edge of disaster.

Ciara watched her brother as he poured the brandy into her glass. It was lucky that Kevin happened to be at home. He'd been a tower of strength over the last few days. Although she'd been surprised when he'd declined to say the funeral mass, arranging for a distant cousin in Niall's family to do the honours instead. Perhaps there was some kind of priestly etiquette involved. She would ask him about it some time.

"Thanks, Kev," Ciara took the drink gratefully, "and thanks for all your help over the last few days. I don't think I could have managed without you."

"Glad to help, love, but you'd have done fine, even if I hadn't been here." He squeezed her arm affectionately. "That was a marvellous tribute you paid to Niall in the church this morning."

Ciara smiled, her lower lip trembling at the memory. It had taken all her physical and mental strength not to break down and cry when she'd stepped up onto the altar to read one of Niall's favourite poems before the assembled congregation, and to pay her own brief tribute to the man she loved before he was finally taken away from her and laid in the cold earth.

"Oh Niall . . ." she thought, "if only I could hold you one more time."

She stifled a sob, knowing that she was only torturing herself. Niall was gone, never to return, and she was now a widow. What a horrible word! Suddenly, it all proved too much for her, and the tears began streaming down her face.

CHAPTER 2

Ciara, everyone who knows you agrees that you are a lovely person, with a kind and generous nature. No one could possibly dislike you, could they? Well, those very people who sing your praises might be very surprised to learn that there is someone who loathes you – even more today than ever before. That person is me.

I am close by, but you don't even know it. Why? Because I've always hidden my feelings so well. The person you see is not the real me – never has been. There is a separate and different me inside that you know nothing about. We all have our secrets, Ciara. I know more than most about secrets, and I have ruthlessly exploited yours.

I've always felt like an actress in a play, pretending to be a child like all the others, yet knowing I was different. Today, I'm an adult, but still that lonely child lurks within, expecting to be hurt and wanting to hurt in return.

The reason why I've always hated you is that you always had everything so easy. You had a loving family, whereas I

14

knew only loneliness. As we became teenagers, all the boys at St Joseph's noticed you, but I never got a look-in because you always stole the limelight.

So why should you have it all? I enjoyed knowing that I had something special with Niall behind your back. You with your simpering ways, your confidence, your fancy clothes . . . My hatred of you sprang from my own deep sense of envy.

I always felt inferior to you, Ciara. You always had the capacity to make me feel ugly and cumbersome beside you. You were small and dainty, the way I longed to be, but instead I felt like a big carthorse beside you. All my life, you've been the one person who's been able to reduce me to that sad, insecure youngster of many years ago.

To overcome that unendingly painful experience, I had to reduce you down in size. This I could achieve by taking from you something that really mattered to you, something that was central to your very identity. By experiencing one aspect of how you lived, your own husband, I could almost believe that I was you.

It didn't matter that you knew nothing about my affair with Niall. It was enough for me that I knew, and that at any time I chose I could destroy your happiness and peace of mind if I wanted to. You have no idea how many hours of pleasure I derived from imagining your shocked face if I should ever decide to let you find out that you weren't the only woman in your husband's life.

And it amused me to think that you might actually come running to me for solace and advice, as you did all those years ago when the boys kept trying to touch you up behind the school bicycle shed. You were both shocked and excited, and you wanted me to give you the go-ahead to experiment, to enter the adult world of forbidden delights. It never crossed your self-centred mind that I, too, might crave those opportunities. In your eyes, I was merely one of your foils, your sounding boards, someone to burden with your own fears and insecurities. The sheer conceit of you; did it never cross your mind that I wanted the boys to want me too?

You probably don't remember much about me then. Like most teenagers you ran with the herd, and I ran with it too, for the feeling of safety in numbers that it gave us when facing a whole new grown-up world. I was the fat, plain one of the group, the one that the boys never even considered. They were too busy chatting up the pretty girls. It didn't matter whether those girls had brains or not, or whether they were nice people or not. The only thing that mattered to the boys was scoring with the prettiest ones, in order to enhance their status among their own male peers.

It was a painful lesson to learn, that a girl's popularity depended on factors over which she had little control. If nature had been kind to her, the boys would be queuing up. But given a slightly different arrangement of molecules, she was devalued and discarded.

I despised you all. I knew I was brighter than all of you put together. Behind the mousy brown hair, big nose and plump face there was a clever, articulate and attractive woman longing to get out. I was determined that some day she would, but back then I just didn't know how.

So I played the clown, the funny fat one the girls never regarded as competition, and with whom the boys talked about their problems dating the other girls. I was sweet and helpful to them all, but inside I seethed. They were all so callous, so insensitive, so wrapped up in their own problems. Did they think that just because I wasn't conventionally pretty and weighed more than most of the other girls, that I was immune to their jibes? Did they think that because I was plain, I didn't have hopes, dreams and longings too? It was they who were inferior, since they could not see what was behind the plain exterior. I also understood that even if one of them had secretly fancied me, he wouldn't have had the guts to ask me out because of what the other boys would say.

I was your friend because I was useful, Ciara. Oh yes, I let you all make use of me. Otherwise, I might have been sitting at home alone, like the other swots at school who were scorned because they had nothing in their lives except their homework. But I was cleverer than all of you put together. I could socialise and get my homework done easily. And I could curry favour by letting you all copy my homework assignments when it suited me.

I also shudder when I think of those awful rugby club dances on Saturday nights, when I became the ideal prop for minding handbags since everyone assumed that I'd never be asked up to dance myself. So I stood on the sidelines in the semi-darkness while the music played, draped in handbags with a fixed smile on my face while all you girls danced past, engrossed in acne-faced beanpoles. Did you all really think I was enjoying myself? I wonder if it ever crossed your minds to think of how I was feeling at all.

At the time, I had hoped that those experimentations of yours behind the bike shed, which of course I encouraged, might result in you becoming pregnant, with all its attendant disgrace. Then you would really have fallen from your pedestal, and I would have had my revenge all those years ago instead. I derived hours of pleasure thinking through the whole scenario, *from the moment when you'd discover that you were pregnant. I imagined you fearfully telling your parents, the rows that would ensue followed by a hasty boat trip to England or to a convent down the country that took in so-called `wayward' girls. That would have clipped your wings for sure!*

Who knows, you might even have come to me for advice. After all, I was the most likely candidate for your confidences, since of all your friends I mattered the least. You saw no need to impress me, so I would have been the perfect recipient to take your problems on board. You might even have thought that I'd be flattered to share your secret!

Would I have kept that trust? It would certainly have given me ammunition to store up for the future, and it would have kept you indebted to me. Because being the only person to know another's secret is a delicious feeling. What a sense of power it gives! I could either have played you like a puppet for years, or I could have ensured that your secret was revealed at a time when it would do you maximum damage.

Alas, you were either too clever or too terrified to do anything with the boys. There never was a pregnancy and, after you'd slapped Terry McKeever's face, word got around that you weren't much fun behind the bike shed any more. That pleased me a lot. I thought that even at that late stage, the boys might come and try me instead. But no, they still kept after you because you were so pretty. So I decided, in all my youthful wisdom, that I would bide my time and some day I would get the opportunity to get my own back on you. It might take years, and you might never even know how I'd achieved my revenge. But I would know, and that was all that mattered.

CHAPTER 3

The morning after the funeral Kate arrived at Ciara's front door, smiling broadly and carrying a box of cream cakes from the local bakery.

"Hi, Ciara," she said, hugging her friend. "Let's get the kettle on, and get working on this lot. How are you feeling today?"

Ciara grimaced. "Rotten, if you want to know the truth. I've just been sending some e-mails. I suddenly realised that neither Marguerite, Dot nor Vera would have known that Niall died," she gulped. "You know, Kate, it seemed so awful, so final, putting it in writing to them."

Kate squeezed Ciara's arm. "Sorry, love. I should have thought of contacting them for you."

"No, it's OK. It was something I needed to do."

"How are they all, anyway? I can hardly believe that you lot have kept in touch all these years."

Ciara smiled. "Well, e-mail certainly makes it a lot easier. Before that, it was just an occasional letter, and a card at Christmas. But I've always felt a special bond with my friends from schooldays. After all, you and I are also friends since back then, Kate."

Kate nodded. "Well, I think you're marvellous for keeping in contact. I'm too lazy to make the effort."

"There's not much effort required to send a card or an e-mail!"

"But you rarely see any of them."

"I know, more's the pity. I haven't seen Marguerite since we left school, and it's five years or more since I've seen Dot. Then again, Dot keeps reminding me that sheep farming is a full-time job. As for Vera, she's so busy with that civil service job of hers, she and I only meet up about once a year anyway! But I like the idea of staying in touch."

Kate sighed. "I wouldn't have the patience to keep writing month after month. I find it hard enough writing for a living!"

There was a sudden silence, and Kate looked at her friend closely. "Are you OK, Ciara?" she asked softly.

Ciara choked back a sob. "You know, Kate, I still wake up each morning expecting him to be there beside me. Then it all hits me again . . ."

"You poor love."

Kate gave Ciara another hug, then put on the kettle, took two mugs from the cupboard and sat down beside her at the kitchen table.

"Did you sleep OK last night? I wish you'd let me come and stay. Just until you feel able to cope on your own . . ."

Ciara shook her head. "Thanks, Kate, but this is

something I just have to get used to. And I might as well begin getting used to it from day one. Oh God, Kate. I miss him so much."

Kate turned away and began making the tea, so that Ciara wouldn't see the tears in her own eyes. For that would be the undoing of them both. After all, Niall had been special for her too.

As she placed a tea bag in each cup, Kate recalled the many memories of her own of which Niall was a major part. Now that he was dead her own secret was safe – at least until she decided what to do about it. She was consumed with guilt, yet she wondered if confession really was good for the soul. Kate managed to turn a sob into a sigh. Evidently, Niall had never told Ciara what had happened that night. Not that she'd ever expected him to. Niall was not the sort of man to burden others with what they didn't need to know, and which might only hurt them anyway. Perhaps that should be her own policy too, at least for the immediate future.

"Here you are, love." Kate passed Ciara a cup of tea and opened the large box of cream cakes. "Look, Ciara. I got your favourites."

Kate pointed to the row of slices and doughnuts, all oozing fresh cream and jam and covered in caster sugar. "Do you remember when we were at school and we'd go into town every Saturday? We'd always end up in the Kylemore or Bewley's, and stuff ourselves with gooey cakes."

Ciara nodded with a smile. "You were still moaning about your weight, even then!"

"Well, right now I don't give a damn!" said Kate,

helping herself to a large cream and jam doughnut. "What's the point in worrying about a few pounds? After all, we could all be dead tomorrow."

There was a moment's silence as Kate realised what she had said, and Ciara strove to ease her friend's embarrassment by pretending she hadn't noticed her unfortunate choice of words. Ciara sighed. Who could spend a lifetime dodging words and references, just to protect someone else's feelings?

"C'mon, Ciara. Eat up," Kate added. "Cream is full of calcium, which you badly need right now to give your system a boost."

Ciara laughed. "You've just made that up!"

"Well, yes I did. But it's partly true. I just left out the fact that all those calories are guaranteed to add several pounds at least. Well, that's what it will do to me. But . . ." Kate wrinkled her nose in mock disgust. "Of course, it'll have no effect on a skinny little thing like you. I hate you, bitch!"

Ciara laughed, and licked the cream from her fingers. Poor old Kate had been battling with her weight all her life, going on endless diets and trying every new gimmick that came on the market. Ciara had always felt guilty that she could eat anything without putting on an ounce, whereas by merely looking at chocolate Kate seemed to put on several pounds.

Just then the doorbell rang, and Ciara made a grimace at Kate. She wasn't in the mood to have their happy twosome disturbed, but when she rose from the table and made her way into the hall she was relieved to see a familiar and welcome outline through the glass.

"It's Dee," Ciara called to Kate. "Better put the kettle on again!"

"Hi," Dee gave Ciara a hug and followed her into the kitchen.

"Oh hi, Kate," she eyed the half-empty cake box, and laughingly produced a cake box herself.

"It looks as though I brought reinforcements just in time!" Deftly, she cut the tape, revealing a further array of cream cakes and pastries.

Happily, the three chomped away, not caring that the cream oozed from their mouths or ended up on their noses. A contented silence reigned, except for the routine chewing, happy sighs and licking of fingers. Ciara looked around her, and was overcome with emotion for these two friends whom she felt so fortunate to have. As different as chalk and cheese, yet both so dependable. She had known Kate and Dee since they'd all started secondary school together. Then Dee and Charlie, Niall's best friend, had started dating and married some years later.

Over the years, all three of them had stayed in touch, even when circumstance had taken one of them abroad or to another area of the country. They'd phoned, written, and later used e-mail so that each of them was kept up-to-date with the important events in each other's lives.

Ciara was deeply fond of Dee, who was always brief and to the point. She was sometimes even hurtfully direct, but at least you always knew where you stood with her. You never had to fear that she would let you go out wearing something hideous for fear of hurting your feelings! Ciara felt privileged to have Dee as a friend; if the worst you had to fear from a friend was the truth, then you were lucky indeed.

And Kate. Dear, sweet Kate, who had known her back in the days when the Reynolds family lived in dire poverty. It was Kate who had covered up for her among her snobby schoolmates, and who had regularly lent her money to buy the things that her parents could never afford to give her. Ciara's eyes filled with tears, and Kate looked at her sympathetically.

"Are you OK, love?"

Ciara tried to smile. "I just feel so empty, so . . ." she shrugged, "so unattached to anything or anyone."

"Don't let Sarah hear you say that!" Kate said with a smile.

"I didn't mean it that way . . ."

"You've got your painting," Dee added with surprising asperity. "You've got a rare talent. You're an acclaimed success. You've got a lot more going for you than most people have."

Ciara looked contrite. "You're right. I do sound so sorry for myself."

Kate hurried round from her side of the table and put her arms around Ciara, giving Dee a warning look as she did so.

"You've every right to feel sad, love. Dee's only trying to point out that you've so much to keep going for. Things will get better. I promise you, they will."

Who am I kidding? Kate thought to herself. Losing the one you love is the most awful thing that can happen. It has blighted my entire life, and everything I've done has been a reaction to losing him. Even my engagement didn't last. What chance did it have when weighed against the trauma of the preceding years? Maybe if I hadn't stayed in such close proximity to him and his family all these years, I would eventually have got over him. If only I'd had the courage all those years ago, to break contact with Ciara permanently . . .

"What do you think of Liam's new woman?" Dee asked between bites.

"She's very glamorous. I'd give anything to have her figure," said Kate, mournfully.

Dee looked at her. "Don't be daft. There's nothing she's got that you haven't."

Kate smiled, pleased at the compliment. But Dee's next remark drained all the colour from her face.

"But you do look as though you're putting on weight again, Kate. Maybe it's time you went back to the gym."

Seeing Kate's shocked expression, Ciara intervened. "I think you look fine, Kate," she lied, "but what Dee means is that since you worked so hard to get that weight off last year, you don't want to let it start creeping on again."

Without doubt, Ciara thought, Kate had been putting on weight lately, but with the pressure of her own problems she hadn't given it much thought. In fact, Kate was also looking quite peaky, an odd combination with an increase in weight. She hoped her friend wasn't ill. She'd heard that certain cancers could affect people that way.

Just then, the doorbell rang and they each looked at the other. Who could it be this time? They were now comfortable as a trio – none of them wanted the balance of their present situation altered.

Ciara went to the door and the others could hear a male voice, then suddenly the room was filled with Kevin's tangy aftershave.

"Hello Dee, hello Kate. I'm not intruding on a girlie tête-à-tête, am I?'

"Yes, you are," said Dee with a smile, "but it's good to see you again, anyway.'

"Hi Kevin," Kate said, "would you like a cup of tea? Hey, you're in luck. There's a cream bun left over, too."

Kevin grinned. "Great. You're sure I'm not intruding? I just thought I'd drop by and see my little sister . . ."

"Hey, less of the `little'!" Ciara chuckled, making a mock swipe at him with a tea towel. "You're only a year and a bit older than me."

Brother and sister smiled at each other, and Kate thought how wonderful it must be to have brothers or sisters. As an only child, she often felt that she'd missed out on the hurly-burly of life in a 'real' family. Life with an elderly aunt hadn't satisfied her craving for the love she'd observed in other people's homes. Therefore, she'd availed of every opportunity to visit the Reynolds' household when she was growing up. Despite their poverty, there was always a warm welcome and a share of whatever food was on the table.

Kate handed Kevin a cup of tea, and he smiled his thanks. Silently, she offered him the box with the remaining cream cake in it, and he lifted it out with a mischievous grin.

"You're trying to fatten me up, Kate!" he chuckled.

Kate smiled, taking in his lean body and noting how handsome he looked out of his clerical garb. She was also aware of how much more relaxed he was on this visit home, unlike previous times when he'd been like a coiled spring. He seemed more sure of himself now, and she wondered if anyone else had noticed it. Perhaps not, on account of everyone's absorption in helping Ciara and Sarah come to terms with Niall's death. Come to think of it, where was Sarah? Kate had hardly seen the child since Niall died. Kate felt deeply sorry for Sarah, feeling an empathy with her as an only child. Kate was aware that in the last few years, Sarah had become a handful and full of teenage angst and moodiness. Kate shuddered as she remembered her own childhood and teenage years. They'd been harrowing and full of youthful insecurities, too. So she could understand what Sarah was going through.

"Where's Sarah?" she asked.

"She's gone to stay with my mother," Ciara explained. "I felt it was better than having the two of us being miserable in the same house." There was sadness in Ciara's voice. Clearly, she and Sarah were unable to offer any comfort to each other at a time when they both needed it so badly.

Suddenly, Kate sat down. She felt very light-headed. The room began to sway a little, and she gripped the table.

"Are you all right, Kate?" Kevin asked, noticing her unsteadiness.

"Yes, I'm fine." she lied, smiling brightly. "I think all those cream cakes have gone to my head!" Then just as quickly as it arrived, the dizzy spell passed.

"We were just talking about Liam's new woman before you arrived," Ciara said. "What do you think of her, Kev?"

"Don't really know. I only met her for the first time after the funeral. Liam seems to like her anyway," he grinned, knowing that that wasn't the kind of reply the trio wanted.

"C'mon, what do you really think of her?" Dee intervened. "She's terribly elegant, isn't she?"

But Kevin refused to be drawn. "Hmm, I suppose she is. I don't know much about designer clothing, but I'd say that the outfit she was wearing cost a pretty penny. What does she do for a living?"

"She's well known in media circles here. She writes regular features for one of the national dailies, and writes a weekly current affairs series which has a big following," Dee explained. "But I suppose you wouldn't know that, being out of the country so long. Anyway, we're asking the questions, Kevin! So what do you, as a man, think of her?"

Kevin knew that he was stepping into a minefield, so he skirted around the subject as disinterestedly as he could. "I suppose she might appeal to some men, but I found her a bit remote."

"But her looks, she is lovely-looking, isn't she?" Dee persisted.

"Yes, I suppose she's a good-looking woman," said Kevin, deciding that he would have to be reasonably honest, "but a bit too skinny for my liking."

"Well, she's not likely to care what you think, is she?" said Kate with acerbity.

"You know what I mean," Kevin added mildly, ignoring Kate's outburst, "for a woman with such impact, she actually seemed rather shy."

"Yes," Dee added, "I thought that as well. I meet her occasionally when we're both doing features for the newspaper, but she tends to keep very much to herself. But Liam obviously adores her, and they seem very happy together."

They all drank their tea, acutely aware that while Liam's new relationship had just begun, Ciara's had abruptly come to an end.

CHAPTER 4

It might have surprised you, Ciara, to know that while you were cavorting around with the boys from St Joseph's, I developed a secret life of my own. But for obvious reasons, I couldn't share confidences the way you and the rest of the group did. This was because the men in my life were a lot older. Perhaps in retrospect, these men saw a vulnerability in me which they chose to exploit. No matter. At the time, I felt that I was the one in control. And I craved control, since so many other areas of my life seemed to have cast me in the role of victim.

You probably don't remember O'Reilly's, the butcher's shop at the corner of the street beside the bus terminus. But I remember Mr O'Reilly – a big swarthy man with black hair, and a face that always looked dirty because his beard grew so fast. He fitted my image of Bluebeard and I was excited by the element of danger that I felt lurked within him.

But there was a glint in his eye that I discovered at the age of thirteen. Each time I was in collecting an order for my aunt, if I was alone in the shop, he would take a long time wrapping up the meat and wink at me each time he caught my eye. He knew that this winking caused me embarrassment, and my embarrassment gave him pleasure. More often than not, I looked away, but sometimes out of defiance, I would hold his stare. Then his eyes would start to undress me and I would feel my cheeks blushing. Then he would give me a satisfied smile, as though he knew what was happening to my body beneath my clothes.

I was both terrified and excited each time my aunt sent me to the shop. I would fervently hope that there would be other customers there, yet perversely I would be disappointed if there were. Perhaps my disappointment showed, because sometimes Mr O'Reilly would ask if I'd mind waiting until he'd served the other people. Mostly, the adults were in a hurry and assumed that this was just Mr O'Reilly's way of showing courtesy to them. But Mr O'Reilly and I knew differently.

Usually, as I waited in the shop for the moment when he and I would be alone together, my mouth would be so dry with fear and excitement that I would have to lick my lips if I was ever going to speak again.

One day, when all the customers had gone, Mr O'Reilly said, "I love the way you lick your lips. Do you know how excited that makes me?"

I shook my head, unable to speak at all, and trembling all over with excitement myself. The idea that I, a mere child, could excite a grown man like Mr O'Reilly was heady stuff indeed. The boys we met after school might not give me a second glance, but clearly Mr O'Reilly could spot my true womanly potential.

Mr O'Reilly leaned across the counter and lowered his voice. "Do you know what I'd like to slide between those lips of yours? My tongue. Then I'd like to stick my tongue somewhere else too. Have the boys in school done that to you yet?"

"No, Mr O'Reilly," was all I could manage to say. Then I grabbed the parcel of meat for the dinner and ran all the way home, almost forgetting to pick up the change from the counter.

I spent the next few days thinking about what Mr O'Reilly had said. In school, the nuns often had to chastise me for not paying attention in class. Clearly, they knew that my mind wasn't on my work. I wonder what they would have said if they'd known what was on my mind?

I imagined Mr O'Reilly and I in the room behind the shop, him kissing me passionately, his tongue probing my mouth. Just like all the boys in school used to try to do to you and the other girls, Ciara. I could only wonder, in my thirteen-year-old innocence, where else he would like to put his tongue.

I soon found out. Philip Breslin – do you remember that gangling, dark-haired boy with pimples, Ciara? The one you once let slobber all over you in the laneway behind the school? That very week he asked me, as a special favour, to hide a book that he was afraid to keep in his bedroom any longer. His parents were planning to re-decorate his room, and he was afraid that they might find it.

Initially, when he approached me, I'd hoped that he was going to ask me out. But, no – that would have been too good to be true. But, at least he had the wit to look embarrassed when he handed me the book. It was all dog-eared. Clearly he'd read it many times, and he turned scarlet when he handed it over. He looked really odd, with his face all red and his pimples standing out like tiny glistening beacons. At that moment, I realised that I just wasn't interested in boys. Men like Mr O'Reilly were much more interesting.

In fact, as it turned out the book he gave me was very instructive. At home in my room, I studied it by torchlight beneath the bedclothes with even more zeal than I'd ever studied my school homework. I was amazed at what I learned. Now at last I discovered what Mr O'Reilly meant.

In a way, I was grateful to Philip Breslin because the book I was minding enabled me to discover that the hair sprouting between my legs was normal. Initially, I had thought something terrible was happening to me, that possibly I had some terrible disease, because my aunt never discussed these matters. I had only learnt about periods through whispered exchanges in the back row of sewing class. But now I was glad of the growth between my legs, because it clearly excited Mr O'Reilly.

I knew this because, when alone in the shop with him one day, he had told me how much he longed to feel my `short and curlies'. I blushed, now knowing what he meant, since the hair on my head was long and straight.

Do you remember Mrs O'Reilly, Ciara? She was a taciturn, stocky woman with hairs on her chin. In my fantasy I loved to think of her shocked expression when she found her husband and me in a romantic embrace. Then Mr O'Reilly would face her and confess that it was me he loved and wanted. He would then tell her to pack her bags and leave the house before he returned from work. The fact that they had seven young children didn't have any place in my fantasy. In dreams, such unpleasant realities could be swept aside.

Of course, Mrs O'Reilly would cry, and beg him to stay with her. However, at that point he would be adamant and she would run from the shop, presumably to pack and leave demurely as he wished. Then Mr O'Reilly and I would be together forever.

Sadly, I never did find out how far my relationship with Mr O'Reilly would have progressed. For on the Saturday that my aunt sent me for two pounds of stewing beef, the shop was closed and the blinds pulled down.

"Isn't it very sad about Mr O'Reilly?" said old Mrs Kenny, who had been walking past and noticed my perplexed expression. "They're taking him to the church at five o'clock. A massive stroke, I believe. May the Lord have mercy on his soul."

It was awful not being able to share my shock and grief with anyone. I felt cheated by his death, and angry at all the sympathy that Mrs O'Reilly and her seven brats were getting. Instead, I sat silently beside my aunt as Father Macken, the new curate, droned on about Mr O'Reilly's virtues. How would he know, I wondered, since he was only new to the parish? Idly, I wondered if Mr O'Reilly had been to confession before he died. If not, all those bad thoughts might now mean that he was roasting in the fires of hell . . . It amused me to think that I might have had some control over his destiny, even if only in the next life.

I wish, Ciara, that I could have told you of my grief and anger at that time, but I never felt able to share my confidences or fears with any of you. I had a specific and subordinate role to play when in your company. Besides, I didn't want your pity. I was the clown, the gopher, the one who magnified your glory and reflected it back to you. My purpose was to give you confidence, not the other way around.

Would you all have been surprised if I'd told you about my banter with the butcher? Would you have pitied me? I wasn't prepared to risk finding out. So I hugged my secret to me, in much the same way as I've kept secret my affair with Niall. It was my own special secret. And secrets are wonderful, aren't they?

CHAPTER 5

Dee let herself into the house by the side door through the kitchen. She was relieved to be home, and away from the false bonhomie of Ciara's house, and glad to be relieved of the responsibility of trying to think up soothing comments and avoiding any references to death.

She kicked off her shoes, crossed the cool tiled floor in her bare feet and put on the kettle. The scene had already been set by the time she'd arrived at Ciara's house. Kate had already mentally wrapped her in cotton wool, frowning over Ciara's head when she thought that Dee was going to say something that would provoke a bout of emotion.

Dee sighed. Maybe Kate knew best. She's a lot more compassionate than I am, she thought. If Kate hadn't been there, I'd probably have stumbled in, made a dozen faux pas within the first five minutes, and made inane comments such as 'Life must go on'.

Filling herself a cup of coffee from the plunge pot, Dee

sat down at the kitchen table. Maybe she was just angry at not being allowed to voice her own grief over Niall. Ciara wasn't the only one who had cared about him.

Dee quickly wiped away a tear. She'd known Niall for most of her adult life. He and Charlie had been friends since schooldays, and Charlie too was quite devastated over Niall's death. If ever two men had cared about each other, then they were the perfect example. They'd quietly supported each other through the various ups and downs of life, being there for each other in times of both crisis and joy.

Dee got up and poured herself another cup of coffee. She thought of Charlie, crying unashamedly at the loss of his friend, his eyes red and swollen from grief. Poor old Charlie – he had always been second-best. He'd just never known it.

A sob escaped from Dee's throat. Ciara wasn't the only one whose life had just been irrevocably altered. Her own plans had been destroyed, too. And she felt like a frightened child, banging futilely against a locked door that isolated her from the world of happiness on the other side.

Dee sighed, remembering Ciara from her own schooldays. She'd shone like a beacon, despite the drab convent school uniform. In fact, it was almost as though she'd effortlessly and unconsciously made it into a fashion accessory of her own. Even then, all those years ago, Ciara had possessed that quality that made her stand apart from the crowd and shine. And while all the other girls had envied her, few had resented her because she was totally unaware of the effect she had on others.

It had been the same with the boys. In her presence they'd immediately become tongue-tied or blushed scarlet. At the club dances they'd almost fallen over their own big ungainly adolescent feet, and each other, in their rush to ask her to dance. But no one had touched her heart until Niall came along.

Dee poured herself another cup of coffee, noting that the pot was now empty. Could she really have drunk so much of it so quickly?

Like all the girls, Dee herself had fancied Niall in those days. But once Ciara had appeared on the scene, with her wispy blond hair and her elfin face, neither Niall nor Ciara had eyes for anyone else.

But then, there had always been Charlie – smaller, stockier and nowhere near as handsome as Niall. He'd been there in the background, always helpful, always eager to lend a hand. With his unruly russet hair standing on end, and an eager expression on his face, he'd reminded her of a terrier, ever ready to fetch and carry at his owner's beck and call. Gradually over the years, he'd worn down her resistance by always being there and gradually making himself indispensable.

In the years immediately after leaving school, Dee had trained in the newsroom of a large Sunday newspaper. There had been other relationships, changes of job, but Charlie had always maintained contact, phoning from time to time to find out how she was. Dee liked the feeling of having someone safe in the background, in case things didn't work out for her elsewhere.

Eventually, she'd taken a job as a columnist on a newspaper in Cork. Charlie still kept in touch occasionally, but when Dee became seriously involved with a local businessman she stopped returning his calls.

When Dee's relationship eventually foundered, she began to think of Charlie again. But by then his letters and phone calls had stopped, and on a visit back to Dublin Dee learnt the cause. Charlie had discovered that one of the secretaries in the accountancy practice where he worked was far from immune to his charms, and there were even rumours of an impending engagement.

Dee had surprised even herself by the speed at which she'd intervened, throwing up her job in Cork, returning to Dublin and quickly dispensing with her rival. If Charlie was going to place an engagement ring on anyone's finger, that finger was going to be hers. Charlie, of course, had been delighted. He was thrilled at being the one to be pursued for a change, and he seemed to believe that his prize was all the greater for having had to wait so much longer to claim it.

Dee sighed. Perhaps that was at the root of her discontent – she'd reacted rather than proacted. She, who prided herself on always making careful well-thought-out decisions, had allowed herself to be cornered into making a rash decision which she'd subsequently regretted. Poor sod, Dee thought, it was just as well that Charlie didn't know the truth. Anyway, he got what he wanted, didn't he? And I've got a good man. We adopted Donal and Terry, who have never given us a moment's trouble and who are both doing well at college. Life could have dealt me a much worse hand. At one time, it looked as though I might have ended up with nothing at all.

Perhaps, Dee thought, when the boys are finished

college I'll think again about leaving Charlie. But what would be the point at this stage? I've missed my golden opportunity. The only man for whom I've ever considered taking such a monumental step is gone forever. She sighed as she recalled his eyes, his gentle mouth, his sudden laugh when she said something outlandish. He'd delighted in her lack of subtlety, whereas most other people were intimidated by it. But because of all the people who'd be affected if they admitted their love, they'd kept their relationship a secret. Now she had nothing left, because nothing was as irrevocable as death.

Ciara's not the only one who's hurting, Dee thought angrily. I'm hurting too, yet there's no one *I* can turn to for consolation. Rising from the table, she angrily threw her empty mug into the kitchen sink. She felt an irrational satisfaction when it landed on Charlie's breakfast dishes, breaking them all into smithereens. She picked out the broken plates from the sink, cutting herself in her carelessness. As she sucked the blood from her finger, the tears gathered behind her eyelids. She knew that she wasn't crying over a cut finger. She was crying for all that might have been.

CHAPTER 6

After Mr O'Reilly died I was consumed with rage and loneliness Ciara. Anger that I'd been robbed yet again of someone special in my life, and loneliness since I now had no one to fuel my fantasies. I hoped that someone interesting might move to the area and take over the shop, but it remained firmly closed.

In desperation, I took to attending church each day after school. This wasn't out of any religious fervour, but the loss of Mr O'Reilly had affected me deeply and the ritual of rattling off a series of prayers gave me a sense of comfort. It seemed at least as good an option as hanging round outside the sweet shop, or going to Ernie's café with you and the other girls to watch you flirt with a gang of pimply boys.

I would sit alone in the darkened church thinking of Mr O'Reilly and wondering where he was now. Had he gone to heaven or hell? Or was there nothing else after we die?

As a small child living on a farm, I'd often hoped in vain that God or the Blessed Virgin might appear to me in the vegetable patch or behind the barn, or perhaps in a burning blackcurrant bush. I'd prayed daily to them, and to an assortment of other saints, for deliverance from my father's drunken wrath. But I sadly concluded that they must be too busy appearing to other people to be of any assistance to me.

Despite usually being alone in the church, word of my religious devotion got back to my aunt who was clearly pleased with this turn of events. "It seems there's hope for everyone," she said gruffly, but I could detect a note of pleasure in her voice. The stupid old cow would have loved to believe I was developing a religious vocation, but that was the farthest thing from my mind.

Being a priest might have appealed to me, since religion was clearly a case of 'jobs for the boys'. Each secular priest usually had his own house, car and housekeeper as well as the adulation and respect of all his parishioners. In contrast, nuns were usually herded together in convents like battery hens. Perhaps that explained why so many of them took out their anger on us poor children when they had us at their mercy in convent school.

I enjoyed the solitude of the church, especially on dark winter evenings when the glow of the candles, lit by devout parishioners, danced on the brass fittings and the smell of incense filled my nostrils. I would sit there in the silence, sometimes pondering on the likelihood of God's existence. I would stare at the tabernacle in the middle of the altar, wondering how that little ornate box was supposed to hold the flesh and blood of Jesus. I derived great amusement from imagining God folded up inside. Was God a contortionist, or was there some other explanation?

My regular attendance at church after school wasn't missed

by Father Macken the new curate, either. One evening, dressed in his long black cassock, he stepped out of a confession box just as I was walking past and for a second I actually thought that the Devil had come to take me to hell.

"Good evening, child," he whispered, in that patronising tone possessed of so many clergy. "I've seen you at Sunday Mass with your aunt, haven't I?"

I nodded meekly. "Yes, Father."

"And I've seen you here a lot lately. Are you praying for a special intention?"

"Yes, Father."

My monosyllabic answers were the result of a lifetime of being told to show 'respect' for men and women of the cloth, combined with my own innate desire to let them know as little as possible about me. Fortunately, Father Macken interpreted my brief replies as being the result of awe and respect.

"Good girl," he said approvingly. "I hope that God will answer your prayers. Hurry on home now – it looks like it's going to start raining soon."

That night, when I was tucked up in my bed, thoughts of Father Macken came unbidden into my head. I wondered what it would be like to run my fingers through his wavy brown hair which had the beginnings of grey at each side of his temples.

I continued attending church every day after that, and gradually my thoughts about God and fantasies about Mr O'Reilly began to fade. It was infinitely preferable to concentrate on a man made of real flesh and blood, rather than one who was already dead and another who consisted of a wafer and a goblet of wine.

Father Macken always seemed pleased to see me, although our conversation was always related in some way to my so-

called prayers. "No luck with the request yet?" he would ask sympathetically.

"No, Father." I would dutifully reply.

However, I could see that he was clearly impressed, and also curious about what could be so important as to detain a young girl on her knees each evening. Fortunately, I had my answer ready for when he would eventually ask. For I knew that curiosity would eventually provoke a query.

One evening, as I was about to head home to my aunt's house for tea, having spent the last half hour thinking of what Father Macken would look like in the bath, he appeared beside me and my heart leapt in my throat.

"Is there anything I can do to help, dear child?" he asked anxiously. "It must be a very important request to keep you here so late in the evenings. Maybe I could add in some prayers too?"

I looked up at him, wondering what he would say if he knew that the only reason I now came to church was to see him. I had transferred all my feelings for Mr O'Reilly to him, and I was anxious for some progress.

"I, I don't know, Father . . ." I said dubiously. "I suppose a few extra prayers might be helpful." I looked at him coyly. "I'm sure your prayers, being a man of the cloth, Father, would hold a lot more weight with God."

Father Macken looked alarmed. "Oh no, no, my dear child. That's not true at all. God answers everyone's prayers, unless, of course, He has His own special reasons for not granting your request."

I looked down at the region where his crotch must be, hidden behind the voluminous folds of his cassock. "Yes, Father," I said meekly.

"Well, I'll have to know what we're praying for," he said cheerfully, and I knew that curiosity was killing him.

"`It's my aunt, Father."

"What do you mean, child?"

"She's not well, Father. In fact, she's very sick."

"My poor child. How sick?"

"Very sick, Father. In fact . . ." I said, warming to my theme, "it's fairly certain that she's going to die soon."

Almost simultaneously he put his arms out to offer me succour, and I moved towards him in a gesture of one surrendering a terrible burden. Then his arms were around me, and I was clinging to him.

"You poor child," he whispered tenderly, "is it, is it cancer?"

I nodded, as though unable to speak from grief. But in fact, I was revelling in the warmth of his embrace. I raised my head and looked at him earnestly.

"But she doesn't know that I know, Father. So you mustn't breathe a word to her, or to anyone else. No one knows except me, and now you, Father. She'd kill me if she discovered that I knew."

"Are you certain, child? There can be no doubt?"

"No, Father, unfortunately not. There was a letter from a cancer specialist on the kitchen table one evening, and I accidentally read it. It said that . . ." I paused for effect, "it said she hadn't got much longer to live."

I doubted if any medical specialist would put such a claim on paper. But thankfully, however, Father Macken didn't seem familiar with this kind of letter either.

"Well at least now, dear child, you'll have me to share your worries and fears with," Father Macken added. "With both of us praying for your aunt, maybe the good Lord will hear us better."

I didn't really mind him calling me 'child', although I would have preferred it if he'd seen me as the woman I was. After all, I was now thirteen years old and not a child any more.

He patted my cheek. "Run along home now. I'll see you here tomorrow after school, and we'll pray together for your aunt." He hesitated. "But you have to accept that maybe it's God's will that her time has come."

"Of course, Father," I nodded. "But at least we can pray for a happy death for her." In fact, I quite liked the idea of praying for my aunt's death!

Out of sight of the church, I hopped, skipped and jumped all the way home. I could still feel the touch of Father Macken's fingers on my cheek where he had stroked it in a comforting gesture. I wished I could have those fingers stroking other parts of my body. The parts that were described in Philip Breslin's book.

"You're in good form this evening," said my aunt disapprovingly as she served us each a meagre helping of stew from the pot that would be expected to last for another two days.

"I got top marks in my Irish essay," I replied, by way of explanation. I always got top marks anyway, so there was nothing to get excited about. Except thoughts of Father Macken.

CHAPTER 7

Ciara took out the box of photographs again. It was silly, she knew, but looking at the old photographs of herself and Niall helped to bring him close to her again. In the first few weeks after his death, getting out the box of photographs had assumed the importance of a ritual for her. It had become part of the process of unwinding, of gradually letting go the ties that bound her to him, and of coming to terms with his death.

It always brought a lump to her throat to look at the photos of Niall holding their new baby daughter, Sarah. He'd looked so happy, proud and awkward at the same time, and she'd felt overwhelmed by love for him. Then there were the pictures of Sarah's first Christmas, and the ridiculously large tricycle that Niall had brought home for her, before she was even walking, a sheepish grin on his boyish face.

Then there were the wedding photos themselves, when she'd floated up the aisle in a cloud of white tulle, never surer of her feelings than at that moment and totally confident of the bright future that lay ahead. Niall had looked so handsome, so eager, so confident too. Their brief honeymoon in Paris had produced a series of poorly focussed and silly photographs of each other, recalling idyllic days and nights drinking wine in little cafés off the Boulevard Saint Michel in Paris, visiting the Louvre and walking hand in hand along the banks of the Seine.

The photographs they accumulated over the years also included many portrayals of friends and family, each batch documenting the gradual changes that had taken place in all their lives. Before her very eyes, Ciara now watched them all grow older, as she, Niall and their contemporaries mellowed into their forties.

There were also photos of Ciara's beloved father Frank, taken just before he died from cirrhosis of the liver. All the years of heavy drinking, which had provided solace from his sense of failure at being unemployed, had finally taken their toll.

There were also the holiday photos, collected over many years – Charlie and Dee, Niall and Ciara getting an all-over tan on the Greek island of Kos, and several of Niall trying unsuccessfully to light a fire on a camping holiday in the Pyrenees. Then there were the ones of little Sarah in a sunhat, playing with her bucket and spade on the beach, Sarah on a donkey, Sarah with a gigantic ice-cream cone, a beard of ice cream spread all over her face.

Ciara sighed. That Sarah of long ago – that happy fun-loving baby – had now turned into an angry teenager. Ciara longed to be close to her daughter, but never had they felt farther apart.

A door upstairs slammed, and Ciara knew that

another confrontation was inevitable. Sarah was home
again from her stay with Annie, but relations continued
to be strained between them. The slamming door was
followed by the sound of stomping feet as Sarah
pounded down the stairs and into the living-room. A
cursory contemptuous glance from Sarah registered her
disapproval at her mother's absorption in the box of
photographs, and immediately put Ciara on the
defensive.

"Y-you're not going out like that?" Ciara asked. The
child looked hideous!

"Why are you always finding fault?" Sarah bristled,
eyes flashing, and Ciara regretted opening her mouth at
all. But what mother could let her daughter go out
looking like that?

"Well, your make-up is far too heavy . . ."

God, she shouldn't have said that. But Sarah did look
a fright – her young, vulnerable face was caked with a
shade of make-up that was completely wrong for her skin
tone. It ended at her jawline, making her face look like a
hideous mask. She wore some kind of glitter gel in her
hair that made her look as though she was wearing a
half-drowned rat on her head. Heavy blusher and bright
red lipstick completed the ghastly picture.

"Jesus, you're never happy!"

Ciara's heart went out to her unhappy daughter, not a
child any longer but not a fully-grown woman yet. Poor
Sarah probably thought she looked the epitome of
sophistication, whereas she looked cheap and available
instead of suave and elegant. Ciara gulped. She looks like
a child prostitute from one of those trendy French

movies, she thought. Why were children always in such a hurry to grow up?

"Look, love – I just don't want you give the wrong impression . . ."

"The wrong impression about what? You're just jealous, you old cow!"

"Sarah! How dare you speak to me like that."

Ciara clamped her mouth shut. Oh God, why had she said that? She was becoming the kind of person Sarah accused her of being! Would there ever come a time when they'd be friends again?

"What would you know about looking good?" Sarah threw the words at her mother contemptuously, casting a withering glance at Ciara's comfortable sweater and jeans. Then she flounced out of the room, and Ciara heard the front door slam with such force that the window panes rattled.

Ciara sat down, momentarily deflated from the exchange. Once again, she's put her two feet in it. What was a mother supposed to do – say nothing and risk letting her daughter get into situations she mightn't be able to handle? On the other hand, her comments hadn't changed anything – Sarah had still gone out looking ridiculous.

Ciara stood up from the table and closed the box of photographs. She no longer felt like looking at them.

God, her mother was impossible these days. Sarah flicked her scarf over her shoulder in a gesture of anger and defiance, as she made her way down the drive and away from the house. When she'd been a child her mother's concern had been like a warm comforting blanket, but now it was suffocating her. When did parents realise that their children were grown up?

Now that Daddy was dead, her mother was being totally unreasonable. What was wrong with staying overnight at Tim O'Driscoll's house? All the rest of the gang would be there. Their parents didn't treat them as though they were babies. And so what if some of her friends were from an older class? Hadn't she pointed out that some of her mother's friends were older too? Of course, her mother had quickly said that it wasn't quite the same when you were her age. But then she *would* say that, wouldn't she? Parents were always quick to move the goalposts when it suited them.

Sarah grimaced as one of her stiletto heels narrowly missed a pothole on the path. Of course, when she'd mentioned staying over at Tim's place, her mother had immediately asked if Tim's parents would be there. Which, of course, they wouldn't. They were away in Spain, and had no idea that their son was throwing a party. Naturally, she'd tried to bluff, but Mummy had decided for no reason at all that it wasn't a fit party for 'her child' to go to. Why was she saddled with such a mean, rotten mother?

As she headed for the bus stop, Sarah wondered why her mother couldn't be like Orla's or Fiona's. They didn't stop their daughters from staying out all night if they wanted to. At least, that's what Orla and Fiona had told her. Sarah had visions of her friends returning home from school each day to a cosy kitchen, filled with the smell of freshly-baked bread and cakes which their mothers were just taking out of the oven. She sighed in exasperation.

When her own mother happened to be at home, she'd be so involved with one of her stupid paintings that she'd forget all about the time. Then she'd throw a frozen pizza in the microwave, and expect her family to be happy with that. Sarah fumed. Her classmate Zoe Merrigan had recently lost her father too, but *her* mother let her wear make-up and bleach her hair! And you'd never see Zoe waiting at a bus stop!

Sarah sighed. If only she had someone like Ita for a mother. She'd been very impressed by the elegant woman who had accompanied Liam to her father's funeral, and she'd been touched by Ita's concern for her loss. Ita had treated her like an adult. Why couldn't her own mother be like that?

Mind you, she didn't really hate her mother, despite her totally unreasonable behaviour. Maybe her mother was going through the menopause. Sarah had read somewhere that this could be an emotionally traumatic time for a woman, especially if it coincided with the woman's daughter growing to maturity, since it accentuated the mother's waning attractiveness while her daughter's was developing to full bloom. That was it, Sarah decided with malicious pleasure. Her mother was jealous of her.

As the bus appeared in the distance, Sarah clenched her teeth with venomous anticipation. She'd practise her withering look in front of a mirror. When she got it right, she'd try it out on her mother, combining it with snide remarks about the menopause and her mother's declining attractiveness. Then, while she momentarily had the advantage, she'd turn on her heel and walk out, leaving her mother speechless for once in her life.

CHAPTER 8

The following day I was already kneeling in the church when Father Macken arrived. After his initial whispered greeting, he joined me in the pew and together we prayed in silence. At least, I assumed he was praying. I bowed my head and tried to look solemn, moving my lips occasionally to make it look as though I was storming the heavens on my aunt's behalf.

Occasionally, I sneaked a covert glance at Father Macken. He had his head in his hands as though cutting off any outside distractions, so I couldn't see his face. But I could study his strong shoulders and the curve of his neck. Watching him made my heart beat faster. I wished fervently that he would end his prayers — how long were we going to kneel there? On the other hand, once the prayers were over, it was likely that he would send me straight home.

Suddenly, I hit upon a plan. Experimentally at first, I tried a sob or two. They sounded quite effective, so I added a few more, increasing the sound level so that Father Macken could hear me. At the same time, I rubbed my eyes fiercely to redden them.

Peering out through my fingers, I could see Father Macken looking at me in alarm. "Are you all right, child?" he asked urgently. "Please don't cry. I know it's all been a terrible burden for you . . ."

"Oh Father," I wept, "I can't help it. Every time I think of my poor aunt, I get so upset. I'm going to be lost without her!"

Even that lie sounded hypocritical to me, but I didn't care. Father Macken had moved closer to me, and I was both frightened and excited at the same time. I desperately craved love and affection, and I was willing to pay for it in any way that I could.

I began to cry loudly, and Father Macken looked around the church in agitation, lest the prayers of other churchgoers might be disturbed. There were a few elderly women kneeling up near the altar, and they turned their heads to see what was happening.

"Come along, child," said Father Macken quietly. "You'd better come with me to the presbytery. You're in no fit state to go home yet. You'll only upset your aunt even more than she's bound to be already."

Together, we left the church and walked down the passageway at the side which led to the presbytery next door. The house was a large grey edifice, built in the same style and stone as the church. It looked cold and forbidding from the outside, but inside it proved to be warm and cosy, with a big log fire burning in the parlour grate.

"God bless Mrs O'Brien," said Father Macken cheerfully, removing the fireguard, and holding his hands in front of the fire to warm them. "She always lights the fire for me before she goes off to do her hospital visitations. Marvellous woman – the nearest thing to a saint."

He looked down at me. I must have looked a mess, for I had genuinely been crying. Not for my aunt, I hasten to add, but out of sheer loneliness and a desperate craving for affection. It was as though the few kind words from Father Macken had unleashed a torrent of pent-up feelings and longings within me. I wanted him to take me in his arms and cradle me tenderly, to tell me that I was a worthwhile person, that I wasn't all bad as my aunt continually inferred.

Perhaps thinking of my aunt's death, even though it wasn't truly imminent, made me realise how terribly alone I was in the world. I'd been off-loaded onto my aunt several years before, and she'd always let me know that I was only there on sufferance. I remembered little about my parents, or why I'd been abandoned by them. Were they dead? I didn't know. But any time I asked my aunt, she refused to discuss the matter. So by all accounts, I had no one who either loved me or wanted me.

"Would you like some tea, child?" Father Macken asked me. I nodded. The prospect of spending further time in the comfort of his parlour, and having his undivided attention, was heaven to me. Leaving me to warm myself by the fire, Father Macken headed out to the kitchen. I could hear the sounds of cupboards opening and closing, the clatter of dishes, then a boiling kettle whistling. Then he returned with a lace-covered tray, which he set down on a small table beside the fire.

"Are you feeling better now?" he asked, as he poured from the large silver pot. I nodded and drank my tea gratefully. It was in a china cup, paper-thin and exquisitely patterned. The clergy certainly knew how to look after themselves! In my aunt's house, we used old chipped cups, while the china remained on display in the china cabinet. How I wished I could

leave the austerity of my aunt's house, and live with Father Macken!

After several cups of tea and most of the plateful of biscuits, I felt that it was impossible to stretch out events for much longer. But I wanted so much to stay in that warm, caring environment. I suddenly realised that I would do anything – yes, anything – to stay there. And perhaps to come back again . . ."

Slowly and purposefully, I arose and walked over to where Father Macken was seated by the fire. "Father," I said shakily, "thank you very much for your help. I don't think I could have coped with this burden otherwise. Can we pray together again soon?"

"Yes, yes, of course," he said softly. "I'll meet you in the church tomorrow at the same time."

"Thank you, Father," I said. He leaned over to shake my hand, but I was quicker than him and I kissed him quickly on the lips. They were soft and tender, just as I had expected, and I felt a quiver of response run through him.

"My God, child!" he recoiled as though I had hit him. "You truly are the Devil's child! Go away from me!"

But I knew that he was frightened of his own instincts rather than of me. I knew about men and their instincts, although priests were supposed to restrain their feelings.

"But Father, I was only saying thank you," I whispered, looking forlorn and rejected. But I didn't move away. In fact, I moved closer to him and tried to take his hand. Taking it, he groaned, pulling me to him, our lips meeting again. It was as though a torrent had been unleashed inside him. Suddenly, he was kissing my neck, my ears, my mouth and muttering feverishly to himself. Then his hands were on my growing breasts, and I began searching among the folds of his cassock.

Yes, there it was, firm and ready, the desires of perhaps a lifetime gathering into one giant tumescence of longing.

Almost as I touched Father Macken's flesh, he erupted, apologising and groaning in pleasure and guilt at the same time. I glowed inwardly. At last I had what I craved most – his undivided attention. This man needed me for his most intimate pleasures – pleasures he couldn't legitimately seek elsewhere. And I was grateful for Philip Breslin's book, because in it I'd discovered the many ways to make a man happy. So far, poor Philip had been too embarrassed to ask for it back again, especially since he knew I was bound to have read it.

When it was over, Father Macken rearranged his clothes and put his head in his hands, sinking to the floor in prayer. "Oh my God, what have I done?" he moaned over and over again, intermittently mumbling a series of Latin prayers. I quietly let myself out of the presbytery and hurried home. I would await further developments.

During the following week, I prayed in the church each day after school but Father Macken never appeared. But I knew he eventually would. And it would be on Tuesday, when Mrs O'Brien went to do her hospital visiting. Sure enough, the following Tuesday he knelt down beside me as I pretended to pray, joining me in prayers for my supposedly dying aunt, whom I had never seen look so hale and hearty.

"Will you come back to the presbytery for a few minutes" he whispered anxiously when we had finished. "I really need to talk to you, about what happened . . ." I nodded.

In retrospect, I do believe that in all honesty he wanted to apologise and assuage his own guilt over what had happened, rather than look for a repeat performance. But I had my own agenda. Rising meekly, I followed him.

Once in the presbytery, I followed him into the kitchen where he was fussing around, trying not to look embarrassed as he placed the china on the tea tray. But I knew that despite his best intentions, he wanted the same thing to happen as had previously.

"Forget about the tea, Father," I said, taking his hand. "I'd rather be with you." He gave that now familiar groan and followed me inside to the parlour. By now, we both knew what was going to happen so we didn't even bother with preliminaries.

In the months that followed, our weekly rituals continued when Mrs O'Brien went hospital visiting. I continued to call him 'Father' because I wanted to assure him that while we'd overstepped one boundary, on every other level I intended to maintain the normal distance between cleric and layperson.

After his initial guilt trips and attempts to deny the strength of his own sexuality, we ceased to discuss my aunt's so-called illness at all. Maybe he, too, hoped that when she died I could move in to the presbytery and be with him always.

One day, when I'd taken him into my mouth and was gently and teasingly bringing him to orgasm, I thought I heard a door slam. My mouth was full so I couldn't easily speak, and Father Macken was clearly so lost in his own pleasure that he heard nothing. Maybe I'd been mistaken, so I continued to bring him to fruition.

Then the door to the parlour opened and there was a gasp. Father Macken jumped up, nearly choking me in the process, as Mrs O'Brien stood rooted to the ground, a look of horror on her face. I don't know how long we three stood there, each of us frozen in time, as though the horror of the situation needed further confirmation. Or else all our brains had ceased to *function, and we were trapped together in a tableau of shock and horror.*

I was the first to move. Without speaking to either of them, I hurried out the door, leaving then to face each other like sparring pit bull terriers. What would happen next, I wondered? Would my aunt be informed, and would a huge scandal ensue?

In vain, I awaited a summons from my aunt, from Father Macken, from the parish priest or even from one of the nuns who taught us. Every time a class was interrupted with a message for the teacher, I felt that this was it. I was about to be called upon to explain my side of the whole sordid story. I remember, Ciara, how you even commented on how edgy I was at that time. One day you came up behind me, and were amused because you accidentally made me jump. If only you had known what was going on!

The following Sunday there was a strange buzz in the church, an undercurrent of gossip and shaking of heads. After Mass, my aunt was accosted in the church grounds by a neighbour who was thrilled to be the first to tell her the news. Her face positively glowing, she told my aunt that Father Macken had left the parish. Just upped and went, she told her, with no explanation. My aunt was horrified and fascinated at the same time. Gossip was her life's blood, and gossip involving the clergy was even better.

I pretended not to listen while my aunt and her neighbour were talking. I did my best to look uninterested, kicking the gravel with what I hoped would be interpreted as a youthful degree of impatience and boredom. In this instance, I was willing to play the role of child who wouldn't be expected to show interest in the hasty departure of a young cleric.

I wondered who would replace him. In the event, it was an elderly man, Father O'Brien, to whom I took an instant dislike. Somehow, he seemed to remind me of someone, or something, I'd long forgotten . . .

The old priest's arrival heralded the end of that period of my life. Why was it, I wondered, that every man I got close to was eventually taken away from me? Perhaps next time, I would be luckier . . .

CHAPTER 9

Ciara woke up to find herself crying. "You bastard, you bastard . . ." she was mumbling, as Sarah rushed into her mother's bedroom and turned on the light.

"Are you OK?" Sarah asked, wide-eyed with fright. She had never seen her mother looking so upset. At least, not since her father died.

Ciara blinked as her eyes adjusted to the light. "Oh, Sarah. God, I was having the most awful dream."

Ciara shivered, and Sarah leaned across, wrapping the duvet around her mother's shoulders. This produced a fresh bout of tears, and Sarah patted her mother as one would soothe a bewildered child. The lateness of the hour seemed to have suspended hostilities between them, at least temporarily. For Sarah, it felt strange to be comforting her mother rather than fighting with her. Lately, fighting was all they ever seemed to do.

"Who were you calling a bastard?"

Ciara smiled now as she wiped her eyes. "Oh, just

someone I knew many years ago. I don't know why I should dream of him now."

"Was he an old boyfriend?"

Sarah had met lots of boys to whom she could apply that particular epithet.

"No – he was someone I worked with, that's all."

"Would you like a cup of tea?"

Ciara was moved by her daughter's concern, but decided not to push their fragile relations any further than necessary.

"Thanks, love, but no. I think I'll just try to get back to sleep again."

"OK. G'night."

"Sarah – thanks."

But her daughter had already turned off the light and left the room.

Alone in the darkness, Ciara shivered again. What on earth had brought that horrible bastard, Alan Moore, into her thoughts? Probably because he'd had the cheek to turn up at Niall's funeral.

Ciara pulled the duvet up around her chin. Before that, it had been a year since she'd last seen Alan Moore. On that occasion, she'd paid the price he'd asked, and since that day of closure he'd no longer had any hold over her. Niall was dead now anyway, so there was nothing further he could do to hurt her.

It was ironic to think that the fear she'd felt a year ago was of absolutely no consequence now. Yet at the time, it had almost destroyed her peace of mind. At least, Niall had been spared the trauma of knowing about those photographs.

Ciara sighed. Perhaps her motives for paying Alan Moore hadn't been entirely altruistic. Certainly, she'd wanted to spare Niall the pain, but she'd also wanted to preserve her husband's good opinion of her which would have been altered forever.

As she lay there, wrapped in her duvet, the memory of those awful few days kept returning to her mind. Especially the day that Alan Moore had phoned . . .

Ciara's heart had almost stopped when she'd heard the name. She'd clutched the telephone receiver so tightly that her knuckles turned white.

"Who did you say?"

"Alan Moore. I was hoping you'd remember me – I'm a photographer with *The Daily News*. I took some photographs of you – oh, it must be twenty-five years ago now. And I see from the newspaper photos of you at your latest exhibition that you're just as pretty as ever."

"Oh."

"How are you keeping?"

Ciara's mouth had gone dry, and she had to lick her lips to ensure that she was capable of uttering any sound at all. "Very well, thank you."

"I've been working abroad for quite a few years, but now I'm living back in Ireland again. Since I've been away, you've been doing really well in your career, haven't you, Ciara? In fact, you've become quite famous! I've seen you at a few receptions lately, but you've always been surrounded by people so I haven't bothered to intrude. But it's nice to keep in touch with old friends, isn't it?"

"Eh, yes. Of course."

"I was hoping that we could get together for a drink, or maybe lunch. I'd like to talk to you about a little proposition I have in mind."

"I-I see."

"Can we meet some time this week?"

"No, I mean yes. Where do you want to-"

"How about the Powerscourt Centre? There's a nice little restaurant there, on the balcony, called Chi Chi's. How about lunch there on Friday, say twelve thirty?"

"Well, yes. OK."

"Terrific. I'll be looking forward to it. See you there at half past twelve. Don't forget!"

As if she could. Ciara put the phone down and buried her face in her hands. What was she going to do? Her worst nightmare had finally come home to roost.

Ciara shuddered. Friday was only two days away. Two interminably long days. Two days of worry and stress. Two nights of tossing and turning without sleep. Because in her heart, she knew exactly what Alan Moore wanted.

CHAPTER 10

You were right, Ciara. Niall was different from the other boys. Although I'd previously preferred older men, Niall at sixteen already possessed a level of maturity that the other boys would take years, if ever, to achieve.

Isn't it funny that I knew Niall before you did, Ciara? And that if you hadn't come along when you did, he and I might have spent the rest of our lives together? Instead, the minute he saw you, he no longer had eyes for anyone else.

Although we girls went to the local convent school and the boys to nearby St Joseph's, the two groups always found ways of bumping into each other! That was the year I was fifteen, and both Niall and I had classes that ended early on a Wednesday afternoon. I would often see him standing outside the small sweet shop with some of his friends. I would walk on, then a few minutes later he would catch up with me, with long strides of his strong muscular legs.

I was, of course, greatly pleased that he enjoyed my company enough to walk home with me each Wednesday. Of all the boys, I liked him best. In fact, everyone did. He had that maturity, that special something that had attracted me both to Mr O'Reilly and Father Macken.

We talked about lots of things that year. It was a vital year for both of us in terms of our physical development. Over the course of one term I watched him grow several inches taller, until he was towering over me. And I was secretly thrilled when sometimes I caught him sneaking a glance at my developing breasts. They'd grown rapidly over the previous summer, and I'd gone from a flat-chested plump child to a woman in the space of several months.

Even my aunt had noticed, and obliquely referred to my need for `some kind of brassiere'. One day she gave me money and sent me to the local drapery store where, she informed me, Mrs Brady would find 'something suitable' for me. Clearly, the matter had been discussed prior to my visit, for the minute the old woman saw me she produced a series of garments that looked as though they'd make ideal harnesses for horses.

I wanted to try on the half-cupped lacy types I'd seen in magazines, and which would have shown off my new assets much better. But Mrs Brady was scandalised at such a proposition, and would only sell me the 'serviceable' ones. Yet, instinctively I knew that if a man was interested in a woman's breasts, he was unlikely to care about the kind of contraption that was holding them.

So when I first noticed Niall looking at my breasts, I began leaving the first few buttons of my school blouse open. I knew that got him excited, but I also knew that since he was such a nice boy, he'd never do more than look. Unless I encouraged him.

One day, the weather was particularly warm, so I feigned

near-collapse from the heat. As we were passing a sweet shop near the quarry, Niall went in and bought us both ice-pops to cool us down. I then suggested that we climb over the quarry fence, dump our schoolbags and rest undisturbed beneath the trees while we consumed them. Niall quickly agreed, and I made sure that he had a good view of my knickers as I climbed over the fence.

Lying in the sun beneath the tree, I languished happily, making sure that most of the buttons on my blouse had 'accidentally' come undone.

"It's lovely here, isn't it?" I remarked, stretching out on the grass. My bra was clearly visible now, and I could see that Niall was feeling a little embarrassed – and hopefully excited – as he tried to look only at my face. Satisfied that things were working the way I wanted them to, I lay back and closed my eyes. That would save his blushes and allow his eyes to rest uninterrupted on my breasts. I knew that while my bra was not particularly attractive, all that would matter to him was what was in it.

After a minute or so, I stretched lazily, letting Niall know that I was about to begin communication again, and allowing him to divert his eyes without embarrassment. I resumed licking my ice-pop which, by now, was exactly the way I wanted it to be – all melting and runny.

Turning to Niall, I held the ice-pop where it was bound to drip on my blouse. I could feel the cold sticky dollops as they fell, but I pretended to be oblivious to them.

Niall gulped with embarrassment. "Your clothes, that ice-pop is dripping on your, eh-"

I squealed in mock dismay. "Oh God! Just look at me!" I said, sitting up and rubbing furiously at the big orange stain on the right cup of my bra. "I'll be killed if my aunt sees it. Ugh! It feels all sticky."

I looked at Niall to see his reaction. "I think I'd better take my bra off."

"What?"

"Well, it's sticking to my skin . . ." I replied reasonably, "and it's very uncomfortable."

"Y-you mean here?" Niall's voice was an incredulous whisper.

"Why not?" I said artlessly, "I can't go home with it covered in orange stains. My aunt would kill me if she saw it. If I put it in my bag, I'll be able to wash it in the bathroom before she finds out."

Without suggesting that he turn his back, I whipped off my school blouse. "Open the back for me, will you?" I asked, turning my back towards him so that he had access to the hooks. As he fumbled, I could feel the warmth of his fingers on my flesh, and it was a heady feeling. As soon as he'd opened the back, I whipped off the bra and turned to face him. He'd turned a shade of deep red, and though he tried to avert his eyes from my breasts, I could see that he was unable to do so.

"Do you like my breasts, Niall?" I asked him, as seductively as I could. "You can touch them if you like."

He groaned and backed away slightly, but not before I gripped his right hand and lifted his fingers to one of them. This time, he didn't back away.

He groaned softly as his fingers caressed my nipples, and I reached forward to feel the front of his school trousers. As I had hoped, there was a huge erection straining against the material. Gently, I rubbed it and pulled him down beside me in the grass. Together we lay there, him feverishly sucking my nipples, me *caressing his hard penis through his open fly. This, I knew, was how to keep a man happy. I might not be as attractive as some of the other girls, but I had exactly the same anatomy. And I'd discovered early in life how to use mine.*

Suddenly he groaned, and I knew that he was about to come. So I speeded up the rhythm of my fingers and he came all over my hand. Embarrassed now, he tried to use his handkerchief to mop it up. He wouldn't look at me, and I could see that he felt in some way humiliated, as though this temporary lapse of control was an aspect of his character that he found difficult to accept.

Quickly, I got up and slipped on my school blouse, then tucked the orange-stained bra into my schoolbag. Still not looking at me, Niall adjusted his own clothing and started walking across the field towards the fence.

"Wait for me!" I called. He slowed down and waited, although still not looking at me. When I caught up with him, I gave his hand a squeeze. "We can do this everyday after school if you like," I whispered.

Niall turned briefly towards me, muttered something non-committal and climbed over the fence onto the road. I followed, and we walked on in silence until we came to the road where I turned off for my aunt's house.

"See you tomorrow!" I said cheerily, but all I got in return was a grunt.

I wasn't surprised by his reaction. I knew Niall was deeply embarrassed, but I also suspected he'd be fantasising about my breasts that night. And that he'd risk further embarrassment the next day, for the chance of a repeat performance.

CHAPTER 11

Ciara shivered as she remembered the lascivious way that Alan Moore had looked at her that day. Even now, the sensation of being undressed by his eyes was just as intense as when it had happened.

He'd been at the restaurant when she'd arrived.

"Ah, Ciara. How lovely to see you," Alan Moore rose to his feet, kissing her cheek warmly. "You're looking wonderful. You're one of those lucky women who actually improve with age. You'll still be a beauty when you're ninety!"

He appraised her with his photographer's eye and she blushed, in spite of herself, at his admiring scrutiny. She tried to smile, but all that her tense facial muscles would allow was a grimace. Relax, she told herself, don't let him know that he's got you on edge.

Alan Moore had aged considerably himself. He had lost most of his hair, and was now sporting a large pot belly – the result of too many receptions and press lunches. But Ciara returned the compliment, telling him how well he too was looking. I can be a hypocrite too, she reasoned.

Taking her hands in his across the table, he looked tenderly into her eyes. "Dear me, you must learn to relax, Ciara. We can't have that lovely face all tensed up, can we?"

Ciara gave him a dazzling smile, which she didn't feel like at all, and tried to extricate her hands from his. But he held onto them, actually tightening his grip as he felt her draw away. Fortunately for Ciara, the waiter arrived at precisely that moment and she was able to withdraw her hands in order to take the menu being offered to her.

"Lamb chops are today's special," the waiter informed them. "I'd also recommend the veal, both of which are supplied directly from our own farms."

Ciara felt like screaming. She fully empathised with the poor sheep and calves that were on today's menu. Like them, she was trapped, with no way of escape. How could she think of food when her stomach was heaving with nerves? Finally, she selected the salmon, wondering guiltily if it was any easier for a fish to die than any other creature. Alan ordered the veal, and Ciara suppressed her distaste as images of sad little calves, bled and dead before they'd even had a chance to live, filled her mind. Typical, she thought. Alan Moore would revel in any kind of exploitation.

"And may we see the wine list?" Alan drawled. "Today is a special day, so I'd like a really special wine to toast my good friend, here. Red or white, Ciara?"

Ciara shrugged her shoulders. She didn't care what

colour the wine was. It could be the colours of the national flag for all she cared. But she kept her composure, trying to look interested and agreeable when the waiter recommended a white 1983 Chardonnay, premier cru. Glancing at the wine list, Ciara noticed that it was the most expensive bottle listed.

"An excellent choice! Only the best will do for my dear friend!" Alan Moore beamed at the waiter, then at Ciara.

When the waiter had departed with their order, Alan Moore continued to make small talk, chatting about his job, the weather, and how lovely Ciara was looking. Ciara did her best to respond to his overtures, trying to look serene and to smile as much as possible. She would not give him the satisfaction of knowing how on edge she really was.

She'd had her hair done earlier that morning, and she had worn her chic new beige dress with a smart black jacket over it. The skirt was short, and showed off her shapely legs. Ciara hoped that it conveyed a casual, relaxed and informal image. She had been determined to look glamorous; not so much to impress Alan Moore as to assure him, and herself, that she was a woman in control. How long is he going to keep me in suspense, she wondered.

During the meal he was unbearably solicitous towards her, attending to her every need at the table, making a great show of passing her salt and pepper, and squeezing her hand at every opportunity. Ciara tried to keep her hands and body well away from him, but it required a constant vigil since the table was small and

Alan Moore seemed possessed of a dozen pair of hands. Ciara found it all very disconcerting. He'd never behaved so flamboyantly towards her before. What was he playing at?

He kept raising his glass – and forcing her to raise hers – in a series of banal toasts to things as disparate as the pursuit of happiness, fine weather for the weekend, and Ireland to win the upcoming international rugby match. Ciara wanted to hit him over the head. He was toying with her, like a cat with a mouse before the final kill. Clearly, he was going to eke out her torment until the very last minute.

When the coffee finally came, Alan reached down by the side of his chair and indicated the flat brown package he now held in his hand.

"I have a little surprise for you, Ciara!" he said coyly, sliding it across the table towards her, like a lover shyly offering his beloved an expensive gift.

Ciara made no move to take it, since she knew exactly what was inside.

"Aren't you going to take a peep?" Alan asked cheerfully. "I was sure that you'd want to take a trip down memory lane. You know, those photos were among the best I've ever taken." He grinned slyly at her. "I'm sure you'd look just as good if I took the same kind of photos today."

Ciara felt sick. There was a lot she'd like to have said to Alan Moore, but she decided to say as little as possible. She didn't trust herself to remain civil if she spoke.

"What exactly do you want?" she asked, looking stonily at him.

"Ah." Alan Moore studied the tablecloth in minute detail before speaking, and Ciara recalled his use of the very same delaying tactics many years before. Ciara longed to lean forward and hit him with the coffee pot, or stab him with one of the knives still on the table. Right now, he seemed to be enjoying this opportunity to make her squirm.

At last he spoke. "I was hoping that you might like to, ah, buy this delightful collection of souvenirs. You might even like to have them framed as a gift for your husband. I'm sure he'd be tickled pink to know what his little darling got up to in her youth . . ."

"Stop it!" As she said it, Ciara instantly regretted her reaction. She was letting Alan Moore see that he had broken through her composure, and he would enjoy that.

"Sorry," he said, not meaning it at all, and wanting her to know that he didn't mean it, "I was sure that you'd be delighted to have them. And, of course, the negatives as well."

"How much?" Ciara asked abruptly.

"Good heavens, Ciara. You're rather direct, aren't you? There's no beating around the bush with you."

He leaned across the table, pursed his lips in a kiss, then whispered the amount he wanted.

Ciara sat bolt upright, her eyes blazing. "You must be joking!"

"Well . . ." said Alan smoothly, "it seems a perfectly reasonable sum to me. That sleazy tabloid, *The Sunday Globe*, would pay a lot more. You know how they love to dish the dirt on celebrities, Ciara. And that's what you are now, my dear – a celebrity. Why, I'm sure you'd get twice that amount from the sale of just one of your paintings."

Ciara sighed. She was beaten and she knew it. Whether she'd worn her best outfit or come in sackcloth and ashes, it wouldn't have made any difference in the end. Alan Moore had his price, and so had she. And she would have to pay his price to save her marriage and her self-respect. Sometimes, she felt that she'd already paid the price ten times over, through years of guilt and shame. But soon, it would all be over and done with for good.

"When can I have the photos and the negatives?"

Alan blew her a kiss from the far side of the table. "As soon as you can produce the money, my sweet Ciara."

"I'll have it on Monday."

"Marvellous," Alan smiled warmly at her, and raised his glass towards her. "It's a pleasure doing business with you, my dear. Let me drink to you – the consummate professional in everything you do."

Alan began pouring the remainder of the wine bottle into Ciara's glass, but she stood up.

"No, thank you. I must be going."

"Oh dear, what a pity. I'd hoped that once we'd got our little business deal sorted out, we could relax together and talk about old times." Leaping to his feet, he made a dramatic show of helping her on with her jacket, and Ciara wondered yet again what he was playing at. "Must you really go? Well, if you insist, my dear. But promise me one thing, Ciara. That you'll have dinner with me on Monday night, so that we can finalise our little deal in amicable surroundings."

He took her hands in his, raised them to his lips and

kissed them flamboyantly. "Please, my dear – indulge an old friend. Then you can have the photos and negatives, and be gone from my life forever." He gave a deep mock sigh, looking at her beseechingly.

And you'll have your bloody money, Ciara thought. She had no other option but to agree. Until the exchange took place, he was still the one in control.

"All right."

"Wonderful! I'll book a table at the Red Rooster for around eight."

Ostentatiously, he picked up the small portfolio of photographs and collected his own coat. Ciara walked on ahead, intending to stop at the cash desk to pay her own half of the bill. Then she changed her mind and walked straight through the foyer and out into the street. To hell with equality, she thought. Today, she wasn't Alan Moore's equal. Until she'd paid him, she would remain his plaything.

Outside the Powerscourt Centre, Ciara quickly turned down into Johnson Court, a narrow side street full of little shops which led into Grafton Street. She wanted to get away from Alan Moore's prying eyes and lose herself in the crowded streets as soon as possible.

Quickly, she darted a glance behind and was thankful to discover that he wasn't heading in the same direction. She'd felt invaded by his proximity, and longed to put miles between them. Unseeing, she passed the big stores and small boutiques of the city's most fashionable area. Normally, she'd have been unable to resist the lure of the brightly-lit windows, but now she hurried by, intent on getting back to the carpark and driving home. Only when she'd closed her own front door on the outside world would she feel safe.

Luckily, Ciara knew that she had more than enough money in her own bank account, so Niall need never know about the payment to Alan Moore. Her last exhibition had brought in several thousand euro, even after the gallery and Liam's commission had been paid. Perhaps Alan Moore is right, she thought ironically. Maybe I am a celebrity after all.

She was grateful now that she and Niall had always kept separate bank accounts. While there had never been any secrecy between them over money, this way they both maintained their independence. Usually, Niall paid the mortgage while she bought the groceries, but this was just a casual arrangement, born of habit. Neither of them ever checked or asked about what the other spent, and this arrangement had served them well. Now for the very first time she was about to deceive him.

Back home, Ciara tried to shake off the terrible anxiety she felt. She would have to present a happy face to Niall when he came home from work, since she couldn't afford to let him suspect that anything was wrong. Hopefully, Sarah would be in a reasonable mood. Under present circumstances, Ciara feared she might overreact to her daughter's constant carping and mood swings.

Unfortunately, Sarah was her usual petulant self. As the three of them sat down at the dinner table, she turned up her nose at the roast Ciara had prepared, reminding her mother that she was on a diet.

"I'll just have some chocolate pudding," she said ungraciously, going to the fridge.

"Sarah, you'll need to eat healthier food than that if you want to get rid of those pimples," Ciara pointed out mildly. "Chocolate can cause spots, you know."

Sarah slammed the fridge door shut. "There you go again, always finding fault! I just can't do anything right, can I? Just because you sell a few bloody pictures, you think you know everything!" She stormed out of the room and pounded up the stairs.

Niall and Ciara both continued eating in silence. The roast was tasty, but Ciara couldn't enjoy it. Apart from feeling sick with tension, she'd eaten the entire salmon cutlet at lunchtime rather than let Alan Moore think he'd caused her to lose her appetite.

Niall didn't seem to be in conversational mood either. He seemed preoccupied, and Ciara caught him looking strangely at her from time to time. Perhaps she was letting her agitation show too much.

Ciara jumped up and began clearing the table, although it was actually Niall's turn since she'd done the cooking. But tonight she was in no mood to squabble about who did what around the house.

"Do you want any dessert?"

"No thanks, just coffee would be fine," Niall stretched. "I had quite a big lunch today."

At the mention of lunch, Ciara blanched but said nothing. But as she carried out the dirty dishes, Niall strolled out to the kitchen after her.

"Speaking of lunch, how was your day?" he asked her, as he took down the coffee mugs from the dresser.

"Oh fine, thanks."

Ciara busied herself cutting cheese and putting

crackers in a bowl, although she knew that Niall didn't want them, and neither did she.

"Did you go anywhere nice?"

"No. I mean, yes. But nowhere special."

Ciara caught his eye, and found Niall looking at her quizzically. An answer was clearly required.

"I-I met an old friend from years back."

Ciara carried the cheese board into the dining room, as Niall followed with the mugs and the coffee pot.

"That was nice," said Niall, as he sat down again. "Was it anyone I know?"

Ciara longed for an earthquake or a bolt of lightning to strike the house, anything that would distract Niall from the details of her lunch date. She'd have to lie. There was no other way out.

"Well, yes. I'm sure you remember Marguerite. I haven't seen her since we left school."

"The big, overweight girl? Yeah, I remember. But I thought she lived somewhere in Europe?"

"Yes, the South of France. She's just home on holiday."

"Isn't she the one with loads of kids?"

"Yes, she has six."

Ciara thought of the family photo that Marguerite had recently sent her. It had arrived as an attachment to a cheery e-mail, and showed her large, jolly friend smiling happily beside a handsome dark-haired man who had his arm protectively around her. On the floor in front of them an assortment of grinning children were seated, ranging in age from around five to fifteen. They all look so happy, Ciara had thought wistfully at the time. How lucky

Marguerite is – I've only got one child, and she hates my guts.

Ciara drank her coffee, noting gratefully that Niall seemed to have dropped the subject. He'd already picked up the evening newspaper and disappeared behind it. She hated lying, but after all it was only a white lie, wasn't it?

For several minutes they sat in silence, Niall reading while Ciara fiddled nervously with the edge of the tablecloth, trying to look as though she hadn't a care in the world. Under normal circumstances, they'd sit together in companionable silence for hours. But this evening, Ciara felt that her nerves were in ribbons.

"Oh, by the way," Niall lowered his newspaper, and Ciara almost jumped with fright. "I won't be home for dinner on Monday evening."

Ciara nodded. This news was like manna from heaven. She'd been wondering how to tell Niall that she herself would be out on Monday night. Now there was no need.

CHAPTER 12

The next day, Niall seemed reluctant to join me for the walk home. So I set out on my own, nonchalantly swinging my schoolbag, as though his presence was of no importance to me. But just as I suspected, he caught up with me before I reached the fence that led into the quarry. And well out of sight of the road, we had another session of panting and touching. This time, he had no hesitation in removing my bra. Almost as soon as we kissed, his fingers were eagerly searching my back for the hooks and I was reaching for the zip of his trousers.

I'd always thought myself too clever to get pregnant. But with hindsight, I realise I'd absolutely no knowledge about how to prevent it. Back then, adults regarded pre-marital pregnancy as a huge disgrace, yet they took no steps to explain how it could be avoided. Merely hoping that youngsters wouldn't follow the dictates of their hormones seemed a poor substitute for practical advice.

Do you remember, Ciara, how we all aired our theories about pregnancy prevention? During breaks between classes, or during sewing class when the atmosphere was less formal, we'd discuss the matter with endless fascination. We were relieved when Vera Malone assured us that it was impossible to get pregnant the first time you did it. But our delight turned to concern when Dot was told by her cousin that you could get pregnant even if you kept your knickers on, because sperm were like germs, and could get in anywhere.

After several weeks of secret visits to the quarry with Niall, and increasingly passionate sessions, I realised that my period was late. At first, I didn't worry too much. I'd read that other things could delay or alter the monthly cycle. We'd been doing mid-term exams and, while I'd never had to worry about getting good marks, maybe I'd been more stressed than I'd realised.

But as time went by, I really began to worry. And my aunt, who I'd thought was oblivious to my comings and goings, commented on the fact that I hadn't been using up the sanitary towels in the bathroom cupboard. "I hope you haven't been up to anything," was her snide comment on the subject.

After three whole months, during which time my schoolwork suffered sufficiently to draw comments from several teachers, I had to accept the inevitable. I was pregnant. Before long, I began to feel ill in the mornings. I couldn't face the porridge prepared by my aunt each morning, but under her beady eyes I forced it down then ran to the quarry where I vomited it all up again. I would lean over the side of the sheer rock face, and when I'd relieved my stomach of its contents I'd lie down in the grass, feeling drained before the day had even begun.

What was I going to do? I'd no way of knowing how to get a pregnancy terminated. I knew that abortions were illegal in

*Ireland, so I'd have to go to England to get one. Dot McNally
had told us that her cousin had once had an abortion in London.
But I certainly wasn't going to ask Dot for help, since she'd
already aired her cousin's problem in front of everyone! No
doubt the cousin had sworn her to secrecy, but Dot could never
keep her mouth shut.*

*I longed to confide in someone, but I knew it was out of the
question. I even thought of telling you, Ciara. Funny, isn't it?
Especially since I'd longed for a similar fate to befall you. But I
couldn't bear to be the recipient of your concern and kindness
– it would just have confirmed my own feelings of inadequacy
in your presence.*

*Telling my aunt was, of course, out of the question. I couldn't
bear to watch the triumphant gloating in her eyes. "I knew you'd
never amount to any good," she'd say, then I'd be frog-marched
down to Father O'Brien, no doubt to receive a lecture on my
foolhardiness and the sacredness of the life that I was carrying
inside me. Then I'd be punished for conceiving this 'sacred' life
by being sent to a convent somewhere down the country. And
when my baby was born, it would be taken away and given to
some childless couple – a man and woman whose relationship
had been 'sanctified' by a church marriage.*

*In sewing class, we'd all discussed the cruel treatment of
women who'd had the misfortune to conceive a child outside
marriage. Everyone had a horror story to tell, of female relatives
who'd suddenly disappeared, taken away to toil in convent
laundries as punishment for their 'sin'.*

*The obvious answer was to tell Niall. In my dreams he was
pleased to hear my news, and we'd plan our wedding. I thought
about the little house that we'd have. Perhaps we'd build it
ourselves, out in the country, where our child would benefit*

from the fresh air and open spaces. In these daydreams, the sun always shone, our child was happy and healthy, and everyone envied us our happiness.

I decided that I'd better tell Niall sooner rather than later, since I didn't want to look hugely pregnant in my wedding dress. A dance was being held at the rugby club the following Saturday night, and I knew that Niall was going to be the DJ. Hopefully, I'd get an opportunity at the interval to have a few discreet words with him. Many times, I rehearsed what I'd say to him and dreamed of how delighted he'd be.

As it happened, fate cruelly intervened. An epidemic of chickenpox broke out in the area, and as I got ready to go to the dance that night (my aunt thought I was going to study at a classmate's house) the first spots appeared on my arms. I tried to hide them by wearing long sleeves, but my beady-eyed aunt noticed that two large spots had appeared on my face and instantly knew what had caused them.

I was given a bottle of calamine lotion and marched upstairs to my room, without even a chance to phone you, Ciara, or any of the other girls who were going to the dance. So for two whole weeks all I could do was scratch my scabs, wait and worry.

At last, my chickenpox was cured and I was relieved to go back to school. After class on my first day back, I looked for Niall outside the sweet shop, but he wasn't hanging out with the usual crowd of boys and girls that congregated there after school. I didn't want to draw attention to the fact that I was looking for him, so I set off home alone. For a whole week I looked for him without success. It was almost as though he'd disappeared off the face of the earth. Maybe he'd developed chickenpox too, I reasoned. Nearly all our class had got it, and St Joseph's had fallen victim to the epidemic as well.

What I didn't know was that he was rushing out of school early to meet you, Ciara. Besotted by you, he wanted to spend every possible moment with you. As long as I live, I will never forget that day when you and Niall joined the student throng outside the sweet shop. You were holding his hand, there was a pink glow of happiness on your pretty face, and I wanted to kill you. Niall was looking sheepish yet proud, in the way that teenage boys do when they are in love. Nothing specific was said, but there was a buzz throughout the group as though everyone had acknowledged that something fundamentally different and unique had happened. There wasn't the usual teasing or ribaldry. Everyone seemed to be behaving differently, as though some rite of passage had just been achieved.

We were all going to the local café for a coffee, and as the group moved off I edged Vera Malone aside and queried what I already suspected.

"Yes, they're going out together," she whispered, all excited. "They met at the rugby club dance – were you not there yourself? Oh shit, I forgot! You had chickenpox. Poor thing, are you feeling OK now?"

I could have strangled kind-hearted Vera at that minute. I didn't want to discuss my chickenpox with her. I wanted to know why my world was falling apart.

"They're going out together, you say?"

Vera giggled and blushed, as though she was personally involved in the romance. "They're madly in love. They're even talking about getting married! Isn't it so exciting?"

I tried to keep a deadpan expression on my face as I looked at you, Ciara, walking ahead of me, holding Niall's hand tightly and gazing up at him like a lovesick calf. And he, with new-found confidence and pride, was clutching your hand tightly. It was as though there was an invisible aura surrounding both of you, from which everyone else was excluded yet party to at the same time. And at that moment, Ciara, I hated you. I hated you for your prettiness, your happiness, but most of all for taking what I'd believed was mine.

If I'd announced my pregnancy by Niall, I could have destroyed your happiness at that moment. I desperately wanted to, but in doing so I'd have risked hurting myself more. Instead, I just stood there, mute among my peers, hating them all. Because I was plain and overweight, it never crossed anyone's mind that I'd been able to seduce the handsomest boy in the school. And I vowed there and then that I'd get him back again some day, if only to prove that I was as good as you. And I vowed that some day in the future – I didn't know where or when – you'd pay in full for what you'd just done to me.

Chapter 13

"You're looking terrific, Ciara, as always."

Alan Moore smiled appreciatively, kissing Ciara's cheek again as she joined him at his table in the Red Rooster restaurant. It was early evening, but already most of the booths were occupied. Laughter and the clinking of glasses could be heard, but the sounds were muted by the luxurious surroundings, creating exactly the perfect ambiance of an expensive restaurant.

Under different circumstances, Ciara would have thoroughly enjoyed dining there. It was terribly expensive, and definitely not the kind of place that people went to for a casual meeting. Captains of industry, judges, bishops, politicians and government ministers were its more usual clientele.

The floor area was tiered, so that diners sat at different levels. This meant that the more elevated cubicles offered the greatest privacy. Surprisingly, Alan Moore was seated at a fairly central table, which was probably the least private of all.

Ciara was puzzled. Given that they were completing a very private transaction, his choice of seating was quite a surprise. Unless of course a more private table hadn't been available at such short notice. That was probably the reason, Ciara concluded. Very expensive restaurants like the Red Rooster were bound to be booked up for weeks in advance, and clearly their regular clientèle would get first preference.

It also occurred to her that the seating arrangement might merely be another way in which Alan Moore hoped to unnerve her. So she made no reference to it, preferring to let him think that she was perfectly at ease no matter where they were sitting.

Ciara had also been surprised at the choice of venue. All weekend, she had pondered on his choice of restaurant, but could make no sense of it. After all, there was absolutely no need for him to pick up the tab for such an expensive dinner, or even dinner at all, when the transaction could have been completed anywhere. They could have simply met in a pub or on a park bench, just like they did in the movies.

On the other hand, maybe Alan Moore intended to leave her to pay the bill. He might intend making that kind of gesture as a final act of contempt towards her. Ciara shrugged her shoulders. If that was his plan, so be it. She would gladly pay, just to be finished with him forever.

With equal attentiveness on this occasion, Alan Moore fussed over her. How ironic, Ciara thought. Anyone watching them would think that he positively doted on her. Even the waiting staff had clearly labelled them as a couple who were probably celebrating some anniversary. Why on earth did they have to go through with this ridiculous charade?

Once again, Ciara had come dressed to the nines. While she knew it would make no difference to the outcome of the evening, her pride would not let her do anything less. On this occasion, she had worn a plain but elegant cap-sleeved velvet dress. Its dark green colour flattered her creamy skin, and she wore her hair piled high in a chignon. She carried the money in a matching dark green handbag which she knew was also big enough to hold the photographs and negatives that she was due to receive in return.

"I have the money."

"Wonderful. And I have the photographs."

"And the negatives too, I hope."

"Yes, of course, my dear. They're all in the same envelope. Depend on it, Ciara." Alan leaned over and blew her a kiss. "I'd never cheat on you."

No, but you'd blackmail me without an ounce of remorse, Ciara thought. But she said nothing.

"And I'd gladly have given you the pictures free gratis, if I hadn't been a bit stuck for cash myself."

Ciara grimaced. "Save me the hard luck stories, Alan." she said curtly.

Alan slid the small package across the table, so surreptitiously and naturally that no one else could possibly have noticed.

"A deal is a deal," he said softly, "and that's all there is to it. as far as I'm concerned. So let's drink to its completion. And to future happiness."

He raised his glass and smiled at her. "C'mon, Ciara. Let me see a big smile. You should be happy, now that you've got what you want."

Ciara felt angry, but she kept a forced smile on her face. The cheek of that bastard, she thought. He was almost implying that he was doing her a favour, rather than blackmailing her!

Ciara took the envelope of banknotes from her handbag and discreetly placed it underneath the saucer of Alan's coffee cup. The notes were in large denominations, so the envelope didn't look as though it contained several thousand euros.

Simultaneously, they both picked up the relevant envelopes. Ciara put hers straight into her handbag, while Alan Moore slipped his into the inside pocket of his jacket. Neither of them bothered to check the contents.

"Isn't it nice that we trust each other?" said Alan.

For a moment, Ciara almost felt as though, now that the whole sordid business was over, he was actually trying to establish some sort of rapport between them. He actually wants me to forgive him, Ciara realised in surprise.

Instead, Ciara smiled back at him, raising her glass in a final toast. "To honest and decent friends," she said softly.

And she was gratified to see that Alan Moore had the decency to blush.

The house was in darkness when Ciara returned home. Sarah was staying over at a friend's house, and hopefully Niall would be asleep by now and wouldn't realise that it was nearly three in the morning.

Closing the front door as quietly as possible, Ciara tiptoed into the kitchen. The heat from the range provided instant comfort and she rubbed her cold hands together to warm them. For they were still frozen from having had to stand around in a cold and poorly-lit back-street for hours.

As if the evening spent with Alan Moore hadn't been bad enough. On leaving the restaurant, she'd hurried along the narrow street to collect her car, eager to put as much distance between her and Alan Moore as possible. Yet when she reached the vehicle, she'd experienced total disbelief. All four tyres were flat! On closer examination, she discovered that each tyre had been slashed several times.

The darkness of the street had been frighteningly oppressive, and she'd felt vulnerable too. Then she'd phoned the Automobile Association on her mobile phone, and waited in her car until they were able to send out a service engineer to help her.

Under different circumstances, she might have phoned Niall. He would have immediately jumped into his own car and come to help her, even if only to provide support while she waited for the AA to arrive. But she felt too guilty to inconvenience him after what had just transpired with Alan Moore. Besides, she was carrying the incriminating photographs, and anyway, she'd just remembered that he'd been out himself that evening. It wouldn't be fair to expect him to come back into the city again.

After her call to the AA, there'd been a further wait in her car, during which time she'd been both terrified and frozen. It seemed ages, although in reality it had only been half an hour, before the bright yellow van arrived on the scene and the friendly serviceman informed her that regrettably, it was impossible to get replacement tyres at such a late hour, so her options were limited. She could either opt to have her car towed home, or he would tow her car to a garage where she could leave it overnight. Then she could get replacement tyres the following morning when the garage opened. Gratefully, Ciara opted to leave the car at a garage overnight, and the AA patrolman kindly drove her home afterwards.

As he dropped her off outside her driveway, the AA man suggested that she contact the police about the incident.

"OK," Ciara promised as she thanked him, "I'll contact them in the morning." Of course, she had no intention of doing so. The night's events had been harrowing enough. She didn't want any further attention drawn to it.

Home at last, Ciara was grateful for the peace and tranquillity of the empty kitchen. With trembling hands, she unwrapped the package she'd been given by Alan Moore and opened the front of the Aga. Pausing only to ensure that she did indeed have the photographs, Ciara lit them with a match and dropped them into the range one by one, watching as the heat curled each one up and they disintegrated. Finally, she checked the negatives, lit them and dropped them in too, watching as the celluloid strips dissolved in the heat. As a final gesture, she crumpled up the wrapping and tossed it in as well. Her spirits lifted. It was over, and she need never feel guilty again.

It was there that Niall found her a few minutes later, when he came downstairs in his dressing-gown. He looked surprised to see her sitting alone in the kitchen staring into the open furnace.

"Where on earth have you been until this hour?"

Ciara felt overcome with fatigue, and not in the mood for answering belligerent questions.

"I had problems with the car," she said abruptly. "Some vandal decided to take a knife to the tyres. I had to wait for the AA."

"Where were you tonight?"

"I was meeting a friend," Ciara replied shortly.

"The same friend you met for lunch, a few days ago?"

"Yes, so what? You were out tonight too, weren't you? But I'm not interrogating *you*, am I?"

Niall shrugged his shoulders and turned away. Ciara was so relieved at having managed to destroy the photographs, that she didn't notice the sad expression on his face. Standing up, she crossed the kitchen and turned on the electric kettle.

"Would you like a cup of tea?"

"No, thanks. I'm heading back upstairs to the office," he said brusquely. "I've some work to finish off for a meeting tomorrow."

"Well, goodnight. I'll see you later," Ciara replied, but Niall had already left the room.

It was almost dawn when Ciara awoke, and realised that Niall wasn't in the bed beside her. Groping for the switch on the bedside lamp, she looked at her watch. It was almost 5 a.m. Surely he couldn't still be working? Slipping out of bed, she tiptoed towards the office at the end of the landing but there was no light visible beneath the closed door. Peeping inside, she realised that Niall was asleep on the studio couch, covered with a duvet from the guest room. Why on earth hadn't he come back to their own double bed? She listened with affection to his gentle snoring, then returned puzzled to their bedroom.

CHAPTER 14

I will never forget the day that I had the abortion. Do you remember, Ciara, the day I disappeared from school and wasn't found for three days? No, I don't suppose you do, secure in the cocoon of your own new-found happiness. There was no room in your consciousness for anyone else, or thoughts about anyone other than Niall.

That particular morning, I set off for school as usual with no intention of ever reaching it. So I had a whole day's head-start before I'd be missed. The teachers would assume that I was out sick, and my aunt would assume that I was at school. It wouldn't be until late afternoon that my aunt would notice my absence.

Having helped myself to the contents of the church collection box the week before – leaving a sufficient interval to ensure both disappearances were unconnected – I headed for the boat at Dun Laoghaire which would take me to Holyhead then by train to London. I changed most of the stolen notes to English ones at a bank in O'Connell Street, where there was little likelihood of anyone knowing me.

I knew nothing about getting an abortion. Nor had I any idea how much an abortion would cost. And since I'd never even left Ireland before, I'd no idea where to find an abortion clinic when I got there. But I had several hundred pounds sterling, and I could only hope that this would be enough.

It was a sad and deeply disturbed young girl that set out for Dun Laoghaire that bitterly cold morning. I longed to take an extra sweater for warmth, but feared that it might later alert my aunt to the fact that my disappearance had been planned. I'll bet on that morning Ciara, as I shivered with cold and fear, you were tucked up in your bed, dreaming happily about the man who'd got me into this predicament.

To allay my aunt's suspicion I left the house in my school uniform, but as soon as I reached the quarry I changed into my Sunday best outfit, which I'd hidden there the night before. Then I put my schoolbooks and uniform into the plastic bag, and hid them carefully beneath some rocks. I'd also left the house earlier than usual, pleading the need to do extra work at school. This early start was essential if I was to get to the boat on time. I also wanted to ensure that I didn't meet any of my classmates on the way.

The boat journey was miserable. It should have been exciting, since it was my first journey abroad but I was both seasick and hungry. I was afraid to spend money on a cup of tea or a sandwich, since I didn't know how much an abortion would cost. I might also need to stay in lodgings for a few nights, since I had no idea how long an abortion took either, or how it would affect me. In fact, I had no idea where I was going once I arrived in London.

By the time we reached Holyhead and were transferred to the train for the rest of the journey, I felt overwhelmed by panic.

Although surrounded by people, I felt terribly alone. On the opposite aisle in the carriage, a young couple sat holding hands, a baby gently sleeping in the crook of the woman's left arm. Watching them, I knew that I would never forget the image of that couple. It would always be a poignant reminder of my own forthcoming loss.

Arriving at Euston Station was a bewildering experience. Everywhere there were people rushing by, and I seemed to be the only one standing still. Purposefully, they hurried from platform to platform, perhaps heading home to loved ones or meeting friends in the city. The thought of other people having friends and loved ones brought tears of longing to my eyes, since I had neither myself. I wanted to climb back into the warmth of the railway carriage and go straight back to Holyhead. But I knew that I didn't have that option.

I must have looked very dejected, because a young man in jeans with a strong Cockney accent came up and offered to carry my bag.

"You look a bit depressed – cheer up!" he said, giving me a broad smile. "You're Irish, aren't you?" I nodded.

These English seemed quite friendly, I thought. Maybe they weren't all the staid, stiff-upper-lip types portrayed in the movies.

"What brings you to London?" he asked.

"I-I'm looking for a job," I lied. "I've just left school, and I thought that I'd have a better chance over here."

He gave me a friendly, appraising look. "Got a place to stay?"

"N-no, not yet."

"Then this is your lucky day! My name's Johnny. I run a kind of a hostel for new arrivals. You can stay there if you like.

It's not great, but at least you'll be warm and dry. And you needn't pay me until you get a job."

My aunt had always warned me not to talk to strangers, and she spoke about 'foreigners' as though they all had two heads. Was it just my aunt's xenophobic conditioning that made me hesitate? Yet I didn't see that I had much other choice.

"OK," I said as casually as I could manage. "Is it far from here?" Not that I would have known where any place in London was!

"No, it's only a few streets from here. C'mon." He took me by the arm protectively, and picked up my bag. "We'll 'ave you there in a few minutes."

We walked through long streets where all the houses looked exactly the same. They were big old houses of a type I'd never seen in Ireland. After we had turned several corners and walked the length of several streets, I'd completely lost my sense of direction. It was now dark and the streets were silent. My companion whistled as we walked along, and all that I could hear was the sound of my own breathing, and the click-clack of my Sunday-best shoes.

At last we reached a dingy-looking house with a light on in the porch. The paint was peeling off the door, and I tried not to retch at the sickly smell that assailed my nostrils. I thought fleetingly of my aunt's immaculate house, and the irony of finding anything good about her lifestyle almost made me smile to myself.

In the hall, the young man took my coat and hung it on the end of the bannister. Then I was taken up a steep flight of stairs covered in threadbare carpet, to a landing that was in similar condition. Opening a door, the young man took me into a room where a girl of around my own age was seated. She was holding *a baby, which she quickly put down when we entered. Suddenly I began to suspect that something was wrong. Why should anyone feel guilty about cuddling a child? But as soon as the child was placed in its makeshift cradle on the floor, it began to howl.*

I looked at the face of my so-called rescuer, and saw that it was now livid with fury.

"Shut that fucking kid up!" he barked at her, with no hint of his earlier charm and concern. He grabbed the girl's arm, and I saw her wince. "Look after this girl here – she's new," he told her, pointing to me. Still holding onto my bag, he turned and left the room, closing the door behind him.

I felt decidedly on edge. I'd just seen a very different side to the man I'd thought of as kind and helpful. Suddenly, I wondered what on earth I was doing there. If I left quickly, I might just manage to find a room somewhere else before it got dark. But Johnny had gone off with my school bag – what on earth for?

As the girl lifted up the baby again it stopped crying, and we appraised each other in silence. I tried a little smile, but it died from lack of any response. At last she spoke.

"`So you're the latest fucking fool," she said, looking at me with a mixture of pity and disgust. "Well, now that you're here, you might as well make the best of it. You'll be sleeping over there." She pointed to a dirty mattress on the floor. "Until Johnny starts you working, that is."

"I beg your pardon?"

I was quite shocked at the idea of having to sleep on the floor, and without even my own room. When I remarked this to the girl, she laughed mirthlessly. "He saw you for the fucking fool that you are. Over here for an abortion, ain't you?"

When I said nothing, she laughed again. "Yeah, it's written all over your stupid Irish face, kid. Well, if you need an abortion, you should have gone straight to old Kitty Hall down in Abercorn Street. But Johnny'll make sure you'll never get there now."

"W-what do you mean?"

"Well, he's taken your coat and your bag, hasn't he? Right now he's probably ripping them both apart for your dosh. I mean, you must have brought money to pay for the abortion, didn't you, ducks?"

Open-mouthed, I was too shocked to speak. As the meaning of her words sank in, I began to realise the danger that I was in.

"Johnny's a fucking parasite," the girl added, by way of explanation. "He picks up innocent young kids from railway stations, then robs all their money and makes them work for him."

"W-what sort of work?" I asked.

She gave a strangled sort of laugh. "On the game, you fool. And you'll be too, in a few days!"

I struggled to understand. What did 'on the game' mean? Perhaps Johnny was going to ask me to work with some local sports team.

"Prostitute – you fucking Irish half-wit! I'm a fuckin' prostitute for Johnny. He knows that the pregnant kids he picks up daren't ever go home again. So they work for him on the streets, and when their babies are born he's got a further hold over them. He'll kill your baby if you don't do the really disgusting tricks. There's blokes who pay him well for young girls."

She gestured to the baby she was holding on her knee. "I was pregnant too when I arrived here from Coventry. Johnny took all my money so that I couldn't have an abortion. Now I've got this little fellow, and Johnny makes me work for him in return for somewhere to live.'

I was about to ask her why she couldn't go home with her child or go to the police, then I realised that I'd be in exactly the same situation. The shame of ostracism back home, and the fear of retribution would be just too hard to bear.

The girl hugged her baby fiercely to her breast, tears now filling her eyes. "He's threatened my Tommy here," she told me, and I felt an even stronger frisson of fear run up my spine. "He said he'd break both his little legs if I didn't do tricks with the dirty old guys."

While I didn't understand what a trick was, I certainly knew that it was time for me to get out of there. Otherwise, I'd soon be trapped there myself.

There was one thing in my favour. Neither the girl nor Johnny realised that my money wasn't in my bag or coat. It was in the pocket of my school knickers, along with my return ticket to Dun Laoghaire. I felt a moment's gratitude towards my aunt for insisting that I wear heavy serge school knickers with built-in pocket.

"Where's the toilet?" I asked the girl. "I'm sure you remember what it's like when you're pregnant . . ."'

In actual fact, I was genuinely dying to go, but I didn't intend remaining in the house that long. Leaving the room, I quickly disregarded the girl's directions and headed straight for the stairs. Almost tripping over the threadbare carpet, I rushed down, fearing at every moment that a door to one of the rooms would suddenly open and I'd be trapped again by my would-be oppressor. As I'd surmised, my coat had been removed from the *bannister and was nowhere to be seen. I managed to reach the front door and pull it open before I heard the sound of footsteps upstairs.*

As I slipped out and ran down the path, I could hear raised voices coming from the open window directly above. Then I heard the sharp crack of a hand on flesh, and a scream that I recognised as coming from the girl with the baby.

"You fucking bitch," I heard Johnny ranting, "you told 'er, didn't you? How many times do I 'ave to tell you to mind your own fucking business?"

Then I heard the thunder of feet coming down the stairs behind me, as I ran out into the street. By now, the urine was flowing freely down my legs and I ran as though possessed. Surely there was someone around that I could appeal to for help? But the streets were deserted, there were virtually no streetlights and all the front doors were firmly closed.

Some clarity of thought must have invaded my brain, because I paused long enough to slip off my shoes. The click-clack of the heels had so far pinpointed the direction of my flight, making it easier for my pursuer to track me. Now, hopefully, it would be less easy for him.

On I ran, now with silent feet, carrying my shoes in one hand while the stones and debris underfoot made me wince constantly with pain. As I'd hoped, my pursuer now assumed that since I couldn't be heard any longer, I must have hidden in one of the gardens. I could hear him opening garden gates and turning over bins as I increased the distance between us.

With heart throbbing painfully, I stopped and listened for the sounds of traffic in the distance to give me a sense of direction back to the main road. Once there, I felt that I'd be relatively safe. What a fool I'd been to go so blithely with a perfect stranger, without even taking note of where he was taking me!

Up ahead, I detected the sound of a bus and bright lights, so I continued running in that direction, being careful to stay in against the garden walls as much as possible to prevent my silhouette showing up against the lights ahead. I'd already lost one of the shoes I was carrying, so now I threw the other one away.

Eventually I reached the main road, and saw with an overwhelming sense of relief that there were numerous people walking about. Some of them eyed me suspiciously when they saw my bare feet, but I felt positively elated. In reality, I wasn't far from tears. Especially when I thought of the ordeal still ahead.

CHAPTER 15

Three weeks after Niall's funeral, Ciara felt able to face the task of going through his possessions. Part of her wanted to leave everything as it was – it was still painful to even contemplate discarding any of his clothing. Every sock and tie seemed steeped in sentimental value.

On the other hand, refraining from tackling the job was mere self-indulgence. There were plenty of less fortunate people who could benefit from the good quality suits and shirts that had been Niall's stock-in-trade for work. She'd take them that very day to one of the local charity shops.

However, she decided to allow herself some small indulgences. She'd keep the old sweater with the patched elbows that Niall had worn around the house and loved so much. And of course, she'd keep his watch and gold neck-chain. Some day she'd give them to Sarah, when her daughter reached the age to appreciate such things.

Ciara smiled as she caught sight of the painting she'd

given Niall as a Christmas present the first year they'd met. She'd been so hard-up that she'd been unable to buy him a 'proper' present. However, he'd always maintained that the painting meant more to him than all the sweaters or scarves in the world.

Ciara was relieved that Sarah was out of the house, since she needed to carry out this task alone. It would be traumatic enough without Sarah's dramatic wailing, tears and tantrums which would undoubtedly end in a battle over what could and could not be disposed of.

Armed with several plastic sacks, Ciara set to work. Everything she took out brought back a flood of memories. Several times, she wept into his clothes as she held them. She could smell the aroma of his aftershave in the cupboard, and was overcome by an acute physical longing for his touch.

Gradually, the wardrobe was emptied, and several plastic bags filled. By this time Ciara was emotionally exhausted, but still determined to carry on. Now she'd tackle the chest of drawers where Niall had kept his socks, underwear and personal documents, things like his driving licence and passport. Ciara wondered what she was supposed to do with these documents. Did she keep them, or did they have to be returned to the relevant authorities? There was still so much to sort out.

Deciding against stopping for a cup of tea, she got through the socks and underwear drawer without too much trauma. Now it was time to sort out the documents, insurance policies, and wads of papers that filled the drawer. This had been Niall's domain – Ciara had never bothered to look at or take any interest in what was stored there. Now, of course, this was a distinct disadvantage since she was unsure of what to throw out and what to keep. Perhaps she should wait and ask Charlie to help her.

Ciara was just about to close the drawer when it seemed to stick and when she eventually managed to prise it free she spotted a photograph jammed in at the back. Taking it out, she looked at it in surprise. Then in shock. It was a photo of Niall lying naked in a double bed, in what looked like a hotel bedroom. And he was laughing at whoever was taking his photograph. Ciara knew she hadn't taken the photo.

Turning it over with trembling hands, she found a scribbled caption on the back. It was dated, and read: "Great speech, Niall, but your performance in bed rates even better! Hope you enjoyed the conference as much as I did."

Ciara's stomach heaved and her bowels contracted in shock. There must be a mistake, a terrible mistake. There had to be some perfectly reasonable explanation, but Ciara couldn't think of one. She sat down on the bed and read the message through again. There was little doubt that it had the chill air of authenticity about it. This was no joke, no office prank. Ciara dropped the photograph and rushed into the ensuite bathroom. There, she threw up the entire contents of her stomach, retching as the acid burnt her throat. Then the shivers came, and she sat trembling on the edge of the bath with a foul taste in her mouth and a terrible ache in her heart.

The slut, Ciara screamed silently from the depths of her insides. How could this woman behave like that with a married man? Has she no shame, no values? Ciara had instantly cast the woman in the role of vile seductress. Yet she was also honest enough with herself to face the real truth. It was clear from the photograph that Niall had been an equally willing participant. She longed to phone somebody for support. Several times, she lifted the phone from its cradle before replacing it. Who would she call, anyway? Her mother? Out of the question. Sarah? She shuddered. Charlie, Dee, Kate, Liam?

Suddenly, she felt alienated from all the people she loved. Because as soon as she told another person what she'd discovered, she'd be publicly admitting that she and Niall hadn't had the perfect marriage that everyone – including herself – thought they'd had. She'd also be annihilating a part of her own identity in the process.

Back in the bedroom, she picked up the photo from where she'd thrown it on the floor and studied what looked like hastily scribbled words. The block letters, written with a ballpoint pen, gave no clue as to who wrote it and the photo itself bore no distinguishing marks. It could have been taken and written on by anyone. Tears filled her eyes once again, and Ciara thought that her heart was going to stop beating with the shock.

Then, for one wild moment, she thought of an obvious solution. If she just burnt the photo now, she could go back to believing that everything was still as it had been. Perhaps in time, she'd even begin to wonder if she hadn't imagined finding the photo. Maybe she could convince herself that it had never happened at all, and Niall would go on being the man she'd thought he was.

Ciara shuddered. No, everything was not as it was. And never would be again. Painful though it was, she had to be truthful to herself.

The silence of the house was like a morgue. Ciara wanted to run out the door, to run away from this horrible piece of celluloid that had destroyed her peace of mind. But instead she went downstairs to the dining-room and opened the antique cocktail cabinet. The array of bottles promised some relief, some numbness from the pain that was ravaging her mind.

Ciara took out the brandy bottle and poured herself a large measure. Although she wasn't a regular drinker, in the absence of a friend to talk to this was the best relief currently to hand. Perhaps if she drank a lot, she would pass out for a while. Right now, oblivion seemed a very attractive proposition.

"You bastard, you bastard," she whispered to an imaginary Niall, over and over again as though it was a mantra. "Was it just a fling because you were bored with me? Did I fail you in some way? I just wish you'd talked to me about it, instead of leaving me in this . . ."

Suddenly, Ciara had another devastating thought. What if this vile seductress was someone she knew? Maybe someone she knew well? Up until now, the 'other woman' had been a shadowy figure, someone she'd caricatured as a cross between the Disney character Cruella De Ville and Glenn Close in *Fatal Attraction*. Suddenly, a frightening thought came to her. Could one of her own friends have been the other woman in Niall's life?

Suddenly, the enormity of this possibility made her

feel physically ill again. This time, she staggered into the downstairs bathroom and stood shivering over the toilet bowl. But although her stomach was heaving, there was nothing left to come up. So she sat on the toilet, thinking that this might ease the cramps in her stomach. It was as though her whole body was in rebellion, each part against the other. Nothing was in harmony any more – neither her body, her mind, her past, nor her future.

Back in the living-room, Ciara took another large mouthful of brandy. It was a ridiculous thought. Neither Kate nor Dee would betray her like that! She was being stupid. There were hundreds of women that it might have been. But inside a tiny, persistent voice kept asking who would have had a better opportunity? By virtue of their work as journalists, both of them had also attended that conference.

Ciara studied the writing on the back of the photo once again. Since it was written hurriedly in block letters, it was impossible to tell whether either of her friends could have written it. Nevertheless, she'd cancel her planned trip into town with Dee the following day. And she'd ignore the phone until she evolved some strategy for coping. In her present state of mind, she didn't want to speak to either friend – if friend indeed they were.

Perhaps a holiday was the answer. It would take her far away from anyone who could hurt her. She'd go somewhere warm where she'd sit alone on a beach and think. She'd swim every day, walk, read, maybe even paint, and in the evening she would have a few glasses of the local wine with her dinner to help her sleep.

The tears came yet again. What had been the turning

point in her life with Niall? Was there a single moment when it had all changed? Then her soul-searching turned to anger. Why was she blaming herself when he was the guilty party? If he'd been unhappy, surely it was his responsibility to tell her? If he hadn't died, was he intending to leave her and Sarah, or was he just staying around until his daughter was old enough to cope?

Ciara felt exhausted at all the possibilities and permutations, and angry at being made to suffer this indignity, pain and fear alone. Taking the now half-full brandy glass, she hurled it across the room where it hit the large mirror over the fireplace smashing into tiny fragments, and cracking the mirror in the process. Ciara laughed hysterically, irrationally pleased with her handiwork. Then she began weeping uncontrollably before she passed out.

CHAPTER 16

The girl with the baby had mentioned the name of a woman who performed abortions. I tried to remember the name, but my brain was too overwrought. I hoped I'd remember later – all I wanted to do was lie down somewhere safe and sleep. But how was I going to achieve this? I had no coat, since Johnny had taken it. I was tired and cold, and the urine that had earlier scalded my legs was now cold, and my knickers were chafing my thighs. I was afraid to go back to Euston Station in case Johnny turned up there and tried to drag me off again. Yet I badly needed somewhere to shelter for the night. My teeth were chattering now, and I was weak from tiredness and hunger.

Eventually, I found a small all-night café run by an elderly Italian couple, where I ordered eggs and chips then sat drinking coffee until my eyelids started to droop. It had the familiarity of the chip shops back home, with its white wall tiles and black plastic banquette seats. For the first hour or so, I kept a constant vigil in case Johnny appeared, but as sleep overtook me I just didn't care any more. Slumped against the side of the cubicle, I nodded off.

When I awoke, it was to the bustle of early-morning diners being served at the counter. The old man behind the counter was dishing up bacon and eggs to several men who looked as though they were either going to, or coming off, shift duty at some nearby factory.

I stretched warily and discovered that the proprietor had covered me with a blanket while I slept. There was also a pair of old trainers, a pair of clean socks and an anorak on the seat beside me. I looked over at the elderly proprietor, and he nodded to indicate that they were for me. Then he silently served me a cup of steaming hot coffee, bacon, egg and toast, for which he would take no money. I thanked him profusely, but he dismissed my thanks with a sweep of his hand. He was probably used to catering for the many waifs and strays that came through Euston Station.

Kitted out in my newly-acquired ensemble, I headed back in the direction of the station. It was still dark, but the first streaks of dawn could be seen on the horizon. The sleep and hot meal had cleared my brain, and I now remembered the name of the woman whom the girl had mentioned and the name of the street where she lived. Now all I had to do was find it.

I felt odd wearing someone else's clothes, someone whom I didn't even know. And I knew that I must have looked a wreck. My comb and toiletries had all been in the bag that Johnny had taken. Would they accept me at an abortion clinic looking as I did? Or would they turn me away because of my appearance? Stupidly, I envisaged a clinic full of doctors in white coats and receptionists sitting at desks decked out with bowls of seasonal flowers. Maybe there would be a waiting list, and I would have to come back another day? And I wondered briefly what had been the reaction to my disappearance back home.

The house, when I eventually found it, didn't look like a clinic at all. It appeared to be a private house, and I began to wonder if I'd got the address wrong. But at that stage I felt that I'd little choice but to check it out. Maybe someone there could re-direct me. So I climbed the steps and rang the bell.

After what seemed an age, a tall elderly woman appeared at the door and barked, "What d'ya want?"

Obviously, I'd called to the wrong place but before I had a chance to explain what I was looking for, the woman said, "Who sent you?"

"I-I got a name from a girl from Coventry. I'm sorry, but I don't know her address. But I must be at the wrong place . . ."

"Hrmmph." She stepped past me and looked up and down the road, to see if anyone else was around. Satisfied, she prodded me into the hallway and directed me down a steep flight of stairs. These English were certainly strange people, I thought. I hadn't even told the woman what I wanted, yet here I was, a perfect stranger being herded into her house.

Momentarily I panicked. Could she be involved with Johnny, the man who'd picked me up at Euston? Was she going to capture me and return me to him? I was almost about to turn and run up the stairs again when I saw the bed and the instruments. I didn't know whether to feel relieved or more terrified.

"Are you . . . I mean, do you do abortions?"

She made a sort of hissing sound, which made her look like a venomous snake about to strike. "Don't mention that word here. Or when you leave either. Do you have enough money? I'm not a charity, you know."

"H-how much does it cost?"

Having named her price, I produced my bundle of notes and

counted out the sum she'd asked for. While it wasn't exactly cheap, I was relieved to find that I would still have a little money left over thanks to the generosity of the parishioners back home. There was a pleasurable irony in having those craw-thumping hypocrites paying for something that would have shocked and abhorred them if they'd known.

Quickly, the woman took the money and stashed it away between the voluminous folds of her breasts.

"`Now take your knickers off and get up on the bed. How many months are you gone?"

Clutching my knickers and the remaining money they contained, I told her the facts as I knew them and did as she instructed. Initially, I was embarrassed at the smell of urine that I felt sure must be wafting towards her from my soiled knickers, but I was quickly distracted by her internal probing.

"Hmmm. This isn't your first time with a man, is it?" she sneered, "Some girls never learn their lesson!"

I had no idea what she was talking about, but her words were quickly lost as a wave of pain came over me.

"Quiet!" she hissed, as I stifled another cry. "Here." She handed me what looked like a piece of towelling. "Bite on that when you want to scream." Which clearly meant that there was more pain to follow. At one stage I almost felt as though I was going to pass out from the pain. In fact, at that moment I wanted desperately to die or to experience oblivion. Then suddenly there was a snip, followed by a muted scream from me.

"There." Triumphantly, the woman held aloft a tiny bleeding bundle. "See, dear, that's all that's left of your little daughter. A fine healthy one she would have been too. But that's life, isn't it? Maybe now you'll learn to keep your legs closed."

113

Perhaps her comments were intended as a deterrent to any future unplanned pregnancies, or else she just took sadistic pleasure in adding to other people's trauma and grief. Either way, her words were ones I'd never forget.

Then I began to cry. Not large sobbing gulps, but a silent inner weeping. Whether it was as a result of the physical pain or the loss I felt when I saw that tragic little bundle of flesh, I will never know. But for the first time since childhood, I felt hot salty tears running down my cheeks, some of them running into my ears as I lay there. I'd surrendered a part of me, and there was no one in the world who cared about what I was going through. Then I thought of Niall and the pain overwhelmed me yet again. The man I loved, the father of the child I'd just surrendered, was in love with you, Ciara, and knew nothing of what was happening to me.

After some time on the bed during which I eventually fell into a nightmarish sleep, the woman woke me up and told me abruptly that it was time for me to leave. I felt groggy and just wanted to continue sleeping, but clearly she wanted rid of me. Within minutes I was out in the street, feeling unsteady on my feet and uncertain of where I was going. There was a wad of blood-stained cotton wool in my knickers, and I had two pain-killing tablets that the woman had handed me as I left. It had taken less than an hour from beginning to end, but I knew that this day would be indelibly seared on my mind.

CHAPTER 17

"Cup of tea, son?"

"Yeah, please, Mam."

Kevin was sitting at the table in his mother's kitchen playing idly with the salt and pepper set, shaking a little salt out into his palm to see if the holes in the top were blocked. Of course, they weren't. His mother kept everything spotless and in working order. Even while she was waiting on the kettle to boil, Annie was wiping the cooker of any imaginary spots of grease.

That woman never sits still, Kevin thought irritably. She was exactly the same as when they'd been children. Although the family had very little in those days, what they had was always kept spick and span. Boots and shoes had to be removed at the front door, and the few cheap pieces of brass on the mantelpiece had been polished daily until they shone. Perhaps that had been their mother's way of keeping some kind of grip on her life. Things had been very precarious during all the years that their father had been unemployed.

Kevin glanced across at the mantelpiece. The same pieces of brass were still there, and still polished to perfection. However, the mantelpiece itself was different. Today his mother lived in a small but comfortable apartment in Donnybrook, a far cry from the council estate where they'd all grown up.

Cillian, with Ciara's help, had provided the finance to enable their parents to leave the council estate several years before Frank died. Now that Cillian was at the top of his profession, Kevin thought sourly, he preferred to hide all traces of his lowly past. Yet even as he despised Cillian's motives Kevin felt envious that despite being the eldest, as a priest with no money of his own he'd been unable to contribute to the cost of the new apartment.

At the time, Cillian had dismissed his elder brother's guilty feelings.

"Forget it," he'd told Kevin affectionately. "The money's no problem to me, and the folks would never expect you to." He'd grinned at his older brother. "Anyway, you're the golden boy. You being a priest has meant more to Mam than anything either Ciara or I could ever do."

Now, Kevin thought guiltily, I'm going to change all that.

"Here you are, love. Would you like a piece of fruit cake? I just made it yesterday?"

Kevin nodded and drank his tea and munched a piece of his mother's cake while she busied herself in the kitchen. Annie was humming to herself, a sure sign that she was happy. That made him feel even more guilty, for he knew that his mother enjoyed the times he spent at home when on leave from the Missions. Apart from the fact that she was thrilled to see him again, it also gave her a chance to show him off to the neighbours.

Kevin distracted himself from his own worries by deliberately thinking again of his sister. Poor Ciara, she and Niall had been the perfect couple. He wished he'd been able to officiate at Niall's funeral service, but it wouldn't have been right. Ciara would understand when he eventually explained why. But first, just as soon as he felt that the moment was right, he had to tell his mother. And he wasn't relishing the thought.

His mother had been so thrilled when he'd entered the priesthood. She'd seemed to feel as though she herself had achieved some monumental step. Which, in a sense, she had. For having a son who was a priest was quite a feather in any Irish mother's cap, or at least it had been back in those days. His mother couldn't have been happier if he'd told her he'd won the football pools. With one sentence, he'd elevated his mother's status in the council housing estate where the family had previously been looked down on because of their father's unemployment and constant drinking. And, of course, their lowly status hadn't been helped by his own earlier lapse.

He remembered how his mother had enjoyed telling the news to the neighbours on either side, especially Mary O'Donoghue next door. That woman had been the bane of his mother's life, tormenting her with sly digs and veiled insults whenever possible. But that day his mother had finally got her own back. Telling that woman that her eldest son was going to be a priest had been his mother's greatest moment of triumph.

Kevin nodded appreciatively as his mother cut him another slice of cake. Would she look quite so happy when he dropped his bombshell? Yet Annie Reynolds had coped with all sorts of adversity throughout her life. His Mam was a great woman. He hated to do this to her, but there was nothing else he could do.

He didn't think Cillian would give a damn one way or the other. His brother was so engrossed in his own life, and in whatever scientific advances were being made in the field of neurology, that not much else touched his consciousness.

He was brought back to the present by his mother's offer of a further slice of cake, which he declined. How would Ciara react to his news he wondered as he drank the refill of tea. He didn't expect his sister to be anything but supportive. Religion meant little to Ciara. In fact, when he'd told her of his vocation all those years ago, she'd been surprised and expressed doubts that someone with his liberal views could submit to the dictates of such a rigid, authoritarian organisation.

Kevin smiled as he remembered the many times they'd discussed that very issue during his visits back to Ireland. He'd been full of the joys of Africa, having grown to love the people and the landscape. And he felt, for the first time since he'd been ordained, that he was making a real contribution. And he'd explained to Ciara that, like many other priests working on the foreign missions, he'd evolved his own way of following the Church's dictates. And he'd pitied his colleagues back home for the moral dilemmas in which many of them found themselves – bound by laws which they felt were archaic, but bound nevertheless by their vows of obedience to implement them.

On the estate where he'd grown up Kevin had seen women worn down by countless pregnancies, homes with too many children and not enough food on the table, men out in the pubs seeking relief from the stresses of home. And all the while, the clergy who forbade them to use artificial contraception were snug in their big parochial houses with plenty to eat and housekeepers to dance attendance on them.

"Mam, I'm leaving the priesthood."

There, he'd said it. The words seemed to hang in the air, almost like tangible entities that could form and re-form of their own free will. It was as though they'd escaped from his mouth, and now they had a life of their own.

Annie, in the act of raising a mug of tea to her lips, now held it suspended in mid-air. It was as though she had become frozen in stone, Kevin thought. Then she replaced the mug on the table, smiling across at him.

"I was wondering when you were going to tell me," she said softly.

Now it was Kevin's turn to look shocked. "You knew?"

"Well, I wasn't certain, but I knew there was something on your mind," she reached across the table and squeezed his hand. "Mothers have an instinct for these things, son."

"And, what do you think?"

"About your decision? Well, I suppose I'm just surprised that it took you so long to make it."

Irrationally, Kevin felt quite peeved. Whatever way he'd expected his mother to react, it wasn't like this. He'd expected shock, horror, maybe even a few tears. But now it seemed as though his own mother had pipped him to the post by anticipating his very actions!

As though to answer his question, Annie spoke again. "I suppose I often worried about whether you'd become a priest for the right reasons."

Kevin coloured. His mother was a shrewd woman. He'd often wondered the same thing himself. But once he'd stepped on that particular merry-go-round there seemed no easy way of getting off. Becoming a priest had gathered a momentum all its own. So many people seemed to be pleased about it, that to back out would have been to disappoint them all. Besides, he'd enjoyed basking in so much approval. It had been a wonderful turnabout, after the shame of what had happened in Dineen's shop. And as a seventeen-year-old he'd been too young to realise that the approval of other people was no substitute for the inner conviction that was the essential ingredient of a true vocation. Nevertheless, he'd been sincere in his belief at the time. It was really only later when he'd come up against the mindless clericalism, and the canon law that had replaced the simple words of Jesus, that he began to wonder if his life was taking the right direction. But Africa had restored his belief that there was a role for him to play. The simplicity of life there and the warmth of the people had given his life meaning and vibrancy.

"I was actually very happy being a priest," Kevin told

his mother. "It's the hierarchy controlling the Church that wore me down." He smiled at her, willing her to understand.

"Well, I'm glad, son, that you've had the courage of your convictions," Annie said. "But what are you going to do now? I mean, you'll have to get a job, won't you?"

Kevin grinned. "A qualification in theology doesn't exactly equip me to work at the cutting-edge of society, does it? Anyway, I have holidays due to me so I'm going to take my time about making any decisions. I've applied to Rome to be released from my vows, but I wouldn't be the first priest to be left in limbo."

Annie grinned. "I thought that place didn't exist any more?"

Kevin gave an exasperated grin. "You know what I mean."

Annie grimaced. "By all accounts, you could be waiting a long time, son. I don't think the Church makes it easy for those who want to leave."

"That's true," Kevin agreed, smiling ruefully and wondering yet again how his mother was so knowledgeable on these topics. He had to admit that she constantly astounded him.

"Maybe you'll have to push them for a decision, son," said Annie, smiling. "By getting married, I mean. Is there a woman out in Africa?"

Kevin coloured. "No, Mam," he said truthfully, "there's no woman there." Then he grinned. "Well, actually, there's a whole continent of them! But I presume you were referring to a special one."

"Yes, son, I was." Annie looked closely at him again. "You know, it's not good for someone of your age to be alone. Maybe now you'll find somebody special."

Kevin nodded, knowing that his mother was thinking of her own much-loved husband Frank, gone but never forgotten. Kevin had thought a lot about his dad while in Africa. It was the kind of place that made a person feel philosophical. Out there, he'd finally begun to understand how his poor father must have suffered from the ignominy of unemployment to the hopeless oblivion of drink, which eventually and irrevocably destroyed his health and prematurely ended his life.

Kevin started as his mother suddenly spoke, smiling.

"Mind you, you've left it a bit late to start hanging round the flesh pots of Dublin," she made an exaggerated study of his face. "But you're not a bad-looking fellow. Obviously, you got that from my side of the family!"

Kevin grinned back. He would tell her about his plans soon, but not just yet.

CHAPTER 18

I'd been out of the country for three days. When I arrived back in Dublin on a cold grey morning I was frozen, my body ached and I longed for the oblivion of sleep. But before I could do that, I had to give the performance of my life.

I reached the quarry early, long before anyone was about, and retrieved the plastic bag containing my school clothes. The early morning frost was still on the ground, and I had to stand there shivering as I changed from my Sunday-best outfit into my school uniform again. Hiding my Sunday clothes in the plastic bag, I carefully hid it underneath the pile of rocks once again. The uniform was crumpled after three days of being squashed under the rocks, but that suited the plan I had in mind.

I wondered if anyone had searched for me. Perhaps my aunt regarded my disappearance as a blessing, and hadn't bothered to notify anyone. If so, that might work even better to my advantage, because she would be the only one needing an explanation. However, it was soon clear that this was not the case.

In my crumpled uniform, I wandered back towards my

aunt's house. I wasn't too sure how I was going to carry off this performance, but I would play it by ear and respond in whatever way seemed most appropriate.

I thought I saw some curtains twitching, but whoever was behind them clearly didn't want to get involved. But I knew that their eyes followed me as I made my way casually down the road.

I soon discovered that my aunt had informed the whole district about my disappearance, revelling in her new-found role of distraught and much put-upon relative. As I reached the corner of the road where she lived, old Mrs Kenny was coming in the opposite direction. Seeing me, she looked as though she'd seen a ghost.

"My God, child," she said, blessing herself, "where have you been? Everyone's been out looking for you. Your poor aunt is nearly out of her mind with worry. We thought something dreadful had happened to you." Keeping up a monologue, she accompanied me to my aunt's door, clearly anxious to be in on the excitement of my homecoming.

By the time my aunt appeared quite a few neighbours had gathered, with Mrs Kenny addressing them all as though she herself had found me and was returning me safely home. My aunt seemed both shocked and relieved to see me, but that relief turned to anger as soon as she'd prised me away from Mrs Kenny and the neighbours and firmly closed the front door on all outside.

"Where have you been these last three days, miss?" she stormed. "Do you know the trouble you've caused? The whole district has been out looking for you. The sergeant thought you'd been murdered! Father Moore has been saying prayers in church after each Mass for you."

She stopped her tirade and looked closely at me, bringing her face so near that I could vividly see the lines on her skin, and the venom in her eyes. "Or have you been off with some boy?" she sneered. "It wouldn't surprise me, you little hussy. You're nothing but a tramp!"

Why was she always calling me horrible names? I wanted to tackle her once and for all, beg her to explain what lay behind these cruel jibes. But this wasn't the time to do it. The local grapevine had brought the news of my return to old Father O'Brien and he was now on the doorstep outside.

"Come in, Father," my aunt gushed, her tone completely changing as she answered his knock. He was still wearing his cassock, having clearly come directly from the church.

"My dear child," he whispered, taking my hands in his, "are you all right? Thank God, the good Lord has spared you. We were all afraid that He'd seen fit to take you from us."

I sighed, and tried to look like a tragic victim. If only he knew that the good Lord in whom he placed so much faith had nothing at all to do with what had been happening to me. But right now I was about to launch myself into the role of bewildered and disoriented child. It felt a strangely familiar role. There was so much of my own past life that I genuinely didn't remember.

"Where have you been all this time, child?" Father O'Brien continued, still holding my hands in his. I wished he'd let go, but it seemed churlish to withdraw my hands just because his were clammy and unpleasant.

"I-I don't know, Father," I replied, looking up into his face as innocently as I could. "The last thing I remember is leaving here to go to school."

"Did anyone – did any strange person offer you sweets or a lift in their car?"

"No Father, I don't think so. But then, I don't really remember anything that happened . . ."

Father O'Brien stood up, thankfully withdrawing his clammy hands from mine, and looked knowingly at my aunt. "I think we should call in Doctor Claffey. It looks as though this young lady may have had some kind of traumatic experience, and I think he's the best person to deal with it."

I sighed inwardly with relief. My ruse had worked, and hopefully my aunt wouldn't dare question or taunt me any further. Of course I still had to deal with Doctor Claffey. But I suspected that he wouldn't push the issue too far.

I was right. The doctor's personal chat with me was perfunctory, after which he prescribed some mild sedatives "to help you sleep". Then he asked me when I'd had my last period. He seemed satisfied when I told him I was actually having a period – after all, I was still bleeding from the abortion. He then assured me that if I had any problems, I was not to hesitate to call at his surgery. Empty, meaningless words. He knew, and I knew, that if pregnancy was my problem, words of sympathy or a few sedative pills wouldn't be of much help.

Even after I'd been sent to bed to rest, I could still hear my aunt and the doctor speaking in low tones downstairs. Eventually I tiptoed down the stairs again in the hopes of eavesdropping on their conversation.

"She's suffering from some kind of trauma," I heard Doctor Claffey say. "When that sort of situation occurs, it's as though the brain refuses to acknowledge what's happened." He sighed. "Whatever happened must be so distressing that she's completely closed it out of her mind. In fact, it's exactly like what happened all those years ago . . ."

At that moment the stairs creaked as I adjusted my position. The conversation stopped abruptly, and I cursed my own stupidity. I was so near to discovering the basis for those terrible taunts from my aunt. Now I'd lost the chance yet again.

"What do you want?" my aunt asked belligerently, opening the parlour door and peering up the stairs at me.

"I-I forgot my rosary beads," I said quickly.

My aunt seemed mollified by this explanation and allowed me to come down into the room to collect them. Under her stern gaze, I fetched them and headed back upstairs, wishing her and the doctor goodnight. But behind my polite exterior I was seething inside. Why were other people allowed to know about aspects of my life that were completely unknown to me? And why did no one want to tell me?

When I returned to school the following Monday, I found that there had been a great deal of interest in my disappearance. Word had got around that something strange had happened to me, and wagging tongues embellished existing theories. At morning prayers, the other girls eyed me curiously, yet no one seemed willing to ask me directly about my absence. I remember how you smiled at me, Ciara, and said, "I'm glad you're back," but you never asked me where I'd been, either. I suppose you simply didn't care, being so wrapped up in your own relationship with Niall. However, I had my own way of ensuring that my version of events would take precedence over any other stories.

"You won't tell a living soul, will you, Dot?" I whispered anxiously to Dorothy McNally, the class gossip, at mid-morning break. She assured me with vigorous nodding of her head. I leaned closer to create a greater air of secrecy and intimacy.

"Are you sure that you won't tell? Promise on your honour."

"I swear I won't tell anyone."

I nodded. "I was in town walking along O'Connell Street, when someone tried to steal my handbag. I clung on to it for dear life, but I was knocked to the ground in the process. But suddenly, this fabulous foreign sailor helped me up. He was tall and tanned, and wearing a gorgeous uniform. To help me get over the shock, he took me into one of the cafés nearby, and bought me a coffee."

"`Oh my God, it sounds so exciting," Dottie's tone was incredulous, her eyes wide and round. "You're so lucky! Nothing like that ever happens to me!"

"It was love at first sight for both of us," I added, copying that misty smile that I'd seen so often on your face, Ciara, when you talked about Niall. "But his ship was sailing that very night, so we agreed that he'd smuggle me on board and I could go back to his home town where we'd be married . . ."

The more I embellished the story, the more I warmed to it. How wonderful if it was true!

"So what happened next?" asked Dottie, all excited. I knew that my secret would be safe in her hands – before the day was over, everyone in the class would have heard the story.

"Well, I knew that my aunt would stop me going if she knew," I explained, "so I just sneaked out of the house and smuggled myself on board his ship. But when we were out at sea, I was discovered by the captain and sent home again." I looked suitably crestfallen. "But we'll continue writing to each other, and we'll get married as soon as I'm eighteen."

Dottie sighed. I could see that she thought it was a lovely story. Love at first sight and unrequited love were favourite themes of hers. To hear of such things happening in real life was almost too much for her to bear – certainly too much for her to keep to herself. Already, I could see that she was straining to get away from me, so that she could tell my tale to her friend Vera Malone. From there my story would take off like wildfire.

I even remember, Ciara, that by the end of the day's classes, you had heard the story. And you, out of all the others, were gracious enough to come and wish me luck and sympathise with me for having to wait until I was eighteen to get married. You hugged me and said that you knew how it felt – you and Niall were hoping to get married as soon as you turned eighteen too . . .

CHAPTER 19

Kate woke up and reached immediately for the packet of pain-killers beside her bed. 'My God, what have I come to?' she asked herself. 'I've a headache first thing in the morning, and I can't even function properly.' Her breath smelled foul, and she rushed to the bathroom and threw up in the sink. God, she thought, what am I going to do? She crawled back into bed and pulled the duvet up around her.

A growing fear gnawed at her insides. Ciara wouldn't speak to her. She'd refused to answer the phone, and she'd pretended to be out when Kate had called to her house. Somehow, Ciara must have found out her secret. Maybe she should have told her right at the beginning, but there never seemed to be the right moment. Besides, wouldn't it have been callous to burden Ciara with further trauma when Niall had only just died? Or was she just making excuses for herself? She rushed into the bathroom and threw up into the sink again.

Anyway, the decision not to tell Ciara hadn't been hers alone. When she'd tentatively suggested that Ciara deserved to know that they'd fallen in love, he'd thought it better to leave well enough alone. They'd go to Ciara together when the time was right, he'd said. Of course he'd known nothing about the baby, because she'd never told him.

She sighed. All this worry wasn't fair on the baby either. She'd read that stress in pregnancy could affect a child's development in all sorts of ways. God, what would she do if it was deformed? It would all be her fault. She'd have to try relaxation or something, but maybe it was too late already. Maybe the poor child already had two heads . . .

Kate padded into the kitchen and turned on the electric kettle. She'd have a cup of tea instead – a small dose of caffeine could hardly do the baby any harm. She was dying for a cigarette, although she's given them up years ago. Could the fact that she'd once smoked have any effect on her child? Suddenly, she had visions of it sitting in its pram, puffing furiously on a cigarette rather than sucking a soother. At the thought, Kate dissolved into hysterical laughter, which ended up as tears running down her face and into the cup she'd just taken down from the shelf.

Life was really strange, Kate thought. All those years ago they'd known each other much more intimately than Ciara or anyone else had ever suspected. And more recently, things had become hot and heavy between them again. She'd become his sounding board, his mentor and this time there was no going back. Sometimes, it seemed as though the years in between had never happened. But there was always a price to pay for happiness, and now she was paying for it in guilt.

Thankfully, Niall had never mentioned to Ciara what had happened at the conference. For Kate, that weekend had really been the start of it all – the time when two people had stopped being friends and finally admitted their love for each other. It had been a sweet and powerful revelation for them both, but one that produced a string of problems and guilt. And now that she was carrying the proof of that love inside her, there could be little hope of hiding her secret much longer.

She could, of course, pretend that the baby she was carrying was someone else's. A one-night-stand perhaps, or an old friend who was briefly in town. Or she could simply claim that at her age, she'd decided to have a child before it was too late. Many career women were making that decision nowadays. And she'd explain that she was thrilled to be having the baby that in her wildest dreams she'd never expected to conceive. Which was perfectly true. She'd always believed that she was unable to have a child. And how envious she'd been when Ciara became pregnant with Sarah.

Kate looked at her watch. Dammit, it was already mid-morning and she'd promised Kevin that she'd write a piece about the plight of some tribe in Africa. It was the last thing she felt like doing, not because she didn't support them in their plight, but simply because she felt so ill. Could she put him off for another day or two? Just until she felt a little better . . . Morning sickness couldn't possibly last all through pregnancy, could it? She sighed and tried to get to her feet. But what was the point in putting Kevin off? If she told him she was ill, she'd only risk him or someone else putting two and two together.

She sighed. No man had stood a chance against the one man she'd always loved, the man in whose wake all other men seemed poor imitations. She sighed again. But at that time, he'd made his own choice elsewhere. And she'd made hers on the rebound. Inevitably, that engagement had ended in tears and recriminations, and once again she'd found herself on her own.

Determinedly, Kate poured herself a cup of tea, although her stomach was heaving and she didn't really want it. One way or another, she was going to have this baby. After all, it was the child of the man she loved most in the world. And even if it was to remain her secret forever, she would still have his child. Turning to the phone on the bedside table, she dialled Ciara's number. Just as she'd expected, there was no answer. Then she rang Dee.

"Dee, have you heard from Ciara? I've tried phoning her several times, but she doesn't answer. But I'm sure she's there."

"I know. She's not answering the phone to me either. I suppose Niall's death is only really hitting her now. She's probably best left alone."

"Y-you don't think that anything else could be bothering her?"

"Like what?"

"I don't know . . ."

Kate sighed inwardly with relief. Maybe it was all in her imagination. If Ciara didn't want to see her other friends either, maybe it wasn't just her she was avoiding. Surely, if Ciara had found out Kate's secret, she'd have contacted Dee for support? Yet Dee sounded perfectly normal.

"Why do you think she won't see us?" Kate asked. "She seemed OK the day we all gorged ourselves on the cream cakes."

"I don't know what's wrong. Maybe she just wants to be alone with her grief." Just like I do, Dee thought.

"But she seemed to be coming to terms with it – I mean, the way she's behaving now is totally out of character."

"It's like she's had a sudden shock or something."

"I – what do you mean?"

"I don't really know, but I'm beginning to wonder if something else is bothering her since she seems to have changed overnight. Maybe she's discovered that the mortgage is seriously in arrears, or that Niall had no pension or something."

"But surely she'd tell us if that happened? Anyway, they're not the kind of things that Niall would have let happen."

"No, I'm sure you're right. Maybe Sarah is playing up? That kid has become a bloody handful lately."

Kate chewed her lip with anxiety. The more she thought about it, the more likely it seemed that Ciara had found out her secret. If only there was someone she could unburden herself to. Could she tell Dee? God, no! Dee would probably be horrified too.

Suddenly, Kate froze. Had Niall said something to Ciara before he died? No, that wasn't possible.

Otherwise, Ciara would have reacted before now. Suddenly, she realised that Dee had been talking to her, and she hadn't heard a single word.

"Sorry, Dee – what did you say?"

"I said that I'm going to ask Charlie to call round to Ciara's house tonight. If she has money problems, Charlie will be able to help her sort them out."

"Good idea. Let me know if you hear anything, will you?"

Ringing off, Kate realised that her hands were trembling.

CHAPTER 20

You might be surprised to learn, Ciara, that my life actually began on a small rural farm. Most people assume I'm from Dublin, and that's what I preferred them to think. Conveniently, I'd moved in with my aunt just as I was moving into secondary school, so it seemed an ideal opportunity to bury my past life completely. Not that I remembered all that much about those years. And the things I did remember were best forgotten.

It was a relief to leave the countryside. Any affinity I might have had with the land was destroyed by the lifestyle that went with it. Life on the farm was characterised by relentless subjugation of women at the hands of brutal, unhappy men. A forceful Church suppressed all passions until, combined with alcohol, they formed a deadly cocktail that regularly exploded in our midst.

As an only child, I spent a lot of time around adults. When the local women would call to our farmhouse, they and my mother would sit in our big kitchen drinking tea and gossiping in low furtive tones. If I crept under the kitchen table, they'd quickly forget all about my existence. In that way, I learned about the endless pregnancies and the miscarriages – some of them induced by the women themselves using various crude and painful methods when another child was just one too many. While tea and sympathy were liberally dispensed, they catalogued their beatings by drunken husbands, displaying the ugly weals and bruises they'd received and applauded each other's subsequent small revenges.

When any of the men came into the kitchen, the tone and the conversation changed dramatically. It became more conciliatory, the topics more general. Crop yields were discussed, or the new barn that a neighbour was building. Clearly, the men were never privy to the secret world that the women shared. Yet it was a world that was created and maintained by fear of the men themselves.

I often wondered if the men knew about the kind of discussions that went on among the women? Eventually, I realised the truth. Whether they knew the details or not, it simply didn't matter to them. The women's opinions were of no importance to them, and I began to suspect that the more reviled the men were by the women the more manly they saw themselves. Yet in their own way, the men were victims too. All of them – men and women alike – were trapped in roles that destroyed all individuality, all decency and all hope.

Strangely, the women were allies only when they were alone with each other sharing the horrors of their daily lives. On Sunday mornings outside church they would parade their Sunday-best outfits, vying with each other for the spotlight, fawning over their husbands and singing their praises to other families and the local clergy. Clearly, this was the world of survival.

I well remember Mrs Keenan who only the night before had cried in my mother's kitchen about her husband's brutality. The following morning after Mass she was singing his praises to the parish priest. "My Dan has just built a whole new set of cupboards in the kitchen," she simpered, while trying to tilt her hat over the big bruise that he'd inflicted on her forehead. And I knew that there were more bruises in places that the priest would never see.

Why didn't the women do anything to change their situation? They seemed to take refuge in their passivity, because they saw no hope of anything ever changing. But if marriage was as bad as it seemed, why did any woman want to marry at all? In my childish wisdom, I concluded that women pursued marriage because there were few, if any, other goals to aspire to. The lot of rural women was tough, and being without a man was seen as infinitely worse than being with a demon who abused you. I longed to tell them to fight back, but that would have drawn attention to my presence and ended my days of discovery beneath the table.

While there was little experience of love among the harsh realities of farming life, there was always an abundance of food. My mother baked bread every day, the hens laid fresh eggs every morning, and the land yielded all the home-grown vegetables and fruit anyone could desire. There were always chickens, pheasants or rabbits hanging in the pantry, and our table never lacked for meat. The cows yielded milk that went to the creamery every day, but there was always more than enough left over to make butter, cream and buttermilk for our own use.

As a small child exposed to so many adult traumas without fully understanding them, food became my relief and my friend in times of need. I ate out of loneliness, I ate for comfort, I ate to momentarily ease the pain of being small, alone and insecure.

I also ate when I was frightened, like the times when my father would hit my mother. He would come back drunk from the local pub and I would hear her cry out, and hear the repeated crack of his hand across her flesh. And filled with unspeakable dread I would run away and hide, usually taking a pile of food with me in case I had to hide out in the barn all night. For I knew that when he was finished with my mother, he would come in search of me.

CHAPTER 21

The phone rang, and Dee picked it up.

"Dee –"

"Ciara! Are you OK? You haven't been answering your phone."

"I know. I've been feeling a bit down. I'm better left on my own."

"Then why are you ringing?" There I go again, Dee thought. I'm sounding totally insensitive.

"I've been checking my diary, and I realised that you and I had arranged to go into town together this afternoon . . ."

"Oh." Dee had completely forgotten about it.

"But I'm afraid I can't go anyway. Kevin needs to talk to me about something."

"No problem." Dee was relieved. She wasn't in the mood for company herself, and certainly not for Ciara's manic efforts at pretending she was fine. "Say hi to Kevin for me. He must be due to go back to Africa soon? It seems like he's been home for ages."

There was a brief silence. "I'm not sure when he's going back."

"Well, have a nice afternoon. Let's get together soon," said Dee, ringing off.

In her bedroom, Dee wandered about disconsolately. She should be working, she had three features to finish, but what the hell. She was too edgy to sit down at her computer and type. Maybe she should go in and write them in the newspaper office itself? Sometimes being part of the media frenzy had the desired effect. She grimaced. But then she'd have to talk to colleagues, and she wasn't in any mood for that. Oh God, she thought, loving someone and losing them plays havoc with your concentration.

Tears came into her eyes as she thought of his handsome face. After months of clandestine meetings, they'd no longer been content to make love furtively in hotel rooms in the afternoon, in fields, or in the back of his car. What had been fun at first now seemed tacky and second-rate.

"I'm going to tell her," he'd finally said one evening, "I can't live this lie any longer, Dee. She must suspect something anyway. I can't make love to her any more, so I find ways to make sure the situation doesn't arise." He laughed harshly at his own unintended pun. "Like bringing files home from the office and pretending to work late so that she goes to bed ahead of me, or else I go to bed early and pretend to be asleep."

He smiled bleakly at Dee, taking her hand in his and stroking it. "But soon she's going to ask me what's wrong, I just know it. So how can I lie to her? I may not love her any more, but she doesn't deserve that."

Dee's heart was beating uncomfortably loud in her chest. She was hearing the words she'd longed to hear, yet the repercussions were terrifying.

He'd gripped her hand tightly. "I want to be with you, Dee – all the time. Not just when we can sneak away to some bloody hotel. I want to set up home openly with you. She can have the house, the furniture. I'll sign it all over to her. I'll give her generous maintenance – she won't need to go to court to get it."

Still Dee said nothing. She was too confused and overwhelmed to open her mouth. Her tongue was dry, and she ran it experimentally over her teeth in a nervous gesture.

He was looking at her now, gently turning her head to face him. "Are you ready to leave Charlie? I know he's going to be upset. I mean, it's even worse because he and I are friends."

Trembling, Dee had looked away. The repercussions of living together would be enormous. They would bring unhappiness to so many people – and hassle for themselves. But this was what she wanted, wasn't it? Of course, it was. But right then, she didn't feel able to cope with all the trauma that would inevitably ensue.

"It's not just our immediate families who'll be affected, is it?" she'd said sadly. "It's also going to spread right through to our friends. Maybe they won't even be our friends any more . . ."

"I know, I know," he squeezed her hand, "but I'm not giving you up. So don't you dare have second thoughts about us!"

She'd smiled back. "As if I would."

So they'd left the situation like that for a while longer. Then it had been her turn to push the pace, when she'd found she could no longer cope with Charlie's sexual demands. When he would climb on her, she'd grit her teeth and lie there woodenly, trying not to cry, and trying to fantasise that it was the man she loved. But her imagination could not make that quantum leap.

"I'm ready to leave," she'd told him. "I can't cope with Charlie's demands any more. I just can't." She'd begun to cry. But she was determined to have her say, the words tumbling out amid her sobs. "The boys are old enough to lead their own lives," she'd added. "After all, they're both at college. They won't like it, but I think they'll realise that their father and I –"

She'd looked at him, at his gaunt face and tortured eyes. He was shaking his head slowly. All of a sudden, he looked tired and old. It gave Dee a shock to see how haggard he was looking.

"I can't leave just now, love," he'd sighed and taken her in his arms. "You know what teenagers are like. We had another major tantrum last night. I think that if I left now it would push the poor kid over the edge. Can we just wait a while longer? It's not long until the school holidays – I think it might be easier then."

And what about me? Dee had wanted to scream. I'm near to the edge too. Your daughter has her whole life ahead of her, while we have so little time left!

How prophetic those unvoiced words had been! All she'd meant was that they'd have less time together than if they'd been younger. But in actual fact, they'd only had a few more months, and there had never been time to live as a couple. Not long after that meeting, she'd stood numbly beside Charlie at her lover's graveside, longing for her own death to ease the torment inside her.

Now springing up from the bed, Dee went to her wardrobe decisively. She'd visit his grave today – it was the perfect time to do it. Ciara was otherwise occupied, and there would be no need to account for her movements to anyone.

As she backed her car out of the driveway, drops of rain began to fall, and Dee cursed inwardly. Driving towards the graveyard, the car's wipers drummed their beat on the windscreen. As they swished back and forth, they seemed to be saying, 'He's dead, he's gone. He's dead, he's gone.'

Stopping at a florist's on the way, Dee selected a single red rose, staring frostily at the young shop assistant as she paid for it. Clearly the youngster was wondering why a middle-aged woman was buying such a romantic symbol of love on a miserable wet afternoon. Dee sighed. The kid probably thought it was obscene for anyone over thirty to have sex, anyway.

Once again, the wipers began their depressing chant, so she turned on the radio to blank out their rhythm. On the first station she found a DJ was asking a listener who she'd be taking with her on the holiday she'd just won. "Oh, my gorgeous husband, of course," she gushed happily. Dee quickly switched off the radio. Another woman's happiness was like a knife twisting inside her, with its visions of idyllic moonlight swims, exotic meals and sensuous love-making.

Arriving at the cemetery, Dee parked her car up the

side street where it was less likely to be spotted by anyone she knew. Then she wondered angrily why she was behaving like a criminal? All she was doing was going to visit the grave of the man she loved.

As yet, none of the newer graves displayed headstones, but she knew exactly which grave was his. On the day of his funeral she'd walked there at Charlie's side, counting every step to occupy her mind and prevent her from losing control.

As the priest had droned the final prayers, Charlie had urged her forward, but she'd released his arm and gestured for him to go alone. She couldn't trust herself to face that final moment, when the first sods of clay thudded onto the coffin. And when the ceremony was over, as they'd walked back to the waiting cars, she'd counted her footsteps all the way back again.

Now, as she stood before his grave again, the tears came unbidden and she knelt in the mud, not caring that her coat was being ruined. As she laid the rose on the grave, a heavy rain shower started which was like a signal that unleashed all her own pent-up grief. As the rain dripped from her hair and clothing, it mingled with the tears that streamed down her face.

Suddenly, she found that she had nothing to say to him here. There hadn't been any need to come to his grave, since he was already in every fibre of her being. Abruptly, she stumbled to her feet and left the graveside without a backward glance, the wet ends of her coat now flapping uncomfortably around her legs.

Among the yew trees, a couple of graveyard workers were sheltering from the rain, resting on their spades and laughing quietly together at some shared joke. They stopped abruptly when she appeared, aware that such ribaldry would seem insensitive to a visitor. Noticing her dripping hair and dishevelled appearance, the older one, a kindly-looking elderly man, asked, "Are you all right, missus?"

"Yeah, I'm fine," Dee replied abruptly. "I just slipped in the mud back there." And before they could offer any further help, she started walking briskly away from them down the centre aisle towards the main gate.

The younger man looked after her receding form. "That woman reminds me of someone," he said softly, scratching his head as if this gesture would aid his memory.

"Thought so meself, son," said the older man, "but for the life of me, I can't think who."

Evidently, the head-scratching paid off, for the younger one turned to the older man. "Do you know who that is?" he asked, looking pleased at his achievement. "Do you remember, Da, those awful people who used to live next door to us years ago? The snooty one who became a painter . . ."

Old Paddy O'Donoghue's eyes lit up as he remembered young Ciara Reynolds and her father Frank, his late, great friend and drinking companion. "I don't think that was young Ciara, son."

"Nah," his son Paul replied, "but it was that friend of hers. She didn't call as often as the one called Kate, but when she did, she was always so rude. She thought she was better than the rest of us."

"You mean young Dee? Ah no, son, she was a good

kid. A bit abrupt, but she meant no harm." He looked after the form receding in the distance. "So that was Dee, was it? She looked very upset, so she must have lost someone very special. May God have mercy on their soul."

Old Paddy scratched his head, it was a family trait. As he stared into space, he was thinking back to all those years ago, when his own wife Mary was alive. How he and Frank Reynolds had laughed at the antics of their two women, who hated the sight of each other! Now Mary was gone, and Frank Reynolds too.

Paddy remembered the day – only a few years ago – when they'd buried his old pal Frank whom he hadn't seen since the Reynolds kids had moved their parents out of the council estate into an up-market apartment.

He'd been in the caretaker's office at the cemetery that day, waiting for the funeral party to leave so that he could fill in the grave. He'd recognised the family as they drove in, and he'd longed to go up to Annie or Ciara and say something. But the same stupid pride that had kept them apart as neighbours still intervened.

Poor snobbish Mary had never wanted the Reynolds to know that he was a gravedigger. She'd constantly told them that he worked for the Corporation, which strictly speaking was true – and even though his wife was long dead, Paddy still felt that he couldn't dishonour her misplaced pride. So he stayed hidden from view as the Reynolds left the cemetery.

And what had those silly feuds between his wife and Annie Reynolds been about? Snobbery and notions on Mary's part. He just wished that his son Paul hadn't been so quick to take up his mother's prejudices. The lad still had a chip on his shoulder about working in a cemetery. Jobs connected with death were often perceived as amusing and macabre by everyone else, but a job was a job and these days you had to be grateful for what you could get. Soon he'd be retiring himself, and, please God, he'd get a few years out of his pension before he ended up in a box himself.

Chapter 22

As a child, Ciara, I longed to be loved and cuddled by my parents, to be shown any sort of affection. I wasn't able to analyse that need as I'd no practical knowledge of what I'd been deprived of. But I knew instinctively that something very real and basic to my welfare had been denied to me. Therefore, when anyone showed any concern for me, I responded as a starving child might seize and devour leftovers.

When I was seven I discovered what had been missing from my life. It was on the day that I and all the other seven-year-olds in the area made their First Holy Communion, a major day in most Irish youngsters' lives. I had a long white dress and veil sent down from Dublin by my aunt, new white shoes and ankle socks which my mother bought in the nearby town, and a little satin handbag which was laden with money, given to me by the neighbours, farmhands and local shopkeepers. Like most of the other children, I was more concerned about how much money I'd collected, and how wonderful I felt in my long dress, than the actual religious significance of the day. For a seven-year-old this day was a rare and exciting occasion indeed.

After the First Communion Mass, we children were brought back to the local convent for lemonade and biscuits, while the adults had tea in the nuns' parlour. After that, all the mothers were taking us to the local cinema, where a special matinee had been arranged for the occasion. My mother and I, along with some neighbours and their children, were driven in style in a big Morris Oxford into the nearest town which was some miles from where we lived. While the adults in the front of the car talked, we children sat quietly in the back seat, eyeing each other's finery, and bragging about how much money we'd got.

By today's standards, the local cinema was no more than a flea-pit. But to me, it was an awesome and exciting place – one that I had never been to before. The adults, lost in their own conversation, merely herded us along. There were lots of questions I wanted to ask, but I knew the adults were too busy talking to answer me. So I contented myself with studying everything and everyone, from the uniformed ushers and ice-cream sellers to the movie posters on the wall and the plush red curtains covering the screen.

There was a tremendous aura of glamour about the place. It was frightening too, but in an exciting way that gave me a terrible pain in my stomach. I worried briefly about what would happen if I got sick in this magnificent place. Apart from ruining my lovely white dress, the ignominy would be unbearable. And I knew for certain that, if I disgraced her, my mother would box my ears and take me straight home.

But this fear was quickly supplanted by awe as the lights dimmed and the enormous red curtains swished back as though by magic. Loud music accompanied this action, and I stared up in amazement as the release certificate, followed by the opening credits, appeared on the screen. I became lost in this wonderful larger-than-life world.

I think the film was Gone with the Wind. All the women in it wore glorious gowns with big full skirts, and I felt just as regal as I sat there in my own full-length white dress. I've never forgotten the moment when, after a series of near-misses and misunderstandings, the hero and heroine kiss passionately to a rousing crescendo of music, holding each other tenderly.

As I sat there in the dark, spooning out the ice cream from my tub, it seemed a wonderfully transcending experience. But my mother and our neighbour tut-tutted loudly all through the scene, complaining afterwards about the 'filth' to the bemused manager. How, I wondered, could such lovely expressions of affection – which made my own toes curl with delight and longing as I watched them – cause the women so much anger? Was it because their own husbands never behaved like that towards them? After all, I'd never heard anything other than a bark or a grunt expressed between my parents. Maybe ordinary people weren't supposed to feel the way people in the movies did.

But it didn't seem wrong to me. In fact, it looked beautiful. And as the film progressed, the couple acquired a baby, whom they now loved as much as each other. I felt overcome by a mixture of envy and delight as the little girl grew from babyhood to around my own age. Her parents clearly adored her, they never spoke a cross word to her and she had all the toys and books she could possibly want. She even had a pony of her own, and she would gallop around the grounds of their beautiful house while her parents looked on adoringly. How fortunate she was, and how I wished that someone would feel that way about me!

But suddenly, tragedy struck. The girl and pony jumped a fence too quickly. There was a scream, a crumpled body, and I knew without a shadow of a doubt that she was dead. Tears fell unchecked into my ice-cream tub and onto my white dress. Embarrassed, I tried to wipe my eyes with the back of my hand, but the boy beside me saw my distress and started to giggle at me, digging his fist into my back as I tried to turn away. His callousness only made me cry all the harder, with the result that my mother leaned over in annoyance and gave me a slap across the side of the head. My happiness exploded like a burst balloon, and for the rest of the film I sat tight-lipped and miserable. It seemed that nothing in life was perfect. Nor in the movies either.

But having seen for myself how people could care for each other, I wanted to experience the same situation myself. I knew that I would never get it from my parents, but maybe someone else could love me? I just wanted someone – anyone – to make me feel good about myself.

For weeks afterwards I fantasised about living with parents who loved me the way the little girl in the film had been loved. They would talk kindly instead of shouting, they would sit down and read stories to me instead of telling me to get out of their way. Maybe they would even buy me a doll of my very own, like the one I'd seen in a shop in the main street on the day I'd made my First Communion. I longed to own that doll, but my mother had taken all my Communion money. She'd said that it was too much for a young child to have, and that she'd put it in the Post Office for me until I was older.

As time went by, I accepted that I was just a nuisance to my parents. Unlike the little girl in the film, I was always being sent off to play or given chores to do, like collecting the eggs, or taking a bale of hay down to the lower field during a cold spell. I eventually accepted that it must be my own fault. Obviously, I wasn't worth loving.

It was a lonely life, since few children lived near to our farm and the ones that did – like the nasty boy who had poked me in the cinema – were not the sort I wanted to play with anyway. I preferred to play quietly by myself rather than be drawn into their tormenting games where there always had to be a victim. And when I played with them, the victim was invariably me.

But sometimes I would talk to Seamus, one of the farm hands. He was much older than me – one day he told me proudly that he was nearly fourteen. He'd left school the year before, he confided, because the teacher at the local Christian Brothers school had told his parents that he wasn't bright enough to pass any exams. And before he left, the brother had hit him so hard that he couldn't hear properly in his left ear.

I felt sorry for poor Seamus. I'd heard it said among the neighbours that he was a bit simple – certainly his guilelessness about his own lack of ability seemed to confirm this, even to my young and inexperienced mind. But I was pleased to think that Seamus saw me as his friend. Clearly, he needed a confidante as much as I did.

Seamus and I were clearly two misfits, so we gravitated towards each other as people out of synch with the rest of the world are prone to do. Coming up the driveway from school each afternoon, I would see him carrying bales of animal feed or repairing the fences. And I would always stop to exchange a few pleasantries with him, knowing that he wouldn't bark at me like my father did.

The other two workers on the farm, Billy and Joe, mostly treated me as though I wasn't there at all, and sometimes I *wondered whether perhaps I was invisible to them like the emperor's clothes in the Hans Christian Andersen fairytale.*

But Seamus could clearly see me. So I fantasised that he was really a prince in disguise, and that one day we would both be transformed into the rulers of some wonderful far-away kingdom and we would have a little girl like the one I'd seen in the film. She would have all the toys and books that she wanted, but I would never allow her to have a pony.

Seamus was a most unlikely prince. Even at thirteen, he was tall and gangly with a ruddy face and teeth that would need more than a toothbrush to get them clean. One of his front teeth was missing, and the remaining ones were heavily tobacco-stained. This was caused, he explained, by many years of smoking. In fact, he confided, he'd started smoking at seven, the age I was now. And he liked being without his front tooth, because it meant that he could comfortably rest a cigarette in the gap while he was working.

"You could probably do the same," he said, looking approvingly at the gap where my own new front teeth had yet to appear. "Do you want to try a cigarette yourself?"

To be approved of by Seamus was one thing – to be offered an opportunity to enter the sophisticated world of grown-ups was a heady experience. I was so excited that I could hardly trust myself to speak, but my shining eyes clearly indicated my delight.

"But we'll have to be careful, y'know," Seamus said, looking all around him to ensure that we were alone. "If anyone saw us, we'd both be in terrible trouble."

I nodded eagerly. The possibility of danger made it even more exciting.

Seamus took a puff from his own ever-present Woodbine.

"In five minutes I'll meet you down by the gate into the lower field. We'll be all right there for a while, 'cos your Da, Joe and Billy are working up in the big field."

I nodded happily. I had no idea how long five minutes was because I didn't have a watch. But then neither did Seamus.

"They say I'm slow," said Seamus, *"but I can run really fast when I want to."*

"I'll just leave off my schoolbag at the house," I told him, *"and I'll be waiting for you behind the hedge."*

I was back in record time, having told my mother that I was going to collect the eggs. Seamus was crouched down behind the hedge, and I noted to my satisfaction that we were no longer visible from the house. He took out a crushed cigarette packet from his back pocket and began to smooth out the broken and half-smoked stubs that were inside it. I felt slightly disappointed that I wasn't even being given a full cigarette of my own, but then beggars couldn't exactly be choosers, could they?

I was nervous and excited as Seamus lit one of the butts. I tried not to think too distastefully of his dirty teeth as I accepted the glowing butt he handed me directly from his mouth, holding it nervously between my fingers as though it possessed a life of its own.

"Hold it like this," he said, demonstrating. I adjusted the butt and placed it between my lips. It tasted terrible but I didn't want to disappoint Seamus, so I sucked in rapidly. Suddenly, my eyes began to water and I felt like getting sick. I dropped the butt on the ground as my head started to swim.

"Are you all right? It takes a bit of getting used to, y'know," said Seamus matter-of-factly as he picked up the butt and began smoking it himself. *"Nobody likes it to begin with. You'll be OK after you've had a few tries."*

All I could do was nod. Why would people persist when it was so horrible, I wondered? I didn't know which part of me felt worse – my head, my mouth or my stomach. But I was so grateful for Seamus's interest and attention that I would have smoked standing on my head if that was what he wanted me to do.

"Want to try again tomorrow?"

I nodded weakly. For his undivided attention, I was willing to try anything.

CHAPTER 23

Kevin enjoyed the feeling of power beneath him as he drove the car out along the road towards Roundwood. He was glad he'd hired a car with a decent-sized engine, even though he knew it wasn't very environmentally friendly. He glanced at his sister beside him, surprised that she hadn't made some comment about over-use of the earth's limited resources.

Ciara was trying her best to look relaxed, but Kevin felt certain that she was thinking of Niall nevertheless. He wished he could say something that might ease his sister's pain.

Coming over Callary Bog Kevin took in a deep breath. This was as good a place as any to tell his sister of his decision. Maybe it was symbolic that he'd chosen to do it after the long climb uphill. As the road evened out, he spoke for the first time since they'd turned off the main road at Kilmacanogue.

"I talked to Mam yesterday."

Ciara looked at him quizzically.

"About leaving the priesthood."

"Really, Kev?" Ciara looked surprised. "I thought you were quite adamant about staying in Africa for the rest of your life."

"I am, but not as a cleric. I'd rather work there as a lay person. I think I can do a lot more that way.'

"What did Mam have to say?"

"Can you believe it," Kevin laughed, "she'd guessed it, even before I said anything to her!"

Ciara smiled at her brother affectionately. "She could always read each of us like a book! Do you remember, when we were kids, she'd always know if we were telling a lie."

"Maybe she was only bluffing. How could she possibly have known?"

Ciara smiled. "Well, I can usually tell when Sarah's leading me up the garden path. At other times, I'm the one who's bluffing . . ." Ciara looked closely at her brother. "Kev, do you regret not having a family? I mean, now that you've decided to leave –"

He smiled. "You mean, now that I've 'wasted' all those years when I might have had kids of my own? Yes, I think I'd have liked having a family, but in a way the kids of the communities I've been working with have become my own kids by extension. Helping them to make a better life for themselves is what a parent does anyway, isn't it?"

Ciara nodded. "Was Mam upset?"

"No, it didn't seem to bother her at all. I expected her

to be upset, especially since she'd been so thrilled all those years ago when I joined up."

Suddenly, Ciara had a thought. "Is that why you didn't officiate at Niall's funeral?"

Kevin nodded, relieved that the matter was now out in the open. "I didn't feel that it would be right. I'd already applied to leave, so technically I didn't feel I was a priest any longer. Yet I couldn't tell you why until I'd told Mam first."

Ciara nodded. "This decision, Kev. Is it something you've been thinking about for some time?"

Kevin nodded. "It's been the back of my mind for the last few years. I know that I can do a lot more out there if I'm not hampered by rules and regulations."

Ciara looked across at Djouce mountain and wondered if the landscape of Africa was in any way similar. Without the rain, of course! Glancing at her, Kevin seemed to read her thoughts.

"It's a wonderful continent, Ciara. The sky seems to go on forever, and the scenery is absolutely spectacular." He reached over and patted her hand. "Maybe you'll come out to visit – when you feel like it, that is. A change of scene might be the very thing you need."

Ciara nodded. The idea was a very pleasing one.

Kevin glanced at his sister. "But Africa's still in turmoil – mostly due to the effects of colonialism and the artificial boundaries that it created long ago. This has led to tribal warfare that's decimated whole populations there."

Ciara looked surprised. "I thought famine was Africa's biggest problem?"

Kevin grimaced. "It's a serious problem all right, but not for the reasons we've been led to believe. Famines aren't always caused by the vagaries of crop yield and weather changes. They happen because poor people – left poor by colonialism and kept poor by their own corrupt governments – are forced to grow cash crops like tobacco, tea, coffee and rubber for us in the West instead of growing food to feed themselves.'

Ciara was aghast. "I never realised that."

Kevin nodded. "Unfortunately, many African governments are only interested in lining their own pockets – they learnt well from their former masters! Where I'm based, the local population are fighting to get a proposed oil pipeline re-routed, but the government won't budge because it's getting big backhanders from the oil company. The government is also planning to bring in companies to mine for titanium and other minerals which, of course, will destroy the local people's way of life." He looked briefly at his sister and smiled. "Sorry about the speech, love. But I do get very angry about it all."

Ciara looked horrified. "How can governments put oil and mineral exploration before their own people's needs?"

Kevin shrugged. "That's nothing new in the Third World, love. Huge money is paid out by these companies for exploration rights. Nobody in power gives a damn about the ordinary people, and the companies are willing to turn a blind eye to people's suffering as long as they get what they want."

Ciara sighed. "But we're just as guilty, aren't we Kev? The so-called First World helps to keep these injustices going. We need the oil for our cars and titanium for our catalytic converters to protect *us* from pollution. So people in these countries have their lives destroyed, in order to preserve our privileged way of life."

Kevin nodded, pleased that his sister was so well informed. "Not many people know that, love. In fact, there are vested interests making sure that we don't know most of what's going on. Worldwide, more and more newspapers, radio and television stations are coming under the control of the same business-oriented clique, who make certain that all protest and independent thought is suppressed."

Ciara sighed. "It's all so depressing, isn't it? If Niall was around, I know he'd love to help . . ." Then she suddenly wondered why she was singing his praises. He'd cheated on her, hadn't he? Yet she had to acknowledge that Niall always refused to take on any projects that smacked of exploitation. Ciara deftly manoeuvred Niall out of the conversation, adding "But maybe Dee or Kate could help. They'd know who to take your story to." As she spoke, she could have bitten off her tongue. She certainly hadn't intended bringing either woman's name into the conversation either!

Kevin nodded. "I've already spoken to Kate about it and she's agreed to write something. But who's likely to print the stuff? Most newspapers won't risk annoying their advertisers."

"Kate never mentioned that she'd been in touch," said Ciara. Then she realised that since she had chosen to isolate herself Kate wouldn't have had the opportunity to tell her anyway. Not that she cared what Kate did.

"I suppose she thought that you'd enough troubles of your own. I mean, it's not long since Niall –"

"So when are you going back?"

Kevin hesitated. "I don't know yet. There are a few things that need sorting out first."

Sensing his reticence, Ciara didn't question Kevin any further. He was probably waiting for his laicisation papers to come from Rome before leaving. He'd tell her what was on his mind when he was ready. She and Kevin had always been close. In fact, she was closer to the brother who lived thousands of miles away, than the one who only lived down the road.

"Is there anything I can do to help?"

Kevin thought for a minute. "Would you do a painting? You know – something that would express the concept of injustice. It doesn't have to be any specific injustice, but since you're so well-known it's bound to generate discussion in the papers. That would be one way of getting the issues covered indirectly."

"Of course. I'll do anything I can."

Kevin was becoming enthusiastic. "Maybe your painting could then go for public auction, to raise money?" He looked tenderly at his sister. "When you feel up to painting again, that is."

Ciara nodded. She'd start work as soon as possible. She felt mildly peeved that Kate was already involved, but she dismissed this feeling as selfish and unworthy. Obviously the more people involved, the better.

As they drove into Roundwood village, Kevin turned to his sister again. "I wouldn't mind a cup of coffee. How about you?"

Ciara nodded, so Kevin drove into the carpark of a large old-fashioned pub, and the two of them ambled inside.

Ciara was surprised to find that she was actually enjoying her outing with Kevin. It was the first time she'd actually relaxed since the discovery of Niall's infidelity. How she wished she could confide in her brother! Several times she'd been on the point of saying something, but had changed her mind. Her own foolish pride wouldn't let her. She still needed everyone to believe that she and Niall had been the perfect couple.

In the comfortable lounge, Ciara settled herself in a corner while Kevin went to the counter to order their coffees.

"Will the laicisation take long?" Ciara asked, when he returned with two cups of coffee and a plate of biscuits.

"It's difficult to say. Given certain circumstances – say, if you wanted to get married – you might be free within a year."

"So, Kev – was a woman a factor in your decision to leave?" Ciara asked, her eyes twinkling.

"Mam asked me that too. Why would either of you think that?"'

Ciara smiled at her brother. "It would seem more romantic, I suppose, if there was someone special waiting in the wings . . ."

With surprise and relief, Kevin looked up as two familiar figures entered the pub. Well, one of them was familiar. The second, he'd met for the first time at Niall's funeral.

"Well, if it isn't Il Papa himself!" said Liam, crossing

the floor and gripping Kevin's hand firmly. "I'm getting into practice, Kev, for when you become the next pope. What will I have to call you – your Holiness?'

Kevin grinned. "Don't put any money on it, Liam, because you'd lose. I'm going to be plain old Kevin from now on."

Liam looked surprised. "Are you serious? My God, I'm hearing so many confessions lately, maybe I'll take over your job!"

Meanwhile, Ciara had risen to greet Liam's companion. "Ita! It's lovely to see you again!"

Ita smiled back shyly. "I hope we're not intruding? Liam spotted the car outside and was positive it was the one Kevin had hired. We had a bet on it – and now I've lost!" Ita coloured. "But I'm glad I lost, because it's so nice to see you again!"

"What would you like to drink?" Kevin asked.

"I'll have a pint," Liam replied.

"A coffee would be lovely," said Ita.

Soon they were all seated with their drinks, Kevin and Liam talking nineteen to the dozen about their favourite football teams. Ciara sat watching their animated faces, wondering how men get so worked up about sport? She smiled at Ita, sharing her amusement.

"Did you play sports at school?" Ciara asked.

"Eh, no. I wasn't particularly good at it," Ita replied.

"I'm surprised. With your height and elegance, I'd have thought you'd be a natural!"

Ita blushed. "Thanks for the compliment, Ciara, but I had two left feet where sports were concerned."

"I used to play camogie in junior school, but I gave it

up when I discovered boys!" Ciara confessed. "By the time I was fourteen I was much more interested in off-field activities!"

Ita smiled but said nothing, and Ciara tried desperately to think of something that would help them to establish some common ground.

"Did you enjoy your schooldays, Ita?"

Ita looked briefly taken aback.

"Sorry. I don't mean to be nosy . . ." Ciara interjected, "it's just that Kate, Dee and I went to the same secondary school. So there's a special bond between us all."

Then her voice faltered. It wasn't true any longer, was it? But having introduced the topic of school, she had to continue with it. "I'm still in contact with several other friends from back then too. There's Marguerite who's married to a French guy and now lives in Nice, Dot who married a sheep farmer and lives in Northern Ireland, and Vera who's now a very senior civil servant!"

Ita nodded. "That's nice."

"We're a very diverse group," Ciara added, "but we still keep in touch, even though we don't get together very often. E-mail makes it much easier. Before that it was just the occasional letter and Christmas card. But we've never, ever, broken the contact."

"Why are you all so close?"

Ciara thought for a moment. "I don't really know – perhaps it's a shared history. I mean, you never forget your schooldays, do you?"

Ita smiled but said nothing. Ciara felt that she'd overstepped some invisible line, and quickly changed the subject.

"Where did you and Liam meet?" she asked, then wondered if that question was also too personal. But Ita seemed happy to answer it.

"We met at a press reception – for the launch of a book on twentieth century painting," Ita told her. "I was there to write up the forgotten role of women. You know, there were many fine women painters whose work has been totally overlooked."

Ciara nodded. She'd intended going to that reception herself, but a commission needed finishing in a hurry. "Did Liam ask you out straightaway?"

"We went to the pub next door after the reception – ostensibly to discuss women painters – but we talked about everything and anything else! Since then, we've hardly spent an evening apart."

Ciara smiled. "I can see that Liam is seriously smitten."

Suddenly, Ciara was remembering her own first meeting with Niall. They'd known instantly that they were meant for each other, and from then on they'd hardly spent a minute apart either. Her eyes clouded over as she remembered. Now all those wonderful memories had been obliterated by the discovery of that photograph. And the smile quickly died on her face.

CHAPTER 24

I enjoyed the excitement of meeting Seamus down at the lower field each day after school. We only managed to meet for a few minutes each time and I could never quite get the hang of smoking, but Seamus didn't seem to mind. Eventually we dropped any attempts at teaching me to smoke. For him, as for me, the smoking was of secondary importance. We were just two lonely kids who were pleased to have someone else to talk to.

"Have you ever been to the pictures?" I asked Seamus one warm sunny afternoon as I lay on the grass behind the hedge, thinking back to the day of my First Communion.

Seamus nodded, puffing happily on a Woodbine. It was pay-day, so he'd been able to buy himself a full packet.

"Yeah, I saw a great picture once," he said proudly, " there was dancing, an' singing, an' everything."

I sighed. Would I ever be taken to the cinema again? I'd probably have to wait until I was an adult and could go there by myself. Or maybe Seamus would take me on the crossbar of his bike.

"I was at the cinema once," I volunteered, "for my First Holy Communion."

Seamus nodded between drags. "It's great, isn't it?"

"I wish things were really like they are in the pictures," I said wistfully.

Seamus looked at me quizzically.

"Well, everyone loves each other. They aren't always fighting, or shouting at each other like they do in real life."

Seamus looked philosophical. "Well, I dunno about that. They showed a trailer along with the other picture I saw, an' it was all about war, an' the people were all killing each other." He looked kindly at me. "But you and me don't fight with each other. Maybe that means that we love each other, like they do in the pictures."

I looked at his big, simple, open face and burst into tears. For the first time in all my seven years, someone had actually said that they might love me!

Seamus looked alarmed.

"I'm not sad, Seamus. I'm happy!" I said, wiping my sniffles on the sleeve of my school cardigan.

"`Maybe when you're a bit older, we could get married," Seamus said kindly.

I nodded happily. It sounded like a great idea. Then I would always have someone to love me.

"But then we'll have to do the things that married people do," he told me solemnly.

"Like what?"

"Kissin' and stuff. Then we have to take all our clothes off, an' I have to lie on top of you."

I sat up. "Who told you that?"

For the first time since he'd come to work on the farm, I

168

actually wondered if Seamus's simple-mindedness had led him to pick up some idle gossip wrongly, or if someone had deliberately misinformed him to poke fun at him. Clearly there could be no truth in such a ludicrous idea. I tried to think of Seamus lying naked on top of me – I'd be crushed to death! It didn't make the slightest sense.

"Well, that's what the lads in the pub told me."

I looked at him with pity, and considerable relief. Clearly the lads had been having a great joke at his expense. Not wishing to cause him any embarrassment, I tried to reason with him. "When we get married, I think we'll just kiss. Then we'll get a baby, and . . ."

"We can't have a baby, at least not until I put my mickey into you."

"What's a mickey?"

He blushed now. "The thing that boys have." Gently he rubbed his crotch, and I noticed that the front of his trousers seemed to be getting tighter as though there was something growing in there and filling up the slack of the material.

Seeing me looking at his crotch, he began opening the front of his trousers. "Do you want to see it?" he asked, getting redder and redder in the face, his eyes becoming glazed as his fingers extracted what looked like a large pink carrot. Then he wrapped his hand around it, and began frantically rubbing it up and down.

Mesmerised, I could only sit and stare at this enormous object. Was he deformed, I wondered? Perhaps this had something to do with him being simple in the head. Perhaps what was missing in his brain had somehow re-located itself below his waistline.

"Go on, put your hand on it," Seamus begged me, and

eager to please him, I reached out and felt its tip. Suddenly he groaned and out shot a stream of thick white fluid. I jumped back. Had I done something terrible to him? Was he going to die?

Suddenly, there was a commotion as my father and the two farm workers appeared.

"What the fuck are you doing!"

"Jesus Christ, he's been at the child."

"I wasn't near her!" Seamus screamed, as my father's fist met his jaw. He stumbled back, grasping at his trousers, which had slipped down his legs and were now hampering his ability to dodge the blows from my father's fists and feet.

Joining my father in the attack, the other two rained blows on poor Seamus's back, and I heard a crack as a bone somewhere broke and a scream as Seamus collapsed under a further barrage of kicks and punches.

Sobbing, I tried to pull them away, but it was useless. Apart from their physical strength, they were all fuelled by an anger that would not be assuaged until poor Seamus had been rendered senseless.

"He didn't go near me!" I screamed, not even knowing what I meant, but wanting to protect the only person who had ever cared about me.

As Seamus lay whimpering on the ground, my father turned to face me. "As for you, you dirty little bitch. Wait 'til I get my hands on you! You'll be sorry you ever knew me – and so will this bastard!"

He aimed another ferocious kick at Seamus's groin, and I heard the poor boy scream in agony. Between them, Billy and Joe lifted Seamus onto his feet. "We'll take him home, boss," Joe said quietly.

"*And tell his mother that he's never to darken my door again! And she can count herself lucky that I haven't killed that retarded bastard altogether!*" *His eyes glittering malevolently, my father loomed over me.* "*As for you, little madam . . .*" *He lowered his voice menacingly, bringing his face close to mine.* "*When I get you home, I'm going to beat every bit of badness out of you, even if it takes me all night to do it!*"

I squirmed under his vice-like grip, stumbling and falling as he hauled me up the long driveway to the house. Once inside, my father ordered my mother to leave the kitchen. "*Go and check on the hens, Nellie,*" *he told her harshly, as he took the leather belt off his trousers. Imploringly, I looked at my mother. Surely word from her could save me?*

But she left the house without demur, and at that moment I hated her as I had never hated anyone before. As the first crack of the belt struck my bare legs, I tried to distract myself by remembering scenes from the film I'd seen on the day of my First Communion. But those happy scenes only served to accentuate the stark differences between my life and theirs. Then I tried to think of Seamus, and how I would run away and marry him when I grew up. But I knew that I'd probably never see Seamus again. In fact, the agony of my father's belt hurt far less than the overwhelming pain of loss that now engulfed me.

CHAPTER 25

Liam was leaning on the crowded bar in Mulligans, when Charlie Somers suddenly appeared. It was early Friday evening, the time when many workers traditionally launched the weekend with a few drinks before heading home.

"Ah, there you are, Liam. Wasn't expecting to see you here. How's she cuttin'?"

"Grand Charlie, never better. I'm heading off shortly but I'll join you in one for the road. A pint?" Liam signalled to the barman, who had already anticipated their need and was pulling the second pint.

Charlie looked at his watch. "No point in leaving for a while anyway – the traffic is manic. I just couldn't face the old bumper-to-bumper routine, so I thought I'd have a pint or two before going home."

Liam handed Charlie his pint, and they both took big gulps in unison.

"Aaah, great stuff," said Liam appreciatively.

"That was some looker I saw you with at Niall's funeral," said Charlie, grinning at him.

"Oh, Ita. Gorgeous, isn't she? I can't believe my good fortune."

"Yeah, she's a real babe all right. Is she your latest?"

Liam smiled and slapped his thigh. "Not just my latest, Charlie. Hopefully, my last! I've really taken to that woman. To be honest, I've never felt like this about any woman before."

Charlie gave a sarcastic grin. "Huh! Seems like I've heard you say that before, old chap."

"Sure, there've been lots of women. I just never fell for any of them. To be honest, I thought I was past all that kind of thing."

Charlie looked at him with amusement. "You're not trying to tell me that you're in love. The great Liam Golden has actually fallen for a woman? Ye gods – it would serve you right if she turned the tables on you!"

Liam smiled. "Yeah, I probably deserve it, but I hope she won't."

Charlie looked at him sceptically. "You're really serious?"

'Of course, I am." Liam looked at Charlie. "I think I was always looking for that special woman. I just never managed to find her. Until now." He punched Charlie affectionately. "Not everyone's as lucky in that department as you."

Charlie nodded in agreement, and smiled into his pint. He'd been very lucky in that area of his life, he conceded. He'd had to chase Dee for a while, but he'd never wanted anyone else. He thought affectionately of the secretary in his office who'd fancied him, and who had inadvertently brought the situation with Dee to a head. Once Dee discovered she had competition, it had all been plain sailing. Charlie sighed happily. It was pleasant to think of two women fighting over him – he wasn't the kind of guy who normally inspired that kind of feeling in anyone. I've certainly been lucky, Charlie mused. The two lads, Terry and Donal, had sailed through their exams, and never given Dee or him any serious grief. It was a pity Dee had never been able to conceive – he'd have liked to see what kind of offspring his own flesh and blood would have produced. Then again, since he wasn't much of a looker maybe it was just as well! They'd probably have been short, stocky and red-haired like himself. Although lately, he'd noticed the red was turning to grey . . . Charlie suddenly realised that Liam had been speaking to him. "What did you say?"

"I said, will you be best man at my wedding?"

"Jesus, has it gone that far already?"

"No, but I hope it will."

"So you're actually going to marry this woman?"

"Ita. Yes, if she'll have me."

"But you hardly know her!" Charlie said in amazement.

Liam smiled. "I seem to remember not all that long ago you were boasting about how quickly you knew that Dee was the only woman for you. And you bored the rest of us rigid with details of your attempts to win her over!"

Remembering, Charlie grinned apologetically. "OK, so I had a few jars too many that night. But it's true, I did know straightaway that she was the only one I wanted."

He patted Liam's shoulder. "So the best of luck, old chap. I hope it works out as well for you as it did for me."

"Thanks, Charlie."

Charlie gestured to the barman, and two more pints quickly appeared. For a few minutes the two men drank in companionable silence, each lost in their own thoughts.

Charlie spoke at last. "I miss him like hell, you know."

"Yeah, I can imagine."

"We were pals since junior school. It's like he was always there. I can't remember a time when we didn't hang out together." Charlie turned to Liam. "He really was one of the good guys. He'd do anyone a good turn. I just can't believe that I'll never see him again."

The two men drank in silence.

"I'm just glad –" Charlie stopped in mid-sentence.

"About what?"

"Oh, nothing."

"C'mon, Charlie – what's on your mind?"

"No, I can't talk about it," Charlie sighed. "A slip of the tongue, Liam. Don't mind me. That second pint has gone to my head already. It's just that there's one thing about Niall I'll never understand."

"So you did know."

Charlie looked up quickly from his pint. "Knew what?"

"Oh, come on, Charlie. I know what you're thinking about. You mean Niall's affair. But I don't think he realised you knew about it."

Charlie looked startled. "Jesus, how did you find out? So I *was* right after all." Then he looked suspiciously at Liam. "Did he tell you about it?"

Liam could see that Charlie was hurt at the idea that Niall would confide in someone else.

"Well, yes, but by accident as it happens. We bumped into each other one night, both of us had too much to drink and it all just tumbled out." Liam rested his hand on Charlie's shoulder. "He was afraid to tell you, Charlie, precisely because you mattered so much to him. I don't think he could bear the thought that you might be disappointed in him. I was just someone conveniently there at the time."

Charlie savoured this information. "Yeah, I suppose I can understand that." He looked back at Liam. "But I'd never have turned away from him. First and foremost, he was always my best pal." Tears gathered in Charlie's eyes. "I'd have told him he was a bloody fool. But I'd never have stopped caring about him. I couldn't have."

Tears were now running down Charlie's face, and he brushed them aside angrily. Liam patted him on the shoulder, and in unison, they took a mouthful of their pints.

Charlie turned back to Liam. "I suppose I'm glad, in a way, that I didn't know for definite about the affair. In fact, I'd never have suspected anything, but one day a hotel receipt fell out of his wallet and he got very defensive about it. That made me wonder if something was up. Then I started noticing other little things, but I never said anything to him. It was cowardly of me, but it was easier not to know because then I didn't feel I had to do anything about it."

Liam nodded. "You can take it as a compliment that he didn't tell you, Charlie. I think he wanted you to go on seeing him as the white-haired boy."

They drank their pints in silence for a while, then Charlie spoke again. "Thank goodness Ciara never found out," he shuddered. "I think it would have killed her."

Liam laughed mirthlessly. "Well, by all accounts, she was having a bit on the side herself."

Charlie looked at him incredulously. "What?"

"Look, maybe I shouldn't have said anything. But according to Niall, that was why he started having the affair – to get even with Ciara."

Charlie looked as though he'd been struck by a bolt of lightning. "I don't believe you."

"Well, that's what Niall told me."

"But Ciara – of all people. Ah no, Liam. It's just not possible."

Liam shrugged his shoulders. "Suit yourself. I'm only telling you what Niall said."

"Jesus! I just can't believe it."

Liam leaned over to Charlie and lowered his voice. "Now, listen Charlie. What I've told you is in strict confidence. Not a word to anyone – not even Dee."

Charlie nodded. "As if I would. Jesus – Ciara having an affair! How did Niall find out?"

"He saw her with this guy several times. Then she lied to him about where she was – said she was out with a woman friend."

Charlie said nothing for a few moments. Then he turned to face Liam. "Do you know who either of them were having their affairs with?"

"I haven't a clue. For all we know Ciara might still be involved with the guy."

"My God." That possibility had never occurred to

Charlie. "But she and Niall loved each other. I'd swear to that."

Liam shrugged his shoulders again. "I only know what Niall told me, and I don't suppose it's any of our business anyway."

"But –" Charlie struggled for the right words, "he was my best friend. It's hard to think –" He left the sentence unfinished.

Liam patted his shoulder. "Look, it's all water under the bridge now, old son. It's probably best if we both forget about what happened in the past."

"But you must be disappointed too, Liam. In Ciara, I mean. After all, she's been a close friend of yours for years."

Liam nodded slowly. "I have to admit I'm, well, surprised. I suppose Ciara is the last person in the world that I'd expect to find in this situation," he grinned. "But then, with my track record, I've no right to judge anybody! Ciara will always be my friend, so I'm going to forget this conversation and you should too."

Charlie nodded. He was still shocked, and the alcohol had made him melancholy. All of a sudden, he wanted to be at home with Dee, surrounded by the familiar things of home since he suddenly felt very much out of his depth.

"Are you sure you won't have another pint?" Liam asked.

Charlie shook his head. "No thanks, Liam. I'm knackered. If you don't mind, I'm going to head off home. The traffic should have eased up by now."

"Are you OK to drive?"

Charlie smiled ruefully. "Yeah, I'm fine. I think the shock of what you've just told me has sobered me up!"

Liam nodded. He was about to head off home himself. And when he got there, he'd ring Ita. God, how he missed that woman when a whole day went by without seeing her!

Saying goodbye, the two men parted company. Liam set off in the direction of his Ballsbridge apartment at a brisk pace, for he'd sensibly left his car at home. As he walked, his thoughts for once weren't of Ita, but of Ciara. He'd no right to be disappointed, he told himself, but he just couldn't help it. Ciara had always been his inspiration, his own reason for believing that there was such a thing as lasting love and commitment. And now, just when he'd found love himself, he'd discovered that his role model had feet of clay.

CHAPTER 26

My father kept a herd of cows on the farm, and we supplied milk to the local dairy. Every morning and evening my father and either Joe or Billy would bring the cows in from the big field to the milking parlour. After the milking had been done, a jug of hot steamy milk would be brought to the house for our own use and the rest would be poured into milk churns which were then left at the farm gate for collection by the local creamery.

Sometimes, when my father wasn't around and Joe and Billy were doing the milking on their own, they would let me have a try at milking a cow myself. I would sit on a little stool, under the cow's udders and try to pull and squeeze simultaneously. It wasn't easy for little fingers to do, and I was always afraid of hurting the poor cows by squeezing too hard. Joe and Billy would laugh at my earnest efforts, but theirs was a companionable laugh, not a mocking one like my father's. And the two farmhands would applaud when I managed to get a stream of fresh, hot bubbling milk clattering into the bucket.

I loved being with the cows – they were beautiful, gentle creatures who were always curious about what was going on. When I'd go down the lane to school in the mornings they would amble over to the hedge to greet me, and some of them would moo gently at me. And I'd talk to them until we reached the point where the field no longer bordered the lane. And they'd stay there, watching, for as long as I turned around to check on them. Did they know that I still existed even after I'd disappeared? I was certain they did, because they'd also be waiting for me at the hedge when I came back from school. I presumed that like the two farm collies, they had an understanding of time that didn't necessitate looking at a watch or clock.

I was forbidden by my father to go into the cows' field, but I would climb the five-bar gate and stroke their broad faces, feeling their steamy, dribbling breath against the palm of my hand. I'd tell them about my day at school, and they would listen intently, gazing rapturously at me with their big earnest brown eyes.

There were always about twenty cows in the field, but sometimes, when the older ones no longer gave much milk they were taken away in a big lorry. When I asked Joe or Billy where they were going, they would explain that they were going on their holidays. I was pleased to think that the poor creatures were enjoying themselves in their old age, and I pictured them frolicking gently in the sunlit fields of a rest home for elderly animals. I heard my father say something to my mother about the glue factory, but I was too afraid that I'd get a clip around the ears if I asked him what he meant.

The year that I was eight, there was great excitement locally because the AI man was coming to the area. Listening to the neighbours converse with each other outside the shop in the nearby village, I got the impression that he was some kind of Santa Claus figure who was bringing his bounty to the locality. Therefore I was quite disappointed when a very ordinary-looking man drove up to our farm in his Ford Anglia.

The cows had already been corralled in the milking shed and after greeting him heartily, my father took him into the shed and the door was firmly closed.

Meanwhile, in the parlour, my mother was setting out her best lace tablecloth complete with dainty cups, saucers and plates from the china cabinet. Then she bustled into the kitchen, extracting a tray of freshly-baked bread and scones from the oven.

"Why is that man here, Mammy?" I bravely ventured to ask.

"Hush, child. He's here on business with your father," I was told. "Anyway, you're far too young to know about these things." With that, she continued her preparations for the AI man's tea.

When he eventually came into the kitchen, washed his hands and was brought into the parlour I hovered around anxiously in the hopes of finding out something about his mission. But as soon as I was spotted, I was sent off to the hen house to collect the eggs. Clearly, this was another aspect of the adult world that was to remain a mystery for the present.

CHAPTER 27

At Dee's insistence, Charlie set out for Ciara's house. He'd been reluctant to go since he'd consumed several pints in Liam's company, but Dee was adamant.

"She's very down at the moment. Maybe she'd having financial problems. If so, you're the ideal person to help her sort them out. Please, Charlie. Just check that she's OK."

As he drove along, Charlie wondered why Niall had never confronted Ciara. Surely that would have been better than retaliating by having an affair himself? He sighed. Not everyone was as lucky as he and Dee. Over the years, they'd grown and matured together, so much so that now they could almost read each other's thoughts and expressions. Their marriage was built on love, trust, and all those old-fashioned values that many people dismissed nowadays. Charlie sighed. He'd always assumed that Niall and Ciara had the same kind of marriage. As he drove along, Charlie wondered if Ciara's affair was still going on? Maybe it was *her* affair that had caused Niall's heart attack?

When Charlie arrived at Ciara's house, there was no reply to his insistent ringing of the doorbell. But he knew that she was at home. Apart from the fact that her car was there, he'd seen young Sarah heading off down the driveway and they'd exchanged brief greetings. Charlie hoped that the poor kid was coping better with Niall's death than he was. Sarah was a bit wild, but a good kid at heart.

So he'd gone around by the side of the house, vaulted over the wall and felt ridiculously pleased at his achievement. Then he knocked on the back door, and receiving no reply he opened the door and walked in.

The minute Charlie saw Ciara's face, he knew that she'd found out about Niall's affair. How she knew, he didn't know. But that look of hurt and sadness on her face was not just the look of bereavement. It told him what he had always instinctively known – that secrets have a nasty way of surfacing, no matter how hard people tried to hide them. He'd seen it happen before. Even years later, a casual remark or a slip of the tongue could bring devastating consequences to those involved.

Charlie knew lots of people who thrived on secrets, and one by one he'd seen many of them toppled from their seemingly secure pedestals into an abyss of disgrace, shame, loneliness and despair. So he'd decided early in life that he'd have no secrets because they weren't worth the catastrophes that invariably followed. So he'd been honest in his business dealings, faithful to his wife, and a fair sportsman on the golf course.

But now, as he stood looking at Ciara's sad face, Charlie felt only anger. After all, she'd started it, hadn't she? What right had she now to feel cheated on?

Her mouth quivered slightly, although she was clearly trying to hide her distress from him. "It's nice of you to call, Charlie," she said, with a weak smile, "even in such an unorthodox manner! But there's no need for you to call. I can manage fine. Right now, I just want to be on my own anyway. I'm sorry, I know that sounds rude, but –"

Charlie made no move to leave. He'd been sent to do a job, and he intended to make sure that Ciara's finances were sorted out before he left again.

"How's Dee? And the boys?"

Charlie confirmed that they were all well, that Dee sent her regards, and that her friends were worried about her. Ciara nodded, but it was clear that she was just making perfunctory conversation. Nothing much was registering with her, Charlie realised.

Nevertheless, Charlie couldn't but respond to her anguish. Years of friendship and affection rose to the surface as she moved instinctively into his arms. He hugged her and kissed her hair.

"You look a bit under the weather," he said non-committally as he held her.

"Yeah, I feel like shit," she agreed. "There are good days and bad days, and this is definitely one of the bad days."

Would she confide in him? If she did, he'd feel duty bound to point out that her own affair had hurt Niall deeply, and might even have contributed to his heart attack. Perhaps some straight-talking and soul-searching could set them back on a course to friendship again. Although nothing would ever be the same again, Charlie knew. Niall was dead, and nothing could ever bring him back.

However, Ciara sat down on the sofa. "I packed away all Niall's clothes the other day," she said. "Tomorrow I'm going to bring them to the local Oxfam shop."

Charlie sat down beside her, not quite knowing what to say.

Jumping up again, Ciara crossed to the drinks cabinet and proceeded to pour them both large measures of gin. "Sorry I've no tonic – will soda do?"

Charlie shrugged to indicate that soda was acceptable, and with unsteady hands Ciara added two measures of soda, watching in dismay as they overflowed and dripped down onto the carpet.

"Oh God, I've made a mess –" Ciara said, looking like a small child who had just committed a misdemeanour.

Yes, there was something decidedly different about Ciara tonight, which Charlie found worrying. There was a recklessness – a barely controlled hysteria – about her, as though she no longer cared what happened to her.

Charlie crossed the room and took both over-flowing glasses from her. "Come on. Sit down, love," he counselled, handing her one of the drinks when she was seated beside him again.

"Thanks, Charlie. I need this right now," she said, raising her glass in a mock toast, then swallowing a large mouthful. Charlie was about to urge restraint, then it occurred to him that a few stiff drinks were probably what she needed to relax her.

"Where's Sarah gone tonight? I saw her heading down the drive."

Ciara grimaced at the mention of her truculent daughter. "She's staying over at her friend Fiona's house. To be honest –" Ciara drew a deep breath, "I'm glad to have her out of the way. She's very difficult to deal with right now. I just don't seem to be able to get through to her, Charlie. She treats me as though I was personally responsible for her father's death."

Charlie said nothing, feeling uncomfortably transparent because of his earlier thoughts. He struggled for something to say, finally managing to make some inane comment about Sarah's tender age and vulnerability.

There was a short silence between them before Ciara jumped up and put on a blues CD. "This matches my mood," she declared brightly. She began to sway to the sad sound as Charlie looked on in discomfort. He wished he could get up and go home, but he felt that it would be churlish to leave Ciara in her present state of mind.

"Come and sit down, love," he said, hoping to stave off any display of emotion, yet the very tenderness in his voice weakened Ciara's resolve and she burst into tears as she fell into his arms on the sofa.

"Oh Charlie!" she wept, as she buried her face in his pullover. "I'm so miserable!" Unable to find anything to say, he held her close, patting her gently on the back as one might soothe a distraught child.

Raising her tear-stained face, Ciara looked appealingly into Charlie's eyes. "I loved him so much, Charlie. I wish it hadn't ended the way it did."

Charlie nodded because he could think of nothing to

say. He didn't know if Ciara was referring to Niall's death, her own affair, or both their affairs. Nor was he certain of his own feelings at this moment. He too felt deeply emotional about Niall's death, and he felt angry and cheated by the loss of his best friend. He longed to attribute blame somewhere, but where he wasn't sure. His feelings about Ciara were mixed up in a cocktail of self-pity, anger and grief that welled up inside him. Suddenly his own face was covered in tears; unbidden, they ran down his cheeks as he clenched his jaw tightly in an effort to stifle the groan that threatened to escape and overwhelm him.

Seeing his distress, Ciara reached for him, and they clung together in their common grief. Gently, they massaged each other to communicate their sympathy for each other. Ciara's hair, which had been tied up in a pony-tail had come undone and Charlie tried unsuccessfully to clip it up again.

As they sat facing each other with tear-stained faces, Ciara leaned back against the sofa and closed her eyes. Watching her, Charlie was stirred by the sight of her dishevelment. Her lovely face, now streaked with mascara, the slightly open mouth, the open blouse that revealed the curve of her bra-less breasts, of which she was totally unaware.

What he now felt was really nothing to do with Ciara's exposed flesh. Charlie had seen her – as she'd seen him – in various stages of undress over the years. They'd all played tennis as a foursome, both families had holidayed abroad together, and many years ago they'd all swum naked in the Aegean sea.

No, it was not her naked flesh that stirred him. It was

her frailty combined with what almost seemed like wantonness as she lay there, a nipple now slightly exposed. Was this how she'd looked when she'd betrayed his best friend?

Suddenly, he was shocked at the feelings he could no longer hide from himself. Her sadness, her raw emotion and her need for his response was part of what produced in him a combination of anger, tenderness and passion in his loins.

Reaching out protectively to cover her, Charlie found himself touching her nipple instead of covering it. Opening her eyes, Ciara stared at him without moving but watching his face closely. The fact that she had not pushed his hand away had a startling effect on him. Leaning forward, he kissed her gently on the lips, only to find her mouth opening willingly to welcome his tongue.

Suddenly, they were clinging together. Then they were on the floor, tearing each other's clothes off, groaning with longing, touching each other's burning flesh. In a frenzy, their bodies fused and with no preliminaries, Charlie entered her. Wrapping her legs around his torso, she bucked back and forth like a wild creature. With a groan, Charlie climaxed as Ciara's own climax followed, her piercing groan filling the room.

Thankfully, Dee was in bed asleep when Charlie arrived home. In the darkness he could manage to hide his guilt and shame. But she woke up as he tried to slide quietly in beside her.

"Hmmm – you're late. Is everything OK with Ciara?" she murmured sleepily.

"Yeah, she's OK. She was a bit upset – she cleared out a lot of Niall's clothes the other day."

What a bastard I am, Charlie thought to himself. Already, I'm telling lies by omission. It was a bitter pill to have to face a side of himself that he hadn't believed existed before. Now he too had a secret like all those other people he'd previously despised.

"Goodnight, love," he said, hoping to ward off any further conversation. Quickly he rolled over onto his stomach and pretended to instantly fall asleep. But while he longed for the oblivion that sleep would bring him, he knew that he was in for a long and sleepless night.

CHAPTER 28

As I approached my ninth birthday, Joe told me that very soon most of the cows would be having calves. I was ecstatic — nothing this exciting had ever happened in my life before!

A few days later, the first of the calves arrived and the cow shed was a hive of activity. I was barred on the grounds that I'd only be in the way, and was confined to the house by my mother. But being so excited about what was happening, I crept down the stairs and out the front door while my mother was hanging out the washing in the kitchen garden.

As I sneaked up to the cowshed, I could hear sounds inside of pulling, shouting, and my father saying, "I have it by the legs, Joe. Watch those feet. Aargh, I've got it!" Then there was a feeble animal cry, and I concluded that a calf had just been born. But where it came from, I had no idea, and what my father and Joe had to do with it was even more puzzling.

I remembered the things Seamus had told me about how people got babies, but that information had been patently ridiculous. The poor lad had clearly been misinformed. Unless

– I suddenly wondered in shock if the AI man had been doing something to the cows . . . with that thing all men had in their trousers. Like the thing Seamus showed me . . . Just then, my mother pounced on me, and I received a clatter across the side of the head and dire threats if I ever dared to disobey her again.

The next day while my father was in town on business, Joe allowed me into the cowshed to see the new arrivals. There were a dozen or more calves suckling their mothers, and the atmosphere was one of glorious contentment.

"After a couple of weeks, we'll wean them all off their mother's milk an' put them onto milk substitute," Joe explained, "since we're already way behind in supplies to the creamery." I pondered on the strangeness of taking calves off their own mother's milk, and giving away what was rightfully theirs for human consumption. But when I questioned Joe, he shrugged his shoulders. "That's the way o' the world," he said. What a strange world it was indeed!

As we prepared to leave the shed, I noticed that one little calf wasn't feeding, but was lying on the ground at its distressed mother's feet. "What's wrong with it?" I asked Joe anxiously.

"Aah, I don't think that little fella will last . . ." he said dismissively. "He was born weak. He'll probably be dead by nightfall. Anyway, he's a bullock, thank God. So his mother's extra milk can go to the creamery."

"Can nothing be done to help him?" I asked anxiously.

"Well, if you want to try feeding some of his mother's milk from a bottle, you're welcome," said Joe, "but for God's sake, don't tell your father that I told you to do it. He has no time for mollycoddling sick animals. If they don't pay their way, they're out."

I nodded. Suddenly, I had a purpose in life – I was going to do my very best to help that little calf live.

Joe found me an old bottle and with his dire warnings ringing in my ears, I rushed off to rinse the teat in the kitchen sink, keeping it well hidden in the palm of my hand as I pretended to wash my own hands with gusto. My mother gave me a dour look. I think she was suspicious of my actions, since voluntary hand washing had never previously been on my agenda.

Back in the barn, I squeezed a little milk from the calf's mother's teat into the bottle, and taking the calf in my arms I tried to get the teat into his mouth. At first he was reluctant, but he was also too weak to resist my efforts. So I soon succeeded in getting some liquid down his throat. While his mother looked on anxiously, I filled a second bottle, and a third. By lunchtime, and several bottles later, I'd managed to get the little fellow standing shakily on his gangling little legs.

"Good for you," said Joe approvingly when I told him and Billy. They were both sitting in the yard, eating their sandwiches and drinking tea from the old earthenware pot that my mother prepared for them at the same time every day.

"Don't get too fond of that bloody animal," Billy warned darkly. "It could still die, y'know."

I nodded. "But it's not going to die," I said triumphantly, "because I'm going to help it get well."

Billy shrugged his shoulders, and I headed back to the cowshed to check on my charge, marvelling at how pleasant life was when my father wasn't around.

The young calf made steady progress, and even my father seemed amused when Joe finally confirmed that he was now doing well thanks to my ministrations. Then his face darkened. "But it's a bloody bullock. What the hell use is that?"

Joe quickly changed the subject, telling my father about a fence that needed fixing. So I headed back to the shed to see how my calf was getting on. For I regarded him as mine now, and I called him 'Moo' after the feeble little sounds that he was gradually beginning to emit. His mother, along with all the other mothers and calves, had now been moved out to the lower field and as Moo grew stronger I would carry him down to visit his mother and collect some of her precious milk for his next bottle. Soon I hoped he would be able to join all the other cows, and suckle his mother's milk for himself.

Joe, Billy, and even my mother found amusement in watching Moo and I making our way around the yard, me coaxing him, he mooing forlornly and hobbling after me. Now he was growing by leaps and bounds, and I was so proud of what we had achieved together. He was almost the same height as me now and I would rub his ears while he snuffled gently, pushing his face into mine and gazing at me with his big brown eyes.

But there was trouble on the horizon. It was time for the calves to be weaned from their mothers' milk and put on milk substitutes. And my father didn't see why Moo should get any. "It's too bloody expensive," he told me curtly, "I'm not spending money on that useless runt."

"Please, Daddy –" I started to say, but Joe gave me a warning glance. He knew that it was useless to argue with my father. But I also knew that Joe would help me later.

"I warned you not to get attached to that animal," Billy said later when he and Joe sneaked me a few scoops of the milk substitute and showed me how to dilute it with water. "Every animal on a farm has to pay its way, and that one's a dead loss."

"What do you mean?" I asked fearfully, but Joe silenced him with a look.

"What Billy means is that since he's a bullock, he can't be left with a dairy herd. He'd be up on every, ahem." He coughed and rephrased his words. "When he's a few months old, he'll have to be sold along with the other bullocks . . ."

Already, a plan was forming in my mind and I approached my father later that evening.

"Daddy, could I buy Moo from you?" I asked. "I could use my First Communion money. Mammy told me that she's put it in the Post Office for me . . ."

My father let out a roar and jumped to his feet. "Enough of this carry-on, you little brat. I told Joe he shouldn't be encouraging you!"

Grabbing me by the ear, he frogmarched me out into the yard. "Where's that bloody animal?" he shouted.

"In the cowshed," I said meekly.

"Well, I'm going to show you what happens when you go against nature," he said wrathfully, dragging me after him. "That calf should have been left to die, as nature intended. I'm going to put an end to all this nonsense –"

Still holding me in a vice-like grip, he went into the tool shed and emerged wielding a large knife in his other hand.

"No! Oh no –" I groaned, the horror of the situation dawning on me. I pulled on the arm that was gripping me to delay our progress to the cowshed. But I was like a mere feather in my father's grip, and I could not hold him back.

Moo was lying in the corner of the shed and when he saw me, he began to rise joyfully to his feet. Obviously, he thought me were going for our usual evening stroll down the lane. Suddenly my father released me, and I fell on the floor whimpering, while that same cruel hand now grabbed Moo and threw him down on the ground again. With lightning speed, *my father drew the knife across his little throat and I watched in horror as the blood of my beloved Moo spilled out from the gaping slit in his neck, making a large red puddle on the floor. Several times, his poor little legs quivered, then suddenly he was still.*

"Now," said my father with quiet satisfaction, "that will teach you to interfere in farm business!" He surveyed Moo's small body, then gathered it up and threw it across his shoulders. "At least we'll get next Sunday's dinner out of him. And maybe a joint for the following Sunday if we're lucky." Then he walked out of the barn without even giving me a backward glance.

For a long time I lay there, sobbing with grief. Then as darkness descended, I crept down to the lower field where the cows were. But they wouldn't come near me, and some of them seemed to be lowing reproachfully. Were they just frightened by my grief, or did they know that something awful had happened to one of their kind? And if they knew, was I now associated, in their gentle and curious minds, with all the evils perpetrated against them by humans? Heartbroken, I wandered back to the house in the dark.

Chapter 29

Sarah had packed make-up, hair gel, new jeans, a very revealing top, and a bottle of her mother's perfume into her duffel bag. If she slipped downstairs now, she could hide the bag in the shrubbery beneath the living-room window and her mother would never suspect a thing.

She smiled at herself in the mirror. She felt very grown-up and very much in control. She'd built up an elaborate story about staying at Fiona's house – which didn't necessitate the full duffel bag – but in reality she was going to Tim's house for the overnight party.

Her friend Fiona was covering for her in case her mother should phone to check out her story. And as back-up, Fiona's younger brother had also been paid to notify her immediately at Tim's house. Of course, if her mother would only get her a mobile phone like Zoe Merrigan had, it would be a lot easier to pull the wool over her mother's eyes. Which, she had to admit, was probably why her mother wouldn't get her one!

Nevertheless, Sarah was happy with her planned deception. Perhaps, she thought, I might even become a spy when I leave school. A job in MI6 or the FBI seemed a more exciting prospect than rotting away in some boring office, or having to study for several more years before taking up some equally boring job. Everything in life was boring to Sarah. She swished a long scarf around her shoulders and tried to look mysterious in the way that she'd seen spies do in the movies.

She didn't really expect her mother to phone. Initially after her father's death, Sarah had resented her mother's endless preoccupation with her own grief. But then she'd realised it could work to her advantage. So why not make the most of it?

Sarah planned to leave the house while her mother was in the drawing-room. Her mother's favourite chair faced away from the window, so she wouldn't be likely to observe Sarah as she left. Then she'd retrieve the duffel bag from the shrubbery and dash down the driveway to where Tim and the others would be waiting in his dad's car.

So far, all had gone according to plan. But as fate would have it, Charlie Somers was driving up to the house just as Sarah was leaving. She'd had to wave cheerfully to him, leaving the duffel bag still hidden, and walk down the driveway without it. But she couldn't possibly go to the party without her make-up and new jeans. So what was she going to do?

Fortunately, Tim had collected her first, and he reluctantly agreed to double back to Sarah's house after collecting the others. Since he'd borrowed his father's car without permission, he was anxious to get it back home in one piece and as quickly as possible. So Tracey had been collected, then Brian Brennan and finally Tim drove back and stopped at the bottom of the driveway to Sarah's house.

"Don't be long," he'd urged her, leaving the engine running. "We don't want to lose any drinking time!"

Sarah kept as close to the shrubbery as possible, relying on the plants to screen her from the house. While Charlie's arrival had been a nuisance, at least her mother would now be occupied in chatting to him so she'd be unlikely to notice Sarah's brief return.

On the other hand, Sarah thought, perhaps she should take a quick peep through the gap in the drawing-room curtains to make sure that her mother was actually there and wasn't spying on her from somewhere else in the house. As she tiptoed up to the window, Sarah thought she heard gasping noises. All sorts of images rushed through her brain – burglars, someone choking, perhaps a wild animal like a fox had wandered in and inadvertently got trapped in the house.

But nothing prepared her for what she saw. She was rooted to the spot in horror as she watched her mother and Charlie tearing each other's clothes off. As she stood there open-mouthed, her mother and Charlie sank to the floor, Charlie climbing on top and pounding his erect organ into her mother. Sarah was rigid with shock. Her mother and Charlie! Apart from the shock of seeing her mother naked on the floor, she could hardly believe that she was having sex with her father's best friend. And her father was only dead a few weeks! She was sickened and disgusted, and doubted if she could ever face her mother again.

Sarah's mouth opened and closed, but no sound came out. She'd never seen a man's penis before, nor had she seen anyone making love. Except in movies, of course, but you never got to see any detail. Unable to cope with the trauma of it all, she forgot all about the duffel bag and ran at breakneck speed down the drive to her friends in the waiting car. Thankfully the others had stayed in the car at the end of the driveway and hadn't witnessed what she had just seen.

"You look like you've seen a ghost!" Tracey said, her arm now around Tim's shoulder. "I thought you were going to collect your new jeans and things?"

"I – Well, you see –" Frantically Sarah groped for words. "Mum has friends in, and it's too difficult to get them." That was certainly true!

"Well, you can borrow my make-up, if you like," said Tracy kindly.

No one else was interested in her explanation – all the others wanted to do was get to the party as quickly as possible. Tim quickly turned the car and headed up the road at well above the speed limit.

"Come here, little darling!" drawled Brian Brennan, the senior school's 'bad boy', who was sitting beside Sarah in the back seat. "I'll keep you warm," he whispered lasciviously. The two in the front laughed as he possessively slipped an arm around Sarah's shoulder, and she could smell stale beer off his breath.

Sarah was more than a little scared of him. Brian was the bane of the teachers' lives, permanently in trouble at school for his arrogance and disobedience. But he was regarded as a hero and non-conformist by all the senior pupils, and a date with him instantly elevated a girl to super-status within the school ranks. Sarah wasn't too sure that she could handle this so-called honour, but she wasn't about to say so. To reject the hero's advances could condemn a girl to social ostracisation, which was more than any fifteen-year-old could bear.

Now he turned her head towards his and began sliding his tongue into her mouth and touching her breasts as though it was his prerogative. She didn't like him touching her, yet fear of rejection by her peers stopped her from objecting. She found the smell of beer and cigarettes from his breath nauseating, but she silently endured his advances and even tried without success to respond to them. Thankfully, Brian didn't seem to notice her lack of enthusiasm. Being so intent on his own gratification, he didn't even consider Sarah's feelings.

She wished she could to talk to Tracey, but she too was otherwise occupied. She appeared to have her hand between Tim's legs, for he let out a groan that sounded very like the ones Sarah had just heard coming from her own drawing-room, and the car swerved dangerously across the road, barely missing a cyclist.

Although she was loath to admit it, Sarah now realised that her mother had been right in not wanting her to spend the night at Tim's house. But it was too late to back out now. If she did, everyone in the class would hear about it the next day and no one would ever ask her anywhere again. Besides, she couldn't exactly go home now, anyway. Not with her mother and Charlie sprawled out on the drawing-room floor . . .

She longed to get away from this idiot beside her, who was trying to ram his tongue so far down her throat that she was almost gagging. Was this what it was all about? Were the words of all those love songs about nothing more than a quick grope, or a bout of thrusting on the floor or in the back seat of a car?

Sarah felt betrayed by the image of love and sex that her mother had inadvertently portrayed to her. Her mother had been at great pains to explain to her the importance of love and respect in relationships. Yet at this very moment she was grappling on the floor with her father's best friend – who was married to one of her mother's best friends!

Brian was now sticking his tongue into her left ear. Did he really expect her to enjoy this? Or was there really something abnormal about her? Now his far-from-gentle hands were trying to worm their way up under her T-shirt.

Could she pretend to be sick? If she said she had her period, would that put him off? No, she'd never get away with that one. Anyway, Tracey would know that she'd only finished her period about two weeks ago. Or was it three? Anyway, it wasn't long enough ago for her to be having another. And even if she whispered the lie to Brian, he was the type who'd announce it to everyone in the car. And Tracey would make an issue of it, since she wouldn't want to be left alone with the two guys.

"Here," said Brian, momentarily extracting his tongue from her ear and thrusting a large bottle into her hand, "you're a bit uptight kid, aren't you? Try a drop of this. It will help you relax."

Sarah took the bottle from him, grateful that she could still hear anything in her left ear and willing to try anything that would ease the tension and misery that she was feeling.

"What is it?" she asked, trying to sound interested rather than concerned.

"Looks like lemonade, doesn't it?" said Brian, clearly thinking himself very clever. "But it's not. There's vodka – lots of vodka – in it. But my folks will never miss it. The booze cabinet at home is just overflowing.'

Letting out a whoop, Brian uncapped the bottle and downed a huge swig of the liquid before passing it back to Sarah. With distaste, she eyed the spittle from his mouth running back into the bottle. But this hardly seemed the time to have scruples about hygiene, especially since she'd already had his beer-smelling and saliva-laden tongue slobbering around inside her mouth. Sarah took the bottle and took a swig, trying to look as though this was something she did every day of the week. When the liquid hit her throat, she almost gagged. There wasn't a lot of lemonade in it, and it burned her tongue and seemed to go right up her nose when she swallowed it.

"Terrific!" said Brian, patting her on the shoulder as though she was some little school-kid who had just tasted her first drink. Which was true, but Sarah wasn't going to let him know it.

"Great!" she replied, holding onto the bottle and taking another swig. This time she was prepared for it, and it slid down her throat with far greater ease.

203

"That's my girl!" said Brian approvingly, as he took another mouthful himself, "I can see that we're really gonna party tonight!" He let out another of his whoops, just as the car turned down the tree-lined avenue towards Tim's house.

"Shut up!" Tim urged. "We don't want the bloody neighbours to hear us arriving. My parents are away – or have you forgotten?"

The four fell silent as Tim turned into the driveway and parked outside the tall red-bricked house. Cans of beer were then silently and surreptitiously carried inside as well as several lemonade bottles which, by now, Sarah realised didn't contain much lemonade.

Inside, the house was carpeted luxuriously in browns and dark greens. Sarah caught a glimpse of antique furniture and a baby grand piano in one of the rooms as they all tiptoed through to the kitchen at the back. Sarah quickly seated herself on a kitchen chair near the sink. At least she wouldn't have to go far if she needed to get sick.

With relief, Sarah noted that Orla and Peter were already there. And several other couples were just arriving. But everyone else was so much older than her – at least eighteen or nineteen – and Tracey was already sixteen. Sarah felt babyish and out of place. People in one group were smoking some kind of joint, and passing it from one to the other. They all seemed so sophisticated in comparison to her.

She also noted that everyone was paired off already. So clearly, she was meant to be with Brian. The thought of having to endure his beer-laden breath made her reach again for one of the lemonade bottles. She took another swig – no one seemed to be using glasses – and noted with satisfaction that it didn't burn as much as it had the first time she'd tried it. Maybe she was getting the hang of it already.

Gradually, as the vodka took effect, she began to feel quite grown-up. And she didn't even mind when Brian positioned himself directly behind her chair, leaning down over her to fondle her breasts. Perhaps she should stop him, but somehow it didn't seem to matter any more. Besides, the sensation was actually quite pleasurable. Almost instinctively, she raised her head to receive his beery kiss, and it didn't taste too bad any more either. Daringly, she even opened her mouth for his tongue.

Brian, despite being intoxicated himself, clearly detected the change in her. "Wowee! We've got a right little go-er here!" he whispered in her ear, drawing her up off the chair into his arms. Music was playing somewhere in the background, and together they started to dance. Sarah now wrapped her arms around his neck, while he continued to massage her breasts. She was genuinely enjoying it now, and she didn't object when he slipped a hand under her T-shirt and began working his fingers into her bra, sliding a strap off her shoulder and groping for her nipple. Her mother had warned her not to let boys touch her, but to hell with her mother. She hadn't set a great example herself this evening, had she?

Tingling sensations were now coursing through her body. Maybe being touched up by Brian wasn't so bad after all. Her head felt decidedly light, and she held onto him tightly for support.

"Let's take a bottle and go somewhere private, eh?" he whispered in her ear.

Sarah nodded. She felt quite unsteady, yet remarkably relaxed. How could she have thought she didn't like Brian? Just because he was always in trouble at school didn't really mean anything. It was unfair that the teachers had a down on him. He was really nice, and she liked the way he caressed her nipples. It was the first time she'd ever let a boy touch her there. She wanted more of it – and more of the vodka in the lemonade bottle.

Their departure didn't go unnoticed. "What's going on here?" asked one of the other boys loudly, in mocking tone. "Brennan, I hope you're not intending to take advantage of that nice young lady?"

Brian laughed back at him. "I certainly am!" he replied, now guiding Sarah's faltering steps up the stairs.

Sarah sighed as she leaned on him. He really was nice, and she knew that he hadn't meant it when he'd said to the other boy that he was going to take advantage of her. That was just the kind of macho talk that boys engaged in. She wondered if it was too soon to consider him her boyfriend. But he was, wasn't he? She didn't think her mother would like him, but then, did she really care?

Upstairs, Brian guided her into one of the bedrooms. Without protest, Sarah let him remove her T-shirt before she lay down on the big bed. Maybe she could drift off to sleep while he fondled her breasts. It would be nice to cuddle up to someone who cared about her, just as she had cuddled up to her parents when she was small.

She held out her arms and Brian climbed in beside her. Vaguely, she noticed that he'd taken off all his clothes, and was pushing his large erection into her hand. She held it, knowing what he wanted her to do, but she protested when he began trying to take her jeans off.

"I'm not going to touch you," he whispered. "I just thought that you'd be more comfortable without your jeans."

"No. Definitely no," Sarah said, as firmly as her slurring tones would allow her. As long as she kept her jeans on, nothing could happen. Why couldn't he be happy just to caress her breasts? That was further than she'd ever let any other boy go before.

"All right, all right," said Brian, a note of desperation in his voice. Things weren't working out quite the way he'd planned. Momentarily, he wondered about leaving her there and trying to pick up one of the other girls downstairs. The problem was, all of them were paired off already. Just his luck to get stuck with an uptight virgin. He'd expected the vodka to do the trick, but clearly it hadn't worked the way he'd wanted it to.

Reluctantly, he fumbled on the floor for his jeans, delving into the back pocket and extracting the precious packet that held several small tablets. He hadn't intended giving her any. He'd hoped to get her in the mood with just the vodka. But desperate situations required desperate means. He'd paid a lot of dough for these pills, so he wasn't anxious to waste them. But he needed a buzz himself, and hopefully one would be enough to encourage Sleeping Beauty to show a bit more interest.

"Darling," he whispered softly, since he couldn't remember her name. "Here – take one of these." Gently he shook her. "It'll stop you feeling sick and drowsy."

It should certainly do that, he hoped, as she took the
tablet and popped it into her mouth, washing it down
with a mouthful of vodka. Before long, he'd be able to get
those jeans off her without any bother.

Sarah looked at him tenderly. He was so considerate.
Not many guys she knew would go to the trouble of
getting her aspirin or paracetamol to cure her headache.

Then she noticed that he was taking a tablet himself.
"Have you a headache too, Brian?" she asked, surprised.

"Yes, my darling," he whispered, slipping his naked
body in between the sheets once again, "but soon you
and I are going to hit the high spots together."

He squeezed her nipples between his fingers, and
began kissing her again. This time, she opened her mouth
to take in his tongue without any reluctance. He was
really so nice – how could she not respond to his
kindness? Maybe she was even falling in love with him.
Maybe she could even go and live with him. Then she
need never go back to her mother again . . .

Maybe, maybe . . . Rainbows began exploding in her
head, and she was overjoyed at the bright colours she
could suddenly see. She held on tightly to Brian, offering
no resistance now as he began to unzip her jeans. Who
needed to be encumbered with clothes when the world
was as bright and beautiful as she was experiencing?
Besides, his hand between her legs was creating the most
amazing sensations. Now she was helping him to pull off
her jeans, and opening her legs wide as yet another
rainbow exploded in her head . . .

Chapter 30

The summer that I was eleven I was suddenly sent to live with my aunt in Dublin. All I remembered was being put on a train by a woman from a neighbouring farm with a few sandwiches wrapped in the waxed paper from a sliced loaf, a bottle of warm milk and a copy of The Beano.

After the long journey to Dublin on a packed train I was met by my aunt, a cold taciturn woman, and taken by bus to her house on the southside of Dublin. Travelling by bus for the first time was an awesome experience for a country child, and I avidly watched all the activity going on in the streets outside. I'd never seen so many houses all packed in tightly together! Nor so many people! The streets seemed to stretch for miles, and I wondered if I'd ever manage to find my way around without getting lost.

But amid the excitement of finding myself in this big new world, I was apprehensive about the total change of scene. The reason for my arrival at my aunt's house was never explained, my parents were no longer mentioned, and if I asked about them I was abruptly silenced. I had no idea why I'd been sent there, although it was a relief to be away from the beatings and the fear that my father had engendered.

However, my mother's elder sister practised her own form of mental torture. Her continual put-downs were clearly designed to let me know that I was an aberration disturbing the otherwise tranquil pattern of her life. I was there on sufferance, and she never let me forget it. It was clear from her own beanpole shape and her attitude towards me that she despised my rural plumpness.

Initially, I tried my best to fit in with my aunt's way of life and to be as helpful as I could. But there was no pleasing her, and I often found myself in trouble for no discernible reason. Nor did I understand her oblique and cruel references to some family problem, the inference being that I was somehow at the centre of it.

Once, when I'd been chastised for some non-existent misdemeanour, she said something very strange to me. "You're a bad one – a home-wrecker!" Yet when I asked for an explanation, I was sent to my room for being cheeky.

My new life nevertheless brought with it some vestiges of the old. Sometimes in my dreams my father would chase me with a pitchfork, and I would run, terrified and screaming, only to wake up with the bedclothes knotted around me and my hair tangled with sweat. At other times I heard him calling me softly, and I would run to him, wanting him to hold me. But in those dreams I could never reach him. As I ran to him, I would get stuck in a mire of thick slimy mud.

Then I would awake, screamimg. Sometimes my aunt would come into the room and scold me for disturbing her slumber. And in my confusion, I'd sometimes think that she was my mother. She would stand there, staring at me as I tried to make sense of what was happening, but she never once comforted or reassured me. After she had gone back to her own bed, I would lie there shivering in my own now-cold sweat, afraid to sleep again until the safety of daylight appeared.

My aunt rarely left the house at all, unless to go to church or gossip with the neighbours. Her home, although elegantly furnished and well-heated in cold weather, was like a morgue. There was never any question of me bringing friends home for tea, and perversely I was glad of it, since no one I knew would have fitted easily into that dark and dismal setting.

My aunt continually carped about the amounts of food that she now had to buy since my arrival, and of the alarming rate at which it disappeared. As I grew older, her pale eyes would rest witheringly on my developing bosom or large thighs, and she would sigh as though I was a disaster thrust unwillingly into her midst. She rarely spoke to me, even at mealtimes, and when she did it was to remark with self-satisfaction at how little food she needed to sustain herself. This, in her eyes, was clearly a virtue. One which, by inference, I did not possess.

Living previously on a farm where food had been plentiful, it was quite a shock to receive barely enough food to keep body and soul together. It was certainly not enough for a growing child. I tried desperately to keep my appetite in check, but the more often food was used as a weapon against me, the more thoughts of it seemed to absorb my whole being. In the same way that food had comforted me as a frightened child, it now seemed to offer me temporary relief from my aunt's indifference.

Night and day I thought about food, any kind of food. I wanted to eat twenty-four hours a day, simply because I wasn't allowed to. I was expected to eat as frugally as my aunt did, but my growing body craved nourishment. Maybe food also represented love and acceptance, which I longed for but never received.

Sometimes late at night, when I was certain that my aunt was asleep, I'd creep downstairs to the kitchen. I'd open the fridge and look in at all the food lining the shelves, studying the contents to see which items were least likely to be missed or which losses could best be camouflaged.

I'd also open the cupboard where all the tins of fruit and vegetables were kept, gazing at them rapturously as a child might gaze at a Christmas window display. I'd count the tins and wonder if my aunt would miss one. Sometimes my cravings became so great that I'd risk my aunt's accusations next time she checked the cupboard. Alone in the dark kitchen, I'd open a can of beans or peas – whichever seemed the most plentiful – and eat the contents cold.

Sometimes, I'd hide a tin or two at the back of the shelf so as to purposefully draw my aunt's comments. If she didn't appear to miss them within a day or two, I knew that it was safe to eat them. On the other hand, if she did promptly comment on their disappearance, I could retrieve them triumphantly, pointing out that they were still there at the back of the shelf and also remarking that perhaps her eyesight was failing. Because I'd discovered that her greatest fear was of growing old and frail. So as surely as she exploited my weaknesses, I exploited hers, and for the next few years we continued to live in this state of almost permanent warfare.

CHAPTER 31

"Let's call around to see Ciara."

Charlie looked at Dee in surprise, hoping that his guilt wasn't showing and that his face hadn't changed colour at the mention of Ciara's name.

It was a week since that night in Ciara's house. Since then Ciara had kept to herself, for which Charlie was extremely grateful. The less he saw of Ciara at present, the better he liked it. He knew that Dee was worried about the fact that Ciara had chosen to isolate herself from her friends, but to Charlie it was a blessing in disguise.

"But she doesn't want to see anyone, does she?" he asked. "Surely it would be better to wait until she's ready to deal with people again?"

Charlie was filling the dishwasher after the evening meal. Terry, their youngest son, had retired to his room to study while Donal was frantically ironing a clean shirt for a date later that evening. Neither Dee nor Charlie had eaten anything. Both had toyed with their food, most of which ended up in the dog's bowl. Charlie knew why he wasn't able to eat, he was still sick with guilt and remorse.

"I'm really worried about Ciara," Dee told her husband. "I don't like the idea of her spending so much time alone in that big house – it's not healthy. And Sarah's no help at all. I keep asking them both over for a meal but Ciara always has some excuse for not coming."

"Well, why don't you go by yourself? I mean you could have a woman-to-woman chat –" Charlie froze in mid-sentence. Maybe that wasn't such a good idea after all! The two of them might inadvertently bring the conversation around to him – "on seconds thoughts, you're right love. We should both go."

Stacking the last of the cups on the top shelf, Charlie closed the dishwasher and pressed the starter switch. Then he reached for his jacket and his car keys. "Do you think maybe we should bring her over a take-away? If she's been stuck in the house all day she won't have thought of eating properly."

"Good idea," Dee rewarded her husband's thoughtfulness with a smile. Sometimes, she thought, Charlie can be a real sweetie. "Why don't we get enough for all three of us? We might feel more like eating ourselves by the time we get there."

"Whatever you think."

Dee looked at her husband. "I'm getting worried about you too, Charlie. You seem to have lost your appetite lately. Are you feeling OK?"

"Yes, fine," he replied vaguely, lapsing back into

silence. The guilt was sitting like a lump in the middle of Charlie's chest. Maybe I really am going to have a heart attack, he thought. That would be his punishment for what he'd done.

At the Lotus Blossom take-away, Dee ordered a selection of dishes they all liked and plenty of fried rice. She was feeling quite hungry now – maybe the strained atmosphere in the house had curbed their appetites earlier that evening. Charlie seemed particularly down. Then again, Dee reasoned, it wasn't really surprising. It was only a few weeks since his closest friend had died. Poor Charlie, Dee thought, sometimes I forget that he's grieving too.

When Ciara opened the door she looked pale and out of sorts, and not particularly pleased to see them. Dee did her best to inject bonhomie into the occasion, but neither Charlie nor Ciara were particularly responsive.

"We've brought your favourite crispy duck dish," Dee informed her. "We probably got too much of everything, but you can always heat it up again tomorrow. I think it tastes even nicer the next day."

"Thanks, Dee," Ciara tried her best to smile. But her greeting to Charlie was strained, which wasn't missed by Dee either. I think we're all too tired and worn out for conversation, she thought. Niall's death has taken its toll on us all.

So they all sat and munched in silence. Ciara found a bottle of white wine in the fridge, which helped to relax the atmosphere a little. Nevertheless, Dee and Charlie were the last people on earth she'd have chosen for company just then.

Emboldened by her glass of wine, Dee chided Ciara

gently. "We've all been so worried about you, love. I know you're bound to be feeling down, but that's the time when you need company the most."

Ciara smiled wanly. "I've just been feeling a bit depressed lately," she lied, "and I'm really better to be on my own when I'm in one of my dark moods. So I've decided to take a holiday soon. Getting away will help me to sort myself out. I've already asked Cillian and Betty if Sarah can stay with them while I'm away." Ciara grimaced. "Needless to say, Sarah wants to stay here in the house on her own. But I've put my foot down – can't you just imagine the parties that would be taking place? Lately she's started hanging around with an older crowd, and I'm not very happy about it."

"I'll come with you."

Ciara momentarily froze, the kettle she was filling for tea now overflowing into the sink. Instantly, she caught Charlie's eye and discovered that he was looking just as shocked as she was. Dee smiled at them both, noting their stunned expressions.

"W-what do you mean?" Ciara asked at last.

"I'll come on holiday with you. I wouldn't mind having a break myself," said Dee.

The last thing Ciara wanted was to have to fall in with anyone else's plans. And Dee of all people!

"Well, why not?" Dee persisted, turning to Charlie. "You know that I always go away with Molly and Edel, my friends from evening class, every spring. We weren't able to go this year because Molly's youngest got measles," she looked from one of them to the other, daring them to show disapproval.

Dammit, Ciara thought. Why did Dee's friend's child have to mess up everything?

"Unless, of course, you prefer to go on your own, Ciara."

"Well, actually –"

"That's settled, then. How soon do you want to go? And where? I've no particular preferences, as long as it's somewhere hot, near a good beach and with lots of cheap wine!"

Ciara and Charlie tried not to look at each other, but the temptation proved too much for them both. Charlie was terrified that given the companionship and availability of cheap booze, the two women might share confidences and confessions. Ciara, in turn, was terrified at the thought of spending two weeks with the woman whose husband she'd recently and inexplicably, made love to. Who might also be the woman who'd had the affair with Niall! Her holiday was turning into a nightmare . . .

The phone rang and Kate reached out to the bedside table.

"Kate?"

"Oh, hi Dee."

"I finally managed to contact Ciara, Charlie and I called over earlier tonight, and I've convinced Ciara that we should take a holiday together leaving as soon as possible. Can you come with us?"

Kate pulled back the duvet and sat on the side of the bed. "Does Ciara know you're asking me to go with you?"

"Of course!" Dee lied, puzzled. "Why on earth

wouldn't she want you along too? Think of the great time we could all have."

"Well, thanks for the offer Dee, but I'm just too busy right now. I couldn't take a break from work at such short notice."

"You could badly do with a change of scene, Kate," Dee replied. "I hope you won't be offended when I say this, but you've been looking wretched these last few weeks. Is anything the matter?"

"No," Kate lied, "I'm just a bit tired. I've been staying up late working on a three-part series on the prison service. I've also got my regular columns to do as well. I just need a bit of extra sleep."

"You could have all the rest you need if you came with Ciara and I."

"No, thanks, Dee, honestly. Another time, maybe."

When Dee rang off, Kate stood up and hurried into the bathroom. Should she pee or get sick first? Both needs were equally urgent. If she didn't feel so awful, she might be able to laugh at the idea of going on holiday with Dee and Ciara. And having morning sickness for the entire fortnight!

The following morning, Dee telephoned even before Ciara was up. Sleepily, Ciara reached for the phone beside her bed.

"Hey, sleepy-head, you're not still in bed, are you?"

"Mmm. Oh hello, Dee."

"You don't sound like a woman who's just about to go on holiday. Haven't you packed your case yet? Aren't you excited?"

"Oh. Yes, of course," Ciara groaned inwardly. If only she hadn't opened her big mouth when Dee and Charlie had called. If only she'd gone and booked a holiday without telling anyone!

"Well, let me tell you the good news. I've just been to the travel agents and if we're able to leave the day after tomorrow, they can offer us two weeks in Turkey in a luxury apartment in Kusadasi for half price! How does that sound?"

"Eh, great. I'll start packing right away."

"Oh, by the way, I asked Kate if she's like to come too."

Ciara's froze. That would double the odds of being on holiday with the woman who'd had the affair with Niall!

"She's been looking a bit peaky lately, so I suggested that the break would do her good. Unfortunately, she's too much work to do right now and can't take a fortnight off at such short notice."

Ciara's heartbeat returned to normal again.

Dee sighed happily. "Anyway, I've no assignments that can't be put off. I'm ahead with my weekly column and I've got until the middle of next month to finish a series on the latest in home appliances." She wrinkled her nose in distain. "Boring, boring! Anyway, there's time enough for me to get cracking on those when we get back. Have you any commissions to finish?"

"Nothing that can't wait either," Ciara replied. She felt guilty that she hadn't yet started Kevin's painting. But if she had to go through with this holiday, she might as well get it over as soon as possible.

CHAPTER 32

After years of enduring my aunt's barbs and minor cruelties, she finally died just before my eighteenth birthday. Since she hadn't made a will – undoubtedly believing that she'd live forever – her house, its contents and her savings eventually came to me as her next of kin. At the same time, the solicitor informed me that on my twenty-first birthday I would also become the beneficiary of a trust fund, established in my name, with the money that came from the sale of my parents' farm. From this information, I assumed they must therefore be dead, although no one ever told me, and I was afraid to ask.

For the first time in my life, I was now free and I was heady with the joy of it all. But I was also shrewd enough to realise that I must put the money to careful use.

I'd just finished school, so I also needed to think about a career. I'd always been a keen observer of life, and I hoped that eventually I might be able put these powers of observation to professional use. I found myself drawn to a career in journalism, but I realised that I'd have to serve my time before

I reached the stage at which people would be willing to pay for those observations!

So I started, as many journalists did back then, as a junior copy-taker with one of the daily newspapers. Then I used my womanly charms to convince a susceptible sub-editor to give me a chance to do sub-editing shifts, because I needed someone to cover up my mistakes as I learned. The sub-editor was only too happy to help me, and to creep into my bed when each shift was over.

Later on, I felt that the time was right to move on, and to cultivate those who could help me take a further step up the ladder. I wanted to move from sub-editing to writing features and hopefully to being a columnist some day. So I began moving in the writers' circles, and drinking in their pubs.

One night, when the editor of a rival newspaper was drinking in our company, I mentioned some of my ideas to him with which he seemed quite impressed. And I suggested, leaning forward so that he could see my cleavage, that I had a hankering to write such features and columns myself.

The following day I got a phone call, inviting me to call to his office to discuss my ideas in greater detail. The rest, as you know, is history, Ciara. He liked my suggestions, and some of those columns of mine are still running all these years later.

Of course, I knew that he was greatly attracted to me – despite having a wife and several young children safely in the suburbs – and that kind of weak man can be easily exploited. Naturally, I was more than willing to use his weakness to develop my own career. I knew that I'd have to sleep with him, and I'd play his game for as long as it suited me. Because ultimately, I'd be the one getting what I wanted. All went according to plan, and as soon as I became an established columnist I dropped him without a backward glance.

The next item on my agenda was to find and marry a man who could give me status, comfort and hopefully the kind of happiness that you'd found so easily, Ciara. If I couldn't have Niall, then perhaps there was someone equally acceptable out there. In due course, I did find a man who I thought fitted all my requirements. But as you will see, Ciara, life has a way of ordering itself that is outside our understanding.

During those early years, Ciara, I no longer felt any need to seek revenge. These were the years during which I built my career and made a new life for myself. I'd put my unhappy past behind me, or so I thought, and I was beginning to feel fulfilled just by being me without constantly needing to review my own life in terms of you and your charmed existence.

But things rarely go according to plan, do they?

CHAPTER 33

There were moments when Ciara felt excited at the prospect of the holiday ahead. At other times she was overwhelmed by panic at the thought of being trapped alone with Dee. Suddenly, she felt an overwhelming need to unburden herself to someone. Perhaps she should ring the Samaritans? Twice, she looked up the phone number of the nearest service, and twice she actually picked up the receiver and began to dial. But each time she put the phone back down again. Perhaps she should get the address of a counsellor and book herself in for a session. But she'd hardly get an appointment at such short notice . . .

She tried desperately to think of someone, anyone, she might confide in. It wasn't that she was short of friends – she was just constrained by her need to keep the image of her happy marriage intact. Ciara sighed. Ringing Dot was out of the question. Much as she loved her old friend, she knew that the details of Niall's affair wouldn't remain confidential for long.

Vera? Definitely not, Ciara decided. Her friend's high-powered lifestyle as personal assistant to a government minister left little time for a personal life. So Vera would hardly be qualified to offer advice on Niall's infidelity, would she? Anyway, Vera was always jet-setting off to some exotic destination with her minister. Suddenly, Ciara wondered if there was more going on in Vera's life than she'd ever told her?

Then Ciara had an idea. She'd phone Marguerite in France. Her old school friend would be helpful and sympathetic, and wouldn't be judgmental. Big, jolly Marguerite with all her children and handsome husband would probably invite her out to Nice for a break, and the idea was suddenly more appealing than going off to Turkey with Dee.

Digging out her personal phone book, Ciara flicked through the pages until she found Marguerite's number. Already, she could feel a weight being lifted from her shoulders. It would feel good to confide in her old friend. She dialled the number several times, but there was no answer. Ciara wrinkled her nose. That was odd. Then again, she'd never phoned Marguerite before, since they normally communicated by e-mail.

Ciara then decided to contact the international operator, and ask them to connect her to the number. Maybe she was dialling the number incorrectly. But the result was the same. "Are you sure you have the right number?" the operator asked kindly.

Damn. Ciara was annoyed with herself. She'd obviously taken down the number wrongly, or left out a digit. She'd have to e-mail Marguerite for the correct number.

Pacing the floor, Ciara then wondered whether she should talk to Kevin. As a former priest he'd been trained in counselling the bereaved and traumatised. Then again, he had enough problems of his own to contend with. And, if she was truthful to herself, she still didn't want him to know about Niall's infidelity.

Suddenly, she had an idea. She'd talk to Ita, the new woman in Liam's life. She'd sensed an empathy in her, and talking to Ita would be like talking to a sympathetic stranger, someone who didn't know anything about the people concerned, yet whom she felt she could trust because of her closeness to Liam. At Niall's funeral, Liam had suggested that she and Ita get together. But it was asking a lot of someone, and especially a comparative stranger. On the other hand, it was an opportunity for her and Ita to forge those bonds that Liam was clearly anxious to encourage.

Ciara stood up and walked towards the telephone. If Ita didn't sound receptive, she'd simply drop the matter. But right now, she was badly in need of someone's support.

Dammit, she couldn't even kill herself properly. She'd swallowed a rake of sleeping tablets the night before and downed them with half a bottle of whiskey. Yet here she was, still alive the following morning, and with a monumental hangover.

Ita closed her eyes again in the hope that reality might

225

go away, or that she might really be dead. But no, reality was intruding yet again, in the form of a telephone ringing somewhere in the background. And that background proved to be beside her bed. She pressed her fingers to her ears. She wasn't going to answer it.

To escape its insistent ringing she got out of bed shakily and went into the custom-built oak kitchen where she began to make herself some toast, using two stale heels of bread that she'd forgotten to throw out. She wrinkled her nose. There was no other food in the apartment, which wasn't exactly surprising. You don't exactly stock the larder when you're not expecting to need food ever again!

The apartment was luxuriously furnished. A Louis Le Broquy, a Jack B Yeats and a Ciara Reynolds hung on the living-room walls, and a large off-white Aubusson rug dominated the centre of the floor. Antique bookcases filled the alcoves on either side of the art nouveau fireplace and a chandelier of Waterford glass hung overhead. Yet none of these things gave Ita any pleasure. She stared around the room now with vacant eyes, seeing nothing but her own pain and inadequacy.

The previous night Liam had told her that he loved her. But the news brought her no joy. She'd never intended this to happen, so she'd deliberately made light of his declaration. Kissing her in his car outside her apartment, he'd said it. At first, she thought she'd imagined it because he'd spoken the words so softly. When she made no response, he said them again. "Ita, I love you."

"Don't be daft," she'd rejoined playfully. "People of

our age don't go around making silly statements like that. Love is for the very young, the inexperienced, the –"

Liam looked at her gravely. "It's true, Ita, and I don't use those words lightly. In fact –" he'd looked earnestly into her face, "I've never said those words to anyone before."

She'd continued to treat his declaration lightly. "You're a good liar, Liam. I could almost believe you!" she'd said teasingly. Yet inwardly, her heart had been pounding so much that she felt she was almost choking.

"It's true, Ita. Sure, there's been lots of women in the past, but I've never felt like this about any of them."

Ita said nothing, still trying to take in the enormity of his declaration and unsure of how to respond. This wasn't supposed to happen. Love just wasn't part of her plans. When they'd started going out together, all she'd wanted was a short-term casual relationship.

Liam spoke urgently. "Ita, I want to marry you. I want to spend the rest of my life with you. Do you understand that? This is no brief affair for me. I want to be able to introduce you as my wife."

There was silence. Ita knew that Liam was hoping that she'd say she loved him too. But she couldn't. So she kept her response flippant.

"Don't be so melodramatic, darling," she'd said, trying to distance herself from him by sounding condescending. "No one gets married these days," she deliberately yawned. "Look, I'm exhausted, Liam. Would you mind if I didn't ask you to stay tonight? I need a good night's sleep."

Hurt and angry, Liam said nothing as she got out of

the car. "Goodnight, darling," she said, her voice momentarily softening. Then she quickly turned and hurried up the path to the apartment entrance.

Once inside her apartment she'd gone straight to the medicine cabinet, followed by the drinks cabinet, then retired to bed with her haul like a squirrel collecting food for a long winter ahead. But unlike the squirrel's cache, hers was intended to end her life rather than prolong it.

It was unfair, she knew, to leave poor Mrs Daly, her cleaning lady, to find her body. The elderly woman was due to clean the apartment the following morning and had her own key for letting herself in. However, to ease Mrs Daly's trauma, Ita had left a sealed envelope for her containing three months' wages in cash.

Anyway, she knew that Mrs Daly enjoyed nothing better than a good gossip, and what could be more newsworthy and entertaining than being the first at a death scene? That would provide the old dear with plenty of gossip, and she'd probably even get her name in the papers. So in a sense, Ita thought, I'm doing Mrs Daly a favour!

Before she'd retired to bed, Ita had sat at her desk by the bedroom window and written Liam a note. He, more than anyone, deserved to know why she was taking this course of action, yet she had no intention of telling him the truth. Instead, she'd written a brief enigmatic note explaining that while she was extremely fond of him there could be no future for them together.

Now, as she re-read the note in the cold light of day, Ita shuddered. It sounded so melodramatic. God, had she really written such rubbish? She'd better organise a better farewell message the next time. And select a more foolproof method for her demise. Quickly, she tore the note into shreds, and hid Mrs Daly's envelope in the desk drawer. For now she'd have to cope with facing Liam again.

The phone rang again, and reluctantly Ita picked it up from beside the bed. If she had to come back to the real world, she might as well start dealing with its demands.

"Hello, Ita. It's Ciara, Ciara Reynolds."

Ita was very surprised to hear Ciara's voice. After all, they'd only met a few times before.

"I, I hope you don't mind me phoning you."

Ita made a polite non-committal reply.

Ciara hesitated, then her words came out in a rush. "I remember Liam said that he'd like us to get together –"

There was a pause. "Yes, that would be nice," Ita replied. "How are you coping, Ciara? It must be a very difficult time for you."

"Sometimes I think I'm going mad –" as she said it, Ciara was surprised at her own openness to this woman who was almost a complete stranger.

There was a staccato laugh at the other end of the line. "I know that feeling, Ciara. More than you could imagine," Ita replied.

"I was wondering," Ciara said hesitantly, "I mean, if you had any time to spare, would you like to call round for something to eat, or maybe a drink, sometime? I need to ask your advice about something."

The urgency in her voice wasn't lost on Ita. "Yes, of course. I'd love to. When would suit you best?" If she had to go on living for a while longer, she might as well step in at the deep end. And Ciara sounded as though she needed somebody's help. How ironic, Ita thought, that I should be the one she's turned to when I'm on the brink of taking my own life.

"Could you manage tomorrow? You see, I'm going away on holiday the day after. And I really need to talk to you before I go. Are you free for lunch? I could make us a steak and salad, or would you prefer something else?"

Ita laughed. "Ciara, tomorrow's fine. But stop worrying about food. Why don't we go out somewhere for lunch instead?"

"No!" Ciara's reply was swift and emphatic, then she immediately became contrite. "Sorry. I mean if you don't mind I'd rather talk to you here, in the privacy of the house . . ."

"Of course. I'll call around at about twelve-thirty. Is that OK? But please, Ciara, don't go to any trouble."

"OK. And thanks, Ita. See you tomorrow."

After Ciara had rung off, Ita stripped the bed of the offending bedclothes. She threw them all, along with her now grubby nightdress, into the linen basket. Then she took a hot shower.

Having dressed, she took fresh bed-linen from the airing cupboard and re-made the bed. Would Liam ever again sleep here beside her, she wondered? Right now, she'd welcome the comfort of his arms. Angrily, she wiped a tear from the corner of her eye, knowing that she'd attempt to kill herself again just as soon as she found a more foolproof method.

CHAPTER 34

When I met my husband-to-be, Ciara, it seemed as though real happiness had come my way at last. We met at a charity reception that I was covering, and we hit it off immediately. We spent most of the evening chatting exclusively to each other, and he asked me out for a meal the following evening.

I was pleased and excited. He was handsome, came from a well-to-do political family, and appeared to have a future that was on the up-and-up. Ted had his finger in all sorts of pies. He owned several hotels, a haulage business and had quite a bit of land that he was expecting would soon be re-zoned for housing. Most important of all, he was single and available.

At that stage, I'd forgotten all about seeking revenge, Ciara. I'd found happiness of my own at last, and I no longer felt any need to punish you. Soon, I expected to have all the things that you had.

The relationship developed rapidly. I spent lavishly on my appearance, buying lots of expensive stylish outfits that enabled me to look my best for the many functions at which Ted liked to show me off. As far as I was concerned, my wardrobe was an investment that paid off handsomely. Within six months Ted asked me to marry him, and I said yes.

Even his large family seemed to approve of me. His father, a retired politician with many important connections, quizzed me about my family background but seemed satisfied with the information that my parents had died when I was a child and that I'd been reared by my aunt. Ted's family seemed primarily concerned about any embarrassing political affiliations in my background. Finding no links with rival parties, I was deemed acceptable to join the Durkan clan.

Ted's mother was a friendly woman and a typical political wife. She was always there to offer support to the family, keeping open house and keeping political enemies at bay while turning a blind eye to the wheeling and dealing of her 'boys'.

She was captivated by my beautiful clothes, my job in the media and my obvious devotion to her son. Clearly, she thought that I fitted the bill perfectly, and I could see she also assumed that with my media connections her family would henceforth bask in favourable publicity when it was needed. As a member of the Durkan dynasty, I'd be expected to ensure that her 'boys' and their various activities received favourable coverage in the media, or at least weren't investigated too thoroughly in the press.

Having passed their scrutiny, my future as Ted's wife was assured. His brothers, two of them TDs, his sisters and their families all accepted me readily. The date was finally set for our wedding.

From being an only child, I now went through the shock of being subsumed into a large and boisterous family. Instead of the privacy that I'd previously taken for granted, I found that now, there was always someone dropping by, offering to help, or just telephoning to say hello. At first, I found it all very difficult, but gradually I grew to enjoy their involvement in my life. At last, I began to feel that I was part of a real family, rather than just an onlooker like I'd always been in the past.

I chose a full-length gown of white satin. The reception was to take place in the town's only five-star hotel, and would be attended by many of the country's leading politicians and business people. I looked forward to my wedding day as the happiest day of my life.

I even intended inviting you to the wedding, Ciara. But when I suggested inviting a few old school friends, the Durkans were far from happy about it. In your case, Ciara, they felt that your opposition to big business and your support for liberal and humanitarian causes was too extreme. They also feared that if any of my journalist colleagues were invited they might use the occasion to probe too deeply into the Durkan family businesses.

Since I was so eager to get married to Ted, I gave way and didn't invite anyone. I felt that once the wedding was over, I'd get around to inviting friends past and present to visit, and establishing my own personal circle of friends.

I longed for the status of being Ted's wife, and I looked forward to our wedding with excitement and hope. Ted had bought us a lovely detached house on an acre of land, amid the rolling countryside just outside the town where his family held sway. The painters and decorators had nearly completed their renovations, and the antique furniture I'd chosen was due to arrive later that week.

Everything in my life was coming up roses. I had a fulfilling career as a columnist, and since meeting Ted I'd also become adept at cooking, entertaining and making small-talk. I felt that finally I'd left the sadness of my past behind, and stepped into the role of successful career woman, wife, and some day soon, I hoped, mother.

Although Ted and I were already sleeping together, either at my apartment or his, we were discreet about it so as not to upset local sensibilities. I still took the Pill, since a pregnancy before marriage would not have fitted into the Durkan family's way of thinking. But it was expected that in time we too would add several little Durkans to the family dynasty.

I looked forward to getting pregnant, and to the adulation it would bring from Ted's family. I'd be able to talk about babies to his mother and married sisters, and when I'd produced a son or daughter I'd really feel a full member of the Durkan clan. This time my pregnancy would be a joyous occasion, unlike my traumatic experience at the age of fifteen. Even still, a day never passed without me thinking of the daughter I'd lost. Needless to say, I'd never told Ted about that sad period of my life. That part of my existence had been buried, never to surface again.

Ted had hinted to his family that we were planning to start a family of our own as soon as possible. Initially, I was peeved at what I felt was a breach of our personal privacy. But I was learning how close and intrusive a large family could be. So I said nothing and pretended to enjoy the nudges and ribald comments that inevitably followed.

One day, just a few weeks before the wedding, Ted snuggled up to me as I sat in the kitchen of our new house, leafing through a sample book of curtain materials.

"Looking forward to our wedding day?" he whispered.

"Of course," I whispered back, "I'm longing to be your wife, Ted."

"Well, my love, it won't be long now. The house is nearly ready for us to move in, the church, reception and honeymoon are all booked, so there's only one formality remaining to be done – our medical check-ups."

"Check-ups?"

"It's just a formality, love, to make sure all the plumbing is in order. Since we want to start a family as soon as possible, we might as well make sure that there are no little problems standing in our way. Besides, we'll need check-ups for insurance purposes anyway."

"OK," I nodded.

Ted smiled. "Great, so I'll make an appointment for you with Dr O'Hara? He's an old friend of the family's. I'm sure you'll like him. Anyway, since he'll be coming to the wedding, you might as well get to meet him beforehand!"

CHAPTER 35

Ciara's hands fluttered like two imprisoned birds, then fell back into her lap again.

"Look, I'm sorry to impose on you like this, Ita. I've no right –" She looked up, pain in her eyes. "But I've got to talk to someone."

Ita looked puzzled. "Wouldn't one of your own friends, Dee or Kate, be more suitable? I'm more than willing to listen, but surely if it's very personal they'd be far better to advise you? After all, you hardly know me . . ."

"I know, and that's exactly why." Ciara drew a deep breath. "I just can't talk to either of them about it, because –" she hesitated, then plunged right in, "I think one of them may be the source of my problem."

Ita sat down, overcome by a sense of foreboding. "Are you sure you're wise to talk to me? Think carefully, Ciara, before you do. I wouldn't want you to feel guilty afterwards."

"Guilty?" Ciara sat upright, her eyes blazing now. "If anyone's guilty, it certainly isn't me. I trusted them both –"

"Ciara, start at the beginning. As long as you're sure you really want to tell me."

"I'm sure. Just promise me that anything I tell you won't go any further?"

"Scout's honour."

"Not even Liam?"

Ita's cheeks blanched at the mention of his name. "Not even Liam. I promise."

Ciara nodded in acknowledgement, and drew a deep breath. This was very difficult for her, and now that she had the floor she was unsure of where to begin. She jumped up from the table and walked to the window, staring out at the distant hills. It was easier not to look at Ita while she was talking. Focussing on the city skyline would make her narrative seem as though she was really talking to herself.

"After Niall died, I discovered that he'd been having an affair."

Ciara could hear Ita's sharp intake of breath.

"I know – I couldn't believe it at first either. We'd been so happy together. We were even planning to go away on holiday –" a sob rose in Ciara's throat. She turned to Ita, her eyes now bright with unshed tears. "Do you know how I found out? I was clearing out the cupboards and drawers in the bedroom, and I found a photograph of Niall that I'd never seen before. When I read what was written on the back of it, I knew without a shadow of a doubt that he'd been having an affair with the woman who'd written that message."

Ita took a deep breath, thinking inwardly that only a fool, an inexperienced fool, would keep such incriminating evidence. Try as she might to distance herself, Ita felt an almost unbearable empathy with the woman standing before her, being no stranger to unhappiness herself. She wished that she had something constructive to say that might help, but she knew that no words of hers could ease the other woman's torment.

Ciara paced the floor. "I just don't know what to do. I feel like I'm trapped in a cage. I can't face anyone, and I want to cry all the time." She looked wildly at Ita. "Will I always feel this way?"

Ita smiled gently. "I'm sure you won't, Ciara. Pain usually eases as you come to terms with it."

Ciara returned to the window, gazing out without seeing. "I can't bear to tell anyone that Niall was having an affair. Because if I do that, I'm changing our marriage and its meaning, and –"

Ita felt her own heart quickening, as she asked the only logical next question. "And you think you know who the other woman was?"

"I'm reasonably sure," Ciara now turned to face her, her eyes glistening with tears of anger. "I was such a naïve fool at first. It never crossed my mind that it could be either of them. In my own mind I'd invented some kind of glamorous scarlet woman who'd whisked him away against his will," she looked out the window again, "and all the time it was happening right under my nose. Can you believe it? One of my own friends!"

"You mean you think it was either Dee or Kate? Surely not!"

Ciara turned around sharply. "I don't think there's any doubt. It has be one of them."

"Surely you can't think your closest friends would do that?"

"Well, who else could it be?"

"For goodness sake, Ciara, there are millions of women it could have been! Why are you so sure it was someone you know? It was probably some woman he met on a business trip, a brief fling that you should just try to forget about –"

Ciara's voice rose. "How can I possibly forget about it, when I don't know why or how it happened? And since he's no longer here, I can't ask him about it! I've got to understand it, and I've got to know who it was, for my own peace of mind!" Ciara dropped limply into a nearby chair. "That's another reason I can't face Dee or Kate at the moment. I'm afraid of what I might say, or do –" she left the sentence unfinished. "Anyway, Ita, you're right about the business trip. The photograph was taken at a seminar in Galway last year. And I know that both Dee and Kate attended it too."

Ita said nothing. As a journalist, she had been at that seminar too. Neither Dee nor Kate had known her at that time, but she'd seen them from afar, knowing that both of them were friends of Niall Delaney's wife.

Ciara sighed. "And there's even worse to come. Later tonight I'm going on holiday with Dee. What am I going to do, alone with her in Turkey for two whole weeks? What if I say something?"

"You've no option but to suspend your doubts for the duration of the holiday," said Ita firmly. "You're not even certain that it was either of them, anyway."

"But who else could it be? I've thought of all the

traditional suspects. There's Sinead, Niall's secretary, but she's utterly besotted with her husband John –" she began counting on her fingers. "Then there's Lily and Alice, the two part-timers in the office –"

"Ciara, for God's sake!"

Ciara stopped momentarily as Ita called her name.

"You're only going to drive yourself insane with this futile search. Besides, would Dee want to go away on holiday with you if she was the guilty party?"

Ciara's eyes blazed. "If she didn't feel guilty about having an affair with my husband, she'd hardly be worried about going on holiday with me, would she?"

Ita rested her hand gently on Ciara's shoulder. "Look, believe in your friends. I'm sure they're both very concerned about you. I noticed how supportive they were at your husband's funeral."

Ciara took a deep breath. "There's something else you should know too. I've done something terrible myself. I had a one-night stand with someone who's married. But I can't tell you any more than that."

"Then aren't you being a bit of a hypocrite yourself?"

Ciara cradled her head in her hands, and Ita was unsure of whether or not she was crying.

"But I didn't start it –" Ciara said, raising her head. "My fling only happened after I'd discovered about Niall's affair!"

"So that makes it all right, does it?" Ita asked reasonably, holding up her hand in supplication as Ciara turned to her. "Look, I'm only playing devil's advocate to help you see what's happening."

"You're right," said Ciara, humbly. "I *am* a bloody

hypocrite. In a sense, I'm as despicable as the woman who had the fling with Niall."

"You're being very hard on yourself. Ease up a bit, Ciara. You've had a tough time lately. Maybe when you can forgive yourself, you can start forgiving others."

"I could never forgive that bitch, whoever she was! Mine was only a one-night stand – a sort of, well, catharsis. Whereas Niall's was a full-blown affair!"

Ita looked at her watch. "I'm sorry, Ciara, but I really must go. I've a dental appointment at two-thirty," which was a downright lie. Who worries about the condition of their teeth when they're intending to end their life?

Ciara jumped up apologetically. "Oh my God, I asked you for lunch and I haven't even made you a cup of tea yet! Please let me get you something to eat. I have it all ready in the kitchen –"

Ita smiled. "Thanks, Ciara, but I'm not hungry. Going to the dentist always makes me feel a bit queasy. We can have lunch together another day soon, but now I must really be going."

Impulsively, Ciara hugged Ita. "Talking to you has really helped. Thanks, Ita. Although I hardly know you, I just knew instinctively that I could be honest with you and that you'd understand." Ciara smiled impishly through tear-laden eyes. "I just hope I haven't bored you so much that you won't call round again!"

Ita laughed, lightly returning the embrace. "I don't think anyone would call our conversation boring . . ."

Ciara touched Ita's arm suddenly, looking directly at her. "Liam loves you. I can see it in his eyes."

Ita smiled, but said nothing.

"How do you feel about him?" Ciara persisted.

Ita shrugged her shoulders. "I'm very fond of him, but –"

It sounded lame, and Ciara knew it too. "So you're playing it cool. Well, maybe you're right, but I can assure you as someone who knows him well that Liam would never let you down." Suddenly, Ciara gripped Ita's arm tightly. "Oh, for God's sake, Ita. Go for it! You'll never regret it. Take the chance of love while it's there. Life's too short to hesitate. I know just how short the time together can be."

Ita smiled, but her eyes were sad. "Goodbye, Ciara," she said. "I hope I've been of some help. Have a lovely holiday." Then she was gone.

Alone in the kitchen, Ciara helped herself to some of the cucumber, onion and tomato salad she'd made for the lunch she'd forgotten to serve, but she wasn't really hungry.

Suddenly, the phone rang.

"Hello?"

"Oh Ciara. Thank God I've m-managed to get you –"

It was Kate, her voice slurred. She's been drinking, Ciara thought with surprise.

"Kate, are you all right?"

"Yesh, I mean no. I've got to talk to you."

Ciara said nothing. She didn't know what to say, even if she'd been able to find her voice. Suddenly her throat had become constricted, and no sound would come out.

"I've wanted to tell you thish for ages, but there just never seemed to be the right time . . ." Kate hiccuped. Clearly she was waiting for Ciara to say something, but once again Ciara said nothing. "Ciara, are you still there? Look, we never meant to fall in love. I'm sorry for not telling you before now. But I think you should know, especially since I'm going to have his baby –" Kate hiccuped again. "Ciara, say something!" she implored. "I couldn't bear it if you won't speak to me."

Suddenly, Ciara found her voice. "You bitch!" she screamed hoarsely. "You expect me to stay friends after, after this? How could you do it to me? Don't ever, I mean ever, come near me again!"

"Ciara, lishen please – we didn't mean it to happen –"

Ciara slammed down the receiver and dissolved into hysterical tears. Now, at last, she knew who the other woman was. And hearing that she was pregnant by Niall was more than she could bear. So much for Ita's platitudes. Clearly the woman had no idea of how devious some people could be.

My God, how could I have been so blind, Ciara thought. All last summer, she'd suspected that Kate might be seeing someone. Often, Kate hadn't been available for their usual outings, excusing herself with vague references to movies she was going to see, the names of which she could never remember afterwards. Amused, Ciara had suspected that there was a man in the background, someone whom Kate did not yet wish to reveal.

Ciara had been glad for her friend, thinking that it was time a new love entered her life. Since Kate's brief engagement all those years ago, there hadn't been any men in her life. And all the time, Ciara thought, I made it easier for her, by never questioning her! I actually helped her to cover up her affair with my husband!

The phone rang again, but Ciara ignored it. As soon as it stopped ringing she would take it off the hook. The cheek of Kate, thinking that she would simply accept her apology! What did Kate expect her to say – no problem, dear. Don't feel guilty. What's a mere husband between friends?!

When it eventually stopped ringing, Ciara took the phone off the hook and went upstairs. Thank God she was going on holiday that very evening. And with Dee. Angrily, she threw her clean underwear, toiletries, dresses, T-shirts and shorts into her suitcase, closing the zip. She was packed now and ready to go. She looked at her watch. Charlie and Dee would be collecting her very soon, then Charlie would drive them both to the airport for their evening flight.

Ciara brushed away a tear. She wasn't going to get all maudlin about the years of friendship she and Kate had shared, the laughs they'd had at school, the agonies they'd experienced over boys. And Kate's generosity – she'd try to forget about that too. Kate who had bailed her out so often when she'd no pocket-money, Kate who'd first introduced her to Niall . . .

With tears running down her cheeks, Ciara filled out the travel labels and tied them onto her suitcase. As soon as the holiday starts, she vowed defiantly, I'll be smiling again. I really will . . .

CHAPTER 36

In time-honoured tradition, the elderly gynaecologist was both friendly and distant at the same time, putting me at ease while he carried out his internal examination. Then he directed me back to the small changing-room, told me to get dressed and come back into his surgery when I was ready.

When I was dressed again, I returned to his office and sat in the chair in front of his desk. He was writing on the pad in front of him, and after what seemed an age I suddenly realised that he was playing for time while he tried to compose what he was going to say to me.

At last he spoke. "Have you carried a child before?" he asked quietly. The room seemed to spin around. I opened my mouth to speak, but no words came out. As I struggled for words, he nodded sympathetically. "It seems to me that you've suffered some major trauma to your womb, or perhaps a botched abortion? I'm sorry to have to tell you this, but —" He knitted his fingers together in the shape of a steeple and continued to stare at them as he spoke. "I'm afraid there is permanent scarring of the tissue inside your womb."

245

His tone sounded so final that I thought he'd finished speaking, so I opened my mouth to ask if this would make pregnancy more difficult. But the words froze on my lips as he delivered his coup de grace.

"I'm afraid, my dear, that you can never have a child."

I clutched the desk. I'm not sure if I tried to stand up. All I remember is the sound of my own voice, rising in a loud wail of denial. It couldn't be true, I told him. Ted and I had planned to have several children like all the other siblings in the Durkan family . . .

Patiently, he sat there until I had finished, looking at me sadly. Then he pressed the intercom and asked his secretary to contact Ted, since I was becoming hysterical.

"No —" I said quickly, "please, no! I need time —"

I couldn't face Ted yet. Besides, I had to decide what I was going to tell him. Perhaps, if I could manage to compose myself, I could even delay telling him for a while. Maybe even until after the wedding. Grabbing my coat, I rushed out of the gynaecologist's office. Did I say goodbye or thank you? I don't even remember.

I wandered around the shops for several hours, had afternoon tea in a small café and bought some new underwear. I felt more relaxed by the time I reached home, having made up my mind that I would stall Ted for a while by telling him that the results of my tests weren't available yet.

Stupidly, I'd underestimated the power of the Durkan family's information network. My mistake had been in attending a gynaecologist of their choice, because it meant that confidentiality was never even a consideration.

I could see by Ted's face that he'd already been told. His face was a dark shade of purple, and I'd never seen him look so angry. "Couldn't you at least have kept your sordid past from fucking up my life?" he roared. "You deceived me, you bitch!"

I might actually have felt sorry for him if he'd shown the slightest concern for me, or for the trauma that I was coping with myself. Instead, he reacted as though my past life was an untidy piece of debris that had surfaced on his horizon with the sole purpose of causing him angst. He never asked me how I'd become pregnant, what age I was when it happened or how I'd coped. His anger was motivated only by concern for his own social position.

Suddenly, all the venom was gone out of him and he began to cry. At that moment I tried, for the sake of what we'd had before, to comfort him by putting my arms around him.

"We could adopt . . ." I said hopefully. But he pushed me away, looking at me as though I was something beneath contempt.

"You must be joking –" he retorted with a harsh laugh. "I don't want someone else's brats. I want my own kids, my own flesh and blood!"

His kids. Not our kids. Clearly, the Durkan dynasty had to go on, and I couldn't deliver the promise of another generation. He began to weep again, but with rage rather than sorrow. So I left the room, put on my coat and left the house by the side door. I was shaking as I headed down towards the woods, hoping that a walk would clear my head and help me to calm down.

Usually, the sights and sounds of spring filled me with pleasure. At any other time, seeing the buds on the trees, the birds collecting twigs and dried grass to build their nests, would have filled me with a primeval sense of hope as nature renewed itself. But today nature seemed to be mocking me. All around me the new was springing from the old, yet I was incapable of fulfilling my own part in nature's plan.

247

"Why me?" I called out, but only the creatures of the woodland heard me. Why, when everything in my life had seemed perfect, did something inevitably happen to destroy it?

And then I thought of you again, Ciara. You had it all – a prestigious career, a healthy daughter, and the man whose child I'd once been carrying. But because he met you I was forced to end the life of my child, and would never now be able to have another. I seethed with anger and hatred for you then. And once again, you became the focus of all the rage that I held inside – against Ted, the Durkans, my aunt, the Church, my brutal rural life and my parents. Revenge was the overriding emotion I felt then, but most of those I hated were beyond my reach. But you weren't, Ciara. So once again, you became the focus of my revenge.

I returned to my own apartment several hours later, unsure of what would happen next, and spent the night tossing and turning in my lonely bed. The following morning, as planned, I attended the funeral of a local dignitary but was totally ignored by the Durkan family who sat tight-lipped in the church watching me from afar with hostile and accusing eyes.

Already, people I'd considered friends began passing me by in the street without a greeting, or looking in the opposite direction. Nor were there any phone calls inviting me to coffee or fund-raising events. As far as these women were concerned, I might as well be dead.

Yet I understood their behaviour. If any of them had shown favouritism or maintained contact with me, it would have meant social and political suicide for them too. Their situation reminded me of the fearful women who'd congregated in my mother's kitchen all those years ago. The only difference separating the two groups was the wealth of the Durkan *family's contemporaries. But the women had just as little power as those of my mother's generation.*

The following morning, Ted called around to my apartment. He stood in the hallway looking awkward and embarrassed, and refused to sit down or accept the cup of tea I offered. Since the news of my infertility had come to light, I realised that I meant little to him as a person. I'd been a commodity, albeit one he would cherish, as long as I fitted the stereotype of the good wife. His need for me wasn't that of a man for a woman he loved. I'd soon be replaced by someone who could fit the mould better, and I knew that already there were several substitutes waiting in the wings.

"I-I've been talking things over with the family –" he began. I felt like screaming. Why did our private lives have to be discussed among his relatives, especially when he wouldn't even talk about these things directly to me? "We, I mean I, I think –" he gulped nervously, like a child trying to remember his lines in a school play. The words finally came out in a tumble. "I can't marry you any more."

I nodded. He was simply confirming what I already knew.

Relief showed instantly on Ted's face. I was now relegated to the role of a burden to be disposed of as quickly as possible so that the Durkan family could continue with their otherwise successful and untroubled lives.

What was I going to do now? Ted and his family had already worked that out too.

"I'd like to think that we can come to some cash settlement," he added, warming to his theme. He always felt on safer ground when he was talking about money rather than emotions. "If we can settle this business amicably, I'm prepared to give you half the value of the house as a once-off payment."

A handsome settlement, I knew, but a poor substitute for a lifetime of love, prestige and security that I thought I'd finally found. I longed to scream at Ted, to tear at his face and hair. But I was beaten. Once again the Durkan family had been able to fix things for their own benefit. I'd be expected to fade quietly from the scene, never to bother them again.

I looked at Ted with hatred in my heart, and reluctantly accepted his offer.

CHAPTER 37

Frantically, Kate dialled Ciara's number over and over again. Each time she got the engaged signal. Clearly Ciara had taken the phone off the hook. She poured herself another measure of whiskey, drinking it all down in one gulp. Maybe it hadn't been such a good idea to try to tell Ciara over the phone. Nor was it very bright to make decisions like that when you'd had too much to drink. But if I hadn't had a drink or two, Kate reasoned, I'd never have had the nerve to tell her in the first place.

She surveyed the almost-empty Jameson bottle. Had it really been full when she started drinking? She dialled Ciara's number again. Still off the hook. Then she tried Ciara's mobile phone, but that was turned off too. Maybe at this very minute Ciara was ringing Dee or someone else to tell them what Kate had done to her . . . She should have waited until after Ciara's holiday. Now, Kate thought, I've gone and blown everything.

She might as well have another drink while she decided what to do. There was just enough left in the bottom of the bottle for a refill. Maybe she'd add a little water to the bottle and swish it around so that she'd be sure to get the very last dregs from it. No point in wasting any of it – it was her only friend right now. She poured the mixture into her glass.

Gulping down the last drop, Kate stood up unsteadily. Why the hell should she feel defensive anyway? Why should she care if Ciara didn't approve? "Fuck you, Ciara!" she said aloud, raising her glass.

Suddenly, Kate had an idea. Why hadn't she thought of it before? She'd drive round to Ciara's house. And she'd keep banging on the door until Ciara let her in. She'd make Ciara listen to her. She'd explain everything, especially about the baby. It had obviously come as quite a shock to Ciara. It had been a shock to Kate herself. After all, she'd been told years before that she'd never be able to have a child. But she fully intended having this baby anyway, no matter what Ciara or anyone else thought.

Sitting in her car, Kate cursed aloud as she searched for the ignition keyhole. Surely it hadn't moved? No, it was there, but somehow she just couldn't get the key to fit into it. She laughed triumphantly when she found it, and eventually succeeded in turning the engine on. As the car throbbed into life, she roared down the driveway and out onto the road, narrowly missing a car that had to swerve violently to avoid her.

Kate laughed as she sped along. She liked driving fast. The quicker she drove, the sooner she'd be at Ciara's house. Then she'd be able to make her friend see sense. As she took the turn leading up onto the new motorway several other cars beeped at her. What the hell was wrong with them? Kate wondered. Maybe she'd forgotten to turn on her lights? No, they were on. She put her foot down further on the accelerator, since she was in a hurry to get to Ciara's. As soon as she explained things to Ciara, everything would be all right.

Why were those drivers coming towards her? Surely they were all supposed to be going in the same direction as Kate herself? Suddenly, Kate realised that she'd gone onto the motorway the wrong way. Dammit, now she remembered seeing those signs that said 'Turn Back', but she'd ignored them because they were only trying to stop her getting to Ciara's house.

She giggled. After all, it was a new motorway. How was she supposed to know which way it was going? Hastily, she pulled over to the side to avoid an oncoming truck, but instead her car skidded and crashed through the barrier, somersaulting in the air before landing upside-down at the bottom of the mound.

Twenty minutes later, the police and the emergency services closed off the road and got a paramedical team down to the upturned vehicle. By torchlight, they surveyed Kate's inert and bloodstained body and sadly shook their heads.

"Get a stretcher down here, lads. As quickly as possible!" someone shouted. "She's breathing, but only just."

"What are her chances?" one member of the team asked the paramedic who was examining her. "Not good, not good at all –" was the reply, "but where there's life, there's always hope," he looked up wearily. Now, it doesn't look as if there's much life, or hope."

BOOK 2

Chapter 1

"Close the door quickly, love. There's a fierce draught," said Annie Reynolds, as her fifteen-year-old daughter Ciara returned home after school. Immediately, Ciara slammed it shut against the force of the wind which threatened to cave in the shabby, ill-fitting door now rattling on its hinges. Throwing down her schoolbag, she hurried over and held her hands to the open fire in the tiny dining-room-cum-kitchen. Her fingers were almost numb with the cold. She'd lost her gloves several weeks before, but hadn't told her parents since she knew there was no money available to buy another pair.

The family's black and white cat lay in front of the fire and Ciara reached down to stroke its fur. It was a scrawny animal, a stray kitten that Ciara had found the year before mewling piteously up near the quarry. Now he was a well-loved, well-fed, neutered tom, but he'd never fully recovered from the deprivations of his youth.

"Would you like a cup of tea, love?" her mother asked. Ciara nodded as she stroked the cat. Her mother's answer to everything was a cup of tea. When the kettle had boiled and the tea had been made in the big chipped teapot, Ciara and her mother sat at the old wooden table surrounded by a clothes-horse and chair-backs laden with shirts and underwear, all of it drying in the heat of the room.

The place might look untidy, but as always, everything was spotlessly clean because Annie Reynolds never let poverty get in the way of her pride as mother and guardian of her family. "Cleanliness is next to godliness," she would say with satisfaction, as she polished the few bits of brass and silver that hadn't yet been taken to the pawnshop.

"How was your day, love?" her mother asked, as she did every single day. And she didn't expect Ciara's answer to vary either.

"Oh, the same as usual," Ciara replied on cue. But she didn't tell her mother that the rest of the class were going to see *Romeo and Juliet* at the Olympia Theatre that night as part of their preparation for their next exams.

Ciara had informed her teacher that she'd a prior baby-sitting arrangement she simply couldn't get out of. She knew that her parents couldn't spare the money for the theatre ticket and bus fare, nor for the after-show snack during which the teacher and pupils would assess the information they'd gleaned from the play.

Ciara's parents had done their best for their children given their limited resources. The weekly wage of a labourer didn't provide enough money for the good things in life. Yet they both wanted something better for their children. Uncertain of how to achieve this, they'd felt that a good education was probably the key to breaking out of the cycle of poverty in which they were permanently trapped.

So they'd enrolled Ciara and her brothers in the best fee-paying schools they could afford, where they hoped their children would receive the kind of education that would enable them to train for careers rather than just jobs.

But the Reynolds' weekly wage wasn't enough to provide the extra money that would enable their children to truly integrate into the circles in which their schooling now placed them. In fact, it was doubtful if Annie and Frank realised the full extent of the opportunities that were on offer. And this was because their three children, realising the sacrifices that their parents were making, never let them know.

Tonight, while her classmates were at the theatre, Ciara decided that she'd paint a scene from the Shakespearean play to relieve her frustration. She would bring it into school tomorrow, so that the teacher would have no reason to pick on her for not being at the theatre with the rest of the class.

Sometimes, Ciara felt that she didn't fit in anywhere. Her education set her apart from the people in the council estate, and some of the local kids called her a snob for not attending the local tech, and for talking 'posh'. Sometimes they even pelted her with stones as she was walking home from school in the evenings.

The estate where the Reynolds lived was regarded by many as a den of petty criminals. This was unfair, however, but Ciara knew that her classmates' parents wouldn't want their children mixing with 'the dregs of society' as she'd heard one parent describe the people from the estate. Sometimes, she wished she had the courage to answer back, to tell them that despite its notoriety her estate also had many decent people living there. Maybe some day, she would . . .

At six o'clock Ciara's father returned from work, his face wreathed in smiles.

"Guess what I found today?" he said, grinning from ear to ear with a look of childlike pleasure on his weather-beaten face.

He looks old, Ciara suddenly thought. Much older than her friends' fathers, although she knew that he was younger than many of them. But the harsh outdoor life had taken its toll, and Ciara felt a stab of pity combined with overwhelming love for this man who was her father.

"What did you find, Dad?" she asked, knowing the ritual that followed would give him immense pleasure.

"You're going to love this, Ciara," he told her happily, his eyes twinkling as he began telling the story of this latest mysterious acquisition. "You know the old national school buildings that are being renovated on the quays?"

Ciara nodded.

"Well, we were clearing the site today and among the things that were being dumped –" his eyes were crinkled up with pleasure, "– was this." He ducked out into the hall and with a flourish, produced an old school easel. "I thought this might be useful for your painting," he told his daughter, willing her to like it. "With this, you won't have to prop up your canvases against a pile of books any more to get the right angle. Look, there are even pegs on it so you can set it at the height you want."

Ciara looked at the battered easel which had

undoubtedly served generations of pupils over the years. And she loved it because of the aura of learning and history it evoked, and because it would give her greater control over both canvases and location. But most of all, she loved it because her father had given it to her.

"Thanks, Dad," she whispered, hugging him and the easel at the same time, "it's exactly what I need. I'm planning to do a bit of painting this evening when I've finished my homework. So I can try it out."

Frank's eyes glowed with pleasure. It made him so happy when he was able to help any of his children, but particularly Ciara he had to admit. She was the apple of his eye. Of course, he loved his sons dearly too, but there was something special about Ciara. Maybe it was just that she was his only daughter, and fathers were supposed to have a special bond with their daughters, weren't they?

Both her parents took inordinate pleasure in Ciara's artistic talent, and they encouraged her to the best of their ability. It was a source of constant joy to them, and astonishment that two people who couldn't draw a straight line had produced a child whose ability asserted itself almost from the day she was born.

As a baby, Ciara had taken to pencil and paper like a duck to water. She'd spent hours drawing coloured shapes and stick figures, which gradually gave way to more recognisable illustrations. As soon as she could talk she learnt the names of the various colours, and wherever Ciara went her box of coloured pencils and drawing paper went too.

At first, her parents regarded this absorption as a marvellous way of keeping her occupied. But as her talent developed, they became her most enthusiastic devotees. Frank's job sometimes involved renovating old office buildings where he'd find bundles of used or leftover office paper that could be used for drawing on, which he'd then bring home with all the pomp and ceremony of someone bearing the crown jewels. Ciara, in turn, responded to all this enthusiasm with a constant supply of colourful drawings which adorned the dingy kitchen walls like a series of bright and colourful explosions.

Over the years neither her interest nor her talent waned. By the time she was fifteen, it was clear to everyone including herself that she would make a career in the world of art.

Around seven o'clock that evening there was a knock at the door. Ciara was surprised but pleased to see her school friend Kate on the doorstep.

"I've left my geography books in school," Kate said apologetically. "I was hoping I could borrow yours. Or maybe we could do our essays together?"

"I thought you were going to see *Romeo and Juliet*?"

Kate shook her head. She'd seen it already. Her aunt had taken her the previous week when the neighbour she'd been going with had suddenly dropped out. But Kate knew that Ciara couldn't afford to go, so she quickly changed the subject.

"What's that – an easel?"

Ciara nodded happily. "Yes, Dad found it today when they were clearing out an old school. I'm going to use it later on when I've got my homework done."

Kate was one of the few friends with whom Ciara felt no embarrassment about her family's lack of social position, and she and Dee were among the few whom Ciara didn't mind calling to the house.

Stepping into the tiny kitchen, Kate was greeted warmly by Annie and Frank. Although Kate lived in the nearby upmarket housing estate she was a friendly, down-to-earth youngster who didn't seem to care about the disparity in their respective lifestyles. Although Kate's aunt's house was equipped with central heating and all modern conveniences, and there was carpet where the Reynolds only had linoleum, Kate sat happily among the drying underwear which was draped over chairs in the Reynolds' kitchen.

"That's a brilliant fire, Mrs Reynolds," said Kate cheerfully to Annie, pulling in closer and warming her hands. With childlike pleasure she watched the flames shooting up the chimney until youthful exuberance got the better of her. "Can I put on a bit of turf, Mrs Reynolds?" she asked.

Annie nodded fondly. With delight, Kate now selected a big chunk of turf, smelling its damp and musty odour before she positioned it carefully among the already burning embers.

"I think you just come here to visit the fire, Kate," Frank quipped. Kate grinned back at him. She always enjoyed being with the Reynolds. After the pretensions of her aunt's house, Kate found that being with the Reynolds was like having a surrogate family.

She particularly liked Frank Reynolds with his craggy, wind-tanned face and his yellow teeth which were due to lack of dental care combined with the cigarettes that he smoked one after another without a break. In her own home she didn't mention what Frank did for a living. Her snobbish aunt would quickly have decided that the daughter of a builder's labourer was not the kind of friend she expected her niece to have.

"Cup of tea, love?" Annie asked. Kate nodded. Hopefully, the offer might include one of Mrs Reynolds' home-made scones. Kate was a big girl who loved her food, and who was always fighting a losing battle with her weight.

After tea and scones, of which Kate had several, the two girls retired to Ciara's tiny bedroom. Their two heads, one dark, one fair, pored over their copybooks on the fold-up plywood desk Frank had built in the corner.

"Are you coming to the dance at the rugby club on Saturday?" Kate asked Ciara as she was leaving. "It's just records, but it should be good fun. All the guys from St Joseph's will be there."

Ciara hesitated, but Kate would brook no argument. "Look, if you haven't got the money, I've enough to pay for both of us. You can pay me back next week."

"OK, I'll pay you back as soon as Dad gives me my pocket-money," Ciara agreed reluctantly. "I'm a bit short because I bought some oil paints this week."

"No problem. See you tomorrow," said Kate, as she placed the money on Ciara's desk. "It should be a bit of fun. Niall Delaney is the DJ and he always plays great music."

"Who's Niall Delaney?"

"He's in fifth year at St Joseph's. He lives just up the road from me, and sometimes we walk home from school together. He's a nice guy, and a dish too."

CHAPTER 2

Ciara hadn't really wanted to go to the dance. Apart from the fact that she'd had to borrow the money from Kate, she didn't have anything nice to wear. She'd worn her only good dress so often that she was embarrassed to appear in it again.

Most of her school friends were able to buy the latest fashions every few weeks, but that was out of the question on her dad's salary. Yet even if she'd had the money to spare, Ciara doubted that she'd be so self-indulgent. Already most of her money was spent on paints. If she'd any extra money, she'd probably buy extra paints anyway!

On the Saturday morning of the dance, Kate, Dee and Ciara took the bus into the city centre where they'd arranged to meet Vera Malone, Marguerite Brown, Dot McNally and whoever else from their class decided to turn up. Meeting in the cafés and ice-cream parlours along O'Connell Street was a Saturday ritual for many school-going teenagers. Different schools frequented different cafés, but schools from the same area frequented the same café. This enabled boys and girls to 'accidentally' meet those they already fancied, or to size up the opposite sex in relaxed surroundings.

But before this boy-girl ritual took place, there was the earlier girls-only ritual of drinking tea and scoffing cream cakes in either Bewley's or the Kylemore café. Here, the girls confessed to each other, in the strictest of confidence, which of the boys they were most keen on and they would plan strategies for attracting the attention of the boys of their choice.

Today, however, shopping was top of the agenda. The boys would have to wait until the dance that night.

"OK," said Dee, wiping the last vestiges of fresh cream from around her mouth, "I'll see you all tonight outside the club at nine o'clock. Don't be late!" She looked at her watch. "I'm off to Arnotts – there's a sale on and I want to get something nice to wear tonight. Where are you all heading?"

"Ciara and I are starting in Clery's, then we're going down Henry Street to look at the dresses," Kate replied. "Ciara's been given her birthday money in advance so she'll be looking stunning tonight!"

Ciara nodded, pleased that for once she could shop as the other girls did. Her birthday wasn't for ages yet, but when she told her Dad about the dance he'd coughed up the money straight from his wage packet, realising that his daughter needed to hold up her head among her peers.

Dee shrugged her shoulders. "You'll look good no matter what you wear, Ciara," she said sourly. "Maybe you should just go in an old sack and give the rest of us a chance!"

Ciara blushed, not sure if Dee was paying her a compliment, or merely being sarcastic. Dee's tongue could lacerate when she was in that kind of mood. Maybe Dee was due her period – Ciara could see several nasty-looking spots on her friend's chin.

Turning to Marguerite, Ciara noticed that she, too, was looking paler than usual and had refused a second cream bun – which wasn't like Marguerite at all.

"Are you OK, Marguerite?" Ciara asked. "You look a bit peaky."

But as always, her jolly friend was quick to dismiss any suggestion that she was in less than top form.

"I'm fine, honestly. I felt a bit queasy earlier, but I'm OK now."

Ciara was relieved. "So where are you and Vera going?"

"We're off to the Palm Grove," Marguerite announced cheerfully, as Vera nodded in unison. "I've some research to do. I think Philip Breslin's cute, and I want to find out if he's going to the dance tonight."

"But he's only a little fellow," said Dee in surprise. "You're at least three inches taller than him!"

"And wider too!" said Marguerite, patting her large rear end and grinning, "but I still think he's cute. Besides, he's only sixteen. He's still got lots of growing to do!"

"I know where *you'd* like him to grow!" said Vera, turning pink at her own daring retort while all the others laughed.

While the others headed off to the Palm Grove café

and Dee went to Arnott's, Kate and Ciara made their way into Clery's department store. In the dress department, Ciara found the rows of beautiful dresses quite daunting and was mesmerised by them all. Kate was having no such problem. She was making oohing and aahing noises like a child in a toy shop and holding up various dresses for Ciara's admiration.

"Look, Ciara. I've found the perfect one for you."

Ciara looked, and could see straight away that Kate was right. It was made of the most beautiful multi-coloured chiffon with a full swing skirt. She fingered the material enviously, then looked at the price tag. She could hardly believe her eyes – it was exactly her size and had been reduced to half price! It was still far from cheap, but already Ciara could imagine herself in it, being swirled around the dance floor by some handsome stranger. She blushed at her own fanciful thoughts.

"It's lovely," she agreed. "Maybe I will try it on. Will you take care of my handbag while I'm in the changing room?"

But Kate was no longer listening to her. Instead, she was waving to a tall, good-looking boy of about seventeen who was walking through the nearby men's department.

"Niall, what are you doing here?"

As Kate waved, he came over to join them and Ciara was thunderstruck. He was absolutely gorgeous! Her heart began to pound, and she could feel her face going red with embarrassment. She hoped he couldn't see how much she was attracted to him.

"Niall, this is Ciara," Kate said, chattering on, oblivious

to the fact that something exciting and wonderful was happening between them. "We're buying new gear for the dance tonight. Do you think it'll be a good night?"

"Should be," said Niall, smiling impishly, his eyes never leaving Ciara's face, "since I'm the DJ!"

"So will you play a special request for me?" said Kate coquettishly.

"If we have the record you want, I'll certainly play it for you," he told her with a smile. But both he and Ciara knew that wasn't exactly what Kate had meant.

Ciara clutched the chiffon dress tightly. She would try it on, and if it fitted she would to buy it, regardless of the price. And she would wear her hair up in an elaborate chignon that would make her look sophisticated and desirable. Tonight she would make an effort like she'd never made before.

"So I'll see you both tonight?"

Ciara and Kate nodded as Niall said goodbye and left the store.

"Is he the boy you mentioned the other night?" asked Ciara, trying to sound casual.

But Kate didn't appear to hear. She was busy rummaging among the dresses again.

"Is Niall a neighbour of yours?" Ciara asked, a little louder this time.

"What? Oh, yes. He lives just up the road from me. He's a fine thing, isn't he?"

Ciara blushed. "Yes, he seems very nice,' she said non-committally.

When Ciara arrived at the club that night she was

disappointed to find that neither Kate, Dee, Dot nor Marguerite were there. They'd all arranged to meet at the entrance to the club, but after standing for several minutes in the chilly night air Ciara began to get worried. She didn't want to be blue from the cold when Niall saw her!

She was too excited at the prospect of seeing Niall again to be angry with her tardy pals, so when Vera Malone turned up along with some of the other girls from her class she paid her entrance fee and headed inside. As usual the girls all stampeded towards the toilets to check their hairstyles, mascara, and tuck in wayward bra straps. With much giggling, plotting and planning, the group of girls eventually stepped out onto the dance-floor, eyeing up the boys who were standing on the opposite side and trying to look totally uninterested in the girls.

Yet while she joined in all the fun and gossip, Ciara couldn't tear her eyes away from the stage where Niall was playing the records. And she wished that her two best friends were there to give her a bit of support. She could have asked them to move a bit nearer to the stage, just in case Niall hadn't seen her . . .

Suddenly, he looked down at the crowds milling around on the dance-floor below, saw her and waved. And Ciara felt as though there was no one else in the hall but her and Niall.

That night she shone as never before. She felt wonderful in her new dress, and now that Niall had spotted her she exuded a confidence and radiance that drew others to her and every boy in the hall wanted to dance with her. She, in turn, was delighted with this turn of events since it gave her a chance to shine in Niall's presence.

She felt his eyes on her all the time as he played the records, and each time she accidentally caught his eye he was looking directly at her. And while she danced she wished there was some way she could let him know – without being forward, of course – that she wished she was dancing with him instead.

Her heart skipped a beat when, at the interval, he jumped down off the stage and came straight over to her. She was chatting with Vera Malone and several other girls, but when he approached it was as though no one else existed. They all seemed to melt away, leaving nobody else in the world except her and Niall.

He claimed her quickly for the first dance after the break, having ensured that another schoolmate could temporarily operate the turntable. The temporary DJ put on several slow numbers, using the occasion to tease Niall by announcing that they were especially for Niall and his lovely new girlfriend. Heads turned and everyone grinned at the embarrassed couple.

"Ciara," Niall whispered, as he held her close, "I thought I'd never get a chance to dance with you. I've been watching all those guys fancying you, and hoping that you wouldn't go off with one of them before I got a chance to dance with you myself."

Ciara laughed and moved closer into his arms, responding to his refreshingly honest candour. "I've been wanting to dance with you too," she whispered shyly.

"Will you wait for me when the dance is over?" Niall

asked her urgently, his face a mixture of hope and uncertainty. "I'd love to walk you home – if that's all right with you, that is."

"Of course," she replied.

It had been that simple and straightforward. There had been none of the agonies and uncertainties, only the strength of their feelings from that moment onwards.

After the dance, Niall packed away the equipment as quickly as possible and joined Ciara where she was waiting for him at the door. Vera and the other girls from school had already left, giving her a knowing smirk and exacting a promise to be told all the details at break-time on Monday morning! Ciara was still perplexed that neither Dee, Kate, Marguerite, nor Dot had turned up, and Vera could throw no light on their whereabouts either. But right now, their absence was of secondary importance. Niall was walking her home and that was all that mattered.

It was a bright starry night as he walked her to her house, which was about a mile from the clubhouse. He'd slipped his arm around her as they walked, but made no further advances. In companionable silence they'd strolled leisurely and happily, both wishing that the night would never end.

When she'd told him where she lived, Ciara had felt a brief moment of panic in case he rejected her. Niall, after all, came from the very upmarket suburb nearby where Kate also lived. But he'd merely squeezed her hand tightly, as though to convey his indifference to her family's financial circumstances.

At last they arrived at the cul-de-sac of tiny council

houses where Ciara lived. She fervently hoped that neither her dad or their opposite neighbour Mr O'Gorman would be drunk again, and shouting bawdy songs at the top of their voices as they staggered home. Or that the gardai hadn't been called yet again to referee the ongoing battle between Mr and Mrs Keating at number 47. Crying children and flying glass was not a sight that she wanted Niall to be greeted with on his first visit there.

She glanced up at the windows of the house next door. Fortunately there was no sign of Mrs O'Donoghue who often sat there, lurking behind her lace curtains as she pried into everyone business. If she spotted Ciara with a boy she'd have his name, rank and serial number circulating around the neighbourhood by lunch-time the following day.

But the night was thankfully silent, and Niall walked her to her door without incident, kissing her gently when they reached the porch. She tried not to seem too eager, in case he thought she was fast, but there was little doubt that her response conveyed feelings that were similar to his. When he'd kissed her it had sent a tingling sensation racing through her body, as though she had received an electric shock.

"How soon can I see you again, Ciara?" he whispered, his fingers playing with a tendril of her hair.

"As soon as you like," she whispered, disregarding all the advice given in women's magazines about seeming 'too keen'. Ciara was keen and she wanted Niall to know it.

"Tomorrow then?"

She nodded happily, giving him her phone number. Thank God they still had a phone in the house! She knew, of course, that payment of the phone bill was long overdue and there was a real danger of it being cut off soon. But tonight, she didn't want to think about anything like that.

"I'll ring you tomorrow after lunch," Niall promised. Ciara nodded happily. Instinctively she knew that he wasn't one of those boys who promised to phone then never did. He would phone – she was certain of it.

He kissed her again tenderly, the electricity between them almost tangible. Then as Ciara slid her key into the front door and let herself in, Niall walked jubilantly back down the road, turning every now and then to wave at her. Standing in the shadows, Ciara waved back, not knowing if he could actually see her but knowing that he knew she was there.

Smiling to herself, she eventually went upstairs, thankful that everyone else was in bed. After the obligatory knock on her parents' bedroom door to let them know she was home safely, she went into her own tiny bedroom. Normally its confines depressed her, but tonight, it looked and felt like a queen's boudoir. In fact, everything in the world was wonderful, Ciara thought, as she admitted to herself that she'd fallen head over heels in love.

CHAPTER 3

The following morning, as the family gathered for breakfast, even those at the table could detect a subtle difference in Ciara. Her father looked at her quizzically over his Sunday newspaper and saw her smiling to herself, lost in some secret thoughts.

Frank sighed to himself. Despite his hangover he recognised the vacant stare, the sparkling eyes, the barely suppressed bubble of excitement that radiated from his daughter. He sneaked a glance at his wife Annie who was poring over the crossword in another section of the paper, a look of deep concentration on her face. His expression softened – didn't he know well himself what it was like to be in love? Hadn't he fallen for Annie the first time they'd met? And he still loved her as much, if not more, as each day passed.

Perhaps he'd better have a discreet word with Annie. Just to make sure that Ciara knew about babies and all that. Please God she'd be sensible enough not to get herself into trouble, but young people in the throes of love had a tendency to forget all about the practicalities involved.

He and Annie had waited until they were married, but today young people seemed to do it as soon as they'd met. It had been a strain for him and Annie to wait, but back then no contraceptives were available so abstinence was the only way of avoiding a pregnancy.

Frank also felt a brief pang of sadness. His little girl was growing up, and soon he'd no longer be the most important man in her life. He caught his wife's eye and they smiled at each other. With the knowledge born of years of closeness, Annie glanced over at Ciara, knowing what was on Frank's mind. She'd spotted it too when Ciara overcooked everyone's breakfast eggs to loud moans from her younger brother Cillian. But Ciara had laughed, apologised and given her brother a kiss on the cheek, much to his confusion and astonishment.

Why wasn't she retaliating, Cillian wondered, like she normally did? There was definitely something strange about his sister this morning. Maybe she was developing some dreadful disease? Cillian intended becoming a doctor when he grew up, so all his thoughts were centred on horrific diseases, gory injuries and surgical experiments.

The night before he'd read about a horrific disease whereby its victims were laughing hysterically one minute, then dropped dead the next. He eyed his sister worriedly. She was definitely excited, but there was no real evidence of hysteria yet. Maybe that would develop later. He'd watch her carefully for any signs.

In one sense, he hoped she wasn't ill because he was very fond of his sister although he'd never let her know it. On the other hand, it would provide a great opportunity to observe such a rare phenomenon at close hand. But could he be clinically detached when his sister's life might be at stake? He abandoned his rock-hard eggs and poured out a bowl of porridge instead. He'd watch his sister carefully and await further developments.

Ciara went to church with the family, but not a word of the priest's feisty sermon registered with her. She was too busy thinking of Niall. She was seeing the world around her in a new light, and it was a world where everything was fresh and different. She felt benevolent towards everyone. Nothing and no one could spoil this beautiful day, this wonderful, beautiful rest of her life.

Unless, of course, he didn't phone. Momentarily stricken now, her heart missed a beat and a small seed of insecurity was sown. But just as quickly it was replaced by the remembrance of his candour and sincerity. Of course he'd phone. Didn't she know that he felt exactly the same way that she did?

Unless, of course, she was mistaken. Maybe he was just one of those boys who told a girl any story in order to score with her. Then he could boast to the other boys about how 'far' he had managed to go with her. But Niall hadn't tried anything at all. He'd only kissed her, and they'd been very gentle kisses at that. And she'd known instinctively that if she'd wanted him to stop, he'd have done so immediately.

But she'd wanted him to kiss her over and over again.

Had she seemed too forward? Did he think that she was easy? By the time the Mass was over, Ciara had gone from elation to despair and back again. Would he phone? Of course he would. Anyway, she'd know in three hours' time.

Twice the phone rang that afternoon, and twice Ciara raced to intercept it. There was a call from one of her mother's friends to whom her mother chatted for over half an hour while Ciara inwardly fumed. What if Niall was trying to phone? What if he thought she'd taken the phone off the hook to avoid his call?

There was also a call for her brother Kevin which, thankfully, had been brief and to the point. She was grateful that her brother and his friends only used the phone for exchanging cryptic comments.

The only cloud on Ciara's horizon was the inexplicable absence of her friends at the dance the night before. She was puzzled, and annoyed with them, especially Dee and Kate, because going to the dance had been so important to her. Part of her was dying to tell them about her and Niall, but another part was angry that they hadn't even bothered to let her know that they wouldn't be turning up. Well, they can ring me first, she thought angrily. I'm not going to bother contacting any of them!

By half past two Ciara was beginning to panic. Niall had said he'd phone 'after lunch'. Surely lunchtime was over by now? In her own home, Sunday lunch was served around half past one, and by now all the clearing up had been done and her parents were stretched out comfortably in the living-room.

Could Niall have forgotten? Maybe last night meant nothing to him. Maybe she should have been more coy, more sophisticated. Not like the silly eager fool she'd been. Maybe . . .

The phone rang suddenly. And Ciara knew, with total certainty, that it was him. The phone seemed to have a special sound to it, a clear, positive sound that proclaimed his feelings even before she answered it. Heart beating wildly, Ciara lifted the receiver.

CHAPTER 4

As Ciara awoke after her wonderful first date with Niall, she found herself scratching furiously at a spot on her leg. Trying to ignore it, she rolled over and pulled the bedclothes over her head. She wanted no distractions as she memorised every moment of her date the previous evening. They'd gone to the local cinema, but she had no recollection of the film. She'd been too acutely aware of his touch, his breath against her cheek, the delicious sense of having found the love of her life.

However, reality now continued to intrude, and Ciara found herself scratching her ankle this time. Then her arm. God almighty, she thought, I hope there aren't fleas in the bed. She vaguely remembered that the cat had been scratching the evening before. That's all I need, she thought sourly, to pass fleas on to Niall. Her face turned pink at the thought of such impending shame. He'd never look at her again!

She stumbled out of bed, feeling decidedly unwell.

Her mouth was dry and her tongue felt coated, and when she stared at herself in the bathroom mirror she let out an anguished wail. There were spots all over her face!

Annie, on hearing her daughter's moans, sprang from her own bed and rushed into the bathroom. One look at Ciara's face and arms was all she needed.

"You've got chickenpox," her mother announced. "For God's sake, don't scratch those spots or you'll be left with the marks for the rest of your life!"

Ciara didn't know whether to feel relieved or enraged. Chickenpox! At least she was saved from the humiliation of having fleas, but this new development meant that she'd be out of school and couldn't see Niall for ages! Tears filled her eyes. Just when everything was going perfectly this had to happen! Maybe Niall would forget her or meet someone else if she wasn't around. It was all too much for her, and she burst into tears.

Annie patted her daughter on the back. "Come on, love. It's not the end of the world. It's just another of those childhood illnesses that all kids get, and it's just as well that you've got it now."

Deftly, Annie grabbed Ciara's hand as she saw her daughter about to alleviate the itch of a particularly ugly pustule on her cheek.

"But the itch is dreadful –"

"I know, love. I'll send one of the lads down to the chemist for some calamine lotion. Kevin – are you up yet?"

A sleepy Kevin appeared at the bathroom door, and he too was breaking out in spots.

"Oh my God," said Annie. "It looks like I'm going to have a house full of invalids. Where's Cillian?"

The future medic appeared, awakened by the commotion in the bathroom, and his eyes lit up with delight when he saw his sister's and brother's condition. A real disease for him to investigate!

"Just you wait," said Annie darkly. "Your own spots won't be far behind. Now, if you'd get dressed quickly, you can go down to McGrath's and get a bottle of calamine lotion."

Off Cillian went, feeling eminently superior to his two spotty siblings. Maybe, if Ciara wasn't too tetchy, she'd allow him to study her spots with a magnifying glass. Of course, if she fell asleep he could sneak up on her and take a look anyway. There was no point in using up favours if you didn't need to.

Down at the chemist's shop, Mrs McGrath informed him that he was lucky to get the very last bottle of calamine lotion in the shop. There had been a terrible run on it over the weekend, since there was an epidemic of chickenpox in the area.

"St Joseph's has lots of pupils out sick today, and I've heard that the nuns at St Brigid's are thinking of closing the school. I don't know what the world's coming to," she added ominously, as though Armageddon was about to strike the neighbourhood and chickenpox was the equal of bubonic plague.

Cillian liked the bit about the school closing down. Hopefully, St Joseph's Junior School which he attended might close for a few weeks. Although Cillian was a bright and intelligent student, he found a lot of his studies quite tiresome since they had nothing whatsoever to do with medicine. Science was the only school subject he could get enthusiastic about. Why waste time studying subjects that you'll never use?

When he'd had this argument with his Dad, Frank had reasonably pointed out that a doctor had to be a well-rounded person, and had to know a bit about everything.

"Besides," Frank had said, "you can't be one hundred per cent sure that you want to be a doctor, son. You might change your mind. After all, you're only eleven. A lot can happen in six years."

But Cillian knew that he wasn't going to change his mind. Still, a few weeks off school would mean that he could go down to the public library and sneak into the adults' section, where all the really good medical books were kept. Right now, he wanted to do some research on chickenpox.

Returning with the calamine lotion, Cillian imparted the news as told to him by Mrs McGrath.

"So you're not the only ones," said Annie to Ciara and Kevin, trying to sound positive as she dabbed the cooling cream on their itchy spots. "Probably half the kids in the area have got it as well. So get back into bed, the pair of you, and try to keep warm. I'll fill a hot water bottle for each of you. Cillian, will you fill the kettle and put it on, please?"

Cillian sighed. If he was going to be turned into a servant for that pair, the sooner his own chickenpox took hold, the better.

As Ciara lay in her bed trying to doze, her thoughts were never far from Niall. She'd have to get a message to him somehow. They'd agreed to meet after school on Wednesday, so she'd have to phone his house and let him know what had happened. But what if he couldn't be bothered waiting for her until she was better? Maybe he'd meet someone else . . .

No such worries were troubling Kevin's brain. He was secretly delighted at having a legitimate reason for missing school – he hadn't finished his Irish essay. Now, he'd have at least a week or two to get it done. He was delighted at the idea of languishing in bed, reading all his favourite adventure stories. Luckily, he'd been to the library the day before and he'd taken out some great books that would keep him occupied for ages!

He felt sorry for poor old Ciara, though. He knew that she'd fallen madly in love with some fellow she'd met at the club dance the previous Saturday. He smiled. She certainly wouldn't want her new Romeo seeing her the way she was at present. She looked awful with all those weeping sores!

Kevin wondered what it would be like to fall in love. Judging by its effect on Ciara, he didn't think he particularly wanted to experience it. His sister had been mooning around all weekend, and now she was miserable because she thought the fellow would go off with some other girl. If love made you that upset, it hardly seemed worth the trouble.

Mind you, he liked Ciara's friend Kate – she was great fun. But he'd stick to his adventure stories where the men were usually too busy battling the elements or keeping their enemies at bay to be bothered much about women. To him, that seemed like the most sensible way of avoiding trouble!

Niall phoned that very evening, which put Ciara in

extremely good humour. They talked for so long on the phone that eventually Annie got annoyed, and started gesticulating to Ciara to get back upstairs to bed before she caught her death of cold.

Niall was sympathetic about her chickenpox, and assured her of his love. Ciara was ecstatic. He'd said he loved her, already! She knew already that she loved *him*, but knowing he felt the same was wonderful! He'd promised to phone again the following evening, and to let her know who else among their friends was absent from school.

"Kate and Dee weren't in school today, so it looks like they've both got chickenpox as well," he added, "Marguerite wasn't around, and I didn't see Dot either. Charlie Somers wasn't feeling too good today. I won't be surprised if he's covered in spots by tomorrow."

"And what about you, Niall?"

Niall chuckled. "Oh, I had chickenpox years ago. I'll probably end up the only pupil in the classroom!"

They chatted on about the possibility of the schools in the area closing, and Ciara made a mental note to ring both Dee and Kate when she'd finished talking to Niall. She now felt guilty about the anger she'd felt. No doubt that explained why neither of them had been at the dance on Saturday night.

But as soon as Ciara finished talking to Niall, Annie hurried her up the stairs to bed. "That's enough phone calls for now. I'm not having you standing around freezing in this hall for a minute longer! You're supposed to be sick – have you forgotten?"

Ciara was too happy to argue with her mother, so she

went upstairs and climbed meekly into bed. She'd telephone her friends the next day. Anyway, all she wanted to do right now was snuggle down in the bed with her hot-water bottle, and re-live every moment and every turn of phrase of her conversation with Niall. He'd said he loved her!

The next day, however, the Reynolds telephone was cut off. Ciara had been looking forward to long chats with Dee and Kate, and to telling them about her relationship with Niall. But for the immediate future, no communication with her friends could take place.

Of course, Niall wouldn't be able to phone either. Ciara felt embarrassed about the outstanding telephone bill, but at least Niall knew she had chickenpox and he'd be waiting for her when she got back to school. She spread more calamine lotion on her spots. They were getting smaller already, and the itch was easing already.

She smiled at her younger brother as he came into her bedroom. Poor Cillian had finally succumbed to the dreaded disease and was feeling very sorry for himself. She ruffled his hair affectionately as she offered the bottle of calamine lotion. It almost felt like a rite of passage!

But Cillian was far from grateful. He was disgusted that she and Kevin were getting better while he was feeling so miserable. He snatched the bottle and stuck out his tongue at her.

CHAPTER 5

It was the first and only time she'd ever seen her father cry. The tears slid silently down his weather-beaten cheeks so silently that at first she hadn't realised what was happening.

Back at school once again, Ciara had just come home from her afternoon classes. She was late, so it hadn't seemed unusual to see her father sitting beside the fire. Her art teacher Mrs Lynch had delayed her, but she'd been glad to stay back because the discussion had been about her chances of getting a scholarship to art college when she left school. Mrs Lynch had been very encouraging, and Ciara was in high spirits when she dashed in the door.

"Dad –"

Seeing her father sitting facing the fire, she launched immediately into an excited monologue. "– Mrs Lynch thinks I've a good chance of getting a scholarship if I work hard between now and the Leaving Certificate."

There was no answer, and it was only when she went over to him that she saw the trembling jaw, the hopelessness in his eyes.

"What's wrong, Dad?" she whispered, instinctively putting her arms around him. He leaned against her, saying nothing but holding her tightly, and Ciara was filled with a terrible sense of foreboding. What could be so bad as to reduce her father to tears? The man who always wore a smile and always had a cheerful word for everyone?

She looked across the kitchen to where her mother stood silently preparing the dinner. Savagely, Annie was slicing carrots on the draining-board, her lips pursed in a thin line. What was going on? Had someone in the family died? Her blood ran cold at the thought. Where were Kevin and Cillian?

As if to relieve her fears, the two boys came running down the stairs and Ciara sighed with relief. Clearly they didn't know what was wrong either, since they both stopped in their tracks as they entered the room. At that point, the cat decided that the room was getting too crowded and headed upstairs for the comfort of Ciara's bed.

"The job," Frank said at last, "it's gone. They sacked me today."

"Oh," Ciara couldn't think of anything to say. She longed to contribute something positive, but her mind was already turning over the implications of this latest news. Kevin and Cillian sat wide-eyed and silent at the table.

"What happened, Dad?"

Frank blew his nose. "Well, you know that I've been trying to get the men unionised for ages?"

Ciara nodded. Against all odds, her father had been trying for months to interest his colleagues in joining the Irish Transport and General Workers Union so that they would be protected from the worst excesses of Burke, their vicious boss. But the men were all so timid and cowed through years of his abuse that they no longer believed they could have any control over their own working conditions.

"Burke didn't like it," said Frank, "because he knows we'd be able to demand proper wages. Some of the lads are just too scared to do anything. They don't seem to realise that if we're all in a union together there's not much that Burke could do to any of us."

Ciara could hear the anger rising in her father's voice.

"Today, can you believe it, Burke said that he was going to start docking pay from some of the men for spending too long in the toilets. The poor lads were only having a quick smoke, and I told Burke that he was way out of line." Frank managed a watery smile.

"So he told me to take my cards and go. I was sacked. And he laughed at me and said wasn't it a pity that I didn't have a union to defend me. So help me, I wanted to break his bloody neck!"

"Well, you handed him the chance to get rid of you on a plate," Annie remarked tartly. She was clearly upset, and was resorting to anger to cover up her fear of the future that lay ahead of them.

"Yes, you're right, love. I did," Frank admitted, "but there wasn't anything else I could do. I couldn't bear to look at the lads' faces. They were just going to let him deny them a few minutes' break without even a murmur!"

"But he's done it now anyway, and you've lost your job for nothing," Annie added.

"Except for a principle," Frank said sadly.

Annie snorted. "We can't dine on principles."

"Don't worry, Dad. I'm sure something will turn up," Ciara interjected, expressing an optimism she didn't feel. Her father had worked at Burke's yard for as long as she could remember and she'd heard the stories about Burke's meanness and cruelty to his workers over and over again. Now all her father's years of hard work, ill-treatment and humiliation at Burke's hands counted for nothing. For without a good reference from his previous job, what chance did he stand of getting another?

On the other hand maybe their luck would change for the better, Ciara reasoned. Maybe he'd even get a job where he didn't have to be out in all kinds of weather, where the boss treated his employees fairly, where there was a union to look after the workers' interests and where the pay would be so much better . . .

She sighed, knowing that it was just wishful thinking. But sometimes things did work out for the best, didn't they? She'd often read books about people who had triumphed over terrible odds.

Frank was well aware that there was much more at stake than just losing his job. If he didn't find another job quickly it would be the end of his hopes of giving his children a chance to escape from the poverty and hopelessness of the council estate. And he'd be leaving them worse off than before, because now they'd know exactly what they were missing. He'd tried to give them a taste of a better life, only to snatch it back from them through his own stupidity.

If only he'd kept his mouth shut when Burke had started sounding off. If only he hadn't risen to the bait that Burke had been dangling in front of him for months, in the hopes of eventually finding an excuse to get rid of him. But today he'd taken that bait, and it had left a bitter taste in his mouth.

Poor Annie. He knew that she was trying to be supportive while also wanting to wring his neck. In one sense, he wished she'd be outwardly angry with him. Anything would be preferable to her tight-lipped silence.

"Don't worry, Dad. You did the right thing, and we're proud of you!" Ciara told her father. "We wouldn't have wanted you to do anything else, would we?" She looked around the room to where her mother stood at the sink, while the two boys sat wide-eyed and worried at the table. They'd never seen their father so upset before.

Annie didn't look too sure if she agreed or not, and there was a split-second delay before she nodded her head. "Yes, I suppose so. There wasn't much else you could do. But what in God's name are we going to do now?"

"I'll start looking for another job tomorrow," Frank promised, trying to convey a confidence he didn't feel. "Don't worry, love. Something will turn up soon."

Annie stirred the pot on top of the cooker. She'd bought a large piece of cheap broiling steak earlier that day and made Irish stew for the evening meal. Under normal circumstances, there would have been enough for the next evening's meal as well. Now, she thought, I'd better add a bit more water and try to eke it out for at least another day . . .

A week went by without any success, and Frank came home each evening looking tired and defeated. As a result, a grey pall of depression hung over the entire Reynolds household. Everyone felt that it would almost be blasphemous to laugh or make a joke.

Annie kept busy as usual. She'd always been an active woman who needed to be working around the house all the time. But now, the trauma of Frank's job loss turned her into a whirling dervish. She scrubbed the house from top to bottom, washed all the curtains, polished the cooker vigorously and shone all the mirrors as though this personal act of defiance would keep any further trouble at bay.

But the air of gloom remained, and everyone else in the house seemed oblivious to Annie's activities. Eventually, Frank began staying in bed for most of the morning since he found no reason to get up. It was also a lot warmer in bed, since there was no longer any fuel to light the fire. The cat sneaked into the bed each morning after Annie left it, finding a cosy spot against Frank's back, thus enabling man and beast to draw solace and warmth from each other.

Since there was no money for the meter, the gas cooker wasn't working. Thankfully, the family still had a small primus stove and half a bottle of paraffin left over from the boys' last school camping trip. Having no cooker meant no hot water either, so the primus was in constant use for washing-up and making cups of tea. At first the boys found it a great novelty, but soon the amusement wore thin.

When he eventually got up around noon Frank would sit huddled in his overcoat in front of the fire grate, as though some imaginary heat was going to reach out to him and warm his numbed psyche. After the first few weeks of unsuccessful job-hunting, he just seemed to lose heart. Now, he sat staring into space while Annie polished and cleaned all around him. How different their reactions were to a crisis, Ciara thought. Her father seemed overwhelmed by it all, whereas her mother tried to carry on as though nothing unusual had happened.

However, Annie was acutely aware that by now Mary O'Donoghue, her nosy and snobbish next-door neighbour, would have noticed that Frank wasn't going out to work. And at the earliest opportunity, she'd corner Annie to find out what was going on.

"If that bitch next door asks about your father, tell her that he's got the flu," she told the three children. "I'm not having her and her ilk gloating over us."

The children nodded. They knew what Mrs O'Donoghue was like. It was her firm belief and she and her family were a cut above everyone else in the council estate because her husband worked for the County Council, and it was her lifelong ambition to ensure that everyone was made aware of this at every possible opportunity.

She constantly delighted in taunting her neighbours, especially the Reynolds, with her steady stream of new possessions. Invariably, she was either hanging new curtains, having the house re-decorated, or the miniscule garden 'landscaped'. She'd even installed diamond-paned windows in place of the standard plain ones, which made the house look completely at odds with the others in the cul-de-sac. Which was exactly what Mary O'Donoghue wanted. Any connection between her and her neighbours was purely accidental.

Her husband Paddy was terrified of her. She'd only to raise an eyebrow and he'd scurry to do her bidding. On the odd occasion that poor Paddy was able to stop to chat over the garden fence with Frank, he'd quickly be called to heel by his wife, and would feel the sharp edge of her tongue for daring to mix with people whom she regarded as their social inferiors.

After a fortnight, Mary O'Donoghue had realised that something more serious than a dose of flu had affected Frank Reynolds. Annie had been hoping that if Frank found a job in the interim, there'd be no need for the O'Donoghues to know what had happened. But since no job was found, it wasn't long before the truth reached Mary O'Donoghue's ears. It was sweet music indeed! She'd been given yet another opportunity to score over her dreadful neighbours who didn't appreciate the fact that they were living beside people of superior quality.

"It must be tough for you now," she said to Annie, hardly bothering to hide her satisfaction. "That's the trouble with labouring work, isn't it?" She placed particular emphasis on the word 'labouring', curling her lip in condescension. "There's no security in it at all. Now, take Mr O'Donoghue –" She never referred to her husband in public as Paddy, as if by doing so she would reduce him down to the level of their neighbours. "He's blessed because he has a state job. And we'll have a nice little pension when he eventually retires. It's a terrible pity that your husband isn't so lucky."

"We'll get by," said Annie, gathering up the mat she'd been thumping with a hard brush and wishing she could apply the brush to Mary O'Donoghue's head. Quickly she went indoors and shut the front door with a resolute bang.

In the privacy of her own kitchen, Annie exploded. "That bloody woman!"

The boys looked at each other warily. They didn't often hear their mother using bad language. They longed to smirk at each other, but were afraid to in case either or both of them got a wallop, since their mother still had the hard brush in her hand.

"That smug, interfering old bitch," Annie went on, "gloating over our misfortune. Her and her diamond-paned windows. I know where I'd like to shove each and every one of those panes!"

The boys couldn't help giggling at the image their mother's outburst conjured up. Their laughter broke Annie's bitter tirade, and she had to smile herself.

"Here's a cup of tea, Mam," said Ciara, bringing her mother's favourite china cup and saucer to the table.

"Thanks, love."

Annie slumped in a chair, her rage dissipated. She closed her eyes and thought of Mary O'Donoghue's smug face. That bitch had been positively gloating. Yet she hadn't even had the decency to offer a helping hand. Not that Annie would ever accept anything from the likes of Mary O'Donoghue. But just to have it offered would have restored her faith in human nature.

Annie sighed. They'd manage somehow, but for the love of God she couldn't imagine how. The few bob that they got from the Social Welfare ensured that they didn't starve, but there was no money left over for anything else. She might be able to get work herself, even if Frank couldn't. But the type of work Annie could get wouldn't be well paid either, but 'any port in a storm' as her own mother used to say.

Tomorrow, Annie decided, she'd check the notice boards in the local shops and hopefully she'd find some sort of work. Maybe someone would want cleaning done, envelopes addressed or children minded. If not, she'd place an advertisement herself. Before she and Frank got married, she'd been a machinist in a clothing factory. Maybe she could do some dressmaking.

If not, they'd have to sell something. The only problem was they didn't have anything of value left. Over the years, the few nice things they'd owned had gradually gone to the pawnshop and they'd never had the money to reclaim them. The children seemed to need an endless stream of clothes, shoes and schoolbooks. This new term had seen the pawning of their much-loved china dinner service, their last item of any real value. Parting with it had really hurt because it had been a wedding present from Annie's late parents.

Annie looked down at her wedding ring, and her eyes misted over at the thought of parting with it. But if it had to go, it had to go. Maybe she could get a brass one somewhere so that Frank need never know.

Fortunately, the month of September was mild and Annie became adept at conjuring up casseroles and stews on the single ring of the primus stove. Ciara and her brothers collected firewood from the nearby quarry at the weekends, and already they'd amassed a substantial pile in the back yard for when the weather turned colder. With their home-made go-kart made from the discarded wheels of an old pram, they loaded on broken branches, strips of decaying bark, sticks and wood chippings left behind after the quarry fell into disuse.

September was also the time when the hedgerows up at the quarry were laden with luscious blackberries. So the children filled boxes, bags and any container they could find, returning home with faces flushed from the effort of hauling the heavily-laden kart and mouths and hands stained red from the blackberries they'd picked and eaten on the way.

Annie longed to bake a blackberry pie for tea, but couldn't because the cooker wasn't working. Nor had she any money to buy flour and butter. But blackberries stewed in a pot on the primus and topped with the cream from the milk made a perfectly edible substitute.

"That was gorgeous Mam," said Ciara, as she cleared her plate. "You're the best cook in the whole world!"

CHAPTER 6

Before long, the month of October arrived, and with it a sudden drop in temperature. This was also the time when bills for the children's school fees were due to be paid. In previous years, finding the money had been a struggle – now it was virtually impossible.

Annie knew that a few weeks' grace was the most that could be expected, and the day of reckoning couldn't be put off indefinitely. The clergy in charge of the schools didn't look kindly on those unable to pay. Nor did they have time for people who advocated trade unionism. If they ever found out that Frank had lost his job through promoting trade unionism, the Reynolds would have another black mark against their names.

There was no one, Annie thought, as class-conscious as a nun or priest. She'd seen it herself during her own schooldays, when the wealthier pupils invariably got preferential treatment. So much, she thought sourly, for their Christian values.

Well, as far as Annie was concerned, no nun or priest was going to treat her children as second-class citizens. So she went down to the Post Office and took out the money for the children's fees from her own private savings account. Thankfully, there'd just been enough to cover the first term, and with luck Frank would be working again by the time the next school bill arrived.

The account had been a secret, known only to Annie. She'd been saving a few shillings each month for ages, intending to take the whole family on a surprise holiday. Now, the holiday would never happen. Still, she reasoned, if the children got a proper education they'd eventually be able to afford their own holidays.

Annie had never had the chance to travel. But she loved reading travel books and newspaper articles on other people's travels. She found it difficult to comprehend that there were places where sunshine and good weather were the norm. But she recalled once seeing President John F Kennedy when he'd visited Dublin shortly before his assassination, and she'd been amazed at how tanned he was compared to her own pale face and those of the crowds around her.

While she'd secretly been saving for the holiday, Annie had regularly collected brochures from the local travel agent, studied the prices and the locations and daydreamed about where she'd take the family when she'd saved enough money. Now, those dreams would have to take a backseat. Disappointment was nothing new to Annie. She'd probably have been surprised if things had turned out otherwise.

Annie now found it difficult to talk to Frank, so often

she didn't bother, finding it impossible to convey a cheerfulness she didn't feel. Helplessly, she watched as her husband descended deeper and deeper into despair, his guilt fuelling further anxieties and creating even bigger barriers between them. There were times when she felt that she hardly knew the man who sat hunched and miserable over the empty fire grate.

Annie, too, felt guilty, and partly to blame for Frank's gloom. Perhaps she hadn't been supportive enough when he'd first told her what had happened at the yard. Had she let him down when he'd needed her most? She was still worried about the future and the children's education, but there was more at stake than just her husband's job. There was his pride and integrity, and their own relationship too. In one sense, she was proud of what he'd done, but had she left it too late to tell him so?

"Mam!"

Ciara was surprised to see Annie sitting at her old hand-operated sewing machine surrounded by swathes of heavy damask fabric. She knew her mother had been a seamstress at a clothing factory before her marriage, but it was years since the old machine had been used.

"I'm making curtains," Annie explained, as the machine needle flew along a seam she was holding with one hand and steering with the other. "I put an ad in a few of the local shops, and already I've got quite a bit of work. So far I've orders for two sets of curtains, one set with matching cushion covers, and I've some dress alterations to do as well."

Ciara felt an overwhelming urge to hug her mother. It

hurt her to see how hard Annie was working to try to make ends meet. Already, she'd taken a morning job in the local hospital laundry which involved walking a mile to get there and another mile back, while the job itself entailed working in a hot, steamy environment. Ciara couldn't but notice how tired her mother looked, how raw and sore her hands were. Hands that were now called upon to perform delicate rows of flawless stitching.

"There's no other way," Annie said abruptly, seeing the look on her daughter's face. "Your father's had no luck at the labour exchange, and there's just no money left. I'm sorry if you don't like it. I'm not exactly delighted about it myself. But we have to get money from somewhere."

"But look at your hands!" said Ciara, taking in the raw and swollen fingers that had already spent several hours in hot water and detergent at the laundry.

"That's the least of our worries," Annie said, dismissing the state of her hands as of no consequence. "Don't worry, love. The skin will grow again in no time. I'd rather have food on the table than a pair of manicured hands any day!"

In contrast, Ciara couldn't help noticing how often her father was absent from the house. And she was aware that he wasn't out looking for work either. He'd have a pint in his hand, and another one already ordered . . .

"I haven't seen you around any morning this week," said Mary O'Donoghue, clearly angling for information.

Annie said nothing, knowing exactly what she was leading up to.

"And last evening, I just happened to look out the window and I saw a big BMW arrive outside your house. I said to myself, the Reynolds must be having visitors from England or America. Until, that is, I saw that it had a Dublin registration."

I'm sure you did, Annie thought. And it wasn't just by accident that you saw the car, you nosy bitch. Anything out of the ordinary happening in the cul-de-sac was guaranteed to get the O'Donoghue curtains twitching.

Annie knew that Mary O'Donoghue didn't, for one instant, believe that the Reynolds had wealthy visitors. She'd correctly guessed that Annie was going out to work in the mornings and taking in sewing work, and she was trying to goad her into a confession.

Mary O'Donoghue made a virtue out of being a housewife, and considered working wives to be piteous creatures whose husbands couldn't support them. Which, Annie conceded, was now true in her own case.

Annie would have liked a career of her own, but it had never been more than a dream. Career opportunities for women hadn't been available when people of her generation were growing up. But that's what I want for Ciara, Annie resolved, the option of having a career if she wants one.

Annie smiled sweetly at Mary O'Donoghue. As far as I'm concerned, she thought, that interfering busybody is getting no information out of me.

"Excuse me, but I've got to go in and put on the lunch," she said. "I find that a leg of lamb takes ages to roast."

She went inside and shut the door, leaving Mary

O'Donoghue open-mouthed. Roast lamb indeed, Annie thought with a smile.

In the kitchen, Annie unwrapped the large leg bone she'd bought from the butcher and placed it in a pot of water on the primus. Up in the fancy estate, people bought leg bones for their dogs. Down in the council estate, the same bone made a meal for a whole family.

CHAPTER 7

On a bitterly cold morning at the beginning of November the men from the Electricity Supply Board came to cut off the electricity.

"I'm sorry, Missus," one of them said to Annie, "but we're only doing our job. Are you sure you can't pay anything off the bill?"

"I'm sorry too," said Annie abruptly, "but I can't pay anything. My husband's out of work."

Embarrassed, the men completed the disconnection and drove off in their van.

Annie sighed. The noose was tightening around their necks, and yet she felt languid at the hopelessness of it all. At least she'd had the foresight to anticipate the disconnection and had bought a box of sturdy household candles. Thank God the sewing machine was hand-operated, since she had curtains and a matching bedspread to finish by the weekend. She'd have to start on them as soon as she came in from her morning job at the hospital in order to avail of the remaining daylight hours. Now that winter was setting in, it was dark by teatime.

Inside the house she made herself a cup of tea on the primus stove, and sat drinking it alone beside the cold and silent fire grate. She spent most of her time alone these days. Frank was still in bed, and when he'd eventually get up and discover that the electricity had been cut off he'd head off to the local pub. Lately, it was the only way he could cope with what was happening to them.

It was ironic that the less money they had, the more Frank was spending in O'Grady's. Still, she didn't begrudge him whatever pleasure he found in his pint, but she was worried sick about the money to pay for it. So far, he hadn't asked her for anything extra from their fast-dwindling kitty. Maybe some of his friends or ex-colleagues were keeping him in pints. It cheered her a little to think that her husband was still held in high esteem by the men he'd worked with. After all, he'd lost his job on their account. Maybe they'd take up a collection among themselves if they realised how bad the Reynolds' situation was?

At first, Kevin and Cillian found the lack of electricity quite a novelty – rather like being away on a camping holiday. But before long, they became bored and fractious since they could only read by torchlight. The electric fires were redundant, and the open fire could no longer be lit since all the wood had been used up. So they all sat huddled in the kitchen, wearing overcoats, gloves and several pairs of socks as the November cold struck with a vengeance.

It became impossible to do homework, yet the three Reynolds children were too embarrassed to tell their teachers what had happened. So they regularly got detention after school.

"At least it's warmer in school than at home," Cillian mumbled to his brother.

Frank found it easy to submerge his sense of hopelessness in the oblivion of a few pints of Guinness each day. What was the point, he reasoned, of sitting at home in the dark when he could be in the warmth of O'Grady's pub with Paddy O'Donoghue from next door? He and Paddy were fugitives seeking sanctuary from the pressures of their daily lives – he from his own sense of failure, Paddy from his harridan of a wife.

The proprietor, Luke O'Grady, was a decent man who let his regular customers run up a tab. But this made it easy for Frank to drink more than he should. With each pint his confidence grew, and by closing time he was ready to take on Burke and the rest of the world as well. Annie bore his mood swings with silent fortitude, for she knew how much he was suffering. But she was deeply worried. What would they do if Frank still had no job by Christmas?

The weather was now bitterly cold. In bed at night, they all piled their coats on top of the bedclothes for extra warmth and wore socks to keep their toes from going numb. The cat's popularity increased dramatically, as they all fought to have him in their beds for extra warmth. But perversely, the cat now refused to favour any of them, preferring to go caterwauling in the back garden with the local toms instead. There were nights when Annie had heard Cillian whimpering, unable to sleep with the cold, but she felt powerless to do anything. Ciara never complained, but Annie knew that she was suffering just as much as the others.

The cold was a great passion-killer too, Annie thought ruefully. There were times when she craved the comfort of love-making, But most nights Frank was either too drunk or too depressed to consummate their relationship. At times, as he lay beside her snoring, she felt a deep and burning resentment towards him. It was as though he'd given up on everything – his wife and family, his ideals, his self-respect.

Annie opened the front door to find the local sergeant standing there, his hand resting on Kevin's shoulder.

"We've got a bit of a problem, ma'am," he began, looking decidedly embarrassed. "This young lad of yours has been caught stealing from Dineen's shop."

"W-what? Oh my God!" Annie's hand went to her mouth in shock, but as she looked at Kevin and clearly saw the guilt in his eyes something snapped inside her and her hand lashed out across his face.

"You young pup!" she screamed, "how could you do this to us. Haven't we enough trouble already?"

"I didn't really mean it, Mam," now Kevin was crying too. "The cakes were just sitting there on the counter. I was starving, so I just reached out and took one. I didn't mean any harm."

"Is-is he going to be prosecuted, sergeant?" Annie asked in as calm a voice as she could muster.

"Well, ma'am, it all depends on whether or not the

people in the shop want to press charges. I'm quite prepared to, eh. I mean, there hasn't been an official complaint made to me directly. I just happened to be in the shop getting something for my tea when this, eh, unfortunate event took place. And being a representative of the law, the owner asked me –"

"Thank you, sergeant," said Annie, "I'll go down to Dineen's this very minute. And I'll bring this lump of misery with me to apologise."

Pausing only to collect her coat and bag, Annie relieved the sergeant of his charge and frogmarched Kevin down the road, maintaining a steady tirade as she did so. Kevin, silent and ashamed, said nothing. He was already in a state of shock from his altercation with the law which was further exacerbated by his mother's stream of expletives, most of which he'd never expected her to know.

In the shop, customers stood aside in alarm as Annie strode in, gripping Kevin by the lapel of his jacket.

"I believe I owe you for a cake that Kevin took, Mr Dineen," said Annie, stony-faced. "I'm sorry about what happened, and he is too."

She poked Kevin in the back. "What have you to say to Mr Dineen?"

"I – I'm sorry," said Kevin looking miserable. "I didn't really mean to take it. It was an accident, really."

Mr Dineen looked both embarrassed and hostile. "That'll be sixpence," he replied frostily, and Annie sighed inwardly with relief. At least if he was letting her pay for the cake, he wasn't intending to prosecute.

But as he took the money, Mr Dineen added frostily,

"And I'd be grateful if neither you nor any of your family came in here any more. I don't want thieves among my customers."

Then he surveyed a list that was pinned on the wall beside the cash register. "I see that you've also had quite a lot of groceries on credit. Would you please settle your bill as soon as possible?" he added.

"I'll settle it now," said Annie, her face aflame with embarrassment, aware that several customers in the shop were listening avidly to this altercation. This would give Mary O'Donoghue lots to gloat about when she found out.

Fortunately, Annie had just been paid for making two sets of curtains, so she delved into her purse and immediately handed over the notes. Then with her head held high she left the shop, pushing Kevin ahead of her.

Annie felt drained. The money she'd just earned from the curtain-making had been intended to cover the electricity bill. Now because of Kevin's stupidity they'd have to remain without heat or light for another while. Another fearful thought struck her as well. Because of this shameful incident, they now had nowhere that would give them groceries on credit any more. And she'd have to walk an extra half-mile to the only other grocery store in the vicinity.

Kevin was only saved from a further tongue-lashing on the way home because of Annie's determination to hold onto her dignity at all costs. Walking up the road past a group of her neighbours she held her head up high, and tried to look as though nothing was the matter. But they weren't slow to detect the tightness of her jaw, and the vice-like grip she was still exerting on Kevin's arm.

Annie felt totally defeated. Her family was falling apart, her whole world was collapsing. She felt like a lost child in a world over which she had no control. Frank, hollow-eyed and silent, didn't even say anything when she told him about the incident in Dineen's shop. Ciara behaved like a church mouse, creeping in and out silently, as though trying not to disturb the already fragile atmosphere. The poor child asked for nothing and ate very little, making Annie feel even worse.

The two boys, she drew in a deep breath, they seemed to be turning into young delinquents. Cillian was in trouble at school for damaging another boy's bicycle, and Kevin's incident in Dineen's shop had almost broken her heart. Didn't they realise that trouble with the law could mean the end of their hopes of going to university or of having a better life when they grew up? Tears pricked her eyes and she brushed them away angrily. Where would it all end?

CHAPTER 8

It was early December. All the streets and shops in the city were brightly decorated and filled with tantalising Christmas goodies. Fairy lights festooned the buildings and stretched from one side of the street to the other, while shoppers below felt as though they were walking through an Aladdin's Cave. Crowds jostled each other good-naturedly as people made their way along, laden down with bags and parcels. At street corners flower sellers sold bundles of holly and mistletoe, traders urged passers-by to buy sparklers and Cheeky Charlies. Already there was a festive spirit in the air.

Kate and Ciara sat in Bewley's café in Westmoreland Street, drinking coffee and eating Bewley's famous almond buns. The café was crowded as always, but Kate had spotted a couple about to leave so they'd quickly moved into the velvet-seated booth along by the wall.

Kate had been shopping, but the space beneath Ciara's chair was devoid of any parcels. She was on her lunch-break from her holiday job in a nearby shoe shop, but even if she'd had time to shop she didn't have the money to buy anything.

"What did you get?" she asked Kate brightly, hoping that she sounded interested rather than envious.

"Well, I got my aunt a sweater," Kate hauled it out of its bag, and Ciara commented favourably on her choice. Kate made a face. "But the old biddy is such a misery, I doubt if it will please her."

"Well, that sweater should please anyone," said Ciara, trying to sound supportive. "But Kate, I won't be able to get you a present this year, so please don't get me anything either."

"All right," Kate agreed, "but Ciara, I'm sure things will get better soon."

As Kate talked on about Christmas, Ciara smiled and tried to look interested but her mind kept wandering. How on earth was she going to get Niall a Christmas present when she had no money? This would be their first Christmas together, and she so much wanted it to be special, but it looked like being the worst Christmas her family had ever had. Her father still hadn't found a job. He'd managed to get a few days casual labouring work on a building site, but nothing else since. And as the days went by, he seemed to sink further and further into depression.

Her poor mother seemed to work night and day, yet she never complained. Her mother's aim was to have the electricity bill paid in time for Christmas. Ciara sighed. It would be nice to have light and heat for Christmas, but they'd have precious little else.

After deducting bus fare and lunch money from her paycheck, Ciara gave the rest of what she earned to Annie. But even with their combined earnings, the family was barely existing. Kevin had tried, without success, to get a holiday job in the neighbourhood and he blamed his failure on the incident in Dineen's shop. After all, nobody wanted to employ a thief. He was now so depressed that Ciara was seriously worried about him too.

Ciara sighed, but quickly turned it into a yawn in case Kate saw her misery. There wouldn't be any luxuries at home this Christmas. They'd never had much, but at least they'd always managed to buy little gifts for each other and have a turkey on the table for Christmas Day. Annie had informed them that this year they'd be lucky if they could afford a chicken, and they'd have to forgo the Christmas tree as well.

Annie had tentatively suggested to Frank that they ask the St Vincent de Paul Society for help, pointing out that the well-known charitable organisation helped many people in financial difficulties, in all sorts of different ways. In fact, she knew of someone whom they'd helped with their electricity bill . . .

Ciara had never seen her father so angry. He appeared to take the suggestion as a slight on his ability to care for his family, and he'd stormed out of the house and gone straight down to the pub. Annie had sighed and given in to his foolish pride. She wouldn't ask the St Vincent de Paul for help – they would soldier on. Maybe something else would turn up soon.

What worried Ciara even more than getting through Christmas was the fact that the school fees for the second term were due by the second week of January. If there wasn't any money to pay them, it would mean humiliation and disgrace. At worst, the three children would have to leave the school, get jobs and give up any hopes of third level education. At best, they'd be allowed to finish out the year, but each of them would pay for it in sarcasm from the nuns and priests running their schools.

"What are you going to do about a present for Niall?" Kate asked, knowing the answer but trying to create an opportunity whereby she could offer Ciara a small loan.

"I don't know. Even if I had any money, I'd feel duty-bound to give it to Mam. How could I buy Niall something when there isn't even enough food on the table at home?"

Kate was one of the few friends who knew about the Reynolds' worsening financial circumstances. Not even Niall had been formally told, although Ciara knew that he was aware her Dad had lost his job. But they never spoke about it because when Niall mentioned it she abruptly cut him off. When she was with him, she wanted to forget her problems and revel in the joy of their newfound love instead.

"I could lend you something. It's not much, but –"

"No, thanks, Kate. I don't want to run up any more debt. Borrowing's been our family's downfall."

"Well then, forget about paying me back. When you're a famous artist, I'll make a fortune from selling all those nasty drawings of the teachers you send me during class! I might even write your biography and tell all your secrets!"

"That's it!" exclaimed Ciara, her face suddenly brightening. "I'll paint a picture for Niall! I've got the paints already, so all I'll need is a new canvas and that won't cost much. Kate, you're a genius!"

Kate smiled back. For months now, she'd watched the Reynolds' situation go from bad to worse. Before her very eyes, she was watching the virtual disintegration of a family. Yet in the home she shared with her aunt there was abundance at every turn. The central heating was always left on, even when there was nobody there. Previously, Kate had accepted all this as simply the way people in Dublin lived, until she discovered that other people, like the Reynolds, led contrastingly different lives.

Across from where Kate and Ciara were sitting, Alan Moore sat watching them as he drank his coffee. He'd finished his morning assignment quicker than expected and was having a leisurely lunch-break before returning to the newspaper office where he worked as a photographer.

He liked Bewley's, everyone did. It had history, character and most important of all from his point of view, it was patronised by the famous and infamous as well as the ordinary punter. Actors strutted their stuff there, politicians hatched plots there, and financiers planned take-overs. It was a great people-watching place. Just before turning his attention to the two girls, Alan had been watching a well-known married actor and his female co-star sharing a pot of tea and he'd wondered idly if they were sharing anything else during off-stage hours.

Alan gave the dark-haired girl a cursory glance. Too

plump, face too round, nose too bumpy. But the other one
– wow! He was immediately struck by her ethereal
quality. In his professional capacity he eyed lots of young
girls, but rarely found that unique quality that he was
now staring at. Her blonde hair fell in wisps over her
delicate face. Enchanted, he watched the change in her
moods as she conversed with her friend. They ranged
from gloom to elation and back again, and he thought
what a wondrously expressive face she had. Suddenly, he
could imagine her lying naked on a bed, smiling shyly
but coquettishly at the camera.

As far as Alan was concerned, guys who wanted to
jerk off over pictures in pornographic magazines had to
be totally screwed up. Why weren't they out there,
getting the real thing? God knows, there was plenty of it
about. On the other hand, those guys were the ones who
put extra tax-free cash in his back pocket. His job as a
newspaper photographer didn't pay him enough to
maintain his extravagant lifestyle. So who was he to
criticise what these guys did in the privacy of their
bedrooms or potting sheds?

Purely in an academic sense, he eyed Ciara's breasts.
From what he could see they were big enough without
being voluptuous – ideal for what he had in mind. Big
boobs were useless from a photographic point of view
because the camera added extra weight to them. On the
other hand, small, well-formed ones could be made to
look voluptuous with glossy make-up, lighting and
camera angles.

Sensing that the two girls were about to leave, he got
up from his table and sauntered across to theirs. "Excuse

me," he said, wearing his brightest smile and handing his business card to Ciara, "I'm a newspaper photographer, and I'd be very interested in taking some professional photographs of you."

He noticed that her initial scepticism turned to genuine interest when he mentioned that she would, of course, be well paid. She would phone, he knew. He could always spot the ones who were interested in the dosh and whose scruples would quickly be rationalised when they found out what was actually involved. He'd seen it countless times before when he'd worked for these magazines. They were all keen enough to do what he wanted, as long as they could be sure that no one they knew would ever find out.

Of course, he'd always assured them that the pictures would only be used in 'foreign' magazines, and the idiots believed him. The truth was, he'd sell them to the highest bidder. It wasn't his problem if Daddy or the boyfriend were into these magazines. Anyway, these guys could hardly confront their little darlings without revealing their own nasty habits, could they?

He'd often masturbated to this particular fantasy himself, and usually had a terrific climax when he thought of Daddy or the boyfriend opening their porn magazine and discovering their own little popsy in the centrefold, wearing nothing but a few staples . . .

"Thank you," said Ciara, taking the card he offered her. "How soon would you want to do them? I'm working every day until Christmas."

Perfect.

"Well, in that case, we could do them at my place

one evening," he said, sounding cooperative and accommodating. He'd never had any intention of doing them anywhere else. He certainly wasn't going to do them in the newspaper studios!

"Ring me at that number any morning before nine," he said, pointing to his extension number in the darkroom. At that early hour nobody else would be there except him, and even if someone else took the message they'd simply think that the 'stud Moore' had found himself yet another girlfriend. Which wouldn't do his reputation any harm at all.

"But don't tell anyone about the photographs at this stage," he added conspiratorially. "This end of the market is highly competitive."

As soon as she'd agree to do the photographs, she wouldn't want anyone to know either, he thought, smiling to himself. Probably not even the plump friend she was with. Mind you, he didn't want anyone knowing what he was up to, either. He certainly didn't need the cops nosing around, and he didn't want anyone else muscling in on his lucrative little corner of the market either.

Having agreed to consider his offer and phone if she was interested, Alan left the two girls and set off for the newspaper office. As they stood in the street outside Bewley's, Kate gave Ciara a quick hug of delight.

"Wow! Maybe he's going to make you into a world-famous model," she said. "Wasn't it Twiggy who was discovered in a restaurant too? Imagine Ciara, if there's good money in it, this could be the answer to all your worries."

Ciara smiled, unsure of whether or not to believe in good luck. "Maybe it'll all come to nothing," she said doubtfully. "Maybe I just won't be what he's looking for. Besides, I really don't want to be a model – the only thing I really want to do is paint. But if I could just get some part-time work modelling, the money would really help out at home."

Then it was back to work for Ciara, but her head was still buzzing and she found it difficult to concentrate on what she was doing. Several times she gave people the wrong shoe size or the wrong style of shoe. Eventually, after a hectic day when everyone in the country wanted new shoes or boots for Christmas, Ciara took the bus home pondering the likelihood of getting work from the photographer who'd approached her earlier that day. Did he really want to take pictures of her, or was it just a joke? She'd heard of these things happening in movies, but never in real life.

Why on earth should he have selected her? There were lots of pretty girls about, and besides, she wasn't interested in modelling as a career. But he had mentioned a substantial fee . . .

CHAPTER 9

The next morning Ciara rang the newspaper during her tea-break and was immediately put through to Alan Moore. He sounded pleased to hear from her, and arranged to pick her up from work the following evening then take her back to his apartment in Donnybrook to do some preliminary shots. She longed to ask him what they were for, who would see them and why he thought she'd be suitable. But there wasn't time, and she didn't want to sound totally naïve. She'd find out soon enough.

All the next day she felt alternately apprehensive and elated. But there was little time to ponder, since all the staff at the shoe shop were rushed off their feet attending to the needs of the whole world's feet, judging by the crowds. By closing time, Ciara felt ready to drop and would happily have settled for going straight home and having an early night to recuperate.

Fortunately, she hadn't arranged to meet Niall that night so no explanations were necessary. In fact, no one knew where she was going except Kate. In keeping with Alan's strictures, she'd told no one else. But it would be a lovely surprise when hopefully she could tell Niall that her photos were appearing in some magazine or newspaper. It would also mean she could help to pay some of the mounting bills at home.

She'd told her mother that she wouldn't be home until later that evening as she was meeting an old friend from junior school. She hated telling her mother a lie, but she was more or less meeting a friend anyway, wasn't she? Annie, weighed down with her own worries, had merely nodded and said: "That's nice. Will I keep your dinner for you for when you get home?" Ciara shook her head. She didn't mind doing without dinner, especially if it meant an extra helping for someone else.

Ciara felt a bit foolish about meeting Alan Moore – maybe people would laugh at the idea of her thinking she could become a model. It would probably all come to nothing, anyway, she decided.

Since she'd no idea where Alan Moore lived, she and Kate had ghoulishly joked about the possibility of Ciara being murdered and they'd agreed a plan whereby Kate would contact the police if Ciara hadn't phoned her by midnight. But since Alan Moore was clearly a bona fide photographer they didn't seriously consider this a possibility.

When she left the shop and found Alan Moore waiting outside, Ciara wasn't sure whether she was disappointed or relieved. She felt awkward and gauche, like a clumsy young animal whose legs wouldn't coordinate properly. As he guided her towards his car, she nearly tripped and fell. How on earth could she, or he, think that she was model material?

As they drove to his apartment Alan talked about the weather, asked what she was studying at school and if she liked her holiday job. If this was meant to put her at her ease, Ciara felt it had failed disastrously. She wanted to ask him about his target market for the photos, how she would have to pose, what she would wear, but he seemed to be deliberately steering clear of the subject.

In his luxury apartment, Ciara was relieved to see several cameras and an assortment of lenses, filters and photographers' paraphernalia. This seemed a reasonable indication that he wasn't planning to murder her!

"Like a drink?"

"Eh, no, thanks. I mean, w-when are we going to do the photographs?"

Alan selected a bottle of vodka from the drinks cabinet and filled himself a large measure. "Are you sure?" he asked, indicating to the bottles. "There's gin, whiskey and brandy."

"No, thanks," said Ciara firmly, "I just need to know a bit about the photographs you're going to take. What do I have to do, and what are they for, exactly?"

"Aah." Alan sat down, raising his glass approvingly at her, as though she had just cracked some mysterious code or won teacher's approval for asking a particularly intelligent question in class.

"Have you heard of, eh, men's magazines?"

Ciara nodded, recalling the few well-thumbed magazines featuring naked women that the boys from St Joseph's had tried unsuccessfully to hide. One day in

Ernie's café, one of the girls had managed to sneak a copy from one of the boys' schoolbags and all the girls had gathered round to discover what was so fascinating to the opposite sex. They'd gazed at the women's open legs, and submissive poses with a mixture of awe and revulsion.

"Yes," Ciara replied, her heart sinking. Suddenly, she was beginning to realise what these photographs were all about.

"Good," Alan nodded his approval once again as though her knowledge meant that he was dealing with a woman of the world instead of a child, and he was grateful that he wouldn't have to waste valuable time explaining.

"You see, Ciara. I work for some continental magazines . . ." He always referred to them as 'continental'. It made them seem so distant and more impersonal. "And I think you'd be a wonderful subject for a series of photos. Nothing too rude, you know. Just a few relaxed, natural shots of you reclining on a bed . . ."

"No!"

Alan looked perplexed, as though surprised at this outburst. Then he brushed an imaginary piece of fluff from his jacket before looking at her again.

"I beg your pardon?"

"I'm sorry, but I'm not interested in doing pornographic photographs," said Ciara adamantly. "I wish you'd told me before now, then I needn't have wasted your time."

"Relax," said Alan, as Ciara made a move to get her coat. "OK, if you don't want to do them, that's fine. But I must point out to you that you'll be turning down a lot of money." He picked up a notebook from beside the phone, scribbled a figure on it and passed it across to Ciara. "That kind of money."

Her mind went into shock as she waited for the blurred figures to come back into focus. Could she be mistaken? The amount he'd written down was more than her poor father earned in a whole year!

Alan watched her carefully. "It's a lot of money for very little work," he added smoothly, "and you needn't worry; these magazines are for a specialist market. They're banned in Ireland, so there's no chance that anyone you know will ever see them. And just think what you could do with all that money – cash into your hand, the minute the session's over."

Ciara was thinking rapidly. It would pay all the school fees for the next year, as well as all the food, electricity and phone bills for months to come. But she just couldn't do it. No amount of money was worth the loss of her self-respect and the shame she'd feel. She shuddered at the thought of dirty old men, or boys like those at St Joseph's, masturbating over her photographs. Already she felt cheapened, yet she'd done nothing.

"I'm sorry, I just couldn't," she said lamely. "It's, oh I can't explain!" Then she felt angry with herself. Why should she have to explain anything to this man?

"Are you quite sure?" Alan added coaxingly. "Take time to think about it, if you like . . ."

"No, no my decision is final," said Ciara, putting on her coat. "Could you please show me where's the nearest bus stop?"

At this point, Alan reluctantly accepted defeat. "I'll drive you back to the city centre, then you can get your bus from there," he said, extending his hand to her. "No hard feelings, then?"

Ciara smiled with relief. Thankfully, there wasn't going to be any unpleasantness. "No, of course not. It's just that I – I couldn't do something like that. I'd feel, oh I don't know – used."

"And, eh, this little matter – it will remain strictly confidential between us?"

"Of course."

Alan sighed. Pity to lose a cute little popsy like this one. He'd been studying her objectively all the time she'd been in the flat, and he was even more convinced now that she'd be perfect for the shoot he'd had in mind. Those eyes were dynamite, and the lips – with a pout and plenty of lip-gloss she'd be an absolute sensation. And she had the kind of translucent skin that photographed really well . . .

Oh well, he thought philosophically, you win some, you lose some. Money-wise, a centrefold of Ciara would have brought him into the big league. But much as he wanted to pressure her further, he realised there was no point. Anyway, he was already playing a dicey game. If any of these little cuties told their parents and they reported him to the police, he could lose his job with the newspaper, as well as his lucrative sideline.

It was also dangerous to get involved with minors, but that was what the magazines demanded these days and the pay-off was worth the risk. Besides, once a girl agreed to be photographed, he was home and dry. From then on, she'd have as much to lose by disclosure as he had.

Alan grimaced as Ciara stepped eagerly into his car.

Back to the drawing-board, old chap, he told himself. Back to the search for another cutie. But it would be some time before he'd find anyone as perfect for the job as Ciara Reynolds. You didn't often come across that combination of blatant sexuality paired with genuine innocence. And when you did, you knew that you could make big money out of it.

But it had all been to no avail. Maybe he should feel angry with her. After all, she'd wasted his evening as well as doing him out of a nice hefty fee. But in fact, he had to admit that he couldn't really dislike her. She had guts.

As she got off the bus, Ciara felt strangely depressed and lethargic. The last thing she wanted to do was phone Kate. She'd have preferred to nurse her strange and confused feelings alone without trying to articulate them to somebody else. But her friend would be anxious and might contact the police if Ciara didn't phone her back! So she slipped into a call-box at the entrance to the estate, grateful that it hadn't been vandalised as was usually the case. Quickly, she inserted the required coins and dialled Kate's number.

"Well, what happened?" Kate's voice was excited on the phone.

"Well, nothing happened in the end," said Ciara, keeping her voice low so that no one else could overhear. "It wasn't quite what I'd expected. He wanted me to do nude pictures for a pornographic magazine."

"What? Oh, my God!" Kate giggled.

"It's not funny."

Ciara found Kate's reaction irksome, yet she didn't

know how she'd expected her friend to react. She felt all mixed up, as though her very identity had been usurped by the night's events.

"Sorry, I'm sure you were disappointed."

"Yes, I was, because he was offering incredible money. But I just couldn't do it, no matter how much he was paying."

"God, no. You poor old thing. You must be feeling rotten too."

Ciara nodded gratefully, momentarily forgetting that Kate couldn't see the gesture. Her tension was beginning to evaporate now that she felt that Kate really did understand how she was feeling.

"Yes, I suppose I am. But I actually felt angry rather than embarrassed when he told me what the pictures were for."

"You, you didn't have to take your clothes off tonight, did you?"

"No, of course not!" Ciara laughed and it felt such a relief. "He explained it to me as soon as we arrived at his place, and I told him straightaway that I wasn't interested. And that was all.'

"He didn't get annoyed, did he? Or make a pass at you?"

"No, he was quite civil about it. To him, I suppose it's just a job. Anyway, he must be used to girls saying no to that kind of offer so it can't have come as much of a surprise to him."

"Was it all very embarrassing?"

"I don't know. No, I think I felt angry rather than anything else."

"And do you feel OK now?"

How perceptive Kate was. "No," said Ciara, near tears, "I feel awful. I mean, what made him think that I might do that kind of thing? Do I look the type?"

"No, of course not."

"I'm going home," said Ciara abruptly. "I'll talk to you tomorrow. Goodnight Kate."

"Goodnight Ciara. Cheer up. It won't seem quite so bad tomorrow."

But when she got home, Ciara hadn't gone straight to bed. Instead, she'd lit the candle beside her bed, then stood naked in her room in front of her dressing-table mirror studying her reflection as dispassionately as possible. She shivered, but it wasn't just from the cold of the unheated room. She found it deeply disturbing to be regarded as suitable material for pornographic photographs. Was there some wanton quality about her that she herself couldn't see? Did other people see her differently than she saw herself?

Now Ciara analysed the feelings she and her friends experienced all those years ago when they'd pored over the boys' pornographic magazine. Their feelings had been primarily of anger. They were angry because the submissive poses of the women reflected back negatively on them too, making them feel as vulnerable and exposed as the women in the pictures. There was no difference between them – they were all women together, and instinctively they knew that what hurt one of them hurt them all.

Ciara remembered being shocked at the exposed genitals. Was this what all women looked like down there, she'd wondered? Those parts that were never talked about, and which few girls would ever think of examining in a mirror. Momentarily, it struck her that men probably knew more about the anatomy of a woman's private parts than women did themselves.

She shuddered now, and reached for her nightdress. It was long, high-necked and made of flannelette, and inside it she felt warm and protected. She looked at herself in the mirror again and liked what she saw this time. This was the real Ciara Reynolds. Pulling on two pairs of old socks to keep her feet from going numb, she slipped into bed, pulling the bedclothes tightly around her. And for the first time in years, she fell asleep sucking her thumb.

CHAPTER 10

By the following evening Ciara was feeling a lot calmer about her experience with Alan Moore. A hectic day in the shoe shop had put things back into perspective, and by now she was almost able to laugh at the whole thing. She might even tell Niall about it at some stage. Not now though. Maybe when she felt completely comfortable about it.

Getting off the bus, she began walking down the road towards the cul-de-sac where she lived. She'd had time to put the incident with Alan Moore into perspective; now she would put it behind her. It was quite funny really. Imagine her having the nerve to think he might have wanted to turn her into a fashion model! She didn't look remotely like Twiggy or any of the other popular models of the day. Nor was it what she wanted to do with her life anyway.

Turning into the cul-de-sac, the first thing Ciara noticed was that her mother was standing on the doorstep and there was another woman, presumably the owner of the large car parked outside, addressing her in loud tones. Unknown to the two women, Mrs O'Donoghue from next door was peeping down at them from an upstairs window.

Ciara tried to take in this confusing scene, but as she got nearer she realised that the woman on the doorstep was actually shouting at her mother. Simultaneously, Mary O'Donoghue noticed Ciara's arrival and retreated behind her curtains, but it was obvious that she was still lurking there and taking in every detail of the scene being enacted below.

"That was an Yves Saint Laurent dress, although I don't suppose you'd know anything about *haute couture*, you stupid woman!"

The harridan on the doorstep was clearly in a rage. She was holding a dress in her arms, and waving it about intermittently as though it was a semaphore flag.

"It's ruined!" the woman added. "I'll sue you for this. You haven't heard the end of the matter by a long shot! And I'll make sure that you never work as a dressmaker again in this town. I'm not without influence, you know. I'll make sure that everyone knows how incompetent and careless you are!"

Annie, her face red with embarrassment and anger, said nothing as the woman stormed down the path of the tiny front garden, brushing past Ciara as she got into her car and drove off at breakneck speed.

Annie was already sobbing by the time Ciara reached her. Having her humiliation witnessed by her own daughter, and anyone else within earshot, was just the final straw. Ciara ran the last few feet and gathered her mother into her arms, guiding her inside. Quickly, she closed the front door, to ensure that their next-door neighbour wasn't provided with any further entertainment at her mother's expense.

"What happened, Mam? Who was that woman? C'mon, I'll make you a nice cup of tea."

"Oh Ciara –" Annie let out a heart-rending wail as Ciara helped her into a chair. "I ruined that woman's expensive dress! I was supposed to shorten the hem by an inch, but I took too much off it by mistake." Annie's eyes were filled with misery. "I don't know what went wrong, love. I think I mixed up the measurements for the dress with the measurements for the curtains. It was too dark to see the bit of paper that I'd written them on, but I was sure it said three inches off the skirt and one inch off the curtains. It must have been the other way around."

Annie's shoulders heaved and her voice shook as she unburdened herself to her daughter. To Ciara, it felt strange to be in such a situation of role reversal.

"It's my own fault. I suppose I was a bit distracted," Annie whispered, "Luke O'Grady came round from the pub with a huge bill that your father's run up. I thought some of his old workmates were buying him drink, but it turns out that he was just putting it on the slate. I know I should be angry with your dad, but he's so depressed these days, love, and he's drinking far too much . . ."

Annie looked up at Ciara with sad red eyes, and Ciara's heart contracted with love for this normally cheerful woman who was now bowed down with fear and worry.

"Then there's the school fees, and I'm worried sick about those two boys. I mean, what could Kevin have been thinking of, that day in Dineens?" As her words tapered off, Annie started to cry again. "If that woman decides to sue me for the price of a new dress –" she sobbed, "what in God's name are we going to do?"

As Annie took the cup of tea that Ciara handed her, she looked up into her daughter's face and Ciara saw a look of terror in her mother's eyes.

"Listen, Mam. She was probably just annoyed. I'm sure it'll all blow over."

Annie drank her tea gratefully. "At least if the curtains are wrong I can do something to rectify that," she said at last, "but after today's episode, I don't know if I can ever take on another sewing job. Even if that woman doesn't carry out her threats, I think I've lost my nerve."

The cup rattled against the saucer as Annie's hand shook. Ciara's mouth felt dry, because she felt herself being pushed inexorably towards a horrendous decision.

"Mam, I'm sure something will turn up soon," Ciara said, giving her mother a quick hug. "Then you won't ever have to think about sewing any more, or even working in the laundry. I just know things are going to get better . . ."

CHAPTER 11

Alan Moore was grinning as he came out of the darkroom. He looked so pleased with himself that the editor's secretary stopped in her tracks and stared at him.

"You look like the cat that's got the cream," she remarked.

"It's the reverse, actually," he grinned back at her, "I'm the cream that's just got the pussy!"

Pleased with his clever pun, and even more pleased with himself, he rubbed his hands together gleefully. That phone call had really made his day. Already he was imagining himself going down to the motorbike dealers, and after an amount of bargaining he'd place his cash on the counter and drive off on the Electra Glide he'd always wanted. Or would he buy the Triumph Bonneville instead? He'd always fancied one of those bikes as well. Maybe he'd get a better deal on that make. Decisions,

decisions! He began whistling happily as he walked down the corridor.

Ciara felt sick with apprehension. If she'd been nervous the first time she'd arranged to meet Alan Moore, this time she felt sick and depressed. It had been a busy day at the shoe shop, but not busy enough to make the time pass quickly. Having made the decision to meet him again, Ciara was anxious to get the whole sordid business over with as quickly as possible. That way, she needn't dwell on it for too long and could just as quickly put it all behind her.

At last it was closing time, and Ciara quickly left the shop. She was anxious to get away before any of the other staff followed and saw her meeting Alan Moore. And worse, she'd had to lie to her mother, telling her that she was staying in town to have a night out with her friends from work.

Alan was waiting outside the shop, and her heart sank. She'd wildly hoped that he wouldn't be there so that she could then go home with a clear conscience. But he was leaning against a street lamp looking smug and confident. Ciara wanted desperately to hit him.

"Hi, Ciara," he said, taking her arm possessively, "I'm really glad you've decided to do these photos. Look, don't take it so seriously. It's great money, and no one you know is ever going to see them."

"If no one's going to see them, what's the point in taking them?" said Ciara sarcastically.

"C'mon, don't be like that. It's just a job. You don't have to like it – you just have to look as though you do."

"Well, I'm actually hating it, if you want to know the truth."

Maybe, Ciara thought, if I don't look happy enough he'll consider me unsuitable. Then it will be his decision to back out, not mine.

In silence, they walked to Alan's car, which was parked down a side street. During the drive to Alan's apartment, he made one or two attempts at conversation, but receiving only monosyllabic answers he abandoned any further attempts until they arrived.

Once inside the apartment, Alan did his best to be the genial host. But to Ciara, the situation felt more like being on a visit to the dentist with the dentist's platitudes doing nothing to dilute the fear of what was going to happen.

As though he was reading her mind, Alan cleared his throat. "Right. Eh, might I suggest Ciara, before we start that you relax with a drink. I can see that you're a bit uptight, and that's going to show up in the photographs."

Ciara felt like screaming at him. Then the pictures would merely be reflecting the true situation! On the other hand, she had to acknowledge that she was there of her own free will and that she could walk out the door if she chose to. But she had made a deal, she needed the money, and she would see it through.

So she nodded meekly, and accepted the large vodka and tonic that Alan poured and handed to her. Perhaps, she thought, if I get drunk the whole nasty business will seem less real and I won't be so inhibited. So she drank her vodka too quickly, then held out her glass for another. Already it was going straight to her head. If she kept drinking at this rate, she'd be more than happy to get into bed! She giggled at her own joke, and Alan smiled encouragingly at her over his own glass, which held tonic only. There would be time enough to celebrate later, he thought. Right now, he needed steady hands to do a professional job.

During the shoot, as the effect of the vodka began to wear off, Ciara was so overcome by such self-disgust that she just wanted to grab her clothes and run as fast as she could out of the apartment. She felt like a piece of meat rather than a woman, and she tried not to think of the leering men who'd be looking at the private areas of her body in the pages of some magazine. Suddenly, Ciara understood that pornography had little to do with sexuality and more to do with men's desire for power and control over women. I'm letting my own sex down, she conceded, and I'm pandering to the very type of man I despise. I'm justifying what I'm doing because I need the money. But I'm selling my body as surely as if I was a prostitute.

Suddenly, she felt overcome by a wave of shame. If any of her friends ever found out, she'd die! And she was filled with dread as she thought of Niall's reaction, or her father's, if they ever saw the pictures. She shivered, and Alan had to tell her to stop moving or she'd ruin his latest shot.

"Are we nearly finished?" she asked sharply. The session seemed to be taking forever.

"Yep, we're nearly there," Alan replied, sounding pleased with his work, "I just want to get one more shot with your legs pulled up. That's right. Now open them wider, so that I can get a full view of your crotch."

How could he be so impersonal about it all? Ciara wondered angrily. Probably like her, he was thinking only of the money.

In fact, Alan was having problems of his own. As he crouched before the camera, he hoped that Ciara couldn't see his erection. God, he had such a horn. Usually, he could take this kind of shot without any difficulty. It was just a well-paid job to him. But this little cutie looked so delectable that he'd love to give her one. That pert little bottom and open legs was one hell of a turn-on.

Luckily, he had enough sense not to mix business with pleasure. Besides, with all the money he was going to make from this job he could have all the cuties, and all the pleasure he wanted . . .

Annie was hard at work at her sewing machine. By the light of a paraffin lamp she'd discovered in the coal shed, she was now re-hemming the curtains that should have been shortened by three inches rather than one. It was only a few days to Christmas and she fervently wished that she was working on a job that would pay, rather than spending several extra hours remedying a problem of her own making.

Fortunately, the client who ordered the curtains hadn't condemned her for her mistake and was perfectly agreeable for her to re-hem them again – at no extra charge, of course. As long as they were ready in time for Christmas. For which Annie was grateful. There might never be any more work after Christmas anyway, especially if that woman with the Yves Saint Laurent dress carried out her threat to blacken Annie's name . . .

It would be a bleak Christmas, Annie accepted. But wasn't Christmas meant to be more than just an orgy of eating, drinking and buying expensive presents? Often, she felt that the event being celebrated was overshadowed by the commercialism that now pervaded every aspect of the season. When she was small, children only got a few pennies and an orange in their Christmas stocking, but it didn't dampen their enjoyment. If anything, they derived more fun out of making their own entertainment. She sighed. Today's children got far too much in her opinion, and they were losing the real meaning of Christmas in the process. But my children certainly won't get too much this year, she thought sadly.

She heard the front door open. A quick glance at the clock told her that it was unlikely to be Frank – he'd stay at the pub until closing time. She smiled as she recognised Ciara's footsteps. Annie was glad that her daughter had been having a night out with her friends – she deserved to enjoy herself. That girl was working too hard at the shoe shop, and so generously handing over most of her pay packet. Annie wished that she didn't have to take the money. By right it should be Ciara's to buy herself whatever she wanted.

"Is that you, love?"

"Yes, Mam."

Ciara entered the room, and Annie was immediately struck by how tired and stressed her daughter looked. So Ciara's next words came as a complete surprise.

"I've got something for you," Ciara placed a bundle of banknotes on the table where Annie was still sewing. At first, Annie could hardly believe the evidence of her own eyes. She blinked, but the notes were still there.

"Mother of Divine Jesus!" she stopped the sewing machine and touched the money, as though to verify its existence. "Where in God's name did this come from?"

"I won it, at bingo," said Ciara, composing her face into a cheerful expression. "I told you our luck was going to change, didn't I?"

She couldn't look directly at her mother, but Ciara needn't have worried. Annie was so shocked and delighted at the pile of money she now gripped in her hand, that she never detected the false gaiety in her daughter's voice.

"My God," was all she could say, over and over again, staring at the money as though it might disappear if she took her eyes off it. Then, as though awakening from a trance, Annie turned to her daughter. "But this money is yours, love."

"No, Mam, it's ours," said Ciara firmly, pressing the proffered notes back into her mother's hand. "There should be enough here to pay all our school fees for the rest of the year, pay the electricity, reconnect the phone, and keep us all going for a while. At least now we can have a proper Christmas!"

BOOK 3

CHAPTER 1

Stepping off the plane in Turkey was like stepping into an oven. From Izmir airport Ciara and Dee along with a group of other tourists, were driven by coach to their various apartments and hotels in Kusadasi, approximately an hour's drive away.

Although tired, the two women were already in high holiday spirits. They'd become caught up in the infectious holiday atmosphere generated by a group of other Irish tourists, who'd been determined to start their holiday even before the plane left Dublin airport! Much good-natured singing, drinking and camaraderie had taken place on the flight, and Ciara had felt her spirits soaring as the plane reached maximum altitude.

Thank goodness Kate hadn't been able to come with them, Ciara thought. Her presence would have made the holiday intolerable. In fact, Ciara thought, I'd have backed out if Kate had been booked to come with us. At least, I can depend on Dee. As long, that was, as she could cope with her own guilt over what had transpired between her and Charlie.

Ciara now studied the landscape as they travelled, watching the women dressed in colourful traditional costumes working in the fields. Many of them waved to the bus as it passed, and Ciara marvelled at the friendliness and warmth of the ordinary Turkish people. Already, she and Dee had encountered many helpful and friendly people at the airport. She felt certain she was going to enjoy her stay here. She'd no immediate worries. Sarah was being taken care of by Cillian and Betty, so all she had to do was enjoy herself.

Ciara was brought out of her reverie by a nudge in the ribs from Dee. "I hear that Turkey is a great place for picking up men," she whispered. "The woman in the travel agency says that there are gorgeous guys available everywhere!"

Ciara laughed, but inwardly she felt a slight frisson of alarm at Dee's mischievous comments. Maybe Dee thought that a holiday romance would do Ciara some good, but she wasn't in the mood for anything like that. Ciara hoped that Dee wouldn't start trying to play matchmaker. She just wanted this holiday to be a time of healing, a chance to gain some strength for the lonely years ahead. She still found it difficult to accept the fact that Niall was gone forever, and that in the final analysis he'd betrayed her. Ciara blushed, suddenly remembering that she had betrayed the woman sitting beside her.

The apartment was cool and spacious. Ciara stretched out contentedly on her bed and surveyed the decor. She loved the elaborately-designed blue tiles that adorned much of the apartment, varieties of which she'd seen on sale in the markets they had passed on the coach. Perhaps she'd buy some for her own en-suite bathroom back home, or at least bring some back as souvenirs.

"Isn't this place gorgeous?" she said to Dee who was already unpacking.

"Hmm, you'd better start unpacking too if you want us to get out in time for a meal. It's quite late, you know, and I'm starving."

After a quick shower, change of clothes and briefing for new arrivals from the resident travel representative, both women were ready to head out towards the town centre. The heat when they stepped out of the apartment was astonishing for so late in the evening. This, combined with the holiday atmosphere in the streets, made them both feel giddy and excited.

They quickly found a delightful outdoor *lokanta* where they dined sumptuously on kebabs and fresh vegetables accompanied by the wonderful discordant sounds of Turkish music.

"Isn't this the life?" said Dee as they raised their glasses in a toast.

Ciara nodded. She was very relaxed and happy, and could actually think of Niall without being overcome by sorrow. And, as long as she was pleasantly merry with Turkish wine, thoughts of Kate's involvement with Niall could be consigned to the deepest recesses of her mind.

The waiters were charming, flirting with them all through the meal, and Dee sparkled as one particularly handsome young waiter paid extra-special attention to her. Finally, he announced that since he was about to go off duty, he'd accompany them to a nearby bar where he'd treat them both to glasses of *raki*, the Turkish national drink.

He was delightful company, and Ciara was amused to notice how flirtatious Dee had become in his presence. She seemed to be deliberately leading him on, and Ciara found herself becoming increasingly embarrassed as the night wore on. Eventually, feeling rather like a gooseberry, she excused herself by pleading tiredness.

"OK, I'll hang on a bit longer with Serpil," said Dee, giving the handsome Lothario a suggestive squeeze. "I have my own key, so don't wait up for me. G'night, Ciara."

As she reached the door Ciara glanced over her shoulder and raised her hand in a farewell gesture, only to discover that the two lovebirds were already fawning over each other and her existence had already been forgotten. Bemused, Ciara wandered up the hill towards the apartment.

It was a beautiful night, and she took deep breaths to draw the humid sweet-smelling air deep into her lungs. She felt strangely at peace here. She thought of other nights, now in the distant past, when she and Niall had wandered arm in arm along other Mediterranean shores. And the memories brought tears to her eyes as she now wondered if they were worth preserving. Had he been seeing the other woman then? Maybe he'd been counting the days till he could get back to her . . .

It was dawn before Dee returned. Ciara had woken early and, finding that her friend's bed hadn't been slept in, she'd become extremely worried. Dee had consumed a lot of *raki* the previous night, and Ciara feared that she might have been taken advantage of by the Turkish Casanova.

"Thank goodness!" said Ciara, sitting up in her bed when she heard Dee's key in the lock. "I've been really worried. I was afraid something might have happened to you."

"Give over, Ciara," Dee snapped. "You're not my jailer."

Ciara sat open-mouthed in surprise. "I – I'm sorry. I was just concerned."

"Well, I'm a big girl now and I make my own decisions. I'll fuck whoever I want, whenever I want. And I don't need you, or anyone else, fussing over me."

Ciara lay down in her bed again. She was shocked, not only by Dee's rudeness but by the fact that she'd clearly spent the night with the Turkish waiter from the previous night. She'd assumed that Dee and Charlie were faithful to each other.

Then colouring, she thought of her own brief lapse with Charlie. Had she been wrong about Dee? Was this Dee's way of letting her know that men, anyone's man, even Niall, were fair game? Maybe Dee knew about Kate's fling with Niall. Maybe they were both laughing at her behind her back! Perhaps Dee had also had an affair with Niall! Or had Dee found out about her and Charlie and was retaliating before a showdown? God, what a mess!

As if she'd heard Ciara's unspoken question, Dee turned to face her. "If you want to spend every night of this holiday in your virginal bed, that's your problem. But I won't be." With that, she threw off her crumpled clothes and stepped into the shower.

Ciara got up and busied herself in the small kitchen making coffee, then carried two full steaming mugs back to the bedroom. But when she entered the room she discovered that Dee had left the shower, got into her bed and was already fast asleep. Despite the tension that had been generated, Ciara smiled to herself. Clearly Dee was worn out from her nocturnal activities!

At least today, she thought, I'm getting my original wish which was to spend some time alone. Picking up her towel, swimsuit and a novel Ciara quietly let herself out of the apartment and headed for the beach.

Being a market town, Kusadasi had no proper beach, so Ciara travelled to nearby Gumbet by *dolmus*, a kind of minibus taxi packed with local people, their animals and bags of fruit and groceries from the local market. Sandwiched between two goats that kept chewing her hair, she'd feared ending up bald until she'd hit upon the idea of distracting them with the fruit she'd brought along for her lunch.

Sitting at last on Gumbet beach, Ciara watched the waves pounding onto the shore and was calmed by its relentless rhythm. The artist in her drew pleasure from the many patterns that the waves made as they tumbled onto the beach, each spray overlapping the remains of the one before, creating a vast patchwork of designs as the foam dispersed over the sands before sliding back into the sea again.

As she walked barefoot along the edge of the spray, Ciara suddenly felt at peace. She hadn't felt that way for a very long time. Some day soon, she vowed, I'll be happy again. I will. I know I will.

CHAPTER 2

Isn't it strange, Ciara, how some of the most important things in our lives happen quite by accident? For years I'd been trying desperately to think of a way to win Niall back from you, yet the means to do so was right under my nose!

On this particular day, I stopped off at the newspaper to see if the colour photographs for one of my weekly features had been processed yet. One of the photographers, Alan Moore, was in the darkroom when I entered. He was looking at a series of photographs taken at a launch you'd attended and making sexist grunting noises to indicate how attractive he thought you were.

Alan was one of the most blatantly chauvinistic men I'd ever met, but because he was so pathetic it was hard to take offence. Besides, I had to work with him regularly, so there was no advantage in taking him to task over his remarks other than to indicate how unworthy of comment I found them.

His passion, apart from women, was motorbikes and he was the proud possessor of a monstrously ugly Harley Davidson and a top-of-the-range Electra Glide. Thankfully, he had to use a car for work assignments! But even when we occasionally travelled on assignment together, he was forever stopping to admire other bikes and discussing the merits of specific models with their owners. Back in the darkroom, if he wasn't leering over photos of semi-naked women he'd photographed at receptions and then tried to chat up, he was drooling over motorbike magazines. His current aim in life was to own a Triumph Bonneville which I gather was an equally monstrous, ugly and noisy contraption.

"Hi," he said, "are you looking for those pics of the Minister? They're on the scanner over there."

Having decided on the picture I wanted to use I was about to leave, but Alan was in a talkative mood. "Not bad pics of Ciara Reynolds, eh?" *he asked rhetorically.* "I took them the other night at an art exhibition in town. She's still quite a looker, isn't she? Although she must be getting on now."

I looked at the pictures on his screen. You certainly looked well, Ciara. You were smiling and chatting to several well-known people, looking effortlessly young and pretty in a simple, well-cut dress. And once again, I felt the unfairness of it all.

"Great body too, looks just as good as it did years ago," *Alan looked directly at me, hoping for a reaction.* "You know Ciara, don't you? But I'll bet you didn't know I once took nude photos of Miss High and Mighty herself!"

Suddenly he had my undivided attention, although I wasn't going to let him know. "No, I didn't. When was that?" *I asked, trying to look only slightly interested. But my heart was pounding with excitement.*

"It was back in . . . Oh, it must be nearly thirty years ago.

She was about fifteen or sixteen. Still at school, but she knew the value of money, that one. She was a bit prudish at first, and terrified that anyone would find out, but like I always say, everyone has their price. Even the clean-living, butter-wouldn't-melt types – they all have their price."

He looked happy at being able to prove the frailty of human nature. Perhaps it made his own failings seem less unworthy.

"What did you do with the photos?" I asked.

"Sold them to a German porno magazine," he boasted. "Made quite a packet for myself too. They were so impressed, they wanted to run another series of her photos. I think it was that mixture of innocence and voluptuousness that got them. But by then she was making a bit of money through selling her paintings, so she wouldn't hear tell of it," he sighed in mock despair. "That was the easiest money I ever made. And it wasn't exactly the most boring job I've ever done either!" he grinned at me. "I wonder what she'd say if she knew that I've kept all the negatives?"

So even you, Ciara, had a dark secret. At last I'd found something that showed you weren't perfect, something that could tarnish your wholesome reputation. Maybe I could now use it to destroy you as you once destroyed me.

Of course, I couldn't afford to let Alan see how interested I was in this piece of news. Nor did I see how I could get possession of the negatives without showing my own hand, and perhaps giving Alan a reason to blackmail me in turn.

"Really?" I said, with a studied shrug of my shoulders. "What on earth have you kept them for?"

"Oh, I don't know," he said sheepishly. "I suppose I just kept them to remind myself of one of the best-paying nixers I ever did. Besides, she was a fine-looking bird then, you know."

I let the sexist terminology pass without comment. I was too busy trying to figure out what my next move should be. I didn't see how I could ask to buy the negatives, nor could I steal them easily, since Alan obviously didn't keep them in the newspaper office! But maybe I could ensure that indirectly I got what I wanted. A plan of sorts was already beginning to form in my mind . . .

All that night I paced the floor at home making endless cups of coffee and trying to figure out how I could best use those photographs to my advantage.

Even if I opted to buy the photos myself, what could I do with them? If I sent them to Niall anonymously, how would that benefit me personally? Even if it meant the end of your marriage, Ciara, that gave me no guarantee that Niall would ever be mine again. If I presented the photos to him in person, what would my reason be? He'd probably hate me for it anyway, and that wouldn't further my own cause at all. Besides, what would Alan Moore think if I asked him to sell me the photos?

Suddenly, the most beautiful plan materialised in my brain. It was so perfect that it almost took my breath away. This way, I was certain that I could achieve everything that I wanted. And it would cost me nothing, except perhaps the bills for a few expensive meals out. And I knew they'd be worth every penny.

Thankfully, I had a reason for being in the newspaper office the following morning since I was due to discuss the content and layout of a new feature series with the editor. Needless to say, I watched keenly for Alan Moore's arrival. Then I had to wait even longer for the right moment to speak to him in private.

351

That opportunity didn't occur until late morning when all the other photographers were out on assignments, and Alan was alone in the studio selecting photos for publication.

"Hi, Alan," I said, breezing in and trying to sound relaxed and friendly, "I wonder if Gary's got the pics of last night's charity bash in the Shelbourne. If there's a good one of the Minister, I might ask Peter to use it with my feature."

Of course, I knew Gary wasn't in yet. Nor did I care.

"Dunno. Want me to check?"

"No, not at all, Alan. Thanks, but there's no rush."

I gave him my most winning smile. He was one of those typical chauvinists who thought that if a woman so much as looked at him, she was bound to be crazy about him.

"What are you working on today?" I asked, leaning across to look at his computer screen and admire the photographs he was sorting through.

"Nothing much. I'm just selecting a few pics to go with the feature on Page Five. Can you believe it, another shower of bloody politicians are going on a junket abroad!" Alan grumbled as he clicked through a selection of photos of the country's lord mayors, TDs and local councillors. "I don't know how those bastards make so much money and get so many perks."

"Well, you could make a nice little nest-egg for yourself," I said softly.

"What do you mean?"

"You've got those negatives of Ciara Reynolds, haven't you? The ones you were telling me about yesterday."

"So what?"

For a moment my nerve almost failed. "So why don't you tell her you've still got them?" I suggested brightly. "I'm sure she'd pay you well to get the originals back. After all, she has a certain image to maintain. She'd hardly want people knowing that she'd been a pornographic model. And I don't see why a clever guy like you shouldn't make a few extra pounds for himself."

I was piling on the flattery which I knew always worked with guys like Alan. But I had to be careful not to make him suspicious as a result. But everything seemed to be working out well. I could see that the cogs in his brain were now turning over and gathering momentum. And while he didn't really like the idea of blackmail, he did like the idea of getting his hands on some easy cash. Perhaps he just needed a gentle prod in the right direction.

"Then you could buy that Triumph Bonneville you're always talking about," I added quietly.

He looked at me through narrowed eyes, and I could see that already his mind was more or less made up. The pathetic fool was thinking of all the women he could impress with a new, deluxe-model motorbike.

"You're hardly telling me this for the good of my health," he said. "What do you expect to get out of it? If you're looking for a percentage . . ."

I quickly held up my hands in a gesture of supplication. "No, no. I don't want anything," I said, laughing at the absurdity of such a thing, "but you could do me a special favour."'

He folded his arms and looked at me suspiciously, as though he didn't believe I could be satisfied with such a small pay-off. Or else he feared that the favour could prove to be more costly than any cash terms.

"Look," I said, "as soon as you've talked to Ciara Reynolds

on the phone, I'd like you to arrange two meetings – say, a preliminary one at lunchtime next Friday. And I'd like you to be particularly friendly towards her."

"What on earth for?"

"No questions asked. Of course, I'll pay for both meals. And have as many bottles of wine as you want."

He continued to look at me suspiciously.

I laughed. "I'm not going to have the money hijacked or anything like that, Alan! I don't even want to know how much you're going to get paid, but good luck to you. If you can get a good price for them, you deserve it." I beamed at him because I was suddenly feeling very happy. "But with your co-operation, Alan, I'd like to arrange a little scenario of my own."

CHAPTER 3

Having left an envelope full of money for Mrs Daly, her weekly cleaning woman who would be the one to find her body, Ita wrote a note for Liam, collected her new supply of tablets from the bathroom cabinet and placed them in readiness on the bedside table. She'd showered, made up her face carefully but sparingly, and changed into a long satin nightdress. She inspected herself in the mirror, and concluded with satisfaction that she looked extremely elegant. This time, she intended to depart life in style. Now, as she sat by the bedside table, poised to take the pills, the doorbell rang.

Damn! She'd had the foresight to take the phone off the hook, but the doorbell was something she hadn't thought about. She hadn't been expecting any callers, which was precisely why she'd opted to end it all this evening. It was probably somebody making door-to-door collections on behalf of some charity, so hopefully they'd go away soon. She'd already left several bequests to charities in her will, so they could go to hell as far as she was concerned.

But the ringing of the doorbell persisted, and in exasperation Ita went out into the hall and switched on the intercom.

"Who's there?" she asked abruptly.

A trembling voice answered. "It's me, Ita. Sarah – Ciara Reynolds' daughter."

"Oh. What do you want?" As soon as she'd said it, Ita realised how harsh her response sounded. But she was annoyed at being disturbed. It wasn't even possible to end your own life in peace! There was always something or somebody getting in the way.

"I – could I talk to you for a minute?"

Ita hesitated, trying frantically to think of some excuse, but nothing believable came into her head.

"Look, if it's too much trouble, I'll go –"

"No, it's OK," Ashamed now, Ita pressed the admission button. "Come on up. I'm on the third floor."

Quickly, Ita swept up the pills and stuffed them under the bed. She took quick stock of the flat and decided that there was no further incriminating evidence on display. Which was just as well, since she could already hear Sarah's footsteps in the corridor outside followed by a hesitant knock on the door.

Opening the door, Ita expected to find the usual bouncy and opinionated teenager before her. But instead, this was a subdued and frightened child. She was wearing far too much make-up and her face had a sad, clown-like quality about it like someone trying to grow up far too fast.

"Are you all right?" Ita asked, wondering if perhaps there was something the matter with Ciara.

Sarah smiled wanly, and Ita's heart went out to her. The child looked so forlorn that it was clear that everything wasn't all right.

"Sorry, Ita, I know it's late, and I can see you're ready for bed. But I need your help. I hope you don't mind me coming to you, but I didn't feel that I could face anyone else." Tears had started to run silently down Sarah's cheeks and she angrily wiped them away. "I'm pregnant, Ita. And I just don't know what to do."

"I presume you haven't told your mother?"

"God, no. I couldn't possibly tell her!"

"But why have you come to see me?"

"I – I don't know. I didn't want to tell anyone in school. They wouldn't know what to do anyway." Sarah drew a deep breath, "I suppose it's because you're not really one of Mummy's close friends. At least, not yet. Maybe you will be, when you and Liam get married –"

"Go on."

"I mean, I couldn't go to Kate or Dee. They might feel that they had to tell her. But you –" Sarah gulped. "It probably sounds stupid, but I just felt that you'd understand. That you wouldn't sit in judgement on me . . ."

Ita laughed mirthlessly. "Good God, Sarah, I've less right than anyone to judge you. If you only knew! Sit down, and tell me how it all happened. Wait, let's go into the kitchen and I'll make us both a cuppa."

Gratefully Sarah followed, and perched herself on a stool at the oak counter while Ita put the kettle on.

"First, Sarah., I have to ask you this. Are you absolutely sure you're pregnant?"

Sarah nodded miserably. "I had a test done at the Well Woman Clinic. There's absolutely no doubt about it."

"Why on earth didn't you use some kind of contraception?" Ita asked, exasperated.

Sarah studied her shoes in minute detail. "I – I mean we –" she looked up at Ita. "Nothing was supposed to happen –" she confessed. "You see, we were both quite drunk." She looked at Ita, expecting to see disapproval, but, when she didn't, she continued. "I was with this guy at a party, and we went upstairs. I just wanted to lie down for a while because I had a terrible headache from all the stuff I was drinking. He gave me something to take to make me feel better – I don't remember much after that."

Ita sighed. The same old story, told by countless generations of pregnant young women the world over. "So what do you want to do, have the baby?"

Sarah looked horrified. "God, no. I couldn't possibly. I'm only fifteen! I could never look after a child. I'm only a child myself!"

The enormity of her own admission brought a fresh wave of tears. Big drops rolled down Sarah's cheeks, and plopped onto the floor. Combined with her mascara and eyeliner, her tears left grey-black patches on the off-white carpet, and seeing what had happened Sarah immediately broke into a fresh bout of crying. Anxiously, she got down on her knees and began rubbing at the stains with a dirty tissue she'd found in her pocket, and Ita had to pull her firmly to her feet.

"For heaven's sake, forget about the carpet. That's not

important now. The important thing is to make arrangements for you to have an abortion. As long as you're really sure that's what you want?"

Sarah nodded.

Thank goodness that in this day and age, Ita reflected, Sarah needn't suffer as countless generations of Irish women did in the past. Abortion was now legally available in Britain, although the Irish were still hypocritical enough to refuse to allow abortions on their own home ground. So Irishwomen still had to make the journey across the Irish Sea to terminate their unwanted pregnancies.

"Tea or coffee?" Ita asked, putting the kettle on to boil.

"Tea, please," Sarah replied, quite forgetting how much more sophisticated coffee was regarded by her friends. Right now, she needed the comfort of what she actually enjoyed best.

Ita brought two mugs to the counter and sat down beside Sarah. "Honestly Sarah, I really do think you should talk to your mother."

"No!" screamed Sarah, "I can't – I won't! And if you're going to make me –"

Sarah had visions once again of her mother writhing on the floor with Charlie Somers. How could she hope for any sympathy from a woman who could behave like that, when her own husband was hardly cold in the grave? "Anyway, she's away on holiday," Sarah added, her tone implying that her mother had more or less abandoned her.

"It's all right, calm down," said Ita soothingly, placing her hand gently on Sarah's arm. "I just felt that I had to say that to you. Because even if your mother's upset at first, she'll want to do what's best for you."

"I'm not telling my mother, and that's final!" said Sarah stubbornly. "If you don't want to help me, then I'll go —" she made a half-hearted attempt to stand up, looking forlorn and vulnerable, almost daring Ita to reject her.

"Sit down, and stop behaving so stupidly," said Ita crossly. "Of course I'll help you. You know that. Have you said anything to the boy involved?"

Sarah sat down again looking horrified at the thought of speaking to Brian about it. "God, no. He'd tell everyone in the school. He's just an immature, self-centred scumbag!"

Ita sighed. At least Sarah had no illusions about getting any support there. Which was probably a good thing. The fewer people involved, the better off Sarah would ultimately be.

"No one knows but you," Sarah finished.

"Are you absolutely sure that you want to go ahead with an abortion? You could wait a few more weeks before making a decision."

Sarah shook her head. "I know what I'm doing, Ita. You might think I'm just a spoilt kid, but I do realise what's involved. And I'd rather get it sorted out while my mother's away."

She looked at Ita with brimming eyes. "But I know that every day, probably for the rest of my life, I'll wonder what this baby would have been like. I'll wonder if it was a boy or a girl and even if I have other kids later on, I'll never forget this one. But my life is only beginning, Ita.

Maybe I'm selfish, but I want a career and a life of my own first."

Ita went to her, enfolding Sarah in her arms, and was surprised to discover that she herself was crying too. As they broke apart, Ita tilted Sarah's chin upwards.

"C'mon, let's have a big smile. I'll come with you to England. And don't worry about money – I have more than enough. We'll get you the very best of care."

Sarah looked gratefully at the older woman through her tears. "Thanks, Ita," she said quietly. "I don't really know how to say this, but I feel as though –" she stopped, looking embarrassed. "Oh, I don't know. It sounds stupid. But it's almost as though, I just had a gut feeling that I could count on you. That you'd be there for me."

Ita said nothing. She felt guilty that it was she rather than Ciara who was comforting and advising Sarah. Yet on a practical level she doubted that Ciara would be able to cope with this extra bombshell, on top of all she'd already been through. Ita sighed. For now, her own plans would have to be put on hold. Maybe in some strange way, there were still things she had to do.

Sarah stood up to go. "Thanks, Ita," she said, hugging the older woman tightly. "I feel a lot better now."

"Good. There's no need for you to worry any more," Ita replied. "I'll make a few phone calls tomorrow and arrange for us to travel. And don't worry about your relatives – I'll invite you on a holiday or something. But if you change your mind you know I'll be there for you, no matter what you decide."

Sarah shook her head sadly. "I won't change my mind."

After Sarah left, Ita took the bottle of tablets from under the bed and put it away in the bathroom cabinet. Thwarted again! But she was no longer angry. She had a mission to complete before she would need those tablets again.

"Hello Betty, it's Ita Byrne. I'm a friend of Ciara's and Liam Golden's."

"Oh yes, I remember meeting you at Niall's funeral."

Ita took a deep breath. "I'm ringing you to ask if Sarah could come to London with me next week. I have to go over on business. We could make a long weekend of it and take in a few shows as well. I'm sure Ciara wouldn't mind."

"That's very kind of you, Ita," Betty replied. "Personally I don't see a problem, although I'd better mention it to Cillian first. I'm sure Sarah would love the trip. After all, it's her mid-term break next week."

Betty was delighted at the prospect of offloading her sister-in-law's stubborn brat onto anyone who'd have her. Sarah was already becoming a disruptive influence on the entire household, even though she'd only been staying with them for a few days so far! She'd persuade Cillian that it was a wonderful opportunity for Sarah, and if he proved recalcitrant she'd pick a row with him until he gave in.

Betty adopted her most caring tone of voice. "The break might actually do the poor child a lot of good, and I'm sure she'd love to go. Have you asked her yet?"

The lie came easily. "No, I wanted to ask your permission first. I think she's been taking her father's death badly. Maybe a change of scene would do her good. Besides –" Ita paused, "I'd really enjoy having her along for company. Spending the evenings alone in a city like London is no fun. But together, Sarah and I can explore and do a bit of shopping as well."

"Sounds really nice," said Betty wistfully.

For one dreadful moment, Ita feared that Betty might suggest coming along herself. But the moment of danger passed, and Betty simply expressed the hope that the two of them would have a great time. Ita sighed with relief. So far everything was going according to plan.

CHAPTER 4

"May I speak to Niall Delaney?"

"`Yes, of course. Who's calling?"

I gave my name to the receptionist, and the next moment Niall was on the line.

"Hi, great to hear from you. What can I do for you?"

"Niall, I have to write a feature about new developments in the field of alternative health. I know that you have the account for one of the companies specialising in this field. Can I treat you to lunch some day this week, say Friday? I need to pick your brains on the subject, and maybe I can give your people some publicity in return."

I knew I was rattling on unnecessarily, but I was worried in case he'd have a prior appointment.

"Friday? Hmm, that's not a good day for me."

My heart sank. "Oh dear. Is there any way you can manage it? My deadline for this piece is next Monday."

It wasn't true, of course. This feature was never going to see the light of day!

"`Wait, maybe I can bring forward my twelve o'clock appointment to eleven thirty. OK, I can sort that out and be free from twelve thirty."

I breathed an inaudible sigh of relief. "That's marvellous, Niall. I'll book a table somewhere nice for around twelve thirty."

I hesitated. "Look, Niall. Don't mention this meeting to anyone, will you? I've heard a rumour that one of the Sundays is planning to run a series on the same subject, and obviously I'd like to get in there first."

Niall laughed. "God, you journalists are as paranoid as the Secret Service! Don't worry. I won't mention it to anyone!"

I laughed in return, but more from relief than in response to his joke.

"Thanks, Niall," I said, sounding immensely grateful. "I'll phone you back when I've booked a table."

I knew exactly where we were going, but I'd wait until the last moment before phoning him back. The reason was because I didn't want you to know where Niall and I were lunching, Ciara. Although there would be no suspicion attached to Niall meeting me, after all we were colleagues and friends, I didn't want Niall mentioning to you where we were dining. Because if you knew, you'd refuse to go there with Alan Moore.

So far, so good. But now that I'd set the plan in motion I could see all the flaws in it. It could still fall through if I was unable to synchronise the arrival onstage of the various players in this little drama. But there was little point in worrying about the second act, until the first act had taken place!

I lifted the phone and dialled Chi Chi's Restaurant in the Powerscourt Centre.

"Hello, I'd like to book a table for two on the balcony please *for lunchtime on Friday. Twelve thirty? The corner table? That's perfect, thank you."*

I arrived at Chi Chi's ten minutes early. I wanted to ensure that I'd been allotted the most strategically-placed table for my plan to work, and I was even prepared to bribe the staff to change it if necessary. I also wanted to be in place by the time Niall arrived, so that he would have to sit in the chair I'd selected for him. I also needed to be sure that from our vantage point we could clearly see the diners on the level below us, but that they couldn't easily see us.

Since it was still early for the lunch trade the restaurant was almost empty, so I tried the seats at several different tables to see how the scene below would unfold. Finally, I settled for the original table I'd booked where potted palms offered considerable cover, yet which would enable both Niall and me to see all that was happening below. Now all I had to do was wait.

Promptly at twelve thirty Niall arrived, joining me at my chosen table. I immediately ordered a bottle of red wine. There was nothing more potent, I found, than a glass of good burgundy to encourage a state of paranoia.

"I've brought you some background information," said Niall, producing a folder full of paper and momentarily shaking me out of my reverie. I'd been so involved with my own plans that I'd forgotten the reason we were meeting!

"Oh, thanks. That's marvellous. But let's have our meal before we talk. I don't know about you, Niall, but I'm absolutely starving!"

Niall smiled, and my heart did a somersault. I desperately wanted this man – he was the only man I'd ever really loved. And soon, if all went as planned, he'd be smiling at me in the *way he'd always smiled at you, Ciara. He'd be smiling tenderly at me as we toasted each other across tiny tables in candle-lit restaurants, and smiling that smile as he lay happily and satisfied beside me in bed . . .*

As our starters were served, Niall and I talked generally about his work and mine. I excelled myself with bright chatter and anecdotes, while all the time I couldn't keep my eyes off the lower level of the restaurant. By now tables were filling up rapidly, and I was inwardly cursing Alan Moore for not having appeared yet.

Then I saw him arrive, and take the table pre-arranged for him and his guest. I sighed with relief. Although that specific table had been booked, the best-laid plans could still have come undone. After all, it would be difficult to dislodge patrons who'd already installed themselves there by mistake. However, everything was going according to plan so far, but I was still nervous. After all, I'd only two chances to get this scenario right.

Then at last I saw you arrive, Ciara. As always, you looked both elegant and trendy. Your smart black jacket was business-like, and your short beige skirt spelt defiance. Yet I knew, by the tension in your jaw that it was all just a front. In reality, you were scared and angry. And if you'd known the plans I had for your husband, you'd have been a lot more frightened.

As you reached the table, Alan leapt up and embraced you like a long-lost friend. Although my own heart was thumping madly, I tried to assess the situation objectively and I happily concluded that, if I hadn't known the true set-up, I'd have assumed that you were either very close friends or lovers. Niall knew that you weren't close friends, so hopefully he'd jump to the other conclusion . . .

"Oh look, Niall. Isn't that Ciara just arriving at that table below?"

"Ciara?"

I was gratified by the surprise in Niall's voice. As I'd hoped, he hadn't told you about our lunch date, Ciara. And as he peered down at you from between the palm fronds, he clearly didn't expect to see you dining out that day.

I took a quick peep myself. Alan Moore now had you gripped in a warm embrace. Good old Alan, I thought, he really is fulfilling his side of our little bargain. But then wasn't he simply ensuring that I'd no reason to blackmail him either?

Niall smiled. "What a coincidence, both of us lunching in the same restaurant and neither knowing about the other!"

I smiled in agreement. "That's Alan Moore. Do you know him, Niall? He's a newspaper photographer – you must know him."

"No, I can't say I've ever met him."

"Nice guy," I said between mouthfuls. "Great photographer, too. He won a big award last year for his coverage of the elections. Used to work in England before he was wooed back to Ireland again. I'd imagine that Ciara meets him regularly at receptions," I paused. "Women just adore him."

"Hmm. I suppose he must be planning to take some photographs of Ciara's paintings."

"Yes, that's probably why they're meeting."

The waiter arrived and took away our plates. After topping up our wine glasses he left and headed for the kitchens to collect our next course.

"He's certainly got a way with women, hasn't he?" I said, laughing as I inclined my head towards the table downstairs

where Alan was now chatting flirtatiously to you, Ciara.
Luckily, Niall couldn't see your face. I'd even ensured you'd be
seated with your back to us so that Niall couldn't see how
unhappy you really were. After all, I wanted him to think that
you were having a wonderful time.

I leaned across and patted Niall's hand gently. "I'm sure
Ciara will tell you all about it tonight."

Our main course soon arrived, and as the waiter served us
I darted a surreptitious glance at the table below. I was happy
to see that Alan was holding onto your hand and looking
affectionately into your eyes. Then I glanced at Niall and saw
that he, too, kept looking down at the table below us.

"How's your steak, Niall?"

"Oh, it's great." Guiltily, he took a quick mouthful. "Really
great, thanks."

Throughout the meal we made desultory conversation.
Niall appeared to have forgotten the reason for our meeting,
and I was glad. Outwardly he seemed relaxed enough, but I
didn't miss the regular glances directed towards the table
downstairs where thankfully Alan was performing with great
aplomb.

I prolonged our own meal until you and Alan got up to
leave, Ciara, at exactly the time he and I had arranged. Niall
and I watched as Alan made a great fuss of kissing your cheek,
and helping you on with your jacket.

"Well, Ciara seems to know him very well, even if you
don't," I said as Alan followed you out of the restaurant. "Isn't
it a giggle that we've spotted them, but they haven't seen us?"
I drank my wine slowly, to ensure that you and Alan Moore
were well out of the way before Niall and I left the restaurant,
Ciara. Eventually I looked at my watch. "Good Lord, is it that

time already?" I asked. "Can you believe it, Niall. We never even got around to discussing the alternative health stuff!"

Niall grinned apologetically. "Sorry. I haven't earned my lunch today, have I? But take a look through the file I've brought you. It should give you most of the background information you need as well as details of the latest research being done on re-discovered plants. If you need any more information, give me a call and I'll see what I can do."

"Thanks, Niall," I said warmly, giving his arm an affectionate but gentle squeeze. And despite his protests I insisted on paying the bill as we left the restaurant. Outside in the street we parted company, each of us heading back to our respective offices. Niall didn't know it, but if my plan continued to work this smoothly, he'd be seeing me again much sooner than he expected . . .

CHAPTER 5

After a solitary but pleasant day, Ciara returned to the apartment to find that Dee was up and dressed.

"Oh great, you're back," Dee said, as though nothing had happened. "It's time we went out for dinner. I'm starving! Did you have a good day?"

"Yes," said Ciara, responding to Dee's good humour, "I had a great time relaxing on the beach at Gumbet. Then I came back and had lunch in one of the cafés down the street, and went for a long walk around the town."

"Great, how long will it take you to get ready?"

"Two minutes," said Ciara, heading into the shower. "By the way, I found out that Ephesus isn't too far away. I've always wanted to see the ancient city and the amphitheatre."

Showering and changing quickly, Ciara was soon ready to go out. She too was feeling hungry, and looking forward to some more delicious Turkish food. Already she was hooked on the incredible range of fruit and vegetables available, and she'd adored the previous evening's meal of fried aubergines for starter, followed by *kofte*, a delicious dish of minced lamb croquettes, washed down with *ayran*, a type of liquid yoghurt that just melted in the mouth.

As she and Dee dined that evening they talked about the food, local customs, and the fabulous leather coats, suits, bags and belts available in the shops. Ciara was concerned about how the leather was obtained, but given the pleasant atmosphere between her and Dee she decided not to express her own personal concerns about animal welfare. Dee's good humour had been restored, but Ciara wondered whether Dee was planning to spend another night with her Turkish Casanova.

After the meal, the two women left the *lokanta* and headed for one of the many *birahanes*, or bars, throughout the town. They opted for a lively bar on the outskirts of the town where they had a panoramic view of the sea. A group of Turkish men chatted across to them from another table and sent them across a complimentary bottle of *raki*. Despite the late hour, the town was still lively with shops and stalls still open, locals and tourists everywhere.

Dee drank with gusto, as though Prohibition might be introduced overnight. She was knocking back two glasses of *raki* for every one Ciara drank, but after her earlier outburst that day Ciara thought it wiser to keep quiet.

Trying to look nonchalant, the men at the nearby table moved to a table closer by and were clearly interested in chatting them up. Ciara found it all rather amusing. She didn't fancy any of them, but she wondered idly if Dee did. After the previous night's escapade, anything could be on the cards! If Dee *was* interested in any of them, hopefully she could slip away quietly without creating any bad feeling. Ciara had been surreptitiously watching Dee, when suddenly their eyes locked and Ciara found herself squirming with embarrassment.

"Go on." said Dee. "Say something. I know you're dying to."

Taken by surprise, Ciara nevertheless decided to take the bull by the horns. "Look, Dee, I just think that maybe we should clear up any misunderstanding –"

"What the hell is there to talk about? I know you don't approve of what I did last night. Well, too bad. I'm not going to sit here and be lectured to by you –"

"I have no intention of lecturing you! I don't care what you do!" Ciara took a deep breath. "As long as, I mean, as long as you don't involve me."

"What do you mean by that?"

"Right now, I'm not interested in getting involved with men myself. Maybe later, but just not yet," she took a deep breath, "and I don't want Charlie thinking I was party to what you're doing." Ciara sighed. Who was she to sound so moralistic? Wasn't she just as guilty over her fling with Charlie?

"Yes," said Dee, pouring herself another glass of wine from the bottle which the group of men had sent across, "I'm sure you don't want to be involved. As long as your little world is OK, to hell with everyone else. Little Miss Goody Two-Shoes always does everything right. Perfect husband, perfect child, perfect life." She raised her glass and looked insolently at Ciara. "Here's to your perfect, perfect life!"

Ignoring the insult, Ciara leaned over and touched Dee's arm. It was burning as though she had a fever. "Dee – why? I thought you and Charlie were happy together . . ."

"You thought. What would you know about anything, except your own perfect, perfect life?"

"My life isn't perfect – my husband's just died!"

"Well, at least you had years of happiness with him!"

Ciara accepted Dee's retort with equanimity. Dee was right – she'd pompously assumed that she had a right to know all about her friends' lives, while refusing to share with them what was going on in her own.

"Look, Dee . . ."

Dee's eyes were glistening, but whether from anger or tears Ciara was uncertain. "It doesn't matter. Nothing really matters any more," she said sadly.

"Of course it does. You're just getting depressed from all the *raki*. Everything will seem better in the morning."

"No, it won't. He's gone, isn't he? I'll never see him again!"

Suddenly, Ciara was afraid to ask who 'he' was.

"You know, I've had a life that you know nothing about Ciara," Dee slurred. "How could I tell you? You with your perfect life! But we're not all lucky enough to marry the man of our dreams. And when you're the loser, you have to collect the crumbs left over by the ones who have it all!" She raised her glass in a mock toast. "You want to know why a so-called happily married woman has affairs behind her husband's back? Well, here's your answer – I'm not happily married. Mind you, Charlie thinks he is. That's how little communication there is between us. He thinks I'm happily married too!" Dee laughed hysterically at her own joke.

Ciara was shocked. She'd always assumed that Dee and Charlie loved each other.

"But what if Charlie found out? About you and these –"

Dee stood up in agitation, faltered, then sat down again, picking up her glass of *raki* and emptying it down her throat. Then she looked across at Ciara with a slightly cynical expression. "Well, are you going to tell him?"

Ciara coloured. "No, of course not. But –"

"Well then, he's not going to find out is he? Besides –" she looked at Ciara, a taunting expression replacing the tearful one, "who knows what he's up to, anyway? Maybe he's having lots of affairs himself. There's so little communication between us, I wouldn't know. In fact –" she looked triumphantly at Ciara, "maybe he's even had a fling with you!"

Ciara blushed deep red, and seeing her obvious discomfort, Dee became instantly apologetic. "Oh God, Ciara. I'm sorry. That was really below the belt. I've had too much to drink." Then she giggled hysterically at her own unintended joke. "Below the belt – what a pun! But you must admit, Ciara, it's a hilarious idea! I can just imagine you and Charlie tearing each other's clothes off in the throes of passion."

Still giggling, Dee reached for the bottle and began refilling their glasses. Ciara was glad of the opportunity to gain some composure, for her cheeks were burning and her mind was full of guilty memories. For one awful moment, she'd been afraid that Dee had guessed the truth or that Charlie had confessed before they'd come away on holiday.

At last, Ciara felt sufficiently composed to continue the conversation. "But I still don't understand –"

"Well, you wouldn't, would you? You see, I never got what I wanted from Charlie. He was always second-best, you know."

Ciara was suddenly filled with dread. What did Dee mean? Could she possibly mean what Ciara desperately feared she might mean?

Dee laughed bitterly. "I tried to tell him a thousand times that I wasn't happy. But he was always rushing off somewhere, usually to play golf – building his career, he called it. And he never had time to discuss it. That way he could ignore the problem, and continue doing exactly what he wanted to do."

"Maybe he did that because he didn't want to hear what you were saying. Because he was terrified at the thought of losing you."

"Well, it's too late now, anyway. There was only ever one man for me – and now he's gone."

Ciara felt as though she was about to have a heart attack. She could barely breathe, and her throat felt so constricted that she could barely speak. She didn't want to hear any more. But Dee clearly intended to keep talking. It was as though having opened the floodgates, nothing could now stop the flow.

The bar was now almost empty. The group of men, noting the women's self-absorption, had given up on them and moved on to more receptive pastures. The air was now filled with the sound of crickets and the distant pounding of a late-night disco.

"I married Charlie on the rebound, Ciara, you must know that. Because you'd managed to bag the prize specimen."

Ciara's heart almost stopped. She gripped the edge of the table, terrified of what Dee was going to say next.

Dee waved her glass, oblivious to the fact that she was spilling half of it on the table. "Oh, Charlie loves me, in his own way. But not the way I want to be loved. He just loves me because I'm there. I'm part of the furniture, I get his meals ready, I fuck him when he wants to be fucked –" she laughed at the shocked expression on Ciara's face. "I needed this holiday to get away and think, Ciara. And I've decided that I'm going to leave Charlie. You see, I've lived a double life for years and I don't want to do it any longer. The only man I ever really loved is dead, and I want my own space to grieve for him as I want."

Ciara sat paralysed with shock, unable to speak.

Dee looked across at Ciara. "Maybe it's time you and I did some straight-talking to each other. Sometimes I'll think I'll burst if I can't let people know the real me. I'm tired of being respectable and fitting in with other people's lives. I'm going to be honest with you Ciara – even if it means the end of our friendship."

Ciara felt her heart pounding. Could it be Dee, rather than Kate, who'd been having an affair with Niall? At that moment, if she could have risen to her feet, she might have thrown her glass of wine over Dee. But she felt like a rabbit frozen in the headlights of a car, powerless to save itself from impending doom. If she could have made a sound, it might have been a scream of rage and pain. But no sound would come out, and she sat mute while Dee spoke on.

"We'd often talked about ending our marriages and going to live together, but –" Dee took another mouthful of *raki*, looking into the depths of the glass as she spoke, oblivious of Ciara's stricken face, "as you know, it never happened. But it would have, if he'd lived –" Dee looked at Ciara. "But then, you know how final death is."

She gestured to the waiter for another bottle of raki, and Ciara sat stricken, waiting for the next instalment of a story she was terrified to hear.

"We were very much in love," said Dee, filling both glasses from the new bottle. "I suppose you're angry with me for not telling you before now, but neither of us intended it to happen."

Ciara swallowed a large mouthful from her own glass of *raki* to help her cope.

"Yes," added Dee, tears now rolling unchecked down her cheeks, "at last I had the only man I'd ever loved, and amazingly he felt the same about me," she looked across at Ciara, her face suddenly gaunt. "Unfortunately, he belonged to someone else." Dee then looked into her glass again. "Please forgive me for not telling you, Ciara. But all I could think of was being in love. I didn't care about anyone else, or how they got hurt." Dee now looked up at Ciara. "Especially you," she sighed. "We'd been secretly meeting for the previous year, and after giving it a lot of thought we finally decided to end our marriages so that we could finally be together."

Ciara felt as though she was having a heart attack. So

it was Dee who had taken that photograph, Dee who had written those sexy messages on the back!

"Anyway, just as we were going to break the news to our partners, Eamonn was diagnosed with terminal cancer."

Ciara sat bolt upright. "W-who?"

Dee looked up at Ciara, surprised. "Eamonn, Eamonn Merrigan. Surely you knew him? He used to play golf with Charlie, Niall and the others. His daughter Zoe is in Sarah's class. I met him in the clubhouse one night when I was waiting to collect Charlie after a game . . ."

Dee's face softened as she spoke his name, and suddenly a terrible weight was lifted from Ciara's shoulders. Momentarily she felt like singing for joy, but the tears in Dee's eyes brought her back to the immediate situation. Anyway, hadn't she known at heart that it was Kate who'd had the affair with Niall?

Of course, Ciara remembered Eamonn Merrigan, a tall, slightly stooped but good-looking man who'd always had a pleasant word for everyone. She'd attended his funeral with Niall shortly before Niall's own heart attack. And she'd never suspected how unhappy poor Dee had been then.

Seeing Ciara's incredulous expression, Dee looked contrite. "Sorry, Ciara. I never told you because I was afraid you'd despise me. I mean, you and Niall were the perfect couple. You made the rest of us feel –" she searched for the word, "inferior."

Dee was sobbing quietly now. "Poor Eamonn only lived for a few months after that. When we knew he hadn't long to live, there seemed no point in putting both our families through even more trauma. So he stayed with his wife, and I stayed with Charlie."

Ciara rose from the table and put her arms around Dee, soothing her as one would comfort a distraught child. Clinging to her, Dee looked up into Ciara's face. "Oh Ciara. It was agony during those last few weeks, when only his family was allowed to visit him in the hospice. We wanted so desperately to spend his last days together! I used to ring him on his mobile phone as often as I could, but we'd both end up in tears because we just wanted to be together. But I never saw him again."

Dee wiped her eyes. "Then I had to go to his funeral with Charlie and stand there trying not to cry, while all the time I wanted to throw myself into his grave."

"I know, love. I know, " Ciara said quietly.

"Oh God, Ciara. Of course, you know! You've been through it too," Dee hiccuped. "I went to visit his grave, you know, the day you cancelled because you had to talk to Kevin. So I went to the cemetery. I just wanted to say my own private goodbye."

This brought on a fresh bout of crying, as Dee clung to her. "I'm sorry Ciara, for making you miserable too – and reminding you of your own loss."

"There's nothing to be sorry about. I'm just glad you've told me at last."

Ciara sighed as she cradled Dee in her arms. It was a beautiful night, but now she felt cold and she just wanted to fall into bed. Briefly, she longed for Niall beside her. Her body still ached for the warmth of his body, the familiar touch of his skin . . . but in the end, he hadn't wanted her. He'd wanted Kate.

Abruptly she stood up. "C'mon, Dee. It's time to hit the sack."

But already, Dee had passed out in her chair, her tear-stained face flung back open and innocent like a child's. Despite her own unsteadiness Ciara managed, with much heaving and hauling and the amused waiter's help, to grip Dee firmly around the waist and eventually get her onto her feet.

Undoubtedly, they'd both have dreadful hangovers in the morning, Ciara thought, as she propelled a sleepy Dee down the street to their apartment. So far, Ciara conceded, the holiday had been full of surprises. And this was only their second day!

CHAPTER 6

"Well, how did I do?"

"You were superb. Did your own business go according to plan?"

"Yeah, no problem. I had her eating out of my hand. She's going to have the money on Monday."

"Brilliant," I said. "Now, how much do I owe you for the lunch?"

Alan proffered the bill. I raised my eyebrows when I saw the amount, and I noted the bottle of premier cru. He'd certainly dined in style at my expense! But I paid him in cash, making no comment. No matter what it cost, it was still excellent value as far as I was concerned.

"OK," I said, "now here's the plan for Monday next . . ."

"Niall, I'm really sorry to phone you at such short notice. I'm an awful nuisance, I know, but I've got to see you urgently about this alternative health feature. Can you please spare me another hour or two?"

There was silence, and I knew that he was trying to think of some excuse to get out of it.

"Look,"' he said at last, "I'm really busy all this week. Couldn't it wait until next week?"

"God, Niall," I said, adding urgency to my voice, "I'm badly stuck for more information. I'm supposed to have this piece finished by Monday, but I've got an extension until Tuesday lunchtime. Look, couldn't we meet briefly on Monday evening? You'd be doing me a huge favour —"

I was really pushing my luck, but if I could pull this one off I'd be home and dry.

I heard Niall sigh. "Well, if you really need the information that badly . . ."

"You're an angel, Niall!" I said warmly, before he had a chance to change his mind. "I'll book a table somewhere for early Monday evening — say, for seven o'clock."

There was a moment's silence. "Couldn't you just call in here to the office?"

I thought rapidly. "Look, I feel bad enough taking up your time, Niall. I'd at least feel better if I thought you were having something decent to eat. Unless, that is, Ciara will have dinner waiting for you —"

Which, of course, I knew you wouldn't, Ciara. Because you were going out on Monday night too!

"No, actually, Ciara is out that night too. Meeting some woman friend. What sort of information do you need?"

"Have you anything on the different ways in which conventional medicines and alternative health products are manufactured? I've been told that conventional medicines use only part of the plant, whereas alternative products use all of the plant . . ."

Niall sighed. "Yes, as far as I know, that's true. I'll see what I can do. But dinner's on me, OK?"

I laughed with relief and delight. "We can argue over who pays the bill on Monday night!"

On Monday night, I was already seated in a secluded cubicle at The Red Rooster when Niall arrived. I'd arranged with Alan that his appointment was for 7.30, so that Niall and I would already be settled in our seats before he and Ciara arrived. Once again, I'd ensured that we had a slightly elevated and secluded cubicle at the back of the split-level restaurant, which enabled us to observe other diners. But diners at other tables, including the one booked for Alan, couldn't easily see ours. Of course, even if we were spotted, Ciara, or Niall decided to greet you, we at least had a valid reason for dining together. But you hadn't . . .

"Hi, Niall. Thanks for going to all this trouble for me. I'll make sure that your clients get a good write-up."

He smiled and sat down, giving me sheaves of paper filled with facts and figures, none of which I gave a damn about since they'd never appear in print. Instead, I was anxious to see his expression when you arrived, Ciara, and especially when you were doted on by Alan Moore yet again.

Niall and I were talking about the increasing popularity of natural healing techniques, when suddenly I looked past him, my mouth open in mock surprise. Turning to see what was attracting my attention, Niall was in time to see you arriving, Ciara. And to watch you walk straight over to where Alan Moore was already sitting.

"Good heavens. I wonder what Ciara is doing here?" I said. "And isn't that Alan Moore she's with, again? I thought you said she was meeting a woman friend . . ."

Niall reacted quickly. "Eh, no – that was cancelled. I think she did mention something about meeting that photographer again, to talk about her exhibition."

I chuckled. "If I didn't know you two were so happy together, I'd almost say they were having an affair!"

Niall smiled tightly but said nothing, toying with his soup spoon agitatedly.

"Would you like us to go over and join them?" I asked, knowing what his answer would be.

"Eh, no. Let's just leave them to their discussions. Besides, we have our own discussions to finish."

"You're right. Anyway, I'm sure Ciara will tell you all about her evening when you get home."

By now, Niall's suspicions were hopefully growing. Forgetting to mention a lunch date could be seen as a genuine error, but now he was wondering what explanation you'd give him about where you'd spent your evening, Ciara. He'd never mention it if you didn't – and of course I knew with certainty that you wouldn't!

Then I smiled at Niall, doing my best to look wistful. "It's so nice for a couple to have separate exciting lives," I said. "In a sense, it gives you both so much more to share. I'm sure that when you go home each evening, you tell Ciara all about your day and she tells you about hers . . ." I sighed deeply for effect.

Niall tried to look interested in the alternative health material, but all the time his head kept turning to look down the aisle at the table where you and Alan Moore sat. Thankfully, Alan was fawning over you yet again, and from our vantage-point it looked as though you were enjoying his attentions. Once again, Ciara, I'd ensured that you were sitting with your back to us.

I could see the package of photographs at the edge of the table on Alan's side, but no one else was likely to notice it unless, like me, they had a vested interest in knowing it was there.

"Are you OK?" I asked Niall brightly, as he looked for about the tenth time at the table below us.

"`Yes, fine," he said, looking embarrassed and altering his position slightly, so that you and Alan were out of his line of sight. Clearly, he was acknowledging his bad-mannered behaviour, and was making a conscious effort not to look at your table any more.

I was elated! Niall was definitely upset by what he'd seen. I didn't resent his concern, Ciara, since his feelings for you would soon change. Love turning to hate, and all that. Then I'd be the one to offer him comfort.

I'd also arranged with Alan that you and he would leave by ten o'clock, Ciara, ensuring that Niall and I could leave in a seemingly natural manner a short time later. But I'd arranged an additional little surprise to ensure that Niall would definitely be convinced of your infidelity. I knew that you intended to get away from Alan Moore as soon as you could. But I'd also ensured that you wouldn't get home until much, much later. And Niall would wonder what you'd been up to during all those unaccounted-for hours . . .

CHAPTER 7

Sitting back in the taxi, Sarah snuggled down into the luxurious leather seating. It represented comfort and safety, which Sarah felt badly in need of. She was scared, very scared. Suddenly she wondered if she should have told her mother about what happened with Brian. After all, her mother was the one who'd always been there when she'd cut her knee or fallen off her bike. Her mother always kissed the injury to make it better, and her magic treatment always worked. Sarah wanted to cry, but she was supposed to be an adult now.

She and Ita had just made their preliminary visit to the private clinic, where everything had been straightforward and the staff more than helpful. She tried not to think about what the clinic staff referred to as her 'little operation'. Maybe if she pretended to herself that she was just here on a short holiday with Ita, it would stop the butterflies in her stomach.

She thought of Brian Brennan and her stomach contracted. How could she ever have slept with that creep? The thought of his greasy black hair, his bad breath and the inane conversation she'd found so witty and sophisticated at the party made her feel sick.

After that night, he'd dumped her anyway. He'd avoided her every time they passed in the school corridor. Maybe the ignorant shit didn't even remember what happened that night. Sarah's own recollection of events was hazy anyway. All she remembered was that in order to cope with her own insecurities she'd had too much to drink, and ended up so sick that she'd missed most of the party anyway.

She shuddered, and Ita slipped an arm around her shoulders, giving her a gentle hug. Sarah looked up and smiled gratefully at the older woman. Ita knew how she was feeling, because she'd told Sarah in confidence that she herself had once had an abortion too. Although she'd made light of it, Sarah suspected that Ita was just doing that to make her feel better. Sarah hoped that Ita had been as lucky as she'd been in having a friend to support her through it all.

"Do you ever – I mean, do you still think of the child you might have had?" Sarah suddenly asked.

Ita thought carefully before answering, knowing that her answer could help or hinder Sarah in her own situation.

"I do, occasionally. But I don't feel any guilt, if that's what you mean. I couldn't have kept the child. I was only about your age too."

She smiled. "Anyway, the time wasn't right for this one. You'll be able to have lots of babies when you're older."

"But you didn't."

Ita patted Sarah's wrist. "I suppose I just never met the right man."

They continued the journey in silence, Sarah gazing out at the hustle and bustle of London which seemed so much more frenetic than Dublin. Driving through the West End, Sarah stared, fascinated, at all the billboards advertising shows that were taking place in and around Shaftsbury Avenue. She noted all the famous names taking part, people whom she'd previously seen only on television. Tonight, she'd see some of those people on stage, since Ita was taking her to a show.

She shuddered. Then tomorrow morning, she would present herself at the clinic for an initial counselling session. Then in the afternoon, 'it' would be done. She couldn't bring herself to say 'abortion' – it was a horrible word. 'Termination' didn't sound much better. She would then stay in the clinic overnight, and Ita would collect her the following morning. Then, Ita had promised her, they would go shopping and buy a really nice dress each!

Sarah's eyes stung with unspilt tears, and she turned towards the window until she could blink them away. Ita had been so good to her, and she was unbelievably generous too. She must have tons of money, Sarah concluded, because since they'd arrived in London, Ita had insisted they take taxis everywhere. And they were staying in a fabulous hotel too.

Sarah felt overwhelming gratitude. Ita had thought of everything! She would have made a wonderful spy, Sarah thought enviously. Tall and elegant, she could imagine her arranging rendezvous with men who looked like film stars, using her allure to extract the necessary secrets from them. Then she would glide off mysteriously into the night. Sarah sighed. Would she ever be as elegant and sophisticated as Ita?

Unbidden, thoughts of Brian Brennan came into her mind. How utterly unromantic it had all been the following morning! She'd woken up to find herself stark naked and Brennan draped around her. He snored too – ugh.

Then there was the shame and embarrassment of extricating herself from Brian's sleepy embrace, of retrieving her foul-smelling clothes that were scattered everywhere, getting dressed and sneaking out of the house.

She hadn't felt able to face anyone so she'd tiptoed down the stairs, nearly breaking her neck on an abandoned beer bottle, but managing to reach the front door without being detected. Once outside, she'd run home as fast as her legs would carry her.

The morning had been cool but the sun was shining, and she'd drawn the fresh air deep into her lungs, gulping like a fish that had just been landed. Her clothes were crumpled and reeked of alcohol and cigarette smoke. A couple, walking along the road towards her, gathered their toddlers close as they passed her.

They think I'm a Traveller, Sarah realised with surprise. For the first time in her young life, she could empathise with the plight of these mistreated people, stigmatised for their unkempt appearance and perilous roadside way of life. Sarah knew that local councils and communities kept moving Travellers on, paying no respect to either their traditions or their safety.

Sarah recalled that her mother had painted scenes from several Travellers' camps. And they'd been bought as investments by the kind of people who'd be the first to run the same Travellers out of town! Her mother, of course, had given the proceeds from the paintings to a Travellers' education project.

Sarah had never given much thought to any of her mother's social concerns, but now as she and Ita drove past Piccadilly Circus, she suddenly felt a strong empathy with her mother. And a desperate wish to feel her mother's arms around her. Then she recalled her mother's disgusting behaviour with Charlie Somers, and the desperate longing faded. How could her mother have behaved like that? Then it suddenly struck her – hadn't she done exactly the same thing?

Sarah started as Ita's touch brought her back to reality.

"Look, Sarah – there's the statue of Eros!"

Sarah looked. God, it was tiny, compared to what she'd expected! In pictures, it always looked much bigger. Nevertheless, she smiled enthusiastically.

"Are you OK, Sarah?" Ita asked anxiously.

"Fine, thanks," said Sarah, trying to sound positive and happy. But she felt more like crying. The thought of what was going to happen to her was very frightening. She patted her stomach surreptitiously, tears prickly against her eyelids. And this little person within her – was it a boy or a girl? Well, tomorrow, whatever it was, its short life would be over.

"Why do men get off so easily?" Sarah said fiercely. It

was a rhetorical question, and Ita took Sarah's hand, massaging it gently in the hopes of soothing the pain within.

Ita sighed to herself. Tonight, she and Sarah would lose themselves in the excitement of the latest West End show that was getting rave reviews. Then tomorrow she would deliver Sarah to the clinic. And when it was all over, she'd return and sit by the child's bed while she recovered.

But before then, Ita had plans of her own to attend to.

Groggily, Sarah woke up to find Ita sitting beside her bed. "Is-is it over?"

"Yes, love. Everything is OK now."

Briefly, Sarah felt relief, then she was swamped by an overwhelming sense of sadness. She began to cry and Ita took her hand, but did not try to hush her. Ita seemed to understand that there was a huge wave of emotion surging through her, and that she had to let it out before she could begin the process of healing.

Gradually, Sarah's sobs became more intermittent, and finally she dozed off again.

Later, Sarah awoke to find Ita still by her bedside. "Have I been asleep for long?"

Ita smiled. "Six hours. You'd win a marathon for sleeping!"

Sarah sighed. "Well, I certainly don't feel very rested after it. I feel as though I've actually run a marathon! Did you go shopping while I was asleep?"

"Of course, not," said Ita with a smile. "I wouldn't

dream of going shopping without you!" She quickly changed the subject. "How are you feeling about it now?"

Sarah looked away. "I had the most awful nightmare, Ita –" her lower lip trembled. "In it, my baby was grown up, but it was still a baby. A giant talking baby. And it kept asking me why I killed it –"

"Sarah, love, there was no choice. You know that yourself," Ita took her hand. "Don't torture yourself any more. You can't spend the rest of your life blaming yourself."

"I still feel so guilty . . ."

"Just remember that your baby, as you call it, was only the beginnings of a possible life. There was no guarantee that it would have lived anyway," Ita smiled. "You know, nature's a lot wiser than us, yet it wastes many potential lives for every one that it creates."

Sarah looked slightly happier. "I guess you're right, Ita. Isn't it more important to care for the lives already in existence? I mean, there are millions of people in the world that no one gives a damn about. Uncle Kevin has often talked to me about the poor people in Africa." Suddenly, Sarah's face broke into a grin. "I've just had a horrific thought! My child might have grown up to look like Brian Brennan! So maybe I've done it a favour!"

Then her laughter turned to hysterical crying, and once again Ita gathered her into her arms.

CHAPTER 8

I waited two days before phoning Niall again.

"Hi, Niall," I said, "I just wanted to say thanks for all your help with the alternative health feature. But I thought I'd better let you know that the article's been postponed for a few weeks."

"Oh. Well, that's the nature of the business, isn't it? I hope the Sundays don't get there ahead of you!"

He sounded fine but I felt that nevertheless, it was time to test the waters. "Niall, are you OK?" I asked, adding a note of concern to my voice. "You sound a bit under the weather, like you've got the flu or something," I chuckled, "or maybe it's a hangover!"

Niall laughed in return, but it was a forced laugh. I could tell that he was upset and I was secretly delighted.

"No, I'm fine. No hangover yet," he paused, "but I might have one tomorrow morning, though. I'm meeting with some of the folks from the PR Institute tonight!"

"Well, I hope you have a terrific evening," I said. "I'll ring you as soon as I know when the article is being published."

After I'd rung off, I got out the telephone directory and looked up the number of the Public Relations Institute.

"Hello," I said to the receptionist, "can you tell me where, and at what time, the Institute's meeting is being held this evening?"

The receptionist put me on hold while she checked. Then she came back on the line, to inform me that it was being held in the conference room of the Burlington Hotel at 8 o'clock.

"Thanks," I said, "I'd forgotten to make a note of it in my diary."

I rang off, then phoned my hairstylist. "Eileen, any chance of a quick wash and blow-dry later today? I've got an unexpected date this evening . . ."

I was seated in the main bar of the Burlington Hotel by around nine o'clock. Nonchalantly, I perched myself on a stool at the counter and engaged in some casual banter with one of the young barmen. I'd brought an evening newspaper to use as a prop, so that if it proved necessary I could avoid the attentions of the many local and foreign businessmen who congregated there in the evenings. Although the bar wasn't exactly a pick-up joint, it was one of the city's nearest equivalents to a singles bar. Except most of the men weren't single.

I sat facing the main entrance to the bar so that I could casually observe anyone entering without looking too obvious about it. One man who was sitting at the bar, Danish or Norwegian I think, tried to initiate a conversation. But I quickly made it clear that I wasn't interested. Another night, he might have been the ideal diversion. Tonight, however, I had bigger fish to fry. And suddenly I saw my prime catch coming into view.

The meeting over, Niall and some of the other PR people entered the bar for drinks just as I'd expected. Some would probably go home after one or two, the rest would stay on for as long as the bar remained open. And I had Niall's own assurance that he was one of those who intended making a night of it! There was no easier target than a disillusioned man.

I focussed my attention on the few women who were in the group. I had to make certain that none of them spent too much time chatting to Niall. Assuming that he was in the vulnerable state I'd hopefully helped to create, I intended to ensure that the shoulder he would cry on would definitely be mine.

"Niall!" I waved across the bar at him and, surprised, he looked up and waved back. Then he detached himself from the woman who had been talking to him, much to her chagrin and my delight, and crossed the bar to greet me.

"What on earth are you doing here?" he asked, a big smile on his face. "I didn't know that this was your kind of territory."

I smiled back. "Oh well, you never know where we press people will turn up!" Then I changed to a rueful expression. "To be honest Niall, I'm not exactly sure what to do next. You see, I was supposed to meet this guy –" I bit my lip, "– he'd agreed to give me exclusive information on the closure of that factory in Cavan, but he hasn't turned up. I've been waiting for him for nearly an hour so I doubt he's going to show up now." I sighed. "I'm pretty pissed off – and I feel so conspicuous with all these lonely businessmen trying to pick up someone for the night. Maybe I should just go home."

"You poor old thing," he said, looking concerned, and patting me affectionately on the arm. "Look, why don't you come over and join us. I'm with some people from the PR Institute. We're just having a few drinks before people head off home."

I looked hesitant. "Are you sure? I mean, wouldn't I be intruding?"

"Intruding? For heaven's sake, no! You're bound to know some of them anyway. Come on over and let me introduce you to Angela Woods — that's the woman I've just been talking to. She's secretary of the Institute. I'm sure she'd love to meet you."

Angela Woods was far from delighted to meet me. She recognised me as a worthy adversary for Niall's attentions, and before long she accepted defeat and opted to go home. Several others left around then too, and before long there was only a core group of about five or six people left.

I'd been closely monitoring Niall's mood throughout the evening. He was drinking heavily, so I plied him with further drinks which he didn't seem altogether aware of, but which he knocked back with gusto. Needless to say, I stayed sober myself. I'd need all my wits to ensure that the situation continued to develop exactly as I'd planned it . . .

CHAPTER 9

After a visit to the local pharmacy for pain-relievers the following morning, both Dee and Ciara went back to bed for a while. Ciara, however, suffered in silence whereas Dee felt the whole world should know how much she was suffering. Later, they decided that they might just as well be ill outdoors as in. After a few hours lounging on the nearby beach at Gumbet they were soon restored to health, and Dee pronounced herself ready for action again that night!

Early in the evening they returned to the apartment for a shower and a change of clothing, before heading out for what Dee hoped would be a 'night on the town'. Ciara was amused at Dee's capacity for recovery, and more relaxed now that Dee's good humour had been restored and the trauma of the previous night hadn't even been mentioned.

In their absence, the travel representative had delivered a note to their apartment informing them that someone called Charlie had phoned. But when Dee found it, she merely grimaced, screwed the note into a tiny ball and fired it into the wastepaper basket. Whatever Charlie wanted, she didn't want to know about it.

After a delicious dinner in a *lokanta* off the marketplace, Ciara and Dee strolled through the streets along with hundreds of other holidaymakers. It was warm, and the air was filled with a delightful mix of fragrances from the wild flowers growing everywhere combined with the luscious fruit on the many street stalls, all of them still open for business.

Many times, they were pleasantly accosted by cheerful young Turkish men, who told them how beautiful they were and tried to pick them up. All the flattery and bonhomie put both women in high spirits.

Having enjoyed the sights, smells and camaraderie of the streets, the duo eventually sat down at one of the tables outside a *birahane*, a beer house where local beers and drinks are served. They ordered *raki* again, and were amazed at how cheap it was to get drunk in Turkey!

"And we don't even have to worry about driving home!" Dee exulted, stretching her arms in the air. "Oh, I just love it here, don't you?"

Ciara nodded. A holiday in Turkey had been an excellent choice. She felt remarkably relaxed, especially since she and Dee had cleared the air the night before. Right now she didn't care about anything other than enjoying herself. She no longer felt any sense of pain or loss. She wasn't even worrying about Sarah. Her mind was free to make the most of whatever happened.

Dee nudged Ciara as two handsome young Turkish men walked by, holding hands. "God, what a waste. They're gorgeous, aren't they? Just our luck that they're gay. Come to think of it, all the men in Turkey are incredibly good-looking, aren't they?"

Ciara nodded. The two men were certainly very attractive. And one of them had actually winked at her as he walked past! She'd been momentarily nonplussed, then wondered if she had actually imagined it. Perhaps the *raki* had gone to her head already!

Dee sat sipping her *raki* and eyeing the local talent, sometimes drawing Ciara's attention to a particularly handsome specimen that took her fancy. But they'd also noticed that Turkish women, at least those married to traditional men, never frequented drinking establishments.

"Maybe there's something to be said for traditional values!" Dee giggled, as she swallowed yet another mouthful of her drink. "We get all the men to chat up!"

Ciara grinned. `Well, yes. But if we lived here, we might be the ones stuck at home while our menfolk were out chatting up the tourists!"

Other tourists were chatting at nearby tables, and a group of Turkish men sent them over complimentary drinks but refused to let them return the compliment. Another group of men went past, laughing and joking to each other, and some of them were holding hands too.

"God," said Dee in mock annoyance, "are you sure we didn't book a holiday in one of the gay capitals of the Middle East? Every good-looking guy I fancy seems to be gay."

Just then, the two men whom they'd admired earlier sat down at the empty table beside them. "Hello," they both said courteously, "you are enjoying your holiday?"

Before long, all four were chatting easily and the young man whom Ciara was certain had winked at her earlier pulled his chair round beside hers. Fleetingly, she wondered why a gay man would appear so overtly interested in her, but she assumed it must just be due to Turkish hospitality.

But when the young man, whose name he told her was Ismail, tried to hold her hand, even the vast amount of *raki* she'd consumed didn't deter her from speaking her mind. In fact, emboldened by alcohol, she was even more direct than she might have been otherwise.

"What on earth are you doing?" she asked, withdrawing her hand quickly. "Aren't you and –" She pointed to the man who was now almost breathing down Dee's cleavage.

"Hakan. His name is Hakan."

"Well, aren't you and Hakan a couple?"

"A couple of what?" Ismail looked at her incredulously for a moment, then his face broke into a big smile. He spoke rapidly to Hakan in Turkish, and they both fell about the place laughing. Then he turned back to Ciara.

"You think we –" Still grinning, he searched for the word in English. "Agh, I do not know the word. You think we –" he pointed to Hakan, who grinned back, "you think he and I, we sleep together? No, it's not true."

"But we saw you holding hands."

Ismail took Ciara's hand in his, and this time she didn't recoil.

"When Turkish men are best friends, they hold hands. But we are not, how you say it?"

"Gay."

"That is true. I like women. I like you."

When eventually the proprietor of the *birahane* began closing up the premises, the two men suggested taking Ciara and Dee to a nearby nightclub. The nightclub like so many in warm countries was in the open-air, and it proved a heady sensation to dance beneath a crescent moon while a warm breeze carried the scent of jasmine and wild honeysuckle through the air. Freed from all the restraints of home, Ciara and Dee danced in frenzied exultation, spurred on by the haunting and discordant Turkish music and the gorgeous men they were dancing with.

In between dancing they relaxed on large floor cushions, snuggling up to Ismail and Hakan and toasting each other in Irish, much to the amusement of the two men who offered to trade lessons in Irish for lessons in Turkish. In the early hours of the morning, the four of them left the nightclub together. By now it was perfectly clear to them all that the men would be staying that night in Ciara's and Dee's apartment.

In their absence, yet another message had been delivered from Charlie. But Dee quickly tore it up and slipped it into the wastepaper basket.

It felt strange and somewhat unreal to make love in a room with other people present, but Ciara was past caring. In the dark each couple behaved as though they were an island unto themselves.

Ciara wondered in passing if Dee or either of the men

had made love in this sort of situation before. She certainly hadn't. But she had to admit that the strangeness of it all increased her sexual excitement. Ismail was a vigorous lover, and she came quickly and with ease. She also found herself smiling in the dark as she heard Dee gasping in ecstasy on the other side of the room. Finally, Ciara drifted off into a deep and trouble-free sleep.

In the morning, the men showed no embarrassment about the night before. All four of them showered together – another new experience for Ciara. Then Ismail and Hakan invited the two women for breakfast at a nearby *lokanta*.

"Then," said Ismail, "we must go to work. But we see you tonight, yes?"

The women nodded, and Ciara suddenly realised that she hadn't asked Ismail anything about himself, his job, or even if he was married. My God, she'd made love to a man whom she knew absolutely nothing about! The experience felt strangely liberating.

After breakfast, when the men left for the leather goods and carpet shops where they worked, Ciara and Dee strolled along the pier near the harbour. Despite her dreadful hangover, Ciara couldn't stop smiling to herself.

Dee looked at her quizzically. "God, Ciara, you're grinning like a Cheshire cat."

"I know," said Ciara apologetically. "I can't believe I've just slept with a man at least ten years younger than me, and that I didn't need to find out his entire family history first!"

"Welcome to the real world," Dee looked at her slyly, "but you seemed to have liked it?"

Ciara nodded. "I feel like – oh, I don't know – a new woman! I feel alive, attractive."

"Maybe now you understand me a little better."

Ciara turned to her friend. "Look, Dee, I'm sorry if I sounded like a pompous old cow. It was all a bit of a shock. I thought you and Charlie were so happy . . ."

Dee's eyes narrowed. "I meant what I said last night. I'm going to ask Charlie for a legal separation when we go back home. Then, after the required number of years, we can get a divorce."

"What? Oh, surely not," Ciara's *joie de vivre* evaporated in an instant. She'd completely forgotten what Dee had said the previous night about leaving Charlie. After all the drink they'd consumed, she'd probably developed alcoholic amnesia. Or else she'd been so relieved at finding out Dee wasn't Niall's lover, that everything else had slipped her mind.

Suddenly, she was stricken. Just as Dee was cleared of guilt over Niall, Ciara had to face her own guilt over Charlie. And its possible consequences. Suddenly she was afraid that when Dee asked Charlie for a separation, he'd assume their marriage was ending because Ciara had told Dee about their fling. Then unwittingly, he'd confirm it, and Ciara's friendship with Dee would be over too . . .

"I just can't keep up the pretence any more," Dee added. "I came on this holiday to think it all through, and I've realised that I can't continue living life second-hand. I want to find some peace of mind, to be alone with my memories of Eamonn, at least for a while."

Ciara nodded. "But don't tell poor Charlie about Eamonn. That would break his heart, Dee. He doesn't deserve that."

Dee nodded, a sad expression on her face. "No, I'd never do that to him. Poor Charlie. He's lost Niall, and now he's losing me. Life's not really fair, is it? I mean, he's never meant any harm, and he's never really done anything wrong," she sighed. "Charlie's problem is that he just hasn't done anything right."

For the rest of their stay in Turkey, Dee and Ciara met Ismail and Hakan each evening. From them, they learnt a lot about Turkish life, and about the way in which modern and traditional society lived uneasily side by side.

"Me, Ciara, I am not married," Ismail explained. "This is because I have difficulty deciding whether to marry a traditional woman, who stays at home with the children, or a modern woman who drives her own car and has a career. In Turkey we have both kinds of women, sometimes within the same family."

Ismail pointed to two women walking along the street together, one in traditional costume, the other in a T-shirt and shorts. "See those women? They are sisters. But the woman in the traditional costume is married to a man who observes the traditional way of life. Her sister is not yet married."

"What will happen when she does marry?"

"It will depend on whether her husband observes the old traditions or has adapted to modern society. Most young men in Turkey today are very modern in their outlook. But sometimes even they prefer to have a traditional wife."

Ciara smiled to herself. That's called having your cake and eating it, she thought!

Ciara was astounded to find herself going happily to bed each night with Ismail, and engaging in passionate and varied sexual activity with him. Previously, she'd never been with any other man except Niall!

"Perhaps some day, I will come to see this Ireland of yours," said Ismail on the last evening of their holiday. Ciara nodded, assuring him that he would be most welcome. But she knew that theirs was merely a holiday romance, and in time it would just be a nostalgic memory for both of them.

That night they made love with even greater fervour and passion than before. And Ciara felt a deep sadness at leaving this man who had done so much to ease her loneliness and pain. Maybe they would meet again sometime, who could tell?

As she and Dee boarded the plane for Dublin the next day, Ciara felt as though the weight of the world was closing in on her. The fun and games were now over, and reality had to be faced. Dee was about to end her marriage, and Ciara could only hope that she herself wouldn't become caught up in the fallout.

She would also have to face Kate. Or preferably, not face her. But one way or another, she knew that there was trauma and unpleasantness ahead.

Ciara fastened her seat belt, and smiled at Dee who

was sitting beside her. She wished she'd told Dee about her faithless ex-friend Kate, but she'd never found the courage. If she'd done so, she might now have an ally when the matter finally came to a head back home. On the other hand, how could she dare ask for support from Dee when she'd let Dee down herself?

CHAPTER 10

Gradually, Niall and I separated from the others, the two of us sitting apart at the bar and talking exclusively to each other. Two of the other men in the group seemed to have successfully picked up women, leaving the remaining few chatting among themselves.

Before long, the bar staff in the hotel began dimming the lights to signify that it was closing time for non-residents, but I still had another ace up my sleeve. Having established my own vulnerability by pretending to have been left in the lurch, I'd created an intimacy that would hopefully enable Niall to unburden himself to me when the time was right. And that time was now approaching.

"Niall," I whispered, "let's go downstairs to the nightclub. We can get more drink down there."

"Yeah, great. I don't want to go home!" he announced. Then he suddenly looked sad. "I've nothing to go home for, anyway."

By now, Niall had become quite garrulous, and I could see

that some of his less inebriated colleagues were looking anxiously across at him. As they prepared to leave, one of them came over to see if he was OK.

"He can't drive home in that state," said the man. "I'll go and arrange a taxi for him."

"Not at all," I said, "I'm quite sober, so I'll make sure he gets home OK. I'll be getting a taxi myself shortly, so I'll drop Niall off on the way."

With obvious relief, the man surrendered the responsibility to me – a precious responsibility I was only too happy to accept. At last, my plan was coming to fruition.

Leaving the bar, we wandered outside into the hotel grounds, then around by the side of the hotel to the nightclub entrance. By now, Niall was leaning on me, his arm draped around my shoulder. It felt good there. My skin tingled at the point where his fingers brushed my skin.

The nightclub was dark and stuffy. The music was loud and there were bodies everywhere, but I managed to find a secluded corner with a comfortable two-seater couch. Niall struggled to his feet to order drinks at the bar, but I urged him to stay and hold onto the seats. Quickly, I ordered a double for him and a non-alcoholic drink for me, then joined him on the couch, sitting as close to him as I dared.

"Thanks, love," he said when I came back, "I should be getting this round, y'know."

I was thrilled to hear him call me 'love', although I knew that he was using it only as a general term of affection.

"Here," I said softly, handing him his drink and raising my own glass in a toast. "Let's drink to happiness."

Solemnly, he raised his glass to mine and we smiled at each other. "Happiness," he echoed. "I used to be happy," he looked forlornly at me, "but now I have nothing to be happy about any more."

*"Oh, c'mon Niall. You're one of the luckiest people I know,"
I said in a warm affectionate tone. "You run a successful
business, have a great daughter and a lovely wife."*

"I thought I had."

"You thought you had what?"

"A lovely wife. But she doesn't love me any more."

*"What do you mean? I always thought you and Ciara –" I
left the sentence hanging in mid-air.*

*"So did I. But do you know what? She's been cheating on
me."*

"Are you sure, Niall? How do you know?"

*At this stage his voice was beginning to slur. "She's carrying
on with the photographer that you know."*

*He looked at me, his eyes glazed, but I couldn't tell if it was
from too much drink or from unshed tears. But the drink was
certainly loosening his tongue, much to my delight. Nor was he
aware that I wasn't drinking myself. I needed all my wits to
keep stoking his paranoia.*

"You saw her with him, too."

*I tried to look surprised. "You mean that day we had lunch
at Chi Chi's? For goodness sake, Niall. They were probably just
meeting to talk business, like we were."*

*He shook his head, looking directly at me. "Then why didn't
she tell me about him? Why did she tell me she was meeting her
old friend Marguerite?"*

I shrugged my shoulders helplessly.

*Niall poured the remainder of his drink straight down his
throat. "I'll tell you why. It's because she's having an affair
with him. They were also at the Red Rooster, and she didn't*

come home until three o'clock the following morning! Of course, she was in his bed – where else could she have been?"

"Niall," I said softly, "let's dance."

Pulling him to his feet, I led him out onto the dance-floor. By now the tempo of the music was slower and more intimate, and the floor was now crowded with smooching couples. I slipped my arms around his neck, and he followed my lead by sliding his arms around my waist. Silently, we moved around the floor, and I was almost afraid to breathe in case I inadvertently broke the spell.

I could feel the warmth of his breath against my ear, and it sent a delicious shiver down my spine. Our bodies seemed to melt into each other, and daringly, I raised my head and kissed him gently on the cheek. He kissed my cheek in turn, then suddenly, our lips met. It was a sweet, but urgent kiss and we continued kissing as we moved around the floor.

Then as if by silent agreement, we left the dance-floor and walked back to where we'd been sitting. In the darkened corner, we continued kissing frantically, our lips and tongues searching each other's mouths. Our hands gently, then more urgently, explored each other's bodies.

"Let's get another drink," I said breathlessly, breaking away from his kisses. There were a few things that needed to be clarified before I would take him to bed and let him make love to me.

Niall was immediately contrite, and struggled to his feet. "Oh God, I'm sorry. I'll get them right away."

I watched as he walked unsteadily to the bar, and I smiled happily to myself. The prize I'd sought for so long was almost mine! But I needed to be sure that he was really convinced of your affair, Ciara. There was too much at stake for me to risk just a one-night stand. I wanted this man for keeps.

When he returned with the drinks, I said gently, "Niall, did you ask Ciara why she was meeting Alan and where they went afterwards? I mean, there's probably some simple explanation."

He laughed harshly. "Like hell, there is! All I got from her were lies. First, she told me she'd been meeting this old school friend. Then, after staying out all night, she told me a cock-and-bull story about someone slashing her tyres! How's that for originality?"

I tried to look sad, but inwardly I was filled with delight. Everything was working perfectly, Ciara. I knew why you were meeting Alan, and why you wouldn't want Niall to know about it. And because of that, you'd played right into my hands! A petty criminal I knew from my court-reporting days had been paid to do a neat job on your tyres, cash up front and no questions asked.

I looked at Niall. "Oh," I said sadly. That single syllable was meant to convey my own sad acceptance of the situation.

I touched his arm. "You poor love. You're just as lonely and let-down tonight as I am. What a sad pair we make – both of us abandoned!"

He grinned. "Then, let's make the most of it." He tipped his glass against mine in an inebriated toast. "This time, let's drink to us!" he said.

I raised my glass to his and we drank in unison, snuggled up together with our bodies pressed against each other.

"Would you like to dance again?" I finally asked him. "I love being able to hold you so close . . ."

"I wish there was somewhere we could go," Niall whispered in my ear, "then you could hold me as close as you like . . ."

Naturally, I'd covered every eventuality. "Actually, there is," I whispered back. "It just so happens that I've booked a *room for myself here in the hotel tonight. I booked it in case I didn't finish the interview until late. After all, I wouldn't want to drive home afterwards, assuming I'd had a few drinks."*

"So, are you inviting me up to your room?"

I laughed. "Yes, you're invited."

CHAPTER 11

Ciara awoke, and at first she couldn't remember where she was. Was she still in Turkey? No, she and Dee had arrived back earlier that evening. She was at home in her own bed, and someone was banging frantically on the front door.

She looked at her bedside clock, which said four in the morning, and sat up with a jolt. Who could be calling at this late hour? Suddenly, she was filled with panic – only the gardai were likely to call during the night. My God, she thought, has something happened to Sarah? No, that wasn't possible. She'd talked to Sarah at Cillian's house as soon as she'd arrived back, and had heard all about Sarah's shopping trip to London with Ita.

Throwing on her dressing-gown, she raced down the stairs, her heart pounding. But instead of the police, she found Charlie standing on the doorstep. His face was haggard, and he pushed past her into the hall without waiting for an invitation.

"You told her – you bitch!"

"Charlie!" Ciara was shocked by his anger.

"You couldn't keep your bloody mouth shut, could you? You had to tell her about us!"

"No, I didn't!"

"Then why does she want to leave me? People don't just throw away their marriages for nothing. At least, decent people don't!"

His eyes flashed venomously. "But I don't suppose someone like you would care, anyway. You wrecked your own marriage with your bloody affair, and broke poor Niall's heart. Why should you care a damn about anyone else's marriage?"

Ciara grabbed his sleeve. "Charlie, what the hell are you talking about?"

Charlie pulled his arm away. "Leave me alone."

"Charlie, I want an answer!"

Eyes blazing, Charlie rounded on her. "How can you play the innocent, when you were out screwing around behind your husband's back? And now you want to destroy my marriage as well."

"Charlie, what are you implying? That I had an affair behind Niall's back? That's not true!"

Charlie sneered at her. "Don't lie to me – even Niall knew about it! He couldn't believe that his sweet, adoring little wife could be such an underhand fucking bitch!"

In a daze, Ciara walked into the sitting-room. Opening the drinks cabinet, she poured two large measures of brandy, silently handing one to Charlie who had followed her into the room. She quickly downed a large mouthful of her own measure, acknowledging that while drink offered no solutions at certain times it was a great stress-reliever.

Ciara sat down, feeling weak and in a state of shock. Was this all a bad dream? Could Niall really have thought she was having an affair? It was ridiculous. She herself was the injured party! She looked up at Charlie, who was draining his glass. Maybe he just wasn't making sense because he was upset. He was bound to be in a state of shock, since Dee had obviously told him their marriage was over.

Ciara stood up and instinctively took Charlie's empty glass to re-fill it. "Charlie, I never had an affair. Please believe me, because I'm telling you the truth." She drew a deep breath. "Niall was the one having the affair."

Charlie turned on her scornfully. "Of course, I know Niall was having an affair, but only because you were having one! He thought it would help him to feel better about what you were doing," Charlie took a swig of his freshly poured drink, "but it only made him feel worse in the long-run."

Ciara re-filled her own glass unsteadily. "What gave Niall the idea that I was having an affair?"

"He saw you with the guy. Several times. And each time you lied to him about where you'd been."

Ciara sank into the chair, feeling sick. So that was how it had happened. In trying to keep Niall from knowing about her sordid past, she'd inadvertently destroyed their future. How well she now recalled those innocent lies, when she'd concocted a story about meeting Marguerite. And fool that she'd been, she'd thought Niall believed her. Yet at the precise moment when she'd finally felt safe, Niall's belief in her had been irrevocably shattered.

Would knowing about the pornographic photographs have been any less hurtful for him than thinking she was having an affair? Probably, but she didn't really know. Right now, she didn't know anything. If someone had asked her what her own name was, she doubted if she could have answered them.

A sob escaped from her throat. How many people knew the exact moment at which their lives were altered forever? It was an interesting concept to ponder, if she was interested in pondering concepts. Right now, she needed a good strong cup of coffee.

Putting down her glass, she looked across at Charlie and was overwhelmed by affection for him. This was a shocking night for both of them.

"Charlie, I'm going to make some coffee. I think you'd better have some if you're contemplating driving home.'

Charlie looked at her, saw the genuine affection in her eyes, and started to cry. "God, Ciara. I'm sorry for the things I said. Did you really mean it when you said you didn't tell Dee about what happened between us? I couldn't believe Dee doesn't want me any more. There had to be a reason . . ."

Ciara stood on her tiptoes and kissed his wet cheek. "It's OK, Charlie. I understand. Tonight's been an eye-opener for me too. But no, I didn't tell Dee, and never would have."

"Look, I shouldn't have said what I did, even if you were having an affair."

Ciara smiled sadly at him. "Charlie, Niall got it

wrong. I wasn't having an affair. There was never anyone else for me but him. But I *did* lie to him, for what I thought was a good reason at the time. And because of those stupid lies, I undid all the previous years of trust."

Charlie looked bleakly at her and blew his nose. `You know, you're lucky really, Ciara. I know Niall is gone –" he started to cry afresh, "but he loved you so much, and always would have, even if he'd lived to be a hundred. Forget about his bloody affair; it had no meaning –"

"I don't want to forget it, Charlie. It happened. There's no point in denying that. But knowing why it happened makes it easier for me to come to terms with it."

Charlie followed Ciara into the kitchen where she put on the kettle. A quick dose of caffeine was what they both needed. She felt selfish talking about her own problems when Charlie was so clearly in need of support. But there was one more question she had to ask. "Charlie, the woman Niall had the affair with. Do you know who it was?"

"I don't know, love. I never met her, and I never even knew her name. In fact, Niall never actually told me about the affair. I just guessed it from his behaviour. Then Liam –"

"Liam knows about it?"

Charlie looked stricken. "Jesus, I shouldn't have said that. I'm sorry, love. But Niall himself told Liam – I don't think he could face telling me, but he needed to tell someone."

"And Liam told you."

"Yeah, well, I'd been talking out of turn, then Liam said you were having an affair too –"

"Which, as I've just said, isn't true."

Taking the cup of coffee Ciara offered, Charlie's face took on an earnest expression. "Anyway, you should forget all about the other woman, Ciara. Niall kept the whole thing quiet. He respected you too much to crow about it. Besides, he wasn't so much having an affair as trying to salvage his poor deflated ego. I don't think anyone else knows about it, except me, Liam and you –"

Ciara looked across at Charlie. "And her," she said softly, almost to herself.

In silence they drank their coffee, each lost in their own thoughts, until finally Ciara spoke. "I'm so sorry about you and Dee. I really am Charlie. We were all so happy once – what's happened to us all?"

Charlie stifled a sob. "I don't know how I'm going to cope without her. At least the boys are old enough to accept it, even if I can't. Oh God, Ciara. What am I going to do?"

Ciara crossed the kitchen to put her arms around him as he sobbed. "And how on earth will I ever face Dee again?" she said sadly, "Now that you've gone and told her what happened between us –"

Charlie pulled away, looking puzzled. "But I didn't. I thought *you* did."

Ciara's eyes lit up with hope. "So she still doesn't know?"

Charlie exhaled with relief. "Well, thank God for that," he said, wiping his brow. "I never actually said anything about it. I just assumed that when she said she was leaving me, it was because you'd confessed while you were having one of your confidential girlie chats on holiday. I was so angry with you, Ciara, that I just rushed out of the house –" he looked embarrassed, "and came straight over here to give you an earful!"

Ciara smiled back at him. Poor old Charlie – it would take him a long time to accept Dee's decision. Things had always been black and white for him. The only thing that was grey was his sad tear-stained face, and the few strands of grey hair now visible in his red thatch. Suddenly, he looked old and tired, and Ciara's heart went out to him. At least Dee hadn't hurt him more than necessary by telling him about Eamonn.

"Charlie, can you and I make a pact tonight, that what happened between us will never ever be mentioned to anyone else?"

"Of course," said Charlie, giving her an affectionate hug. "It was a mistake, we both know that, but you're still a dear friend, Ciara."

"Does Dee know that you're here?" asked Ciara suddenly.

"God, no. She thinks I'm out driving around trying to come to terms with the separation."

She gave him a quick hug. "Then go on home, Charlie. Things won't look so bad in the morning."

What a meaningless platitude, she thought, even as she said it. But Charlie smiled back at her, as though her words had the power to make him feel better about everything.

Then suddenly, he looked stricken and started to cry again. "Oh God, can you believe it? I've been so wrapped up in my own problems that I forgot to tell you about Kate –"

Ciara froze.

"I phoned you in Turkey several times, but Dee said you didn't get my messages. Well, Kate's in hospital. She'd been in intensive care since the day you left on holiday. In the beginning it looked as though she wasn't going to pull through, but she's out of danger now."

"What happened?" Ciara asked, hardly able to speak, her voice coming out in a whisper.

"She was drunk and she drove up onto the new motorway in the wrong direction. I don't know where she was going, but they reckon she was travelling at a ridiculous speed."

"What time did it happen?"

Charlie looked puzzled. "I dunno, sometime in the early evening I think. It was probably about the time that I was driving you and Dee to the airport. As soon as I found out I tried to let you know, but I didn't hear about it until Kevin phoned the next morning. I think he was called in to give her the last rites."

Images of Kate at school, Kate playing hockey, Kate helping her with her homework came unbidden into Ciara's mind. Happy smiling Kate, the Kate she had loved so dearly – the Kate who had let her down.

Ciara wasn't sure how she felt. Shouldn't she feel a primitive sense of justice that Kate had been punished for stealing her friend's husband? Yet it wasn't all Kate's fault – Niall had been a willing participant too. Was it possible to hate someone on the one hand, and feel a terrible sense of loss on the other?

She started to cry softly. After all, look how she'd behaved herself only a few weeks before! Wasn't Dee equally as entitled to feel hatred, if she knew what Ciara herself done? Suddenly, the whole world seemed upside down.

Charlie tried to put his arms around her again to comfort her, but she moved away from him. "Go home, Charlie," she told him gently. "There's only so much I can take in right now."

Charlie nodded, understanding exactly what she meant. He too felt drained from the events of the evening.

As he drove away, Ciara watched the car until it disappeared out of sight. Poor, sad, unhappy Charlie, she thought. And poor, sad, broken-hearted Dee. And here was she, caught in the middle, and party to both their secrets.

She made herself another cup of coffee. Now, at least, she knew that Niall had really loved her. She would sleep long and fitfully tonight. And she wished fervently that Charlie and Dee would be able to do the same.

And Kate? She would deal with that problem in the morning. Right now, what she needed most was a good night's sleep.

CHAPTER 12

"Excuse me, I hope I'm not intruding –"

"No, not at all." She was a friendly young woman who clearly welcomed the diversion of a stranger on her doorstep.

"`I'm doing research for a book I'm writing on abortionists of the sixties and seventies," I lied. "I believe a woman called Nurse Kitty Hall used to live here?"

For a long time, Ciara, I'd felt an overwhelming urge to re-trace the steps I'd taken all those years ago in London. Perhaps I felt that by seeing the street and the house again, I could reduce the memories down to size and lessen their ability to still hurt me. I hoped that the street, which had loomed enormous in my 15-year-old mind, was in reality just a small dingy place and that by visiting it again I could bury once and for all the memories that had haunted me during all those intervening years. It would serve as a catharsis, just like writing these memoirs, Ciara, and enable me to leave the pain behind forever.

The young woman's eyes lit up with delight when she heard that I was a writer. Clearly, this was an opportunity for her to revel in the notoriety of her home. She didn't even ask for any *identification, although I always carried my press card in my pocket.*

"Oh, don't talk to me about that one!" she said cheerfully. "You have no idea of the stories we've heard since we moved here. We didn't know anything about what went on until after we'd bought the house. Estate agents never tell you these things, do they?"

I smiled at her, and at the little boy who was clinging to her skirts. Clearly that gesture helped to ingratiate me, and pulling the child aside, she gestured towards the hall with her free hand.

"Would you like to come in? I'm afraid the place is very untidy."

"Thanks, that's very kind of you."

Stepping into the hall, I felt none of the horror that I'd felt on my previous visit there. The decor was different now, and there was an untidy, warm and lived-in feel to the place.

"Apparently, Kitty Hall was quite a character," the young woman said. "She performed all the abortions downstairs in the basement. Would you like to see it? We've converted the area into a kitchen, so I'll make us a cup of coffee while you're looking around. Simon, leave the lady alone."

A small sticky hand had grabbed the hem of my skirt, leaving a stain that looked like melted chocolate. I glared at young Simon behind his mother's back, and he quickly withdrew his hand. But in reality, the stain didn't matter. I was far more eager to hear about the previous owner's exploits than worrying about such a minor inconvenience.

I looked around the downstairs area, especially at the area where the dreaded couch had been. Now there were toys scattered around the floor, a fire burning in the small fifties-

style grate and a half-knit child's jumper lying alongside a bag of matching wool on the arm of a well-worn sofa. And where I had once smelled antiseptic, there was now only the comforting aroma of fresh coffee.

"What happened to her?"

"Nurse Hall? Oh, she died years ago." The woman put the two coffee mugs on the kitchen counter. "Milk? Sugar? I might even have a drop of cream, if you'd like it."

"No, no, this is wonderful," I said, taking the coffee gratefully. "Did you ever hear any stories about her?"

"Oh, lots," said the young woman, helping herself to a chocolate biscuit from the packet which she then offered to me. I declined, but now I knew for certain the origin of the stain on my skirt. "The neighbours around here could tell you, especially old Mrs Kickham next door. Nurse Hall had a trail of young girls forever knocking at her door. Sometimes, they'd get the address wrong and call to Mrs Kickham's by mistake."

"So the neighbours all knew about her?"

"Well, I think a lot of them knew. But you know what British reserve is like – stiff upper lip, mind your own business and all that."

The woman aimed a sudden swipe at young Simon, who was trying to climb up onto the counter, intending to help himself to the remainder of the biscuits. Then she went on talking as though nothing had happened. "Mrs Kickham said that she'd often thought of notifying the police, but she felt sorry for all those girls. What would they do if they couldn't get the kind of help Nurse Hall provided? Even though abortions became legal in the late sixties, most of these young girls couldn't afford to go to expensive clinics."

"How did Mrs Kickham know what went on?"

"She found out from the girls themselves. Sometimes they called to her house by mistake, Mrs Kickham being next door and all that."

She paused. "More coffee? No? Nurse Hall was a moralistic old cow who didn't approve of girls having sex outside marriage. Yet she was quite happy to exploit their vulnerability for cash." The young woman looked at me grimly. "Probably a frustrated old bitch herself."

This was getting nearer to the kind of information that I was looking for. "How do you know all that?"

"Oh, I've heard what I know from Mrs Kickham. You should go and see her yourself. She's lived here for years – quite ancient herself, poor dear. She knew Nurse Hall personally. Well, they used to say hello when they met in the street."

I put down my coffee mug and stood up. "Yes, that's a good idea. Do you think she'd be there if I called now?"

"Oh, yes. The poor old thing rarely goes out. It's her arthritis, you know. But she loves having someone to talk to. Tell her I told you to call."

Giving young Simon an affectionate smile that I didn't feel, and which he knew I didn't mean, I left the kitchen and climbed the stairs to the hall. The woman accompanied me, chattering all the while about how exciting it must be to be writing a book and how she'd love to write one herself, if only she had the time. Murmuring my thanks, I extricated myself and headed down the garden path, recalling the day when I'd previously left that house under vastly different circumstances.

At first, there was no answer from Mrs Kickham's house next door, and I was about to leave when I spotted the old woman's silhouette through the glass panel in the hall door. She was shuffling slowly towards it, and I hoped I hadn't disturbed her from an afternoon nap, in case the interruption wouldn't dispose her too favourably towards me.

However, I needn't have worried. She was clearly as delighted at having company as her young neighbour, and full of apologies for the delay in answering the door.

"It's my arthritis, dear," she told me, "but if you're selling anything, I'm not interested."

"No, no," I hastily assured her, "your next-door neighbour thought you might be able to help me with some information, for a book I'm writing."

"Oh, young Alison? Charming child. She and her young man have been very good to me. You know, helping to put the bins out, and looking after my cat when I go to visit my sister," she peered closely at me now. "But how can I help you?"

"I'm looking for information on Nurse Hall. Alison said you were the best person to talk to."

"Yes, yes, she used to live next door. Dreadful woman. Nurse Hall I mean, not Alison. All those poor young girls –" she looked momentarily distressed, before looking me up and down. "You're writing a book, you say?"

"Yes, I'm documenting the history of abortions in the sixties and seventies," I lied. Who on earth would want to read, much less buy, a book like that?

"Well dear, I'd be glad to help," said old Mrs Kickham. "I used to see her every day, you know. Nine o'clock sharp each morning, regular as clockwork, she'd set out for the corner shop to get her newspaper." Suddenly, she looked at me in alarm. "You're not digging up scandal for one of those dreadful tabloid newspapers, are you? Because if you are –"

"No, of course, not," I assured her. "My book is based on

people like you, who can provide valuable insights into the ethos of that time."

"W-will I be mentioned in this book?"

I hedged my bets. "It's entirely up to you. You can be credited, or remain anonymous if you prefer."

I could see the old dear visibly swell with pride. She would want her name in lights. And she was dying to tell me all that she knew.

"Well, come inside, dear, because I need to sit down," she said. "My old legs aren't what they used to be. That's the problem with old age."

I followed her into the old-fashioned parlour, which looked as though nothing in it had been touched for the previous fifty years. But everything was clean and freshly polished, bearing testimony to a lifetime of care and attention.

"Did she perform many abortions?" I asked.

"I couldn't say exactly how many, dear. But young girls were forever turning up on her doorstep. And on mine too, when they'd get the address wrong," she sighed. "I used to feel so sorry for them, and sometimes when they were very upset I'd invite them in for a cuppa. You know, it's such a big decision. Some of them didn't want to go through with it, but they had no other choice. They knew they'd be thrown out of home if they told their parents they were pregnant. Most of them were terrified of the pain. There were some really horrific cases, where girls had been made pregnant by their brothers or fathers," the old woman shuddered. "What kind of animals are these men?" she asked rhetorically.

I didn't bother to inform her that in my opinion, animals were less cruel and infinitely superior to humans in almost every respect.

Then the old woman's face brightened. "There was one little girl in particular, an Irish girl like yourself. The poor child was so upset that I brought her in for a cuppa and a chat. She badly needed to talk to someone. She'd been taken advantage of by a young curate back home in Ireland and she was sure that she was in the family way. Needless to say, the cleric didn't want to know anything about it. She'd very little money and knew no one over here, and I was so sorry for her that I invited her to stay here after she'd had the, er, business done."

She stopped talking, and I began to fear that the old woman had fallen asleep. But she was merely lost in her own thoughts, and I waited patiently until she was ready to continue. I wished she'd move on to a more interesting aspect of Nurse Hall's escapades, but I was afraid to show my impatience lest I lose her goodwill.

"That young girl kept in touch with me for years, you know, even after she went back to Ireland," the old woman said at last, "and I'd get a Christmas card from her each year. Eventually through, the cards stopped. I think she got married, so it wasn't really surprising," the old woman sighed. "I suppose she wouldn't want her new husband knowing how she'd met me."

She sighed, and I smiled at her in sympathy. Was there no way I could get her away from this boring preamble? I'd no need to hear this other girl's story. But it seemed churlish to leave, when the old woman was clearly enjoying her reminiscences.

If I'd left at that moment, I might never have discovered the truth of what happened all those years before. But there are defining moments in life, and sometimes we are blessed, or cursed, by knowing the exact moment when everything changed. Mine was just about to happen.

CHAPTER 13

Ita smoothed out the long satin nightdress. It really was a beauty. She'd even put satin sheets on the bed this time, so the room looked like a movie set from the forties. I'm a total fraud, she thought complacently, but at last, I'm actually going to do something about it.

She'd finished washing her hair, blow-dried it and used the electric tongs to curl it at the ends. She rarely used the tongs, knowing that it could dry out her hair and cause split ends, but what the hell did it matter now? This was the last time she'd ever style her hair. Unless the undertakers did things like that? There were probably people especially employed to tart up corpses. It was an amusing, if ghoulish, thought. And she remembered how, during her childhood, certain women in the neighbourhood would arrive at the house after someone died and lay out the corpse.

She'd decided against make-up, it would only stain the pillowcases. Besides, she wanted to look elegant in death, not like a hideous doll with a painted face. She looked in the mirror. Perhaps a little eyeshadow, and a slight pencilling-in of her eyebrows, but nothing more.

She was surprised at how methodically she'd set about organising her own demise. She'd planned it unemotionally, as though she'd been organising a social event. She'd even made a list of all the things that needed to be done before she was ready to go, like ensuring that her will was up-to-date, and leaving money out for her cleaner Mrs Daly. She'd even bought fresh lilies for beside her bed. A theatrical touch, she supposed, but she really wanted the place to look nice. She also liked the idea of being able to smell the fragrance of her favourite flowers as she lay waiting for death.

Ita wished she could see Sarah for one last time. She felt guilty at leaving the child now that they'd established such a close bond. But Sarah's secret was safe, and would always be safe, unless Sarah herself ever chose to reveal it.

Finally, Ita sat down at her computer, copied a file onto a disk, placed it in an envelope, sealed and addressed it, then placed it on her desk. She smiled whimsically as she did it – she was the consummate journalist right to the end! Then she shut down her computer for the very last time.

Now undressed, Ita slipped on her satin nightdress, enjoying the luxurious sensation of the material against her skin. Soon she would be ready.

Ita walked resolutely to the bathroom, taking the bottle of tablets from the medicine cabinet and bringing it to the bedside table, where she'd already poured herself a glass of water. She might as well get on with it. She could dither indefinitely, but what was the point of putting it off for another hour, another day? She was still going to do it anyway. Besides, the irrevocable decision had been made already, when she'd posted her final letter to Liam.

She'd left the house that afternoon, and headed to the nearest postbox, in time for the postal collection. That would ensure that Liam received her letter the following morning. Too late to stop her, but at least she'd tried to assure him of the special place he would hold in her heart forever. Then again, how long was forever? Once she was gone, there would be no forever for her any more.

As she'd walked to the postbox, she'd noted with surprise how her senses made her acutely aware of everything around her. And she surveyed it all with a poignancy she hadn't expected to feel. She noticed the carefully tended gardens, the blossoms that had been blown off the trees during a recent shower and which now lined the sides of the street like confetti. She passed an elderly couple, and wondered idly how they would feel if they knew they were probably the last people to see her alive? She smiled at her own self-induced melodrama. Maybe she should have written movie scripts instead of becoming a journalist!

Even the puddles held a childlike fascination for her, and suddenly everything around was dear and precious to her. Perhaps, she thought, this is how a death row prisoner feels when they take their last walk before being executed. But she dismissed the fanciful comparison. In the case of the criminal, society was sanctioning their death. In her case, she was acting as her own executioner. She'd dropped the letter into the box and hurried back to her apartment.

She now surveyed the pills dispassionately. Hopefully, she would just fall asleep. But even if it hurt a bit, there was no physical pain on earth that could compare with the agony that existed inside her head. Soon, she'd be released from all the torment that had filled her entire being for as long as she could remember.

Sitting on the side of her bed, she slipped the first tablet into her mouth and swallowed it. It was a strange feeling. She could still change her mind if she wanted to. But then she swallowed a dozen more in quick succession, gagging slightly at their bitter taste. Soon, she thought, I'll have reached the point of no return . . .

There, it was done. She felt a moment of triumph as she surveyed the empty bottle. Now it was time to get into bed and settle down for her long sleep . . .

Suddenly she remembered the paintings on the dining-room wall, and jumping off the bed, she went into the living-room to have a final look. With a feeling of intense pleasure, she surveyed the Jack B Yeats, the Louis Le Brocquy and the Ciara Reynolds. She'd left them all to Liam in her will, knowing they'd mean more to him than to anyone else.

Suddenly, she wished she could be there when he discovered that the paintings were his! What a pity she couldn't have given them to him in person and witnessed the joy and incredulity on his face. Maybe it wasn't too late to call him, to just hear his voice one more time, to tell him that there was a lovely surprise in store for him. But it was too late now, wasn't it? Maybe if she dialled his number, she could listen to his voice on his answering service . . .

Ita returned to the bedroom and picked up the receiver. Then she put it down again. Was it really fair to call him? Yet she longed to be soothed by hearing him say, for the last time, that he loved her. No one had ever truly loved her before. Resolutely, she put the receiver back and lay down on the bed. Oh, Liam, she thought, I wish I could have loved you the way you love me, but the timing was all wrong.

Then all of a sudden, she was overcome by fear. She was afraid to die alone, afraid to die at all. Already she could feel her body being overcome by a terrible lassitude. Initially she fought it, like someone who was drowning and reaching out in vain to find a helping hand. But it was too late now . . .

Gradually, the abyss came to meet her, and she was falling, falling, down, down . . . Her body shuddered, then it was still. And as the darkness engulfed her, she gave up the struggle at last.

CHAPTER 14

As I sat in the old woman's parlour my mind was in neutral as she droned on. As soon as it was polite, I would leave her to her memories. She was rambling on about some unfortunate Irish girl, who'd had an abortion all those years ago. Then suddenly, I was jolted by the impact of her next words.

"But," the old dear said, "when she went back to Ireland after the abortion, she wrote and told me she hadn't been pregnant at all!"

I sat up in my chair. "What do you mean?"

"Begging your pardon, dear. A lot of Irish girls were terribly naïve back then. Most of them got into trouble because they didn't even know how people got pregnant! Men would tell them that what they were doing wasn't any harm, or tell them that they couldn't get pregnant the first time, then the poor girls would be surprised when they ended up in the family way!"

"But you said this girl —"

"Yes, poor girl. Can you believe it, I've even forgotten her *name. Now what was it? Anyway, she didn't understand how girls got pregnant either! She thought the local priest had made her pregnant. But when she discovered the true facts of life, and not the mixed-up version she'd heard from her friends, she realised that she couldn't have been pregnant since the priest had only put his hand up her skirt after choir practice!"*

"But, I thought you said she had an abortion . . ."

"Yes, that's what I'm trying to tell you. Kitty Hall took her money and pretended to do the abortion anyway. Can you believe it?"

The old woman sighed. "That dreadful woman took advantage of those poor girls' ignorance. Even when they weren't pregnant, she took their money and pretended to do an abortion anyway. To make it seem real she hurt them too, and she used to hold up what was supposed to be a dead baby afterwards."

I could hardly find my voice. "How do you know that?"

"Oh, she told me so herself, dear. Proud as Punch about it too. One morning she invited me in for coffee, and told me she was 'retiring'. In the course of conversation I got up the courage to ask her if she'd ever had girls call who weren't actually pregnant," Mrs Kickham pursed her lips. "She got a great laugh out of telling me that she made good money from naïve Irish girls like that. When she examined them and realised that they weren't pregnant, she pretended to do the abortion anyway. It was easy money after all, and she enjoyed showing them a foetus afterwards, although it was only a piece of steak she was about to cook for her own dinner," Mrs Kickham sighed. "How many poor women today are grieving for aborted babies that never were?"

I was rooted to the seat as the old woman continued. "Kitty

Hall liked to make out that she was doing these girls a favour by discouraging them from getting pregnant again. But I believe she was just a bitter old woman who was probably ditched by a man herself, and she couldn't bear to see other women, even frightened kids, getting male attention." Mrs Kickham retreated once again into her own private reverie.

I sat there stunned, because now I'd discovered what had happened to me as well. In retrospect, I realised that Niall and I hadn't really gone far enough for me to get pregnant, but I'd always assumed that I must have been pregnant since Kitty Hall had taken my money and shown me what I assumed was my dead baby. My head began to spin, since the repercussions were too frightening for me to grasp all at once.

"Are you all right, dear?" the old woman asked. "You've suddenly gone a bit pale. Would you like a cuppa to warm you up?"

I shook my head. A triple brandy might have done the trick, but the last thing on earth I wanted was tea.

Together we sat in silence, each of us lost in our own thoughts. By tacit agreement, the discussion was now over. The old woman was worn out from the excitement of her revelations, and I was reeling in shock from the impact of her words.

"Thank you for your help," I said, picking up my shoulder bag. "Please don't get up. I can see myself out."

"All right dear, and good luck with your book. Will you send me a copy when it's published? Wait a moment, I'd better write out my name for you, in case you're quoting me."

Guiltily, I waited while she wrote out her name and address on a scrap of paper. At least I'd given her an afternoon's entertainment.

As I walked down that back street in London, I finally realised that there had never been any justification for what I'd done to you, Ciara. And all the years in between, I'd mourned for a child that never was, attributing my infertility to the abortion and avenging myself against you and Niall with no justification.

But I still didn't have all the answers. I now remembered that Kitty Hall had made a sneering comment to me, which I hadn't understood at the time. She'd said, "This isn't your first time with a man, is it?" Had she assumed from the condition of my womb, that I'd either had an earlier abortion or suffered some other kind of trauma to my womb? If so, did this mean that there was still something even more awful in my past, of which I wasn't aware? Was it something so horrific that I'd chosen to suppress it, even from myself?

CHAPTER 15

Whistling happily, Liam closed the door of his apartment and headed down the corridor. The sun was shining, it was a beautiful morning and he was happy to be alive. As he took the lift to the ground floor, he made a face at his reflection in the mirror for he was in a giddy humour.

Today, he hoped to complete negotiations with an artist he felt was going to become another real 'biggie' in the future. After that, he was due to attend an end-of-term student exhibition at one of the regional colleges. He loved attending this kind of exhibition where the work was fresh and uninhibited, where there was always the possibility of discovering a major new talent, followed by the joy of nurturing and developing it.

What gallery owner or art teacher didn't dream of finding a budding new talent? He remembered the thrill of discovering Ciara Reynolds all those years ago. He had a lucky knack for talent-spotting, and he felt certain that today was going to be a lucky day. And to round off the evening, he was taking Ita out for dinner. He hadn't seen her for two whole days, and he was filled with an almost overwhelming need to be with her.

He fingered his pocket. Inside, in an old-fashioned jewellery box, was his grandmother's engagement ring, which he intended presenting to Ita that evening. He'd had it since his mother gave it to him all those years ago. The ring had been destined for someone special, and now at last he'd found her. He was still whistling as he stepped out of the lift.

Just as he went to check his mailbox in the hall, the postman arrived. Perfect timing. What better proof did he need that it was going to be a good day?

"Morning, Jim. Great day, isn't it?"

Jim sighed, rubbing his back. "Too hot for me, Liam. We're not used to this kind of weather y'know," he said darkly. "The body can't adapt that quickly."

Liam laughed. "C'mon, Jim, cheer up! We could do with a bit of good weather. I'll bet you the farmers are pleased about it anyway!"

"I never met a farmer who was pleased with the weather, no matter what it was like," said Jim, determined to be negative. "I hope these aren't all bills," he added, handing a bundle of envelopes to Liam.

Liam surveyed his post casually as Jim placed the other residents' post in the appropriate boxes. He grimaced at the electricity bill, was it already two months since the last one? They seemed to arrive with amazing regularity! Good, an invitation to a Royal Hibernian Academy exhibition the week after next. They were always interesting.

He frowned. A handwritten letter from Ita? Impossible – it was probably from somebody whose writing looked like hers. He eyed the cream envelope suspiciously, then tore it open, his heart sinking as he did so. If it was from Ita, did that mean she was giving him the heave-ho? Yet why else would she write, when she was due to see him that very evening?

"Cheerio, Liam."

Absent-mindedly, Liam looked up, just in time to observe the retreating figure of the postman. "Oh goodbye, Jim. See you tomorrow."

Slowly, Liam removed the single sheet of cream-coloured notepaper from the envelope with a terrible sense of foreboding.

Jim the postman had just reached the end of the driveway when he heard the howl. At first, he thought it was a dog that had been run over, then suddenly he realised that it had come from the hall of the apartment block where he'd just left Liam. Dropping his postbag, he raced back up the driveway as quickly as his elderly legs and his lumbago would allow him.

In the hallway, Liam was sitting crouched on the floor, his post scattered all around him with a grey expression on his face, his eyes staring out ahead into some unfathomable darkness. Initially, Jim thought the poor fellow must have had a heart attack.

"Liam, for God's sake, man. Are you all right?"

But Liam was incapable of giving any reply. His body had become convulsed, and old Jim wondered if he was having an epileptic fit instead. Reaching for the wall phone in the lobby, he picked it up and began to dial the general emergency number. They'd know what to do, or what particular service to send.

"No."Suddenly, Liam was on his feet. "Jim, have you got the van with you?"

Jim nodded.

"Then will you take me round to the apartments on Beech Road, immediately?"

Jim hesitated. Now that he'd established that Liam wasn't dying, he was less keen to get involved. Besides, he still had to deliver post to several roads in the area, and some people became very cranky if they didn't get their post on time.

"Well . . ."

"Please, Jim. I'm not fit to drive. My –" Liam hesitated briefly, then the tears came in a rush, "– the woman I was going to marry, she's killed herself. God knows why. I've got a key to her apartment, so I need to get there urgently."

"Holy God!" Quickly, Jim made the sign of the cross and mumbled a prayer. Then both men hurried down the driveway and climbed into the postal van, Jim flying along like a racing driver on the Mondello circuit. Then it suddenly crossed his mind that if the woman was dead, she wasn't going anywhere in a hurry so he slowed down since it wasn't worth the risk of losing points off his driving licence.

At the apartments, Jim was only too happy to disgorge his deeply distressed passenger. He wasn't used to dealing with men who cried. Besides, in his haste to oblige Liam, he'd abandoned his sack of post and he could be in serious trouble if anyone found it before he got back to collect it.

"Is there anything I can do?" he asked half-heartedly, and was greatly relieved when Liam declined any further help.

"Oh, wait, Jim –"

Liam began searching in his pocket for a piece of paper and a pen, finding his handkerchief first and wiping his tear-stained face with it. "Would you phone someone for me?"

Jim nodded, glad that Liam didn't want him to go into the apartment with him. He wasn't too keen on dead bodies. Especially now, since he was getting perilously near to retirement age. He wasn't too keen on being reminded of his own mortality.

Liam wrote Ciara's name and phone number on the paper, and handed it to Jim. "Please ask her to come to this address as soon as possible, and Jim –"

Jim waited, looking away so that he wouldn't have to see Liam's tear-stained face again.

"– tell her that Ita is dead."

"I beg your pardon?"

"I'm sorry to trouble you, missus. My name is Jim. I'm the postman for the Ivy apartments in Ballsbridge. Liam Golden asked me to phone you."

Ciara's heartbeat quickened. "Is he all right?"

"Yes, well I think so. But he's very upset. He said to tell you that Ita is dead. And he wants you to go round there as soon as you can."

"To his place?"

"No, missus, to her place. I've just dropped him off there."

"Oh my God." Shocked, Ciara barely remembered to thank the old man for his call. Gathering up her coat, bag and car keys, Ciara was out of the house within seconds. Although she'd never been there, she knew roughly where Ita's apartment was. Liam had often mentioned little anecdotes about Ita's life in the Donnybrook complex, so at least she knew where to go. Which was just as well, since she'd forgotten to ask the postman, and he'd either assumed she knew or had been too shocked to volunteer the information.

What on earth could have happened to Ita? Ciara had been too stunned herself to even think of asking what had happened. Had the poor woman accidentally electrocuted herself? Or had someone broken into her apartment and murdered her?

Realising that speculation was pointless, Ciara concentrated on driving. Now that she had more time to think, the full impact of never seeing Ita again began to register. And she was overcome by a deep sadness, for she'd liked the woman very much. And with frightening clarity, she realised the traumatic effect that this would have on poor Liam.

All it took was one look at Liam's face to assure her that the message had been accurate. He'd been waiting for her at the ground floor entrance to the apartment block, perhaps remembering that she didn't know the actual apartment number. Silently, she and Liam stood locked together in an embrace, just as they'd held each other in Ciara's house on the day of Niall's funeral.

Ciara could feel Liam's body shuddering as he held her close, and a sob escaped from his lips as he buried his face in her hair. Then suddenly Liam was crying, big gulping sobs that rendered any conversation impossible.

"Is she?"

Liam nodded. "She killed herself. Why, for God's sake? I just don't understand –"

Upstairs in the third floor apartment bedroom, still holding Liam's hand, Ciara gazed at the immobile form lying on the bed. Ita looked too glamorous, too vibrant to be dead.

Liam gazed without speaking at Ita's lovely face in repose. She didn't look dead. At any moment, he expected her to open those beautiful big eyes and smile at him. Yet he had to admit that she looked more at peace now than she'd ever been during the short time he'd known her. She looked almost triumphant now, as though she'd finally achieved something of monumental importance to her.

He leaned forward and stroked her face, feeling the cold marble-like texture where there had once been softness and warmth. And he gently caressed the eyelids that were closed now, as though in sleep.

Ciara touched his arm. "Have you called anyone else, love?"

Liam shook his head.

Although still in a daze, Ciara lifted the receiver of the phone beside the bed, and dialled the emergency services.

CHAPTER 16

I'd just arrived at the newspaper when my boss called me into his office. "I've a really interesting assignment for you this week. You like dealing with historical issues, don't you?"

"Yes, I do," I said, smiling at the editor, "but I know you too well, Peter. When you start hyping something before you've even told me what it's about, I know it's going to be awful!"

Peter Loftus pretended to look upset, but I could see that the corners of his mouth were twitching. "Moi? As if I'd ask you to do a news feature you wouldn't enjoy! Seriously though, I thought you'd like getting your teeth into this one." He handed me a small cutting from a regional newspaper. "This old bird's just kicked the bucket. She was serving life for murdering her husband on their farm thirty-five years ago. But after a few years in prison, she ended up in the loony bin. An interesting case. You're too young to remember it, of course, but I was a junior reporter at the time and I covered the court case. It was a nine-day wonder when it happened. There weren't many murders in this country back then, so it got massive coverage in all the papers." He smiled benignly at me. "I'd like you to research the background to the case, and see if you can come up with any new theories as to why it happened. Depending on what you can find, we'll run a full-page feature with pics on page six." He handed me a file of press cuttings. "Here's a few items to get you started, but you may need to spend some time in the National Library if our own files aren't detailed enough."

I nodded as I took the file. It didn't seem a particularly onerous piece. I'd be able to wrap it in a day or two at the most.

"Oh, by the way —" Peter called after me as I left his office and walked down the corridor towards the features department, "— there was a child, a little girl as I recall. Try to find out what happened to her, will you?"

Suddenly, I was overcome by the most chilling sense of déja vu. My heart was pounding, and I wanted to drop the file and run out of the building. I didn't want to read what was in the newspaper cuttings, and I didn't want to write the story. I was filled with a terrible sense of foreboding.

In the features office, I sat for ages just staring at the file without opening it. Fortunately, most of my colleagues were engrossed in their own projects, so no one paid any attention to me. Maybe I could refuse to do the assignment. If I told Peter I wasn't feeling well, hopefully he'd assign it to someone else. That way, I could avoid facing the demons that I feared were lurking inside that file. If I didn't know what was in there, it couldn't hurt me.

But I wasn't a journalist for nothing. Curiosity got the better of me, and I eventually opened the folder and looked inside. The old yellowed newspaper pages swam before my eyes as I saw my mother's face looking back at me. There were *photographs of her being led into court, photos of the farm where I grew up, and photos of the slurry pit where my father's body had been found.*

My heart was palpitating. I just couldn't do the story. I would plead illness and Peter would have to assign it elsewhere. Then I realised that another journalist would then begin digging for information on the child, and I couldn't risk that. I would do the story, but on my terms. No one would ever discover what had happened to the little girl, since I'd claim that she'd emigrated to Australia or America and had never been heard of again.

Looking down at the news cuttings swimming before my eyes, I realised I'd finally been given the opportunity of discovering what really happened to my family. While I remembered my early childhood, and my later life in Dublin with my aunt, there was a huge gap in between. I'd always suspected that something awful had happened, something so awful that my mind refused to allow it in. Maybe now if I steeled myself, I could finally face the demons that lurked in my family history.

CHAPTER 17

Kevin sat on a chair beside Kate's hospital bed, holding her hand tightly. He was almost afraid to believe that she was out of danger. He'd hardly left her bedside since she'd been admitted, except to sleep briefly for a few hours. Then he was back at her side again, willing her to get better, mopping her brow and generally getting in the nurses' way. But they tolerated him good-humouredly. They realised that if anyone could give Kate Egan the will to survive, it was this tall gangling man who, someone said, was a priest working in Africa.

He watched Kate's heartbeat flicker on the monitor. How many men knew the beat of their loved one's heart as intimately as he did? He'd been watching it for over two weeks now, at first with fear and trepidation, then with relief and joy. She was going to make it. His beloved Kate was going to survive.

And the baby. He'd never even suspected that Kate might be pregnant! It had come as a complete surprise when the doctor on duty expressed concern for the child she was carrying. "B-baby?" he'd asked stupidly, shocked and thrilled at the same time. Kate and he were having a baby!

"Yes, Ms Egan is five months pregnant," the doctor had told him. "At this stage, the condition of both mother and child is fairly stable. So she has a good chance of delivering to term. For while, it was touch-and-go. We were afraid that we might lose both of them."

When the doctor left, Kevin had sat staring at Kate's outline beneath the bedclothes, pondering joyously on the fact that his child was growing in there! And to think that she'd never told him. Come to think of it, he'd thought Kate had been looking peaky and off-colour lately, but hadn't liked to mention it to her. And all the time, it was because she'd been carrying his child!

He hoped fervently that their child would live, but it was secondary in importance to his beloved Kate. He didn't know the baby, although in a primitive way, he loved it anyway because it was theirs and it represented the physical embodiment of their love. But the one person that really mattered was Kate. If she lost this baby, they could always try for another when she was well enough. But if he lost her . . . He shuddered. He wouldn't even think about that possibility. He'd wasted enough time already.

He was there beside her when she opened her eyes for the first time since the accident. And his own eyes filled with tears as she looked around her in surprise, then she smiled with pleasure at finding him there.

"Kev – where am I?"

"You're in hospital, love. You've had an accident. But you're OK," he squeezed her hand. "You'll be well again in no time."

Kate smiled back at him. If Kevin was beside her, everything was bound to be all right. Yet there was something nagging at the back of her brain, something that was still disturbing her peace of mind. Suddenly, she remembered. The baby!

As she cried out, and her hand quickly moved to her stomach, Kevin smiled tenderly at her. "It's OK," he assured her. "Our baby is doing fine."

Kate smiled with relief and clutched his hand.

"Why didn't you tell me, love. About the baby?"

Kate sighed. "I didn't want to make things any worse for you. I mean, you'd already made the tough decision to leave the priesthood. I didn't want you to feel that I was going to be another millstone round your neck. If I told you, I'd be tying you down with responsibilities before you'd even had a chance to taste your freedom."

Kevin squeezed her hand. "Freedom? Is that what you think? My God, I want you! And our baby! I love you, both of you, you know that!" he grinned. "Anyway, how dare you refer to my family as a millstone!"

Suddenly, Kate looked solemn again. She vaguely remembered that something else had happened. It was something to do with Ciara. She struggled through the fog, trying to remember. Yes, at last it was all coming back to her. Ciara was furious with her. Ciara had said that she never wanted to see her again. Clearly, Ciara blamed her for Kevin leaving the priesthood.

Suddenly, she grabbed Kevin's arm. "Kev, Ciara is

very angry with me. Could you go and see her, please?"

"Of course. But why is she –"

Just then, the duty sister bustled in, smiling broadly when she saw that Kate was finally awake. "Call the doctor on duty, quickly!" she told the junior ward nurse. "Tell him Ms Egan has regained consciousness."

Suddenly, the ward was a hive of activity as one by one, all the nursing staff on the floor came in to see Kate for themselves. She'd become quite a *cause célèbre* with all of them hoping and praying for her full recovery and the baby's survival. Then the doctor on duty arrived, followed by several specialists, and Kevin retired happily to the corridor outside.

What did Kate mean, he wondered, when she'd said that Ciara was angry with her? Maybe Kate was still slightly concussed, and had got her wires crossed. After all, those two had been friends since their schooldays. In fact, it was through Ciara that he'd first met Kate all those years ago, long before he'd even considered entering the priesthood. What could possibly cause a rift between them?

Suddenly he had a weird thought. Surely it couldn't be because of his relationship with Kate? That didn't sound like his sister at all. He sighed. She'd hardly be peeved, would she, because they'd kept their relationship a secret? Was she hurt that they hadn't taken her into their confidence?

Now that he thought about it, Ciara hadn't called to the hospital since Kate had been admitted. He knew she'd been away on holidays when the accident happened, but she'd been back for several days now.

Perhaps he'd better go and see his sister. He felt guilty that he'd only seen her twice since Niall's funeral, and one of those occasions being the day they'd driven out to Wicklow. He also wanted his sister to know that he hadn't left the priesthood because of Kate, not that anything like that would worry Ciara anyway. He'd made the decision to leave long before he and Kate had fallen in love. In fact, theirs had only been a friendship before that. There had been no physical relationship to begin with. That had come later, when they'd become so unbelievably close that it became the next inevitable step.

He and Kate had always been very fond of each other, even back in their schooldays when Kate was a regular caller to the Reynolds house. They'd always shared a special empathy, and he'd actually fancied Kate long before he decided to become a priest! Kate had recently confessed to him that she, too, had loved him all those years ago and had been devastated when he'd decided to become a priest. And while he'd been overjoyed to know that he'd always been important to her, he was saddened to think that he was the reason for the failure of her engagement, which had taken place on the rebound.

Less than two years ago, they'd bumped into each other in Grafton Street when Kevin had been home from Africa on holidays. They'd stopped for a cup of coffee at a nearby café, and Kevin suddenly found himself pouring out all his doubts about his vocation to Kate. It had been like old times again.

"Why did you become a priest in the first place?" Kate had asked him that day. And he'd had to confess that he just didn't know.

"It seemed the right thing at the time. I suppose I just got carried away by the whole religious fervour thing, and the idea of working in the Missions. I've never changed my mind about working in Africa; there's so much that needs to be done there."

Kate smiled mischievously. "Do you force the gospels down their throats, or try to convert them?"

"Definitely not," said Kevin, "although technically, that's part of what we're supposed to do. Historically, the Church in the field, whether in Africa, South America or wherever, has always been on the side of the dispossessed rather than the dictators, landowners and big business, because the clergy see the injustices at first hand. But too often, the institutions of the Church have been slow to speak out against the regimes that cause these people's sufferings." He smiled. "If there is a God, I don't think that he, or she, would ever choose to be on the establishment side! Jesus himself was a revolutionary!"

Kevin had grinned apologetically, realising that he'd been hogging the conversation and talking very loudly. He looked at Kate solemnly. "If I'm truly honest, I think that I also felt so guilty about stealing that cake in Dineen's shop."

Kate had looked at him with surprise, but she didn't smile back. "You're not saying you became a priest to make up for stealing a bloody cake?"

"No, not exactly. But I know I upset Mam badly at the time. It was an awful time for the whole family with Da out of work, and there was I making things worse. I knew that if I decided on the priesthood, Mam would be really happy. And I wanted to make her happy more than anything in the world," he sighed. `You know the scenario, Kate. Priests were always highly regarded in the community and still are in some places. I wanted to make up to her for what I had done. She and Dad had struggled so hard to give us kids a better start than they'd had."

He smiled, willing her to understand. "At seventeen, you only think of the immediate future, without realising that your life is only just beginning. Your own narrow world hasn't enabled you to discover all the options that are out there, and your immaturity leads you to believe that you know it all anyway." Kevin gently squeezed her arm. "Sorry for rambling on, Kate, but it's your own fault. You're a great listener, and it's just like old times. Now tell me, what's happening in your own life?"

They'd discussed Kate's job, her brief engagement, her sporadic and largely disappointing love life, Ciara's last exhibition, Cillian's appointment as director of the city's newest neurosurgery unit and Kevin's own deep and abiding love for Africa.

"Why don't you come out and see it for yourself?" Kevin had asked suddenly, surprising himself by the earnestness with which he issued the invitation. "You'll love it. It's a magnificent place, and the people are wonderful." He looked at her earnestly. "Please say you'll come, Kate. There's just so much out there that you could write about. Maybe your newspaper would commission you to do a series on Africa?"

Suddenly, more than anything else he'd wanted to share his beautiful Africa with Kate, to be the one to show her the vast and glorious skylines, to take her through the huge safari parks, and show her the many conservation projects underway to restore endangered species to their original habitats. She'd be able to travel with him while he carried out his pastoral work, meet people from the many tribes and townships he visited and learn about their customs and way of life. And instinctively, he knew that she'd come to love the people as much as he did.

To his joy, Kate promised to give the matter consideration. In truth, she'd been excited at the prospect of seeing Africa for the very first time, and, of course, seeing Kevin again . . .

On his return to Africa, Kevin got himself a laptop so that they could keep in regular contact by e-mail. A few months later, Kate headed out to Africa for a three-week stay during which time she sent back several colour pieces to her newspaper.

By unspoken agreement, he and Kate had played down their friendship among family and friends. At that stage, they were simply good friends anyway, and neither of them wanted people making snide innuendoes. Kate had simply told everyone that she was going to Africa on holiday, and would make contact with Kevin while she was out there. It seemed the most natural thing in the world anyway.

But they'd both subconsciously known, even then, that something was happening again between them. Kevin had been relieved to discover that there was no special man in Kate's life. And he'd been thrilled when she'd phoned to tell him the date of her arrival.

As he'd stood waiting in the small African airport, he'd scanned all the faces anxiously, afraid that at the last minute something might have happened and she wouldn't be able to come. Then suddenly she'd been standing there, and no one else in the whole world had existed but her.

Someone coughed gently, interrupting his reverie, and Kevin turned to find the duty sister beside him.

"Eh, Father . . ."

"Kevin is the name," he said, smiling. "I'm not a cleric any more."

"Well, eh –" embarrassed, she didn't repeat his name. "Kate would like you to sit with her again now. The doctors have finished examining her, and they're very pleased with her progress."

"Sister –"

"Yes, eh, Kevin?"

"Kate and I are getting married as soon as she's well again."

CHAPTER 18

*As I looked at the newspaper cuttings from all those years ago,
I finally had to confront the horror that my mind had blotted
out since I was a child. A story that would also explain how I'd
wrongly blamed you, Ciara, for something that was never your
fault.*

*That fateful day, all those years ago, there was plenty of
excitement in the neighbourhood. Our county had just won the
All-Ireland Hurling Final. Train-loads of local supporters,
including my father, the parish priest, local businessmen and
farmers, had gone up to Croke Park in Dublin for the final, all
of them decked out in the county colours.*

*And they'd returned triumphant that evening to frenzied local
celebrations. All the pubs in the area were crowded to capacity,
and as I went into the village on an errand for my mother, I
saw drinkers standing out on the streets, glasses in hand, in fine
festive fettle. One man even gave me a few coins as I passed by.*

*I knew, even as a small child, that drinking in pubs was
something done mainly by the men of the locality. Some of the
women would adjourn together to the snug, a separate area*

partitioned off from the main bar, where they would drink 'medicinal' porter, which was reckoned to cure all sorts of female ills. But in general, drinking was a male preserve and one which I knew made them more jovial, raucous, and all too frequently violent towards their wives and children. The men might look forward to Saturday nights, but they were dreaded by most of the families left at home.

I'd often witnessed my father's violence towards my mother, and had personally experienced his rage on many occasions. The pain of those backhanders across my head had taught me to keep well out of his way when he'd been to the pub. I'd sit shaking in my room as I heard him hit my mother over and over again, and I'd sob quietly as I heard her screams. I longed to grow up so that I could go and save her. But then I'd wonder – why couldn't she leave him and take me with her?

The All-Ireland celebrations were still in full swing, but I'd been sent off to bed early. I'd begged my mother to let me stay up longer since I, too, had been affected by the excitement in the air, and was skittish and over-active. But while I was feverish with excitement, my mother was contrastingly apprehensive and unwilling to allow me any leeway. She was always on edge when my father was out drinking, but surely, I thought, nothing bad could happen on this wonderful night of celebration?

Sulking, I went to my room, where I opened the window and stood looking out across the darkened fields to the nearby village where the raised voices of the revellers in the pubs were carried through the still evening air. Sometimes in the darkness I could see the glow of a pipe or cigarette in the boreen, as a farmer or farmhand stopped to light up while on his way to join the celebrations with his neighbours. An occasional car went by, or a dog barked in the distance.

Eventually, I got bored and retired to bed. I fell into an uneasy sleep, and had no idea what time it was when I awoke. It was still dark, yet through my open bedroom window I could hear sounds of revelry coming from somewhere close at hand. Climbing out of bed, I tiptoed to the window but could see nothing. It seemed to me that the sounds were coming from the direction of the barn, which was hidden from my view by the row of outhouses directly below my window.

Immediately, I was alert and filled with the inquisitiveness of a ten-year old. Barefoot, I tiptoed out onto the landing and checked the time on the old grandfather clock outside my room. It was nearly four in the morning. What could possibly be happening outside at this late hour?

I felt excited as I crept down the stairs. What had been a unique day looked like turning into a unique night too. Carefully, I negotiated the edge of each step, trying to ensure that I stepped on the parts least likely to creak. If my mother caught me leaving the house in the middle of the night, there would be hell to pay.

Later, I often wished that the stairs had creaked, that my mother had ordered me back to bed, or that I'd never woken up in the first place. For what happened next will help you to understand, Ciara, all that subsequently happened to both of us.

Out in the yard, I followed the sounds of revelry, which led me to the big barn. The door was open and the inside area was lit by a single bulb. It was unusual to see the barn lit up – usually that only happened when my father and his neighbours were filling the barns with hay before the end-of-summer rains came.

Inside, my father and several of the local farmers were sitting around on the floor, all of them clearly the worse for wear with some of them propped up against the bales of hay that were stacked at varying heights throughout the barn. Some of them were still wearing caps or scarves in the county colours, and there were bottles of drink strewn all around. Someone had already vomited on the floor just inside the door.

But what was difficult for my 10-year-old brain to comprehend was the fact that most of them had their trousers pulled down and were fondling their genitals with one hand, while swilling down bottles of beer with the other. Instinct told me that I'd stumbled into some strictly male preserve, and that I'd better leave as quickly as possible. But I was mesmerised, and in my anxiety to learn about the adult world I lingered just a second too long.

Several magazines, with pictures of naked women in them, lay open on the ground and one of the men had positioned himself over one of them and was pulling on his organ until it erupted all over the picture. I stood aghast as he grunted in satisfaction, then lay down to sleep with his trousers still open.

In another corner, my father was lying on his back against a hay bale, a similar magazine beside him. He was snoring gently, his trousers open too and a strange limp thing like a dead snake hanging out. Was this the same kind of thing I'd seen in Seamus's trousers?

Suddenly, as I stepped backwards to avoid standing in the vomit, I slipped. Quickly, I struggled to my feet, but not before being spotted by one of the neighbouring farmers.

"Well, if it isn't Miss High and Mighty," he said, slurring his words as he tried to scramble to his feet. Looking around at the others, most of whom appeared comatose, he raised his beer bottle in mock salute and roared, addressing no one in particular. "Well, lads. Ye were lookin' for women, weren't ye? Well, there's a little one right here!"

He turned towards me as I cowered in the shadow of a hay bale, awaiting an opportunity to flee. "C'mere child —" he held out his hand to take mine, but as I recoiled from him he became angry. "C'mere, you little bitch!" he roared. "Come over here child, when I call ye!"

He stumbled to his feet with the intention of coming after me, so I turned to run out of the barn. But another drunken neighbour who'd been lying unseen just inside the door, grabbed me by the hem of my nightdress before I could escape. His hands were as big as hams, and his breath smelled of stale beer and tobacco. I felt ill at the smell of him, and terrified by the grip he was exerting on me. I kicked my legs in an attempt to break away from him, but despite the amount of drink he'd consumed, his hold on me was like a vice.

"She's mine now," he called out. "You can keep the dirty magazines. I've got the real thing!" He leered at the man who'd previously tried to grab me, and who'd by now stumbled across the barn to re-claim me. But the second man held me aloft over his head to prevent the first man grabbing me. Terrified, I feared that one or both of them would lose their balance and I'd be dropped down onto the ground. I screamed as I was thrown aloft again, but he caught me firmly enough as I fell, this time turning me upside down so that the nightdress fell over my face and my bottom was bare. Laughing, he slapped it in a self-congratulatory manner, stinging my flesh with the impact of his hand.

Suddenly, my father came to life, scrambling to his feet. "Leave her alone. That's my daughter!" he roared. The others momentarily froze and I sobbed with relief. I expected my father to be cross with me for my intrusion into this male preserve, but I was certain that at least my deliverance was now at hand.

But instead, my father grabbed me roughly from the others.

"I'll be the first!" he roared. The thing that had been hanging limply from his trousers was now big and stiff, and he forced me down on my knees and forced it into me from behind as though I was an animal. I bit my lip and cried silently as the pain seared through me. What was my father doing to me? Why was he hurting me like this? What had I done to deserve such punishment?

"You liked lookin' at that half-wit Seamus's mickey, didn't ye?" he roared. "You dirty little bitch! See now how you like a real man's one!"

At last he was finished. I was wet and I felt as though my insides had been ripped apart. But my ordeal was far from over. As he lay back once again against the bales of hay, my father magnanimously waved his hand in a gesture of permission to the others. I was merely a possession to him with which he could afford to be generous to his friends.

Quickly, I was seized by another burly farmer who made me cry out again in pain as he entered me. This brought gales of laughter from the other men. My pain was clearly a signal to them that they were having a good time. I didn't exist for them as a person in my own right. As far as they were concerned, I'd no rights at all. Then I was passed like a piece of meat to the next man who, equally oblivious of my feelings, bucked back and forth inside me like a demon possessed.

At last I escaped, sobbing, from the barn and ran silently across the courtyard and into the house. Alone in my room, I cried with shame and pain. I understood little about what had happened, yet instinctively I knew that my life would never be the same again.

I bled for most of the next day, so I stayed in my room, mopping it up with old newspapers and trying to avoid both

*my mother and my father. I told my mother I was feeling sick –
never had I spoken more truthfully! I felt wretched. I had
terrible pains in what I assumed was my stomach, and I felt
feverish and disoriented.*

*Eventually, my mother noticed blood on the sheets of the
bed, since the newspapers hadn't been sufficient to stem the
flow. "You must have started your periods," was all she said to
me, giving me a wad of cotton wool to put between my legs.*

*What were periods? I longed for answers, someone to
confide in. But there was no one whom I could trust. So I
stayed alone in my room, crying and dozing.*

*After lunch, the door to my bedroom opened and in walked
my father. I clutched the bedclothes around me in terror. But he
smiled at me, a grotesque, sadistic smile. Pressing money into
my hand he leaned over the bed, and lowering his voice he
warned me that if I ever told anyone about what had happened
he would beat me so hard that I wouldn't be able to stand up
afterwards. Terrified, all I could do was nod as he left the room.*

*Never had I been given so much money in my life. But I had
no desire to spend it, since it seemed to tangibly represent the
trauma of that terrible night, and anything I bought with it
would carry the same stigma.*

*Sometimes in school I'd look around at my classmates, and
wonder if any of them were suffering as I was. If so, they hid
their dark secrets as well as I did.*

*I often thought of running away, but where does a ten-year-
old child go? So I stayed, watching my father go to Mass each
Sunday, receive communion at the altar and chat to the parish
priest afterwards, while I continued to endure his brutality in
private. Until the time finally came when I could take his abuse
no longer.*

CHAPTER 19

Kevin sat down at the table in Ciara's kitchen. His sister had been pleasantly surprised at his visit – she was always delighted to see her favourite brother. But her happy expression turned to dark fury when it became clear that he was there to plead Kate's case.

"Ciara, Kate's really upset that you haven't been to visit her in hospital."

Ciara's expression turned to one of fury. "Kate's upset? So well she might be! That woman has a bloody nerve!"

Kevin was shocked at his sister's vehemence. It was unlike her to react that way to anyone, never mind to someone as dear, and as ill, as Kate. "Look, love. She knows she's upset you, but she hopes that we can all sort it out between us. I mean, it's not like you to take this so personally."

"For Christ's sake, Kevin, how can you defend her like that? After what she's done –"

"Aren't you being a bit over-dramatic, love?" Kevin asked mildly. "Surely what Kate does with her life is her own business? I mean –"

Angry tears blinded Ciara's eyes. How dare her own brother take Kate's side! "Not when it's with my family, it isn't!" she screamed. "That bitch! How could you take her side against me, Kev?"

"Ciara, love! What on earth are you talking about?" Kevin quickly crossed the room and tried to put his arms around her, but Ciara pushed him aside.

"Get away from me, you, you bastard! How could you possibly defend her, after what she's done? You're just as bad as she is!"

"Is it because of the baby? Surely you'd have the decency to wish her well –"

"Wish her well? I'll see her in hell first!" Ciara began to weep. "How could she pretend to be my friend, while all the while she was carrying on behind my back!"

Kevin sat down, resting his head in his hands. "Jesus, Ciara, I just don't understand you any more. You were always the great liberal, the one who never judged other people –"

They both sat at opposite ends of the table, the silence broken only by Ciara's sobbing and the ticking of the clock on the mantelpiece.

"I think you should know, Ciara, that Kate had nothing to do with me leaving the priesthood if that's what's bugging you," Kevin said at last, "and even if she had, I still don't think you've got any right to behave this way."

Ciara raised her tear-stained face in surprise. "What do you mean?"

"Well, to be honest, I never expected this reaction from you. I don't know what's happened between you two, but it's not going to stop Kate and I having the baby and getting married. I'm just sorry that you can't be happy for us."

"Wait a minute, what do you mean about you and Kate?"

Kevin looked blank. "We're not going to change our minds just because you don't approve," he said quietly.

Suddenly, Ciara was screaming angrily. "You mean you're going to marry Kate, to provide a father for Niall's baby?"

"Niall's baby?" Kevin shouted back. "What the hell are you going on about? Why would Kate be having Niall's baby? She's having mine!"

Ciara sat down again, her eyes wide with astonishment, still unable to take it all in.

"You mean, Kate is expecting *your* baby?"

"That's what I bloody well said, isn't it? Why can't you just be happy for us?"

"But I am. Oh God, Kev, I never realised!" Ciara rushed across to her brother and threw her arms around him, fresh tears running down her face.

Kevin smiled with relief. "Well, actually, you weren't supposed to realise. Things developed gradually between Kate and me when she first came out to visit me in Africa. But we decided not to tell anyone until I'd actually left the priesthood."

He laughed. "But we were eventually caught out by Niall at a conference last year. Kate was writing up the conference for her newspaper, and since I was home on leave I went along too. Kate's press colleagues were all there, but we were incredibly discreet. But Niall spotted me coming out of Kate's room early one morning! He just grinned and said nothing, but Kate was really worried that he might mention it to you."

Ciara smiled. "Niall never mentioned a thing about it." That was typically Niall, always discreet. Then suddenly she realised that he'd been conducting his own affair at the same conference! That was where the incriminating photograph had been taken.

Then Kevin suddenly recalled Ciara's earlier outburst. "And what's all this about Kate having Niall's baby?"

Ciara smiled guiltily. "Oh, nothing Kev. Don't pay any attention to me. Somehow, I got my wires crossed. But everything's OK now, and I really am thrilled for both of you. When do you think I can go and see Kate?"

Kevin looked at her, grinned, then picked up his car keys and linked his arm in hers. "Since Kate is longing to see you, I suggest that there's no time like the present!"

CHAPTER 20

It was a bright sunny morning when I took my father's hand and led him to the shed at the far end of the yard. I was surprised that he came so willingly. Usually he had little time for me, except when he wanted to start touching me.

"Come on, Daddy," I said coquettishly, placing my small hand in his big one, "I've made you a lovely meal on my toy cooker."

He appeared to find nothing odd about my unusual compliance. Usually he had to bribe me, or threaten to beat me to get me into that shed. I was eleven now, a little old for playing with toy cookers, but it suited me to appear more childish when my father was around. He didn't like the idea of his little girl growing up, and for my own safety I'd humour him. Since that night when he and his friends had raped me repeatedly in the barn, he'd become a regular visitor to my room at night, and at other times he'd drag me into the shed or the barn and threaten severe beatings if I didn't comply.

Now he came into the shed, and settled down on the old crate, as he always did when he intended to abuse me. He pulled me to him. "So what's my little girl doing today?" he wheedled. "Making something nice for her Daddy to eat?"

For a few seconds he humoured me by pretending to eat the raw cabbage concoction I'd prepared. He made exaggerated chomping noises of enjoyment, then pulled me to him again and began touching me in that way I hated so much. I endured for the very last time the pain and the shame, knowing that soon it would be over forever.

When he'd finished hurting me, Daddy reached, as always, for the whiskey bottle that he kept hidden on the top shelf. He unscrewed the cap, and I held my breath and waited. Thankfully, he didn't seem to notice that there was more in the bottle than before. Then he threw back his head and guzzled it down his throat.

For a moment, time stood seemed to stand still. I heard a lark in one of the nearby fields, and heard the distant drone of one of our neighbours' tractors. The sun continued to shine vividly in the mid-morning sky, and through the shed door I could see the glorious array of wild dog-daisies that had somehow rooted themselves in the dirt of the yard outside.

The only incongruous sound was that of my Daddy groaning as he clutched his chest. I watched in awe, mixed with surprise and jubilation, as his huge frame crumpled, reeling at first in disorientation then falling to the ground. As he fell, he reached out, clutching at shelves, cannoning into walls and I heard the splintering of glass as both the whiskey bottle and his body finally hit the ground.

I looked at him for a long time in the silence that followed. Now he would hurt me no longer. I'm sorry Daddy, I told him, please try to understand. You were always hurting me, and I had to make you stop . . .

It seemed to me as though time then stood still, but only a few minutes could have elapsed before I heard my mother's hurried footsteps and saw her anxious face appear at the door.

"What's going on? I thought I heard glass breaking —" Her voice broke off as she surveyed the body of my father on the ground, his trousers open in the front. I heard her sharp intake of breath as she surveyed the scene. Then she looked at me, her eyes narrowing. "What in God's name have you done?" she whispered, her voice edged with fear.

"I'm sorry, Mammy," I said, as calmly as I could, "but Daddy was always hurting me. So I had to stop him . . ."

With one quick move, she crossed the shed to the old cupboard and flung open the doors. She lifted out the jar of rat poison and surveyed its contents. She looked over at me accusingly, but said nothing. Then she replaced the jar and closed the door. For what seemed an age, she stood there staring at me with a strange look in her eyes. I wished that she'd say something, for I feared her silence more than I feared her wrath.

"I'm sorry Mammy," I said once again. "I just had to stop him hurting me."

This time, my words seemed to break into her trance and galvanise her into action. Quickly, she crossed the floor towards me and I thought for one moment that she was going to hit me. But instead she motioned silently for me to assist her. Together, with much pulling and pushing, we dragged my father's big frame out into the yard. At first I wasn't sure where we were taking him. Then I realised that we were heading towards the slurry pit beside the cattle shed.

Several times, we had to stop because of the heat and the exertion. But never for longer than to draw breath. Relentlessly, my mother would begin pulling again, not caring how my father's head now bounced unceremoniously along the ground. Thinking that it was all a great game, the two farm dogs snapped and danced around us as we dragged him along. To them, it was a great diversion, and they pulled at my father's clothing with their teeth, barking excitedly as though he meant no more to them than a dead sheep.

The slurry pit was deep, and I'd always been warned to stay well away from it. Now I was closer to it than I'd ever been before, and I couldn't help reeling slightly from the foul fumes emanating from it. For a brief moment my mother and I hovered on its brink, the fumes almost enveloping us as we heaved my father's body in. I watched with a mixture of horror and fascination as the mass of smelling slime seemed to claw at his body like a living thing, pulling him gradually down inside. For one fanciful moment, just before his face disappeared into the mire, it almost seemed as though he was still alive. An arm briefly hovered above the surface. Then suddenly, all trace of him was gone.

My mother and I never again spoke of what happened. In fact, we never ever spoke to each other again. Around midday Joe, one of the farmhands, called to the house. Needing a decision about something, he enquired after my father's whereabouts. My mother's non-committal reply was not very helpful, so fearing that my father might have met with an accident he and the other farmhand began searching around the yard, in and out of the sheds and up through the fields.

After three days of searching, his body was eventually found. The local gardai and doctor were immediately called in, and a post-mortem arranged. Throughout all the fuss – the steady stream of neighbours dropping by to stare, to offer condolences and hear the latest snippets of gossip, the visits of gardai and officials – my mother stood looking on, dry-eyed and stoical. She spoke to no one, not even to me. It was as though she was living in a separate world of her own. Perhaps it was the only way she could cope with what had happened, and the inevitability of what was still to come.

On an equally bright sunny morning a few days later, my mother was vigorously scrubbing pots in the kitchen and I was playing in the yard with my doll's tea set. My mother seemed to be cleaning the pots with more vigour than I'd ever witnessed before, as though someone other than herself was about to sit in judgement on them. Were we expecting visitors, I wondered? Suddenly, a police car and the local doctor's car arrived in the yard. I watched as they held a brief consultation before heading en masse towards the kitchen door.

I tried to eavesdrop from outside, but they'd closed the door behind them so I could hear nothing. I pressed my ear to the door in vain, then I tried standing on an upturned flower pot. I managed to climb up onto the sill of the small open kitchen window, but as soon as I got there I lost my balance, fell and cut my knee. The pain made me want to cry, as did the brief glimpse I caught of my mother's sad face in the window before I hit the ground.

As I nursed my cut knee the Garda came out, followed by the doctor with my mother leaning heavily on his arm as though all the strength had been drained out of her.

"Where are you going Mammy?" I called, but she didn't answer. In fact, nobody answered. They all got back into the cars, this time with my mother sitting primly beside the doctor in the front seat of his Bentley.

"Mammy, can I come too?" I called, running across to the cars, suddenly frightened at being left alone. But my mother never even looked at me. She continued to look straight ahead *unseeingly as the cars gathered momentum and headed down the driveway. I ran after them, crying and calling her name.*

It wasn't long before a woman from a nearby farm came up the driveway on her bicycle, informing me that she going to take me to her house on the back carrier. She informed me that I'd be staying with her and her family until my future was decided.

"Where's my Mammy gone?" I asked, but all I received was some non-committal reply. It was as though my mother simply didn't exist any more.

I ran inside and quickly collected the few clothes I owned. I also gathered together all the money I'd been given by my father over the previous year. There was quite a tidy sum, witness to the terror I'd been subjected to as he ensured my compliance through threats and bribes. But I knew that I might need it wherever I was going. So I stuffed the notes down each side of the ankle socks I was wearing.

Instinctively, I knew that I'd never go back to the farmhouse again. And the memories of that awful childhood buried themselves deep in my subconscious, because the reality of what had happened was too painful to bear.

Yet it was those very memories that made me who I was, a person you never truly knew, Ciara. And those hidden memories were still guiding my actions years later, even though I never even knew it myself. I've always been shackled to my past, and it affected every decision I've ever made.

I realise now that when I fantasised about men as a teenager, it was to block out the memories of my own horrendous past. Mr O'Reilly, Father Macken and Niall were just symptoms of my longing for love, and I approached them on a sexual level because I knew of no other way of relating to a man. After all, Ciara, I'd never learnt that real love asks for nothing in return.

CHAPTER 21

It was a cold morning as they left the crematorium. There were countless press, television and public relations people at Ita's funeral service, many attracted as much by the notoriety of the occasion as by any real interest in the deceased. Some people came because they knew that other press colleagues would be there, making it important to be seen there. It was also an opportunity for others to make business contacts, and hear whatever media gossip was doing the rounds. Ciara saw Alan Moore there, and he gave her an insolent grin. Abruptly, she looked away.

"Mam –"

Ciara felt a rush of happiness as Sarah spontaneously linked her arm in hers. It had been a long time since her daughter had made any overtures towards her, apart from screaming at her. Perhaps this was a new beginning.

"– did Ita ever say anything to you about me?"

"No, why do you ask?"

"Oh, nothing," Sarah shrugged her shoulders. "I just wondered –"

Ciara looked at her daughter's earnest, but sad face. Clearly Ita had come to mean a lot to her.

"Well, I know she was very fond of you," Ciara added. "I think she enjoyed having you around."

"I'm glad," Sarah said. "She was very good to me, taking me to London and all that."

"I think that she felt you were almost like a daughter to her."

Sarah looked happily surprised. "You know, I felt that way too –" she coloured. "I don't mean she could take your place or anything."

Ciara patted her daughter's arm. "Don't worry. I'm not jealous. Well, maybe just a little bit! But you were special to her, I've no doubt about that."

Sarah smiled, wiping away a tear. She wished she could tell her mother about Ita's kindness and understanding when she'd badly needed a friend. Maybe when she had babies of her own, other babies, she'd tell her mother about her 'holiday' in London. Sarah choked back a tear. It was strange how Ita's death had brought her and her mother close again. Poor old Mummy could be a right pain at times, but at the back of it all she had a good heart. Besides, with Daddy gone, they really should be more supportive of each other.

Sarah often wondered about the night she'd witnessed her mother and Charlie rollicking on the floor of the drawing-room. Since then, she'd been watching Charlie closely every time he was near her mother, but she couldn't detect any special glances or secret signals passing between them. In fact, they looked and behaved just like they'd always done. If she hadn't actually seen them with her own eyes, she might have believed that her mind was playing tricks.

But she'd been eavesdropping when Mummy was talking to Gran on the phone the day before, and she'd heard something about Dee and Charlie breaking up. Mind you, she'd only heard one side of the conversation so she wasn't entirely sure of the details. She'd made a roundabout enquiry from Terry, Dee and Charlie's son. Well, she'd vaguely asked him if he'd any news or if anything strange or startling was happening in his life. But for her pains all she'd got was his usual monosyllabic answer.

If it was true, she hoped her mother wasn't responsible for the break-up. And she fervently hoped that there wasn't any possibility of Charlie becoming her stepfather! That would mean that those two boring farts, Terry and Donal, would be her stepbrothers! Hopefully, her mother had just made a stupid mistake over Charlie, and there would be no further repercussions. After all, she'd made mistakes herself, so it was gratifying to see that her mother could make them too.

Sarah looked over her shoulder, to where Liam was being helped along by Kevin and Charlie. He looked distraught, his eyes wild and unseeing. How could he have aged so much in just a few days? She was frightened as she surveyed his grey face, the bags under his eyes, the stumbling gait that made him look like an old man. Sarah was suddenly overwhelmed by affection for Liam. He'd been a friend of Mummy's for so long that she couldn't imagine their house without the sound of his booming voice, his laughter and jokes at parties and family get-togethers. In fact, he really was one of the family. Yet now he looked so lost and sad. She wished she could do or say something that would bring back the old smile to his face, but she felt too young and inadequate for the task.

"Poor Liam. He looks awful, doesn't he, Mam?"

Ciara nodded, looking back sadly to where Liam was now receiving condolences from a well-wisher. His innate good nature made him respond courteously, but he looked spaced out, almost like a drug addict. He was merely going through the motions, without any of it registering with him.

"Go on, Mam. I think you should be with him," Sarah said, giving her mother's arm a squeeze. "Of all the people here today, you're the one who's closest to him. And you really understand how he feels. You know, after Daddy dying and all that."

"Are you coming too?"

"No, I'll go and join Gran," Sarah said, looking ahead to where Annie was walking alone towards the funeral cars. "She looks as though she could do with some company too. But right now, Mam, Liam needs you more than any of us."

CHAPTER 22

When I started writing this story of mine, Ciara, I had no intention of ever letting anyone else see it. But as my story draws to a close, I've gradually come to realise that the very least I owe you is the truth. So I will leave you a disk of these pathetic ramblings of mine.

Now, at last, you're about to discover who your husband's 'scarlet woman' was. By now, you'll know that both Dee and Kate are innocent, so as Ita, I must arise and take a bow. My final bow before I end this sad, despicable life of mine.

You're undoubtedly surprised and bewildered, since the Ita you've known has been portrayed as a successful journalist with a fine career and the love of a wonderful man, your own dear friend Liam. Why on earth would she want to hurt you? And since you've only met her recently, how could she harbour such deep resentments and have such an intimate knowledge of your life?

Well, Ciara, I didn't start my life as Ita. The glamorous woman you came to know was a manufactured product, the *result of cosmetic changes. That's why you didn't recognise me when you met me again.*

You see, Ciara, when my aunt conveniently died just after we'd left school, the timing was perfect for me to begin a new life. There was no need for continuity. The old me could, quite literally, disappear. Then a year or two later, the elegant and sophisticated Ita appeared on the scene.

How did I transform myself? Firstly, I went to a health farm in England for several weeks where I was pummelled and pushed into shedding two stone in weight.

Next, I had my nose altered. Gone was the unsightly bump that was my legacy from my father's side of the family. I now had a slender, slightly upturned nose that I marvelled at day and night. Initially in the mornings I'd leap out of bed and rush for the mirror, half afraid that it would have vanished overnight. But it was still there, and I began to become more certain of its permanence as time went on. Finally, I had my jaw re-shaped, and I was truly astonished at how different it made me look.

All these changes meant spending several months in hospital, and made a dent in the money I'd inherited. It was also a very lonely, frightening and painful time, and the days dragged by without the distraction of people dropping in during visiting hours. But that was how I chose to do it. I wanted no one to witness the process whereby the ugly duckling became a presentable swan. When the surgical changes were fully healed, I arranged a series of visits to an orthodontist in London to have my teeth straightened. Then, in a final act of defiance to the world, I changed my hair colour from mousy brown to glorious blonde.

I also marvelled at the change in people's attitudes towards me. Whereas previously, when I'd been large and unattractive, no one had given me a second glance or felt my opinions were worthy of any consideration, now, suddenly, my opinions were valued.

Most of all, I saw the change in men's attitudes. I now fitted the stereotype, so I was worthy of their attention. It angered me to think that their response was still based on how I looked, just as they'd judged and rejected me all those years ago.

But Niall hadn't rejected me. At the quarry, he'd seen and responded to my womanly potential, and I'd fallen deeply in love with him as a result. Despite the pain of loss I experienced when he fell for you, Ciara, if anything my love for him became even more deeply etched into my heart. I believed he was the only man for me. A fanciful notion, perhaps, but it made total sense to a child who had never received acceptance before.

But how, I'm sure you're wondering Ciara, did I manage to keep track of all that was happening in your life, since as Ita Byrne we'd never met until Niall's funeral? The answer is really quite simple. You told me everything yourself.

Don't you remember your old friend Marguerite, who hung around on the fringes of your charmed little group, smiling and making jokes? You thought she was funny, and she played the clown in order to be your friend. Then she salvaged her pride by inventing her love affair with a sailor, seeing the respect in your eyes when you discovered, via arch-gossip Dot McNally, that she'd somehow managed to get a boyfriend of her own.

But I'm sure you're still puzzled, Ciara. If big Marguerite changed her name and face to become Ita, who is the woman you've been writing to and e-mailing all these years? After all, you recently received a jolly family portrait from Marguerite, showing her with André and their family. In it she is as big and *jolly as ever, full of news about her life and about how her kids are doing in school.*

A pure invention, Ciara. I kept the original Marguerite alive in order to keep in contact with you, and to be kept informed about all that was happening in your life. You became my very own informant on the major and minor happenings in your life with Niall.

As for the photos, I paid for them as I needed them. In France, I found a woman who looked very like Marguerite, so over the years I've paid her to pose for me. Sometimes, I'd take photos of her with her family, or maybe pictures of her standing in the street, or in the marketplace, all designed to show you what a full and exciting life she was leading. Once, I took a photo of her standing in the doorway of a typical French villa. Then I sent it to you as Marguerite's home. The woman herself believes that I'm carrying out research for some scientific project on women and ageing, but I doubt if she really cares as long as she receives her money regularly.

With e-mail, all that I needed in order to keep up the deception was a French e-mail address. I could, of course, have simply used a worldwide service provider address, but since I was regularly in France for the photos anyway, it involved no extra effort to be totally authentic. Before e-mail, I simply posted an occasional letter from whatever destination my job took me to. Surely, Ciara, you must sometimes have envied Marguerite's wonderful lifestyle, travelling regularly with André on business trips? And wasn't it a pity that the one time you were visiting Nice for an exhibition, Marguerite just happened to be away in America?

Of course, Niall never knew that Ita Byrne, columnist and feature writer, was also the fifteen-year-old girl with whom he'd shared his first love-making sessions up at the quarry. I wonder how he'd have felt if he'd known that during all those years in between, I'd watched both your lives and careers, and planned to win him back again?

Without doubt, I was a good journalist. But would poor old Marguerite Brown have achieved as much success as the glamorous Ita Byrne did? I doubt it. Nor would Marguerite ever gain the attentions of someone like Ted Durkan. As the archetypal successful businessman, Ted wanted a trophy wife. I shudder to think what he, or any of his family, would have thought of poor Marguerite.

Well, Ciara, could you ever have guessed that the lovely Ita with her money, career and elegant lifestyle, could carry so much hatred and pain inside? However, you must remember that Ita was only a body, an exterior that hid the damaged person within. Because I was still Marguerite inside.

Sadly, I discovered that no amount of external changes can cover up one's inner feelings. That kind of pain stays with you. You carry it around like a lead weight because there's no escaping a legacy of brutality and the feelings of worthlessness that it engenders. So I decided that there was only one way to end it all, the only way I could find personal peace, and atone for what I'd done to you.

CHAPTER 23

They all stood together in the airport, a small group of friends and relations, watching the clock and savouring those last minutes together before it was time for Kevin and Kate to board their flight to Africa. All formalities had been completed, luggage had been dispatched, and boarding passes had been issued. Now it was time for the goodbyes.

Kate hugged Ciara tightly. "I hate leaving you now. I feel I shouldn't be so happy when you're all alone."

"Don't be daft. I'm just happy that you're happy," said Ciara, smiling. "What would be the point of us both being sad? Besides," she gestured towards Kevin, "you're making someone I love the happiest man on earth."

Kate's and Ciara's tears mingled as they embraced each other affectionately, while Kevin hovered in the background beaming happily, his mother by his side.

"I'm losing you again," said Annie, but she was smiling. "First it was to the Church, now it's to the mother of your own child. My grandchild."

She squeezed his arm, and he could feel the tremor of emotion in her grip. She's getting old, he suddenly thought with surprise. He'd always thought of his mother as invincible, but now for the first time he noticed the deep lines etched on her face, the sagging line of her jaw and the frail hands with the bones showing through the thinning flesh. Quickly he embraced her, so that she wouldn't see the tears in his eyes.

"I'm so happy for you, son," Annie said at last as they broke apart. "That's all any mother wants. To see her children happily settled."

"Thanks, Mam. I am happy. Happier than I ever thought I could be."

Just then Kate joined them, sliding easily into Kevin's embrace. "You'll come out to see us soon, won't you?" Kate asked Annie anxiously, resting her arm lightly on Annie's frail one. "I'm going to miss you so much –" she looked from Annie to Kevin and grinned, "– but I promise to take good care of your son!"

"I know you will, love. Just you mind that he takes good care of you –" Annie smiled wistfully, "– and my precious grandchild."

Liam was now standing beside Ciara. Already, they'd fallen into the habit of being there for each other, of going places together, of travelling together when they were attending the same function. Each had found warmth and acceptance in the other's company. Since each had faced death at close hand, they understood each other's silences and could anticipate each other's needs and mood swings.

And now, despite their own individual sorrows, they

each took pleasure in watching other people's lives taking on a new dimension. And they drew sustenance from the knowledge that love continued, even if it was only for other people. Perhaps it provided them with a deep-seated hope that life wouldn't always be as bleak as it presently was.

"Good old Kev. I think he and Kate are perfect together," Liam said to Ciara. "I'm just surprised that I never thought of them as a likely couple. I mean, look at them. They're just so right for each other, aren't they?"

Ciara nodded. "It's funny, seeing my brother and one of my best friends together. And yet, in another way, it's perfectly logical isn't it?"

"You mean that since they're both special to you, it stands to reason that they'd have a lot in common too?"

"Yes, that's exactly what I mean," Ciara looked at Liam, pleasantly surprised as she always was lately by his astuteness and empathy with her own thoughts. There were times when they didn't even need to speak in order to know what the other was thinking or feeling.

Sarah joined her grandmother, Kate and Kevin. She'd wandered off from the group, claiming that she needed to go to the toilet but that hadn't been true at all. She hadn't wanted them all to see her crying – it was such a soppy, childish thing to do. At this stage, she just wished the parting was all over, because these last few minutes were agony and she had an awful feeling that all her attempts to appear grown-up would dissolve in a flood of tears when the actual moment of parting arrived.

"You'll come out too, Sarah, won't you?"

"To Africa?"

"Of course," said Kate. "You've an open invitation at any time. How about next summer, during your school holidays? I had a word with your mother, and she thinks it's a great idea."

"Oh Kate, that would be terrific!" said Sarah, momentarily forgetting to be sophisticated and aloof, and hugging her mother's friend warmly. Already she could feel tears forming in the corner of each eye, but she no longer cared who saw them. Besides, she should be used to crying by now, she'd done an awful lot of it lately. After the shock of her father's death, there'd been the trauma of her own abortion, her terrible feelings of loss at Ita's suicide and Liam's devastation at losing the woman he loved. It had been a terrible period in Sarah's life, but suddenly Kate had given her something to look forward to.

"There's a catch, of course –" Kevin added with a grin, as he joined Kate and Sarah. "You'll have to help out with minding your new cousin!"

Sarah blinked back her tears and grinned. She was looking forward to having a cousin, a new member of the family. Briefly, she thought of her own aborted child. And she was grateful that her sudden tears could be passed off as appropriate for the occasion.

Cillian and Betty arrived just in time to wish the departing couple a safe journey. Typical, thought Ciara, smiling. Cillian was always late for everything. Perhaps he'd cultivated being late as a way of letting people know how busy and important he was.

Anxiously, Ciara looked around. Dee hadn't turned up. Or Charlie. Surely they'd want to wish Kevin and

Kate happiness for their future? Surely neither of them would allow the pain of their own break-up to blight such a happy occasion?

Ciara had seen them both on separate occasions since their decision to part, but had learned nothing conclusive from either of them. As yet neither of them had moved out of the house and they were attending marriage counselling sessions together. All their friends had been shocked and devastated by the news of their break-up, and were doing their best to give them both support.

Suddenly Annie was at Ciara's side, almost reading her thoughts. "No sign of Dee or Charlie? It's nearly time for Kev and Kate to go through. I don't think they can risk waiting much longer, or they'll miss their flight."

"I know, Mam. I don't know what's happened. I was sure they'd be here."

Suddenly, there was a flurry of activity and Dee arrived, followed by Charlie. "God, we're so sorry. We had a puncture on our way here!" Dee rushed up to Kevin and Kate, embracing them both warmly. "Thank goodness we got here just in time. I'd hate to have missed saying goodbye."

"It's not goodbye, anyway," said Kate, hugging her friend tightly. "It's only *au revoir* until you can come out to see us. Maybe it would do you good to get away for a while, when you and Charlie –" Kate couldn't bring herself to say the words 'break up', and there were tears in her eyes as she hugged Dee tightly.

"We may not be splitting up after all," Dee quietly told her friend. "Charlie and I have been doing a lot of talking lately, more than we've done in years."

"That's great news!" Kate whispered.

Dee smiled fondly at her friend. "Well, it's early days yet. But I'll keep you posted about what's happening."

Charlie, having said his goodbyes to Kevin, now came across to hug Kate. And Ciara, who'd just caught the tale-end of Dee's conversation with Kate, took her friend hastily aside.

"Did I hear you say to Kate . . ."

"Yeah, you did. Look, Ciara. I just don't know. Maybe I'm not doing this for the right reasons. Maybe I'm just being selfish –"

Ciara squeezed her arm in support.

"– but Charlie really needs me. Maybe I'm not doing him any favours by staying. Maybe he'd eventually sort out his life without me. But I've seen him differently in the last few weeks, Ciara. He really loves me, you know, and it's enough for him to have me back. He's not asking for anything else. And because of that, I want to give him more. Does that make sense?"

Ciara nodded. "Totally."

"That in itself made me realise that I really respect him. Maybe eventually, I could even resurrect that old tingle again."

The women smiled as they hugged each other.

"I'll never forget Eamonn," Dee added, "but he's dead and Charlie's alive. What's the sense in us leading separate, lonely lives? Maybe I'm just a coward, but on the other hand maybe we can try for a little happiness together."

Ciara looked across at Charlie who was chatting animatedly to Annie, Sarah, Liam, Kate and Kevin. She felt a rush of affection for him, and was glad that Dee and he were going to give their marriage another try. She could tell that he was happy again. Maybe this was a new beginning for them both.

After a final round of hugs and promises to e-mail, Kate and Kevin walked hand-in-hand through the departures gate. Ciara held her mother's hand tightly as Annie watched her eldest son disappear out of sight. And Ciara knew instinctively that her mother was wondering if she'd ever see him again.

"C'mon, Mam. I'll drive you and Sarah back," Ciara whispered, giving her mother a much-needed hug. "I know what you need right now – a nice cup of tea."

After Ita's funeral and the departure of Kevin and Kate for Africa, Ciara eventually found time to think about her own future. As she sat alone by the fire one evening, she felt restless. There was something bothering her, but she couldn't quite figure out what it was.

Adding another log to the fire, she watched as it quickly caught fire. Was it really only three months since Niall's funeral? In some ways, it felt like a lifetime ago. In other ways, the memories were as painful as if it had only been yesterday.

Sarah was out for the evening with friends, and to Ciara's surprise she'd informed her mother of the exact time she'd be back. She also seemed to have dropped those older friends of whom Ciara had disapproved.

At Ita's funeral, too, Sarah had excelled herself. She'd been helpful to everyone, and deeply concerned about Liam. Perhaps, Ciara thought, she's growing up at last.

490

For some reason, her daughter had taken a great shine to Ita, and Ciara was sorry that the child had lost someone else who'd clearly come to mean a lot to her.

The afters for Ita's funeral had been held in Ciara's house, and it had felt strange to have her house packed again so soon with people attending another funeral. But it had seemed appropriate to hold it there. Caterers had supplied the food, and the local off-licence had sent round a large selection of drinks. Ciara knew that Liam would feel happier being somewhere that he felt comfortable, and where he could get drunk and fall asleep if he wanted to.

Ciara sighed. Poor Liam was a very different man from the one who'd comforted her at Niall's funeral. This time, Ciara was trying to give him the same care and support that he'd given to her just three months before.

That had also been the first time she'd met Ita. Who'd have thought, as she'd thanked Ita for coming to Niall's funeral, that she'd be attending Ita's own funeral just three months later? Ciara found it impossible to understand why such a beautiful and elegant woman had chosen to kill herself. Especially since she'd recently met Liam, who was clearly in love with her. Why would a woman, with everything to look forward to, take her own life?

Since Ita's death, there had been no time for Ciara to examine the small sealed envelope that the police sergeant had handed to her. It contained a computer disk, and she'd been amazed to discover that Ita had addressed it to her. She was surprised, since she and Ita had hardly known each other. Yet deep down, Ciara was filled with a strange sense of foreboding.

Reluctantly, she now rose from the warmth of the fire, went upstairs to her studio and turned on her computer. Opening the file, she was surprised to see that it began with her name. She began reading, and before long she was lost in the text which, astonishingly, took her right back to her own schooldays . . .

CHAPTER 24

Can you imagine how awful I felt, Ciara, the day you chose to confide in me? Your grief at Niall's infidelity was like a knife through my heart, especially since I was the cause of it. And to discover that you now distrusted your closest friends, people who loved you and would never harm you, was to discover yet another repercussion of what I'd done to you. Like ripples in a pool, the effects of my vendetta had spread out into areas I'd never even considered.

Having discovered that Niall never caused either a pregnancy or my infertility, I now realised that my damaged womb and inability to conceive was the result of the brutal treatment I'd received at the hands of my father and his drunken friends all those years ago. Nurse Hall may have perpetrated a fraud on innocent young girls, but the damage to my womb had already been done.

And it was those injuries that prevented me from having a child and living happily ever after with Ted. Perhaps the 'happily ever after' would never have happened anyway.

Having discovered the kind of man he was when thwarted, it's unlikely we'd have had the kind of idyllic marriage and life-long love affair that you and Niall had. Please, Ciara, believe in the solidity and strength of your marriage to Niall, because he loved you so very much.

My own brief relationship with Niall never developed in the way I'd wanted it to. For years I'd dreamed of winning him from you, and in my dreams we'd live happily ever after once I'd got him. But for him, our brief affair was merely a way of healing his wounded pride and of secretly and childishly getting back at you for the affair he believed you were having with Alan Moore. But gradually, he became ashamed of what he was doing, and when he looked at me he saw his own weakness mirrored back to him. And he grew to hate what he saw.

Then, when I finally discovered that my vendetta against you had no basis in fact, the raison d'être *for my affair with Niall evaporated and was replaced with guilt and self-loathing. So when we mutually agreed to end our little liaison, I told Niall that I knew for certain you'd never had an affair with Alan Moore. It was my parting gift to him, but in telling him I may have done more harm than good. I thought he'd be relieved, but then I realised that in finding you innocent, he found himself more guilty. And that guilt may have contributed to his heart attack. If so, then I must also accept my share of the blame for that.*

Regrettably, Ciara, being loved by Liam only exacerbated my own sense of alienation. At last, I'd found what I'd craved since the days when poor Seamus and I shared cigarette butts in the lower field. Yet when it finally happened, the timing was all wrong.

Even if I'd managed to tell him about the things that happened to me as a child, all of which he'd accept in that open-hearted way of his, I could never tell him about the terrible things I'd done to you without any justification. Ultimately, I'll be doing him a greater favour by leaving him free to love someone who is worthy of him.

I wonder if there really is an afterlife, and if I'll meet my father again? I feel no remorse for what I did to him. If I could, I'd do it over and over again, for all eternity.

Why did my mother take the blame for my father's murder? I wish with all my heart that I knew. Was it a genuine act of love on my mother's part, the first she'd ever shown towards me? Had she really been unaware of what was going on? Or had she become so demoralised that she was incapable of saving either of us? Surely, at those kitchen counselling sessions, she could have confided in some of the other women? Or was the pride of a family more sacrosanct than the safety of its most vulnerable member? Perhaps she found it preferable to confess to murder, rather than let it be known that her daughter had become the object of her husband's lust.

My past life also explains the jibes my aunt made about me being sexually precocious. It must have been quite a shock for a virginal spinster to have a wanton niece under her roof! Clearly, she transferred blame for the abuse onto me, and in her eyes I became the trouble-maker rather than the victim.

Of course, she was right. I was sexually precocious. As the victim of my father and his friends, I'd learnt early in life that sex was the only currency exchanged between men and women. And this manifested itself in the compulsion to keep creating opportunities for further abuse. Maybe without even consciously knowing why, I later justified my vendetta against you, Ciara, because pornography was used to fuel those men's sexual violence.

In conclusion, Ciara, although I've no right to ask, I'd like to ask you a favour. Is it so awful of me not to want Liam to know how unworthy of his love I really was? Is it so terribly wrong of me to want him to continue thinking well of me? Perhaps it is. Perhaps it would be too cruel to leave him grieving for the person he thought I was, rather than the person I really was. So, Ciara, I will leave the decision to you. Do what you see fit with these sad, pathetic ramblings. Being the caring person you are, I know you'll use them wisely.

Since I have no other demands upon my estate, I'm leaving my apartment to Sarah in my will. Perhaps, in some small way, it will enable her to explore options and make the kind of choices that were once denied to you and me. In living a fulfilled life, maybe she can give my own pathetic life some meaning.

It seems strange to be writing my very last words to you, Ciara. You, who ultimately was the least deserving of my hatred.

So, Ciara, I've chosen to even the score myself. As my own judge and jury, I've found myself guilty as charged. My final act will be to carry out the sentence of death. Forgive me, Ciara, if you can. I allowed my pain to diminish me as a human being, but I believe that you'll grow stronger as a result of yours.

Sincerely,

Ita

CHAPTER 25

In the early hours of the morning, Ciara finished reading Ita's story. She was cold, her muscles were stiff and aching and she was overcome with longing for a cup of tea.

Downstairs in the living-room, the unattended fire was by now reduced to smouldering ashes. But Ciara threw on a few pieces of turf, in the hopes that it could still be revived. She was far from sleepy. She filled and switched on the electric kettle.

While she waited for the water to boil, Ciara suddenly felt in the mood for painting again. In a strange way Ita's revelations had generated a new enthusiasm for her work. When she thought of how much time Ita had wasted on revenge, Ciara realised how valuable every moment was. In a strange way she felt as though Ita, by her confession, had set her on a course to freedom again. Freedom from the doubts and uncertainties about her marriage. Freedom to begin her life again.

Although drained, she felt strangely at peace. So many questions had finally been answered. It was too early to feel anything but anger and hatred for Ita. On the other hand, she had to accept that Ita couldn't have manipulated her and Niall if the elements of insecurity and distrust hadn't been there already.

Why had she never thought of Ita and Niall? For heaven's sake, her name had been Marguerite at school, which Ita was short for! Ciara now admitted to herself that she'd never given much thought to poor Marguerite's feelings. How selfish they'd all been back then, thinking only of their own popularity ratings!

Ciara, who prided herself on never forgetting a face, was astonished that she'd never spotted any similarities between Marguerite and Ita. But then how could she have realised the extent to which Ita had changed herself? Especially when she herself was still getting regular e-mails from Marguerite in France!

Ciara now made herself a cup of tea, and brought it to the table. Before she'd begin painting, there was something important she had to do first. Taking down her box of photographs, she sat at the table. Slowly she spread the photos out like a pack of playing cards, picking out individual ones at random. Yes, there was the one of the whole family the Christmas before last. It had been a happy Christmas, one of the happiest she'd known, and no one could ever take that away from her. And there was the cherished photograph of her father Frank, looking old and frail from the cirrhosis of the liver that had led to his death just weeks later. How she wished he was here now, to hold her and love her unconditionally as he'd always done when she was a little girl.

A collection of old black and white prints brought back memories of an earlier time, when she, Kevin and Cillian had built sandcastles on the beach at Sandymount, and buried their father's feet in the sand as he lay snoozing. Now she came to the photographs taken on the day that she and Niall got married. She'd been a glowing bride then, full of confidence about the future. Looking closely at her own young and joyful face, Ciara realised how like her Sarah had become. And it made her feel ridiculously pleased. It felt like further proof of the growing bond between them.

Ciara had been amazed at the recent changes in Sarah's behaviour. It was as though she'd suddenly matured by leaps and bounds. That shopping trip to London with Ita had clearly done her a world of good. So perhaps she had Ita to thank for something after all.

Ciara sipped her tea while looking at the photographs of Sarah at Disney World, photos from the year when she and Niall went with Charlie and Dee to Marbella, all of them laughing and sun-tanned, photos of her and Liam at her first solo exhibition.

Finally, Ciara took out and studied the old photo of Niall that she'd carried everywhere in her pocket while they were teenagers. How handsome he'd been, even then! Ita had certainly right about that. Niall had been a man among boys, even at sixteen.

In the end, we were both to blame, she thought. Me for taking my happiness for granted, Niall for being so ready to believe that I needed to find fulfilment elsewhere.

Where do I go from here? Niall's life is over, a life on which I built so many of my own hopes and dreams. I'm older and wiser now, and I know that no one can live their life through someone else. I'm just glad to know that he did truly love me, and that all those years we shared together weren't a lie.

Ciara put all the photographs back in the box and closed the lid. Now she felt that she had finally exorcised all the demons. Not so long ago these photographs had been a source of indescribable pain to her. They had yielded a power over her that could crush her spirit with each memory they held. Now, they were just memories wrapped in celluloid, reminders of the passing of time. She would remember, but now the memories would serve to urge her on to new pastures.

And soon, she thought with pleasure, there'll be new photographs to add to the collection. The ones taken with Kate and Kevin at the airport, and soon there'll be photographs of Kevin's and Kate's new baby. A cousin for Sarah.

Ciara thought again of poor Liam, probably down at the pub drinking too many early evening pints. She'd ring his mobile phone and ask him over for dinner later that evening. She'd plead loneliness herself, in the hopes of getting him over. Since Sarah was staying with Annie, it would be just the two of them. It was a pleasant prospect. She would make a casserole, which Liam loved, and open a bottle of Liam's favourite wine.

Suddenly, a germ of a thought danced through her head but was gone just as quickly. Her, and Liam? It was so strange a thought that she could barely acknowledge it. But it wasn't an unpleasant one. In a strange way, their lives had been converging for years, situations and times inexorably pulling them together. Maybe some day there might come a time that was destined to be theirs alone?

Quickly, Ciara dismissed the thought. It was preposterous. It was almost sacrilegious to entertain such thoughts while poor Liam was grieving. And wasn't she still grieving herself? She was in no hurry to have another relationship anyway. Yet the thought persisted. And she wondered if, like the way in which debris from a forest fire produced stronger growth the following season, the pain that she and Liam had been through might one day forge an even deeper bond between them.

Suddenly she recalled the evening, just after Ita's funeral, when she'd called round to Liam's apartment to keep him company. They'd been sitting at the table in his kitchen drinking tea and chatting about old times, and both had become briefly lost in their own memories.

Then Liam had broken the silence. "Ciara –"

"Yes, Liam?"

There was another brief silence before he finally spoke. "Did you have an affair before Niall died?"

Ciara looked him straight in the eye. "No, Liam, I didn't."

"Oh," he smiled at her. "I often wondered, but it just didn't seem like your style at all."

"You're right, an affair's just not my style."

Their eyes locked, and Ciara had felt a frisson of excitement run through her. Liam wouldn't have asked about it, if it hadn't mattered to him.

"Another cup of tea, Liam?"

"Yeah, thanks love."

She liked the way he said 'love'. He'd always called her that, even when Niall was alive, and it seemed so comforting and natural. As Ciara boiled the kettle again, she had been smiling.

Now, finishing her tea, Ciara went upstairs to her studio. She unwrapped the fresh canvas that had stood unused for months, and placed it on the old easel her father had brought home to the tiny council house all those years ago. She could still recall the joy on his face as he presented it to her, his love for her clearly evident, his eyes twinkling with unbridled delight.

In some ways, those old memories were the most vivid of all. Perhaps this was a positive sign, reminding her that the bittersweet memories of her years with Niall were not the only ones that would sustain her in the future.

After priming her canvas, Ciara selected several brushes and tubes of colour and filled a dish with a mixture of turpentine and linseed oil. Later this year, she thought, I'll definitely go to Africa, for Kate's and Kevin's wedding and the birth of their child. And maybe I'll stay there for a while, to paint the vast skies that Kevin has so often spoke about. And Sarah will come out during the school holidays. But first, she'd start the painting for Kevin.

She knew exactly what she was going to paint. Alan Moore's delight in his pornographic work still haunted her, so she would paint sad, innocent children's eyes that held depths of pain, having learnt to trust no one. In a way, she might also be painting Ita's pain, because the

502

pain and suffering of exploited children was the same the world over. She would let the painting speak out on behalf of the used, the abused and the exploited who were unable to speak for themselves.

Suddenly, she had a thought. Perhaps it was time for her, too, to speak out about her own experience as a pornographic model. People might be shocked, she supposed. Would her own mother be upset? Maybe, but Annie was a strong woman who would surely give her daughter her full support. And what about Sarah? Soon she'd be a grown woman herself. Maybe it would be good for her to know that her own mother had once been young, vulnerable and foolish too.

She'd also talk to Liam about those pornographic photos. She didn't want there to be any secrets between them. Secrets festered, causing misunderstandings and pain. She was testimony to that herself.

Suddenly, she thought of Ita and realised with surprise that her own feelings of guilt gave her a sharp and penetrating insight into Ita's mind. How could I ever blame you, she thought, I who thought the worst of my own friends? I, who didn't realise the insecurities that my own husband was feeling? On a scale of one to ten, am I any less guilty than you? In fact, through my pornographic photos, I may ultimately have harmed far more people than you ever did. The fact that I didn't intend to makes me no less guilty.

Would she tell Liam about Ita's computer disk? For the moment, she'd do nothing. Perhaps time and circumstances would eventually help her to make the right decision. If she did show it to him, she'd have to be certain that her motivation was the right one and that she wasn't using it to lower Liam's esteem for Ita so that she could replace Ita in his affections. Ciara felt herself blush. Why was she thinking so often of Liam?

Selecting a clean rag to wipe her brushes, Ciara picked up each tube of paint in turn and started to squeeze out the colours onto her palette. She was almost ready to begin. Finally she slipped on her old paint-stained smock, the same one she'd been using since her college days, although it was covered with stains from top to bottom. But she loved its familiarity, and the fact that it carried with it the traces of all her former work. In a sense, her entire history as a painter was represented within its grubby folds. It felt better than the most expensive designer-label coat, and it seemed to embrace her like an old and dear friend.

Then Ciara picked up a brush and began to paint.

THE END